Accidental Destiny Thief

Thief

Book 1

Tam Delakor

EXPLICIT 18+
X
Explicit Language
Graphic Sexual Content
Mature Content
Graphic Violence
Rated X for explicit content - adults only
IBRS

Contents

Chapter 1
Thursday's Suck!

Destiny doesn't exist. There, I said it. No one else has the guts to. Fate is just a made-up word to get gullible saps to do stupid things, all for some inane sense of duty or whatever. I hate to be the bearer of bad news, but they lied to you.

There is no such thing as 'the chosen one.' And there certainly isn't eternal glory waiting for you at the end of the line. You know what's down there? Shit. Just a giant ball of pain and suffering that only turns you into a martyr, all so they can spread even more lies about how it was your destiny. It's a vicious cycle, one utilized by the powers that be to continue the process to get even more idiots to do what they want. The only real Destiny I know of works at the Pink Dragon and charges $25 for a minute-and-a-half lap dance.

I know what you must be thinking. "Oh, Turtle, how can you say that? I was chosen by fate! Destiny picked me to be a hero!" It's a story I've heard a thousand times since the Rift appeared. The day the entire universe was shaken upside down, and everything changed. A day that brought thousands of fantastical worlds into our reality and *really* messed up my vibe.

It happened on a Thursday, which should tell you everything you need to know. I mean, what cataclysmic, reality-altering event happens on a Thursday? It couldn't wait until after the weekend? Some of us had plans, thank you very much! And no, it doesn't matter that my plans involved sitting in my tiny one-bedroom apartment with my three-legged corgi, watching cartoons, and eating pizza. Plans are plans.

Anyway, it all started on a Thursday. I'd just finished taking a shower, getting ready for my shift at the shitty hole-in-the-wall bar down the street. Thursdays were always a hassle. The owner, in his infinite dumbassery, instituted the ever-popular 'Thirsty Thursday' policy, making all PBRs and Natty Lights a dollar. And anyone who knows anything knows that a deal like that doesn't bring out the most refined patrons.

The bar was going to be filled with drunken frat boys trying to impress whatever poor woman they could find with how fast they could make an ass out of themselves. And who gets to clean up the mess when one of them inevitably takes it too far and crosses the line? Me. But I shouldn't complain too much about it. I was lucky I even had a job as it was. No one was lining up to hire a 23-year-old college dropout. My size and ability to fight was the only thing I had going for me.

I've always been a big guy. Growing up, I didn't have the sitcom homelife, if you know what I mean. An older brother who essentially tortured me, a father who drank and blamed me for all of his problems, and a mother who was too scared to stand up for herself or her child and accepted the abuse we got. So, it's safe to say I haven't really liked people very much. I spent most of my time growing up either reading or working out. Both allowed me to take a break away from the giant shit show my life was back then.

I figured if I got strong enough, no one would be able to hurt me anymore. It did end up helping me get my father and brother to stop being physical with me, but it also made me a target for others who wanted someone to look down on. My anger used to get me into a lot of trouble back then. For years, I fought the hard way until a neighbor who was a retired boxer took me under his wing and showed me how to do it right. He also taught me how to manage my anger issues better. It took years, but if not for him, my story would've gone down a very different path.

I started using my head more than my fists, but I occasionally still had to crack a few skulls to get my point across. Unfortunately, that drew attention to me, and not in a good way. Eventually, I caught the eye of the owner of a crappy bar just off campus, and he wanted my help running the door. He played on my desire to keep people safe, and I soon gave in and accepted. It was long hours, crap pay, and I had to deal with drunken idiots on a nightly basis. But it allowed me to keep food in my stomach and a roof over my head, so I can't complain too much about it.

I finished drying off from the shower and grabbed my black T-shirt and blue jeans. I used to make fun of it, asking if the owner wanted the 'best cooler in the business,' but I think it went over his head. My genius is often underappreciated. I had some of my classic rock playing from the Bluetooth speaker in my bedroom, and Champion lay on the small couch, watching me with one eye.

Quickly brushing my beard, I took one last look at myself in the mirror before clicking off the light and grabbing my phone and wallet. I reached down and scratched Champion on his head as I turned off the music and turned on his favorite TV show, the Best British Bake Showdown, or whatever it's called. For some reason, that dog loves watching English people make cake and shake hands.

"Alright, boy," I said as I turned to leave. "Be good. Em will be by in a few to take you potty."

Champion didn't so much as look back at me, his attention focused solely on the television. Chuckling, I shook my head and walked out the door, locking it behind me. The worn floorboards of the apartment hallway creaked as I made my way to the far side and down the uncomfortably narrow stairs. I lived on the fourth floor of one of the oldest apartment buildings in town, and it desperately needed a remodel. It was one of those old mansions from the early 1900s that someone decided to make into apartments in a mad cash dive.

Of the eleven residents, I was by far the youngest, with the next in her mid-sixties. The landlord only came around once a month to collect rent and then would disappear again. So, when anything broke around the building, I became the de facto go-to person for the other residents. I didn't mind, really. Everyone was pretty chill, and many would cook me something nice or offer to help me take care of Champion on my long nights.

Just as I reached the bottom of the stairs, the door of room 101 slowly cracked open, revealing a big pair of brown eyes peeking at me from behind. "Hey, Mrs. Atkin. How's that ceiling fan holding up?"

The door opened wider, revealing the frail woman smiling back at me. Mrs. Atkin had lived in the building the longest, and I was always surprised by how well she could still get around. For a woman in her early eighties, she was pretty spry when she wanted to be. She'd always been really nice to me and Champion since we moved in almost two years ago.

"Oh, it's fine, sweetie," she said, her cracked voice holding a bit of a tremor she'd been trying to hide the past six months. "Are you working late tonight?"

"Yes, Ma'am," I said with a smile. "But don't worry, I'll be good to go tomorrow morning to take you to your appointment. So, make sure you get your beauty sleep tonight, okay?"

Chuckling, Mrs. Atkin shook her head and closed her door as I turned and exited the building. In the distance, I thought I heard some kind of siren going off, but I quickly shut it out by hitting play on my music and sticking in my earbuds. I walked down the street toward the edge of the college campus, letting the solid tunes blaring in my ears help amp me up for what was most likely going to be another monotonous night of drunken college kids and crappy techno music.

As I walked, I realized there were a lot of cars on the road for a Thursday in the middle of the semester. It was usually only at the end of the semester that so many people were rushing to leave this town. Yet, I still didn't see anything to be concerned about.

When I was about two blocks from the bar, the familiar tune of my ringtone rang in my ear. Chuckling, I pulled my phone out of my pocket and saw the expected picture of the caller ID looking back at me.

Incoming Call: Honey Badger

Swiping up, I pulled out an earbud so I could talk. "Hey, Honey Bear, why are you calling me? You know I'm almost there, right?"

"What have I told you about calling me that, pendejo?!" the sultry voice snapped on the other end of the line.

Laughing, I shook my head at my own joke. Honey Hernandez had been my best friend since, well, forever. We grew up next door to each other and were both loners as kids. So, eventually, we became loners together. I always had a crush on her, but I never really knew how to express that properly. Instead, I pretended to like the same books and games she did. That plan backfired when I realized I really enjoyed those stories and became obsessed with reading them. Honey wasn't much into working out, though. She never needed to. She was one of those blessed with somehow having the perfect figure no matter what.

Everyone thought we were secretly dating for a long time, but that was never in the cards for us. She was my best friend, and I loved everything about her. But besides some typical teenage hormone stuff, nothing romantic happened between us, despite how much of a crush I still have on her.

There was only one time I thought I might've scared her away. I'd lost myself in a fit of rage as a teenager and ended up putting her stepfather in the hospital for a week. But she stuck by my side even closer after that, treating me like a savior rather than the beast I'd turned into. We'd become inseparable after that night, and I loved her even more for not running away after seeing the monster inside me.

When she came out as bisexual in high school and got a girlfriend, I used that as my reason not to make any moves on her. Somewhere deep inside, I thought it was her way of letting me know she wasn't interested in me like that. Unfortunately, her family was even more pieces of flaming dogshit than my own, and they finally kicked her out at the ripe old age of sixteen.

Honey was a survivor, though. She wasn't one to let something like that get her down. My family ignored anything I did by then, so I let her crash in my room until we graduated high school. We'd both decided to get the hell out of that ass-backward town the second we could. After Honey had broken up with her girlfriend who didn't want to leave, we packed her car and moved to Krayden for college. Little did we know, neither of us was made for that life, and both dropped out after a year or so.

I started dating my ex soon after and moved in with her, while Honey met a lovely woman at a coffeehouse the next town over. She and Sara have been together ever since and have even started talking about getting married. Meanwhile, I got cheated on, dumped, and left in massive debt for my troubles. Yay me!

"What's up?" I asked, rounding the final corner and bringing the bar into view. "I'm literally right down the street."

"What do you mean, what's up?!" Honey yelled; her accent always got more pronounced when she was agitated. When she began using Spanglish, I knew she was really upset. "Open your ojos! Do you *not* see what's going on out there?!"

Confused, I stopped and looked around. That's when I noticed it was worse than just a bit more traffic than usual. The entire street was almost bumper to bumper, with people abandoning their cars and running away, looking back in terror as they did. Furrowing my brows, I turned to see what they were all looking at, and I almost dropped my phone when I saw it.

What I could only describe as a tear had formed high in the sky. A strange pulsing light tinged with blue and purple radiated out as its edges grew longer, and several smaller ones formed around it. I stared in disbelief while the sky above me ripped in half. A sharp static sound brought me out of my stupor just in time to hear Honey's faded words calling out to me. Then my phone went completely dead.

Staring at the black screen, I tried again to understand what was happening. I looked behind, wondering if I should return to the apartment. The others wouldn't know what was going on, and I wanted to be able to help them if something bad went down. Then I kicked myself. The sky was *literally* ripping apart; something bad was *already* going down!

I took off running toward the bar, intending to grab Honey before I did anything else. I wouldn't leave her alone when the world was falling apart. Bursting through the door, I looked around frantically for the woman. I was surprised by how many people were there, acting as if the entire world outside wasn't about to be torn apart.

"Turtle!" Honey called out from behind the bar, waving me over.

"Hey! What the fuck is going on?!" I asked, forcing myself between a pair of peacocking frat boys. "Why are people here right now?!"

Honey shot her hands up in the air and shook her head. Her dark, curly hair was pulled back into a messy bun, yet strands still fell across her face. She blew the rogue locks away and wiped her hands on her gray tank top, which stood in contrast against her naturally tan skin. Honey was petite, standing at not even five and a half feet tall—more than a foot shorter than I was. Yet her large breasts and slim figure made her stand out in any crowd. I once joked that her legs stopped growing in middle school, but her chest must've never gotten the memo. She kicked me in the nuts in response.

"¡No sé! Pero, I'm not staying. I can't get my car out of the lot. Can you give me a ride back to mi casa?"

Nodding, I grabbed her hand, pulling her from behind the bar. "Yeah, it's back at my place. Let's get going before—"

"And just where do you think you're going?!" A loud voice boomed just behind us.

I cringed before turning to see Mr. Pittman, the bar owner, staring us both down. His face was beet red, and sweat poured down his balding head. This man was a walking heart attack and diabetes commercial if I've ever seen one. He stabbed one of his chubby fingers toward Honey and me before pointing back at the bar.

"We have customers waiting! Get back to work!"

"Are you fucking serious?" I shouted, waving my hand outside at the increasing chaos. "Do you *not* see what's happening out there right now?"

Mr. Pittman scoffed and crossed his arms in front of his chest. "I don't care what's happening out there! This is my bar, and we're open for business. So do your jobs like I pay you for, or you're fired!"

"Screw you!" Honey spat at the man. That Latin temper of hers had gotten her into a lot of trouble over the years. Trouble I usually had to clean up. "I'm going to be with mi familia."

We turned to leave, but then Mr. Pittman had to make the mistake of opening his fat mouth one last time. "Family? Ha! Hate to break it to you, *chicka*, but a wetback and redneck dyke with a cat isn't a family."

I stopped in my tracks, dropping Honey's hand as I turned back to the man. He raised his chin and sneered at me as I stepped toward him. "Oh, did I hurt your feelings, boy? What are you go—"

He never finished as I slammed my fist hard into his jaw, feeling the crack of bone underneath my knuckles. The fat man dropped like a brick, lying motionless on the floor as the patrons around him cheered. I grabbed Honey's hand again, leading her out of the bar. We rushed down the street, which had grown exponentially more crowded. I looked up and cursed as I saw that in the few minutes I'd been in the bar, the tear in the sky had almost tripled in size, with dozens of smaller branches reaching off it.

"What in the hell is going on?" Honey asked, her voice shaking as we rushed down an alleyway toward my apartment.

"I don't know!" I yelled back, suddenly stopping just as someone on a moped sped less than an inch in front of us.

A massive explosion echoed through the buildings from somewhere in the distance, causing the ground to shake under our feet. Screams rang out from all around as the panic increased for everyone trying to run. A loud whooshing from above caused us to look up just in time to see five fighter jets fly past, straight toward the tear. For the briefest of moments, I had some hope. If the military were there, they'd handle whatever it was, right?

Boy, was I wrong! As if watching the sky being ripped apart wasn't shocking enough, what happened next was beyond insane. As the fighter jets approached the tear, the pulsing light from beyond grew more intense. Without warning, two of the jets exploded into massive fireballs in midair. Honey and I watched in horror as the remaining jets swerved to miss the falling wreckage as a gigantic, clawed hand reached through the tear.

It looked like it was made of pure darkness, as if the light itself dared not try to touch it. The clawed fingers wrapped around two of the jets and crushed them as easily as if they were made of tissue paper. More screams rang out as a deafening roar shook the very fabric of our reality. Gripping Honey's hand even tighter, I pulled, dragging her to my apartment as fast as I could.

"What the fuck, what the fuck?!" Honey continued to whisper as we finally made it through the door of my apartment building.

"It's okay. It's going to be okay," I said, pulling her into a tight hug.

I'd known Honey my entire life. She doesn't get rattled easily. She was one of those women who wouldn't bat an eye at almost anything. To see her shaken this bad made me feel even more uneasy. We stood there holding each other for several minutes as the adrenaline continued to course through our bodies.

"I-I need to get back to S-Sara . . ." Honey said, finally breaking our embrace.

"Of course," I said as I looked up the stairs. "I'll go grab my keys and Champion. Give me five minutes to check and make sure everyone's all right here first, okay?"

Nodding, Honey turned and walked to Room 101. "I'll check on the ones down here."

I ran up the stairs as I heard Mrs. Atkin's door creak open. I didn't know what was going on, but everything was falling to shit in a very fast way. The floorboards moaned as I ran down my hall, slamming my key into the lock. On the other side of the door, I heard Champion barking frantically, causing me to all but smash through.

To my amazement, the small dog wasn't barking out the window at the absolute chaos that was taking place. Instead, he was barking at the TV, which was now just static. I shook my head in disbelief as I approached the hook holding my car keys. The world was literally coming apart, and the dog only cared that it interrupted his show.

I put the keys in my pocket before opening the small table drawer underneath the hooks. There lay my S&W 686 plus, freshly cleaned and oiled less than two days ago. I quickly strapped the holster to my waist and grabbed two boxes that had '.357 Mag' printed on the top. I wasn't sure what was happening, but considering I got this gun in case of an emergency, I couldn't think of a more fitting situation for it.

The building shook, causing me to stumble and grab the table for balance. Champion finally stopped barking at the TV and looked around the room as if just realizing something was wrong. I walked to the window and looked outside, my breath catching. What I was seeing wasn't computing in my mind. What I could only describe as massive tentacles waved through the sky from beyond the tear, smashing several skyscrapers as if they were a child's building blocks.

"Turtle!" Honey yelled from somewhere downstairs, breaking me from the horrific sight outside.

I turned and ran out the door, calling for Champion to follow me. I didn't need to wonder if he would or not. Even though he only had three short legs, that dog could run when he wanted. As I reached the top of the steps, the tan fur ball jumped past me and ran down the stairs. I was the only resident on the fourth floor, so I didn't have to worry about checking the other rooms.

I jumped down to the third floor and pounded on everyone's doors, checking in to make sure they were all still okay. It never ceases to amaze me what old people can sleep through. Almost none of them even realized something was happening outside. I mean, why would they? It was already after five pm. It was well past their bedtime.

I finished with the third floor and made it to the second when I came across Honey standing at the landing, holding Champion tightly in her arms. "I got these already. I told everyone to stay inside or go to Mrs. Atkin's apartment until they hear otherwise."

Nodding, I looked around once more. "Good. Thank you. Now, let's hurry. It's getting even worse out there."

We took off down the stairs and went out the door once again. Pandemonium wasn't even close to describing the sight we ran into. The long tentacle-looking things had completely leveled several buildings further in town. Giant pillars of smoke rose high into the air from all over, and the sounds of countless people screaming bounced from every direction.

Grabbing onto Honey's hand again, I pulled her toward the parking garage down the street where I kept my car. I barely needed to drive anywhere the past few years, but thankfully, I never got rid of my old beat-up Pontiac. Champion followed us as we ducked through parked cars and up the sidewalk to the garage elevator. Just before I hit the call button, Honey stopped, pulling me backward.

I looked at her, confused about why she was standing there, staring wide-eyed down the street. Then I turned and saw what caught her attention. Four cars were crumpled together in a horrifying mass of twisted metal and flames. What was worse, they completely blocked the garage's exit. There was only one other way out of the old structure, but since that was on the street we used coming back from the bar, I knew I couldn't get out that way.

Honey's resolve broke, and she let out a soft sob. The fear and frustration were getting to her. I didn't know what to do. Instinctively, I wrapped my arms around her and began stroking her hair, trying to stay strong for her. Champion barked and started walking back toward our apartment building.

I turned to call him back, but something caught my eye as I looked down the way. Mrs. Atkin had come outside, slowly pushing her walker down the ramp toward the street. My heart froze as I saw someone on a motorcycle weaving through the stalled cars before jumping onto the sidewalk to avoid the blockage.

"NO!" I yelled, pushing my body as fast as I could back toward the elderly woman.

Listen, I know I'm not the most intelligent man in the world. I never claimed to be. But when you see someone you care about in mortal danger, common sense kind of flies out the window. I ran right toward them as if I could outrun that motorcycle from more than a block away.

I'd only gotten a few feet before it reached Mrs. Atkin, who hadn't seen or heard the approaching danger. She was so focused on looking up at the unbelievable sight above that she didn't see him until it was too late. To my horror, I saw the woman who'd been so kind to me for years go down as the motorist tried to swerve but failed. The driver was thrown from his seat, slamming hard into a parked car, and Mrs. Atkin lay motionless on the ground.

I ran as fast as I could, hoping if I could get to her, I might still be able to do something. A scream behind me broke through the shock, causing me to turn just in time to see Honey's eyes wide in terror, calling my name. It didn't take me long to see why. One of the massive tentacles had come slamming down directly at me from above. I had just enough time to try to raise my hands in a feeble attempt to protect myself before a crushing weight slammed me into the pavement, and everything went dark.

Chapter 2

A Convincing Proposal

I hate alarms. The constant beeping, the annoying buzzing. All they do is ruin a good night's sleep and make you have to deal with shitty reality yet again. I think if I could ever go back in time, I'd find the person who created the alarm clock and beat him to death with a wooden spoon.

The recurrent beeping of my alarm broke through the darkness, causing me to immediately regret every life decision I ever made that led me to set it. But the more I lay there, the more it would beep at me. Grumbling every curse I could think of, I slammed my hand down on the annoying contraption. It took a few smacks, but the beeps eventually stopped, and I was left with sweet silence yet again.

That was until the beeping started once more. "FUCK YOU!"

I grabbed the alarm clock and threw it across the room as hard as I could. My efforts were rewarded with a loud crash and the sound of plastic and metal breaking. I sighed, letting my heavy eyelids close, wishing for the sweet relief of slumber to drag me back. But it never did. I lay silent for several minutes, wondering who actually won that fight. I'm awake, but the alarm clock is broken. So, tie, I guess?

The soft sound of my door gently opening and closing let me know I was no longer alone. I felt a heavy warmth climb onto the bed beside me and slender arms wrapped around my midsection. Locks of curly hair tickled my nose as Honey pressed her face into my bare chest. I laid my arm across her shoulder, pulling her even closer. Instinctively, I began stroking my fingers through her hair, causing her to let out a deep exhale.

It was apparent she'd just taken a shower since I could smell the subtle hint of her lavender body wash radiating off her warm skin. She was wearing a thin shirt and very short shorts, allowing me to feel her smooth legs rub over my own. Her heavy breasts pressed into me as she let out a soft sigh.

"That's like the tenth alarm clock you've broken this year, love," Honey said, a hint of a smile in her voice.

"Why do you think I don't use my phone anymore?" I chuckled. "Alarm clocks are much cheaper to replace. And make great alternatives to therapy."

We lay in silence for several minutes, simply existing with one another. "Sara said she's going to be making breakfast soon. Do you want eggs or pancakes today?"

Sighing, I slowly opened my eyes. "You know y'all don't have to keep doing this, right?"

Lifting her head, Honey gave me a questioning look. "What do you mean?"

Resigning to finally get up, I sat, causing Honey to sit with me. I leaned against the headboard and looked at my oldest and dearest friend. It never ceased to amaze me just how beautiful Honey always appeared. Here she was, first thing in the morning, yet she could easily be on the cover of any magazine right then and there. Her deep brown eyes studied me, almost as if she were daring me to say what I was about to.

"Y'all don't have to do this," I said, gesturing around the room. "I mean, it's been ten years. Y'all don't have to keep treating me like a broken little bird that needs to be cared for."

Honey glared at me, and my sphincter instinctively clenched. I've seen her angry more times than I can count and God help whoever made her that way. There were quite a few times I was on the receiving end of her Latina temper, and it was not a place I wanted to be again—especially this early in the morning.

Before she could say anything, I raised my hand in an attempt to calm the coming storm. "I'm not saying I don't appreciate everything you and Sara have done for me. I'm pretty sure we both know I'd probably be dead in a ditch somewhere if it weren't for y'all. But you know I don't want to be a burden."

With a long sigh, Honey shook her head and bit her lip. I could tell she was still unhappy, but at least I think I stamped out most of the fire. "You're not a burden, Turtle. We love you. We're family. And families stick together and help each other, right?"

Snorting, I rolled my eyes. "You don't remember my family very well, do you?"

Honey pulled back and punched me in the chest. It was meant to be playful, but there was still some heat behind it. "Your family is who you choose, not who shares your name. You know that. Besides, the only one from yours we claim, is Lana."

"And me, right?" I asked, arching an eyebrow at her.

"Hmmm," Honey made a show of trying to think about it. "Not sure. The jury's still out. But Lana, she belongs to us now."

Chuckling, I nodded. "Yeah, she's the only good one. Speaking of, she should be calling soon. I sent her the last payment for this semester's tuition yesterday."

"Really?! That's great! Tell her we said hi and can't wait for her to come visit on break."

Rotating my head quickly, I was rewarded with a loud crack from my neck. "Oh god, that felt good."

"Well, hurry up and get dressed," Honey said, standing from the bed and heading to the door. "I'll tell Sara to make you a tofu omelet."

"Don't you dare!" I yelled, shooting Honey a stern glare.

She turned and stuck her tongue out at me, giving me her usual mischievous smile before rushing down the hall toward the kitchen. Grumbling, I ran to the door, flinging it open and sticking my head out. "Sara! Don't you dare listen to her! She's an evil, disgusting woman who doesn't deserve your cooking."

Laughter echoed from the kitchen. A heavily southern-accented voice called back to me. "You say that like I don't already know."

"Burnt toast and water for Honey!"

"Deal!" Sara agreed, followed by a loud pop and a squeal of laughter from the two women.

I closed my door and walked past dozens of shelves lined with hundreds of well-read books to my dresser against the far wall. Standing in front of it, I studied myself in the large, attached mirror. It was something I'd done almost every day since I left the hospital all those years ago. Using the tips of my fingers, I slowly traced the long, jagged scars that covered most of my torso. I could still feel the metal pieces they used to replace the bones that had been all but ground into dust.

You ever watch one of those videos where someone suffers such a terrible accident that you know they couldn't survive? Like there's no way someone could walk away from it, yet in the end, they came out the other side? Well, when you're the one who goes through that horrifying incident, you still feel that same disbelief—that same utter confoundment about how you survived. But you can look in the mirror and see that it really did happen, and somehow, you're still standing.

I'm not getting sappy, and I don't think I'm anything special. Thousands, if not millions, were injured all those years ago during what's now called the First Rift Event, or FRE for short. And plenty out there had it much worse than I did. In fact, I was one of the luckiest. Because as I lay bleeding in the middle of the street, barely clinging to life, the 'miracle' happened.

Miracle . . . don't make me laugh. They call it that because it's meant to give hope like we hadn't just had our entire reality torn to shreds before our eyes. Honestly, they could've kept their 'miracle' and shoved it up their ass for all I cared. Yet, I wasn't given a choice, was I?

From what Honey said, after I was flattened like a cartoon coyote, but just before she could reach me, a brilliant white light shot from the tear in the sky, bathing everything in its rays. She said it filled her with such a deep sense of peace; all the terror we'd just gone through seemingly disappeared. When she could finally open her eyes from the brightness, the tear in the sky had shrunk considerably, and the tentacles and claws destroying the city had all vanished.

She thought I was dead, but when she got to me, my entire body was encased in some kind of cocoon of light. After several hours of her trying to call for help, some men wearing strange military uniforms showed up and took me away. Every time she told me about it, she'd start crying hysterically, saying she thought she'd never see me again.

Yet, two months later, she got a call from an unknown number saying she should come pick me up from the local hospital less than a mile from her house. I'd just opened my eyes when she walked through the door of my room. I'd never seen her cry so much as she wrapped her arms around my neck, pressing my face firmly into her ample chest. I thought I might actually die of asphyxiation from her holding me in her breasts for so long. It's not the worst way a guy could die, that's for sure.

She told me she and Sara agreed that I'd be moving in with them and that they'd help take care of me from then on. I tried to protest but was quickly shown that my thoughts were irrelevant. Honey's one of the most stubborn people I've ever known. And when she gets it in her head that she's going to do something, it would take an act of God to get her to change her mind.

The smell of bacon cooking snapped me back to reality, causing my mouth to water. Is there a better smell out there? That's a trick question; the answer's no. Smiling, I grabbed my RRS polo and a pair of khaki pants. The heavy boots the company requires us to wear are cumbersome, but I still feel like a badass lacing them up. There's just something about thick, steel-toed leather boots that drive up the testosterone, you know?

Exiting my room, I went down the hallway until I reached the dining area. Across the room was the open kitchen, where a barely dressed Sara danced while flipping a pancake. She was an entire six inches shorter than Honey, standing just under five foot tall, and had long, blonde hair that she kept pulled back in a simple ponytail. Her almost porcelain skin was smooth and lacked any sort of blemish or freckle. Unlike Honey, Sara went with me to the gym several times a week, and it showed.

She had a very athletic build, with toned abs and incredibly defined legs. And while she wasn't as endowed as Honey in the chest department, her pride and joy was her ass. She worked hard on it, and it was literally the most perfect ass I'd ever seen. There were many times I thought if she and Honey hadn't been together, I might've tried to make a move on her. Even though she was from the Deep South, she took pride in breaking most of the stereotypes people had thought about her. She was pansexual, and she and

Honey were polyamorous and had an open marriage, but there are still some lines you don't cross.

It appeared Sara didn't have to work today since she stood there wearing nothing but one of my T-shirts I put in the laundry days ago. I had to quickly look away to avoid getting a massive hard-on watching her cook like that.

"Makin bacon pancakes . . . " Sara sang, shaking her ass while dancing to her made-up song.

"Someone's in a good mood," I said with a laugh, sitting at the table to try and hide my growing erection.

Sara turned and shot me a toothy grin. Her hazel eyes twinkled as she put the pancake she finished on a plate with several others and brought them to me.

"You can say that," she said, setting the plate in front of me. She leaned in and gave me a sweet kiss on the forehead. Her lips were plump and soft as she lingered slightly against my skin. "Eat up, stud!"

Shaking my head, I chuckled again, picking up the fork and knife from the table. "Could I get—"

I was cut off by Honey setting a large cup of coffee in front of me, a smirk on her face. "God forbid you go a single morning without a cup of coffee."

I rolled my eyes at her as I sipped from the piping-hot mug. "It's for the greater good, thank you very much. I'm just a better person when I've had my coffee."

"Amen to that!" Sara cheered, taking a sip from her own mug at the same time.

Honey rolled her eyes and shook her head. "You two should just fuck already."

Sara winked at me and then popped Honey on the ass before heading back to the kitchen. "All in due time, babe."

It had become a regular joke between them, each trying to embarrass me by being overtly sexual. It started as just small quips here and there, but over the past couple of years, it's turned into lingering touches and kisses or claims in some way that one or the other wanted to sleep with me. Since I knew neither of them was serious about it and was only trying to fluster me, their comments and intimate signs of affection didn't have the embarrassing effect they hoped for. Yet, for some reason, it's continued and has become almost a daily thing with them.

I laughed at their joking before digging into the delicious stack of bacon pancakes. Now, I'm not saying that they were on the same level as the ambrosia of the Gods. I'm saying they were even better. Sara was a phenomenal chef, and she had never made anything that wasn't out of this world fantastic.

"Oh, God," I said, leaning back in my chair and rubbing my distended belly after finishing my eleventh pancake. "I don't want to stop eating, but I'm afraid I'll shit my pants if I keep going."

"Sexy," Honey said, rolling her eyes as she drank her morning tea.

"You know me," I said with a wink.

We sat silently for several minutes while Sara continued humming and dancing in the kitchen. I looked over at the energetic woman and then back at Honey, raising an eyebrow with the obvious question. I saw the slight blush on Honey's cheeks as she tried to cover her face with her mug. I smirked, letting her know I saw it. She glared back at me, squinting her eyes in warning.

I laughed loudly, causing her to glare even harder. "Come on, what's going on?"

Sighing, Honey set her mug down and focused on the table. She used the tip of her fingernail to pick at an imaginary spot on the wood. I've seen her do it thousands of times, usually when she wasn't sure what to say or if she thought it would be embarrassing. It took her a minute before she could look me in the eyes.

"We got the call last night," she said, her voice almost shaking with the news. "We . . . we're approved for the adoption license!"

I was floored by the announcement. They'd been trying for years to get approved for adoption, but for one reason or another, their application was always denied. I never understood why, though. It wasn't because of their open marriage either, since polyamory and even polygamy had been accepted for years by now.

These women are two of the most amazing, loving people I've ever met. I mean, hell, look how they helped me! That first year I was out of the hospital, I was basically like a toddler, yet they took care of me better than anyone else could've possibly been able to.

"Seriously?! That's fantastic!" I yelled, jumping up and rushing toward her.

Honey squealed as I lifted her from her chair and embraced her tightly. Her legs dangled in the air as I swung her around while she slapped at me in protest. "Okay! Okay! Stop. Put me down!"

"No!" I laughed, hugging her tighter.

Sara came rushing into the room, her face beaming with happiness. I decided she needed in on the hugging action too. I reached out and pulled her in with my right arm while keeping Honey held with my left. I lifted Sara as well, and we all shared a happy embrace. After a minute, I finally let them down, and they stepped back with red, smiling faces.

"You're too freaking strong," Honey said, taking a deep breath. "You almost snapped me in half!"

"Aw," Sara said, wrapping her arm around Honey's waist. "I like his hugs. Makes me feel so small when I'm in his arms."

"That's because you *are* small," Honey said with a laugh, pulling Sara close and kissing her.

I smiled at them, so happy that the pair finally got their wish. A slight buzz on my wrist brought me back to reality, and I looked down at the RRS-issued watch I had to always keep on me. "Shit, I gotta go."

Honey and Sara looked at me, each with large smiles on their faces. "Aww, okay. Try not to work too hard today. We're meeting at the tavern at seven tonight to celebrate. And you're going to be there, Mister!"

I smiled and tipped an imaginary hat to them as I turned to leave. Walking outside the house we all shared, I stopped to look up at the Rift high above. Ten years had passed, and most people had already gotten used to it being there. It was just another part of everyday life now. But they don't see what I see when I look at the softly pulsing light radiating from its edges.

I sighed and walked out of the front gate, making my way toward the massive structure that now took up more than three square miles in the small neighborhood- the Krayden branch of the RRS. You know those jokes about government agencies being inept and pointless for what they should be? Well, that's not the RRS.

The Rift Research Services was an agency no one had heard of ten years ago. Yet, they'd all but taken over the world by the time I woke up from my injuries. Right after the FRE, they showed up out of nowhere. At first, no one was giving them the time of day. But when the Second Rift Event happened, everything changed. About six months after I was allowed to leave the hospital, one of those annoying all-system alerts on everyone's phones went off worldwide. The message was simple yet confusing.

RRS ALERTS

"PREPARE FOR RIFT EVENT IN 5 MINUTES."

No one understood what any of that meant. But within minutes, the light from the Rift began to pulse faster and brighter. I was told that everyone affected by the 'miracle' began to glow just like we had after the FRE. I was alone enjoying some 'me time,' if you catch my drift. My boxers were down around my knees, and I was watching a particularly spicy video about a guy and his two roommates when I felt a soothing warmth wrap around me. Then, a soft, cooling sensation began to fill my chest before spreading out to every fiber of my being.

I must've passed out because by the time I opened my eyes again, it was dusk, and both Honey and Sara had been standing over me with tears in their eyes. They wrapped me in hugs when they saw I was conscious again, saying how worried they were when they got the alert. It was pretty embarrassing when I realized my cock was still out, yet neither of the women seemed to care as they all but laid on top of me. I still didn't know what exactly happened, so we decided to try to do some digging the next day.

We never got the chance. At 7:00 am, there was a loud banging on the front door, and three men wearing RRS fatigues pushed their way into our home and surrounded the couch I was using as a bed. They hooked me up to several machines, poked and prodded me for hours, asking all kinds of strange questions. And then, just as quickly as they showed up, they left without another word. For a week, we were at a loss.

Then, Dr. Saph showed up. She was the walking definition of a MILF if I ever saw one. If I had to guess, I would've said she was in her early 40s, with fiery red hair and deep green eyes. Her massive chest was barely contained in the white blouse she wore. Though she was a very sexy woman, she was undoubtedly intelligent. I was still pretty weak at that point, so she sat in a chair right beside the couch I was lying on to discuss everything with me.

There was a kindness behind her eyes I didn't expect from a government bureaucrat. She was the first to sit down and talk to me like I was a real person and not just some kind of test subject. She told me the RRS had existed for many years before the Rift Events. It just wasn't until after the FRE that the world's governments finally took them seriously. That was when she dropped the biggest bombshell I ever thought possible.

"There are countless worlds out there, Tom," she said, her eyes looking over my bare chest before recomposing herself. "You read fantasy books, right? Play video games? Well, then, you know the basic premise. While no movie or book comes close to the reality of it, many share bits of the truth. There are more Realms out there than grains of sand on the beach. We at the RRS have dedicated our lives to studying them and believe we've found a way to create a better world. Worlds, actually. For all out there, not just us."

I studied her intently, my bullshit meter going crazy with that last bit. "Sorry, Doc. But you're right. I *have* seen a lot of movies. And anyone who tries to say they want to create a better world for others is usually set to be revealed as the third-quarter villain."

Dr. Saph chuckled and nodded in agreement. "Oh, I understand your concerns. Normally, I'd say you're right. But I've been with this organization for a long time now. We're not controlled by any one government, so we don't let politics affect our work. And we're not sponsored by crazy billionaires who think of themselves as rocket scientists. Creating a better world is for everyone, not just the rich or powerful. It's for people like your friends Honey and Sara. Like your niece, Lana. Like you."

I was still skeptical, but I must admit that this particular villain pitch didn't sound too bad. "Okay, say I believe all of that. What exactly do you want from me?"

"Well, Tom, you'll play a vital role in all of this," she said, her smile growing wider. "You see, every Realm out there is connected through the Pathways or what's being called the Rift. Unbelievable power resides within it and flows into the universe randomly.

It's completely unpredictable most times. But as you might have noticed during this last Rift Event, we could predict when it would happen by studying the pulse patterns emitted from the Rift itself. What we didn't know was what exactly it would do."

"And? What did it do?"

"It brought magic to our world," Dr. Saph said with awe and wonder, her gaze fixed on me.

It took everything in me not to roll my eyes at her. "Magic? Seriously? You expect people to actually buy that crap?"

Dr. Saph didn't even flinch. It was easy to tell she'd already given this same speech countless times. "We have a tear in the very fabric of our reality that let unspeakable horrors through that almost killed you. Then, you were miraculously saved by an intangible force that not even our greatest scientific minds could figure out. And you think magic is off the table?"

I bit my tongue. She got me there. After everything I saw, why not magic? It's as good an explanation as any at this point. Yet I was still confused about how she knew any of this.

"So, I have magic? Is that what you're saying?"

Giving a nod, Dr. Saph pulled out a piece of paper from the file she carried. "It seems like you got one of the most rare abilities out there, Tom. While some gained extra strength or the ability to wield fire with their bare hands, you've been given the power to jump."

I cocked my eyebrow at her in confusion. "Jump? Like . . . a frog?"

Dr. Saph chuckled and shook her head, her massive breasts jiggling and pressing at the already strained buttons of her blouse. "Of course not. Jump is simply the term we use when referring to traveling through the Rift. Your energy signature aligns with that of the Pathways. In fact, it aligns better than anyone else we've ever seen. You have the potential to travel to any Realm with just a single thought. Think of it, Tom. With you and others like you, we can help spread throughout the Rift and gather untold information to help us better the entire universe!"

I was dumbfounded. This lady had to be a quack. There was no way any of it was real. I looked around the room, hoping to find some camera or see Honey somewhere trying to prank me. Yet, there was none of that. Dr. Saph was completely serious.

"This is your destiny, Tom," Dr. Saph said, leaning closer and placing her hand on my thigh. I felt the warmth of her skin radiate through the thin sheet I had over me, causing my blood flow to start going in a different direction. "You have the power to help decide the fate of everyone in the universe. And all you have to do is help us."

"Help you do what?" I asked warily.

The alarm bells were definitely going off in the back of my mind, but I just couldn't help it. I've been an avid fantasy reader and game player my entire life. And I just had a drop-dead gorgeous woman essentially give me the 'you're our only hope' speech. Of course, my inner nerd was dying to believe her.

"We're going to send special individuals into the Realms searching for powerful artifacts. Items we believe will help us not only protect ourselves from further attacks but also give us the knowledge we need to ensure peace for all. And it'll be possible thanks to people like you, who answered the call of destiny."

I let out a long sigh as I let her words sink in. Thinking back on that day, I wish I could tell her to take her offer and shove it so far up her ass the next guy she'd try to dupe would smell the shit on her breath. But Dr. Saph was an intelligent woman and knew just what to say to keep someone on the hook, especially when she started rubbing my thigh a lot higher than I expected her to.

It was apparent I hadn't been entirely sold on what she was telling me. She also knew she could play that damn 'destiny' card and get the inner hero most of us have raring to go. Like I said before, we're gullible saps, each and every one of us. Well, it was between that and her hand finding its way to my now rock-hard dick, slowly massaging it over the sheet. I had almost no blood going to my brain. Before I realized what was happening, Dr. Saph pulled down the sheet, reached into my boxers, and freed my fully erect cock, which she held firmly in her hand.

Her skin was smooth as it glided up and down my hardened shaft. Using her thumb, she wiped some of the precum that had begun to bead at the tip. She released my cock and stuck her thumb in her mouth, making sure to keep her eyes locked onto mine. Sliding from her chair onto her knees, she gripped my shaft again and rubbed it along her smooth cheek until the head was just below her thick, red lips.

I felt her hot breath as she opened her mouth and let her tongue lightly lick just under my cockhead, sending a wave of immense pleasure coursing through my body. It had been over a year since the last time I'd had any kind of sex with someone, and I was surprised I didn't bust my entire load right then and there. She licked again as she began to stroke a bit faster than before.

"Well, Tom? What do you say?"

Her firm yet gentle grip mixed with the hot wetness of her mouth as her lips fully wrapped around my shaft only let me think of a single question to ask. "Okay, what do I have to do?

Chapter 3

So Many Questions, So Little Time

Ten years is a long time. I can't even tell you all the shit I've seen since the day I signed on the dotted line with the RRS. Don't get me wrong, it hasn't been all bad. Hell, there've been some really great things that have come from it. Travel, prestige, money, women. Oh God, the women! Screw the preppiest frat boy trying to flash all his daddy's money to impress someone at the bar. Walk in wearing an RRS shirt and mention you're a Rifter; let's just say you're in for a very sleepless night.

Rifter was the title they gave those of us who could 'jump' through the Rift. We were the rarest of all those who got abilities from the SRE. There are only three of us working out of the Krayden facility. Worldwide, there are less than twenty in total, including the five that refused to join the agency. From what I gathered about the Realms, we had the highest concentration of Rifters out there. Most others had maybe a dozen if that.

After my recovery, I walked into two big surprises when I arrived for orientation. First, Dr. Saph wasn't just a hot recruiter but the Director of the entire RRS and was stationed out of the Krayden Facility. I thought it would be weird between us, but it really wasn't. One thing I learned rather quickly about her was that she's very good at separating her personal and professional life. Even after years of working under her, in more than one way, if you catch my drift, I knew very little about her. I knew she'd gone to college in Krayden and that she immediately left for Europe and was stationed there until just before the FRE. There might have been mention of a daughter at some point, but it was at a time that my attention was focused . . . elsewhere. But that's about it.

The second surprise was my job title. Due to my PT, I started a few months after the other Rifters, yet I somehow was given the position of Head Rifter. And not just for the Krayden branch, either. I oversaw *all* the Rifters in our Realm, which was exciting and terrifying all at once. But I handled it like I handled everything else in my life, like a boss!

As I turned down the next street, the massive wall surrounding the RRS facility appeared. If there's one constant for any government agency, they don't do pretty. What was essentially a solid concrete slab that stood fifteen feet high and two feet thick, surrounded the entire facility. All-in-all, the Krayden branch of the RRS took up the equivalent of three square miles. It was entirely out of place in the middle of a residential neighborhood. But that was by design, apparently.

I'm not sure if it's true or not, but someone told me that during the FRE, this was the first place something from beyond the Rift touched down. And whatever it was leveled a twenty-block radius in the blink of an eye. The RRS showed up almost immediately and quarantined the entire neighborhood. By the time I was released from the hospital, they'd already started construction on the facility. I've never heard of any government agency moving as fast as they did.

They had the entire thing finished within nine months. Go figure. There's a pothole in the middle of Garner Street that's been there since before I moved that still hasn't been fixed. Yet, a new, state-of-the-art research facility that takes up two-thirds of an entire neighborhood? No sweat! Pricks.

A soft buzzing came from my pocket as I continued toward the southern pedestrian entrance, drawing my attention back to reality. I pulled out my phone and smiled, seeing the picture of the only person from my family I actually give a shit about.

Incoming Call: Lana-Banana

Lana was the only child of my asshole of a brother and was by far one of my most favorite people in the world. If anyone could give me hope for the future, it was her. This girl was one of the most intelligent people I've ever met, and I knew without a shadow of a doubt she'd change the world.

"Hey, kiddo! What are you doing up so early? Isn't it, like, 6:00 am there?"

Lana let out a soft chuckle on the other end of the line. "Yeah, but it's fine. I have labs I need to get ready for."

"Jesus," I grumbled. "I don't know how you do it. Mornings are evil."

"I would've never thought you felt that way. Remind me, just how many alarm clocks have you broken so far this year?"

"You know what? Screw you! They make them so fragile these days. I'm pretty sure it's all a ploy from Big Alarm Clock to force us to keep buying them."

"Or," Lana said, dragging out her word slightly. "You could be normal and use your phone like the rest of us. And, you know, not throw it across the entire house for doing what you tell it to do?"

"Nah," I said, shaking my head as if she could see me. "Hard pass."

Lana let out another soft laugh, and I heard some rustling of fabric before she tried to stifle a yawn. "Well, Uncle T, I can't talk long right now. I just wanted to say thank you again for helping me with the tuition for this semester. The RRS programs are fascinating but expensive. There's no way I could afford to keep taking them with just my part-time job."

I smiled, happy that I could do something to help her follow her dreams. She was barely eleven when Rift Events occurred, and just like with us all, her life had been changed forever. Luckily, she hadn't been hurt during the FRE. But she saw the extent of my injuries when Honey had brought her to visit me shortly after I was released from the hospital. Then, when the SRE happened and I got my ability, Lana became fixated on joining the RRS.

Over the years, I tried to talk her out of it. I was a sucker and signed my soul away, but deep down, I've always known there was something not right about the agency. There were things that didn't add up on paper, and I always suspected there was some shady shit happening behind the scenes. Yet, the money was good, and there was no proof they were doing anything wrong, so I stuck around. I still didn't want Lana involved with them, though.

But, just like everyone else in my family, she's too stubborn. I'm just glad that trait skipped me. Lana focused all her studies on learning about space and physics and everything else you'd think you'd need to know about dimensional rifts that allow people to travel to alternate worlds across the cosmos.

Which is a lot. And it costs a *lot* of money to do it. Even with the steep discount I could get by using my Head Rifter position, it still costs over $10k per semester just for the RRS courses. That didn't even include her regular school tuition, either! Now, I've worked with countless dumbasses over the years, so I know most who work at the agency don't have any of those same degrees. But Lana wasn't one to settle for just being another drone in the hive. She wanted to make a difference.

"Guess what?" she asked, the excitement growing in her voice. "One of my instructors this year is a Taritian! Can you believe that?"

"Really? That does sound awesome," I said, trying to give my best pretend voice.

Taritians aren't anything special; they just like to pretend they are. They were one of the first races we made peaceful contact with shortly after the SRE. Standing over seven feet tall, their bodies were covered in strange blue feathers that shimmered anytime they moved. Their faces were what always freaked me out, though. They all wore these blank white masks with big beaks coming out of the middle. It reminded me of the old plague doctor masks people used during the Black Death.

The thing is, so far, I've yet to figure out *why* they wear them. I've been to Taritia countless times, and their atmosphere is identical to ours. They breathe oxygen, and you *cannot* get them to shut up about how immune they are to pretty much all diseases and pathogens. And I know that mask isn't their natural face, either, because I've seen one without it. They look like a strange combination of that big yellow bird on that kid's show mixed with the smaller blue one who's always trying to fuck a chicken. Man, I can't believe we let kids watch stuff like that.

"What's their name? I might know them," I said, trying to show Lana I was as invested in her excitement as she was.

"It's Go . . .Gordinalilaod? Shit, I can't pronounce it! Why isn't my translator chip working yet?!"

I laughed loudly, knowing her frustration. "That's because you're not letting it do the work for you. You just got it last week, so don't worry about it. Most people take a month or two before everything starts flowing naturally. But once it does, you'll be able to speak and understand every known language without effort. Until then, they should tell you the human name to call your instructor for those who don't have the chip yet. Almost no one can pronounce their language correctly without one."

Now that we had access to new Realms, one of the first things we had to do was find a way to communicate with them. Luckily, the Taritians already had developed a chip that could be implanted just behind the ear, and it would instantly translate what you heard and said into the language of the person you were talking to. *If* they were in the Database, that is. First contacts were always a bit on the rough side until we could get them added in. At first, only RRS employees got the chips, but now, almost everyone on Earth has one. At least those that were 21 and over. They didn't allow anyone younger to get them. Don't ask me why, either. I don't know, and it's above my pay grade to ask.

"Hmm," Lana hummed, her mind now obviously fixating on trying to impress her new professor by learning to pronounce their name in their native language. "Well, I need to go. I hope you have a great day! You're in for a treat."

"Wait, what?" I asked, stopping just before I got to the security gate. "What do you mean?"

Lana chuckled, and I heard the smile in her voice. "You got called in this morning, right?"

"Yeah?"

"I was the one who found the jump point!" She exclaimed happily. "Late last night, I found an anomaly with some of the readings. After I reported it to the instructor, they confirmed it was a brand-new jump point! They called it in as I was walking away, and I just so happened to overhear your name get mentioned."

I stared at the towering wall above me, letting that news sink in. New jump points were hard to come by these days. Certain conditions had to be met to jump into a new Realm successfully. Most of the time, we're sent coordinates to where we're going and then jump to an established area. Jumping blind into a new realm was borderline suicidal.

"Alright, Uncle T! Have a great day, and I can't wait to hear about the new Realm when you get back," Lana said, hanging up the phone before I could respond.

Looking at the black screen for a moment, I smiled. I'm so proud of that girl, and I can't wait to see what she can do when given proper resources and guidance. Shoving my phone back into my pocket, I approached the door and slid my ID over to the Winly guard sitting outside. The Winly were, on average, about nine feet tall and were some of the scariest SOBs out there. They had thick, dark gray skin and pitch-black eyes. People were deathly afraid of the hulking beast, as they reminded almost every one of the stereotypical cave trolls from old fantasy movies.

"Hey, Gregg," I said, smiling slightly at the security guard. "How's it going today?"

"Not Gregg," the Winly grunted before pushing my ID back and hitting a button to open the door for me.

"Alright, have a good one, Gregg," I said, walking past the stand and into the narrow corridor.

"NOT GREGG!" He yelled angrily after me.

Security for the RRS was no joke. From start to finish, it usually took me twenty minutes to go through seven checkpoints, which included everything from showing my ID to a full body scan. And just like with Gregg, almost none of the security team has any sense of humor. I thought I might actually get tased the first time

I jokingly asked the man patting me down if he was going to give me a reach around while he was back there.

My watch buzzed again, letting me know I was late for the briefing. Shaking my head, I buckled my belt as I left the last checkpoint. "One of these days, y'all need to buy me dinner!"

Nothing. Not even a smile. Humorless twats. Sighing, I picked up my pace and headed down the twisting maze of the RRS Krayden facility. I've been with them for ten years and still don't know where eighty percent of the corridors lead. But I didn't really *need* to know. I had my little piece, and I was okay with that.

"Hey, Turtle," a diminutive voice called out as I rushed past a small sitting area lined with hard plastic furniture. "Turtle!"

Without stopping, I tilted my head back and looked down toward where the voice was coming from. Running from halfway down the hall, a very short man was waving his tiny arms at me. Haladro was an imp. Well, not really, but that's the best way I could describe them the first time I met the race. I think they're really called the Pridactonir or something like that. But I mean, come on. He's three-foot-tall and has red skin, horns, and a pointed tail. If that isn't an imp, I don't know what is.

"Hey, Hal! I can't talk right now, buddy. Running late."

"I know," Hal continued running, trying to catch up to me. "I was sent to find you. I have a note for you."

That got my attention, so I slowed and let the small man catch up. I can't tell you how much you just don't fully get used to seeing magical creatures wearing a mustard yellow button-down shirt and tie. I swear if Hal wore glasses and didn't have horns, I'd bet anything he'd be trying to sell me paper as an assistant to the regional manager somewhere.

Hal finally caught up and almost doubled over trying to catch his breath. I watched with a bit of amusement as he tried to collect himself. "You okay, buddy?"

Nodding, Hal looked up with a half-smile. "Yeah, I've been looking for you for thirty minutes. These halls are not made for someone like me."

"Why didn't you just hit my watch?"

Shaking his head, Hal pulled a folded piece of paper from his back pocket, handing it to me. "I was told no communication over the frequency. For your eyes only."

Curiosity got the best of me, and I grabbed the paper. A wave of warm energy pulsed around me the minute I touched it. My eyes widened as I looked back at Hal, who seemed to be staring at absolutely nothing. I turned around to confirm my suspicion, and I was right. Everyone else walking around us was frozen, as if time had stopped for everyone but me.

I looked down at the paper in my hand, turning it over again and again, but I didn't see anything on the outside. This wasn't my first Time Stop. It was one of the innate powers Hal's people had. It's one reason they were so valuable to the RRS. It guaranteed that no one except the intended person or group would be aware of it. You could have entire conversations without any worry of someone overhearing. Everything would just return to normal, and barely a blink of a second would've passed for everyone else.

I opened the note but was even more confused by what was written inside. It was a string of numbers and letters in extremely precise block handwriting. After doing this for so long, I recognized it as coordinates for a jump; I just didn't know to where. I'd never come anywhere close to those coordinates before.

The edges of the paper slowly began to turn black as a small flame flicked at the corners. The sudden heat surprised me, causing me to drop it and shake my slightly singed fingertips. The moment the paper touched the floor, it erupted in a bright flash of light and disintegrated instantly. Another pulse spread throughout the hall, and everyone around began to move as if nothing had happened.

I stared in shock and confusion at the tiny bits of ash on the floor before looking back at Hal. The imp was just standing there with a strained smile on his face. "Okay, Hal, what was that? Who sent me coordinates like that instead of just buzzing them straight to my watch like usual? I didn't even have a chance to write it down."

Shaking his head slowly, Hal looked around as if trying to find whatever answer I was looking for. "I'm not sure what you're talking about, Turtle. What coordinates? Wait, did you get new coordinates? Where are you going?"

With a long sigh, I tilted my head back and closed my eyes in frustration. I'd forgotten the other reason the RRS likes to use the imps. If they perform a Time Stop, their minds get wiped when finished. No mess, no worries about security leaks. A magical memory wipe is pretty much a one-way trip, so there's no way someone could learn anything from them.

"Never mind," I said, turning to walk back toward the briefing room. "I'll see you later, Hal."

I entered the conference room and slipped in the back door as Director Wallace reviewed the new inoculation policy. "Lots of strange diseases out there, folks. Ensure you get your updated shots before the end of the week."

I stopped listening the minute he opened his mouth; my mind focused on the strange note Hal had given me. Who would send me something like that? Those coordinates didn't make any sense. With everything I've ever known about jumping the Rift, there wasn't anything in that area. It was just dead space way out in no-man's land. Besides, there wasn't even a way to get out there if I wanted to.

Jumps require an incredible amount of energy. There are so many variables to consider, from how many people you're taking to the most minute details like what size lip balm you have in your pocket. Yes, I use lip balm. Got a problem with that?

According to Dr. Saph, I was named Head Rifter because I somehow had one of the strongest connections to the Rift. That made it much easier for me to make the actual jumps. Yet, even with that extra advantage, I could only perform a dozen or so in a day. And that would drain me to the point of passing out. To get anywhere close to those coordinates would require thousands of jumps—probably more.

Let me put it into a better perspective for you. Imagine the entire Rift that we know about is our solar system. Most Rifters can jump the equivalent of a state or two at a time, with the average being able to make seven jumps daily, whether in a row or spread out. On the other hand, I can jump to the moon in one go. Luckily, we can make consecutive jumps in the Pathways and don't have to pull out to make the next. But those coordinates wouldn't even be in our solar system in this scenario. It'd be in Alpha Centauri somewhere.

"So, give them all a hand and wish them the best today!" Dr. Wallace's voice echoed off the sterile walls of the room.

The claps of everyone brought me back, and I started clapping along without knowing what was happening. I looked around and saw several people looking at me with half-smiles or nods of acknowledgment. I kicked myself for not paying more attention. I always told my parents that I had ADD or something. But did they believe me? No. Instead, I have the attention span of a golden retriever who saw a squirrel.

"You have no idea what's going on, do you?" a woman with a smooth English accent whispered behind me.

"Of course I do," I said, turning and looking down into familiar green eyes.

Arabella Anderson had transferred to Krayden almost four years ago from the UK and was what the RRS called a Healer. And, yes, it's precisely what it sounds like. After the SRE, she found she could tap into a person's life energy and help heal them. I never really understood what she was talking about when she tried to describe it to me, though. All I know is if you get hurt, Ara will fix you.

I remember playing video games when I was younger; no one ever wanted to be the healer. They were considered weak and not as fun. But now that I'm going out into these worlds with people getting put into dangerous situations all the time, I can promise you the healer is pretty damn important. It's an unspoken rule that when push comes to shove, the two people you protect during a hairy situation are the Rifter and the Healer.

Ara narrowed her eyes at me, her long, red curls outlining her freckled face. "So why are you clapping then?"

I looked around, hoping to find some clue to the answer. "Uh . . . They're . . . bringing back taco Tuesday?"

Ara snorted and let out a single laugh, slapping me hard on the arm. Now, I'm a big guy. Well over six and a half feet tall and easily two fifty of solid muscle. This little girl barely came to my chest and looked like a strong wind would send her back across the Atlantic. But that slap caused me to wince and rub the reddening skin.

"Ouch!" I hissed, trying to play up the pain. "That's not fair to use your power like that. I thought nurses are supposed to help people feel better, not worse!"

Shaking her head, Ara tried to tuck strands of her unruly hair behind her ears. "You're just getting weak, *Turtle*."

"Woman, please," I said, shooting her a cocky grin. "I could lift you with one finger if I wanted."

Ara's smile widened even more as she leaned in, her voice low with a slight growl. "I bet you could do a lot with one finger if I let you."

I laughed, shaking my head. Ara had always been fun to hang around, and I was lucky she requested to be on my team when she transferred. She was brilliant and funny and was one of the only people I've ever met who could match my sense of humor. I won't lie; I've had a major crush on her for years. And with how she acts a lot of the time, I knew there was a good chance she had some kind of feelings for me as well. However, since I was her superior, I never wanted to cross any boundaries that could make her uncomfortable if I was wrong. Not to mention, it was against agency policy, and I wouldn't do anything that would jeopardize Ara's career like that. She just liked to make it hard for me sometimes. Pun not intended.

Ara's smile fell slightly, and she quickly looked around before leaning back toward me. "They announced we're going to explore a new jump point today."

"We?" I asked, shocked they were sending Ara with us. "Usually, it's just me and the Shield."

Shrugging, Ara winked at me. "I guess we just make a good team. Besides, you'll want me there when you hear who your Shield is."

I groaned and looked up toward the heavens, wishing with every fiber of my being that another Rift Event would happen and, this time, finish the job of taking me out. "Please, don't tell me—"

"Chet," Ara said with a smirk.

"Fuuuuck . . ." I moaned, shaking my head. "He's so annoying! Why can't I have Barret or even Jay?"

Shrugging once again, Ara gave me a sympathetic smile. "At least you'll have me?"

I smiled at her and nodded. She was right. Ara always made the jumps fun, even on mundane, monotonous trips. It still sucked having Chet be the one I had to deal with.

He was what they called a 'Shield.' After the SRE, we quickly learned that we couldn't jump with many kinds of weapons. Don't ask me why. It just doesn't work. Every single Rifter has tried countless times and under many different circumstances. If anyone in the group were holding a firearm or explosive or anything like that, the weapon would be left behind. So that's why we relied on groups known as the Swords and the Shields, who were given offensive and defensive abilities during the SRE.

In regards to the Shields, think of them basically as tanks. They have swift reflexes with almost super-human strength; some can even create a barrier to protect others. Chet was the Head Shield and one of the strongest of them all. He also seemed to have a brain about the size of a peanut. He's the perfect sap that buys into absolutely anything the RRS tells him. I can't stress this point enough; he's a massive tool.

The meeting finally broke up as Ara and I exited the room and headed down the corridor toward my prep room. When I jump, I usually don't need to prep anything anymore. As long as I have my coordinates and a general knowledge of what I'm taking, I can go from anywhere. However, like with any government agency, there are procedures to follow.

"So, I was thinking of going to the pub for trivia tonight," Ara said as we walked through the twisting corridors. "I know last time we got really close to winning. So . . . I was wondering if . . . you'd like to be my partner again? I'll buy you a bevy after, win or lose!"

"Ha!" I laughed and nodded, remembering our near win. "We would've won if it wasn't for that stupid last question. I mean, who the hell knows that East Timor has the highest tax rate as a percentage of GDP?! That was just bullshit! Well, trivia does sound like a lot of fun, but unfortunately, I can't tonight. My roommates just got approved for an adoption license, so we're going out to celebrate."

"Oh," Ara said, a slight catch in her voice. "That's g-great! Tell them I said congrats. And if you get done early with that and feel like hanging out after, let me know. I'll probably be up late tonight . . ."

I nodded and smiled down at her. "Thanks! Yeah, for sure. It'll depend on how many jumps they have planned today. I'm basically just a glorified multi-realm rideshare. But if they don't run me dry, that could be fun. You still have that old Playstation?"

Ara chuckled and bobbed her head. "Yeah! We could play a few rounds of that fighting game you got me. And you know, you can always just stay the night if you get too tired . . ."

We rounded the last corner and suddenly stopped, seeing several people outside my prep room. The blood ran cold in my veins as they all turned to look directly at me. The five highest-ranked individuals in the entire RRS stood quietly, studying me as if looking for some kind of weakness. Listen, I'm not one to get intimidated easily. But seeing your boss's boss's boss glare at you can make the old twig and berries shrink a bit.

"Rifter TTL, are you ready for your jump?" Director Gram Wallace asked, his beady eyes boring deep into me.

"Uh . . . Yes, sir," I said, glancing at Ara, who seemed to step back and now stood partially hidden behind me. "Healer Anderson and I are ready for the jump."

"Where's your containment case?" General David Norvik, the World Council's military liaison, asked.

"Containment case, sir?"

"Yes, son, your containment case," the General snapped back. "Or do you need to be reminded about the rules of being a Rifter?"

I shook my head, trying to force myself to think. Rules of being a Rifter? I remember being told them a long time ago. But after a while, you just start doing whatever. It's like with every job. You're taught how they want you to do something, and then you find the way that actually works and do it that way instead. I thought hard until it finally clicked in the back of my mind.

"Rule Number One: Never jump with an uncontained shard," I said, my eyes widening with the realization. "Sir, is there a possibility of actually finding a shard on this jump?"

The men simply nodded before turning back to each other, talking quietly. I was stunned at the thought of finally finding a shard. "Holy . . ."

"Shit," Ara finished from just behind.

Chapter 4

From Bad To Shitstorm

A shard. Like a real, *actual* shard. I couldn't believe what they were saying. When Dr. Saph recruited me, she told me that the purpose of the RRS was to help spread throughout the Realms in search of powerful artifacts that could help us defend ourselves from another attack and bring peace to everyone. Those were the shards.

According to the RRS, the shards were once part of a single . . . thing. No one knows what it was in the beginning. Some said it was a sword; others said a shield. Some say it wasn't anything we would've even recognized. But no matter who tells the story, everyone agrees that a massively powerful *thing* once existed somewhere.

Then, just like every fantasy book, comic, show, game, etc., a big bad shattered it. When it broke, it released a powerful blast that ripped through the very fabric of time and space, creating what we know as the Rift. Shards of the item scattered into the countless Realms, each still containing pieces of its former power. There was no consensus about what they looked like or even how many there were. They're just . . . out there somewhere, and it's our job to find them.

Sounds like a load of bull, right? That's what I thought this whole time, at least. Ten years of doing this, I've never even heard of a shard being found, let alone recovered by the RRS. But the fact that the five most powerful people in the world now stood before my prep door made me question my previous thoughts on the subject.

"An actual shard?!" Ara whispered, gripping my arm from behind as tightly as she could. "Turtle! A shard!"

"Yeah, I heard," I hissed, trying to get her to calm down before the very important men who signed our paychecks saw her acting like a little girl drooling over a piece of candy. "Be cool. Okay? It's no big deal. We're going to treat this like any other jump. Alright? You with me?"

Ara squeezed my arm tighter against her chest, and I became very aware that she wasn't wearing a bra. Her soft breasts wrapped around my arm, and I felt the tip of one of her nipples harden against my skin. I quickly turned, pulling my arm away as I walked around a corner and down the hall. Spinning on her heels, Ara chased me, obviously confused about where I was going.

"What are you—"

"Rule One," I said, walking into a supply closet at the end of the hall. "Never jump with an uncontained shard. I stopped keeping containments in my prep room a while ago. But I'm pretty sure . . . Yup! Here's one."

She gave me a quizzical look, tilting her head to the side as she thought. "Why don't you keep them in your prep room?"

Shrugging, I wiped some dust off the large metal container that looked like it should be a prop from a lousy heist movie rather than a real piece of state-of-the-art equipment. "They get in the way, and I don't even remember the last time I trained with one."

"Aren't you required to do the yearly training like the rest of us?"

I gave her a cocky smile and winked before heading back down the hallway. "I knew I forgot to do *something* the last seven years or so. I guess it's good that the agency follows *some* governmental stereotypes. Like failing to follow up on test outs."

Ara stopped walking, her mouth agape. "Are you serious?! I've been doing those stupid—"

"Hey, keep up," I snapped my fingers at her as I continued to head back to the prep room. "Pitter-patter, little lady."

Ara let out a low growl and began to catch up to me quickly. I chuckled, knowing she'd probably find a way to get back at me for that. We rounded the corner again, but the corridor was empty this time. There was no sign of the superior officers anywhere. I hesitated, wondering if they'd entered my prep room, though it wasn't big enough for all of them.

Stepping past me, Ara let her arm fly backward just enough that the back of her hand slapped me directly in the balls, sending a lightning bolt of pain through my entire body. I yelped and doubled over, gripping my screaming manhood as firmly as I dared. "God damn it! You got 'em both . . ."

"Pitter-patter," Ara said without breaking her stride as she continued toward the prep room.

"Fuck you," I was barely able to whisper as I hobbled after her.

Ara entered the prep room first, but I was just behind. I was finally able to stand back up as I walked through the door. The room was barely the size of my bedroom, with shelves lining the walls filled with tools and bins from all over. A large table was pushed to the side, stacked with binders and more bins of random things from my past few weeks of jumps. Ara stood in shock as she stared around the room.

"You're . . . filthy," she exclaimed, turning to look at me in surprise.

"Hey! I'm not filthy. This is organized chaos. Is this really your first time coming into my prep room?"

Ara continued to look around as she nodded. "Yeah, you usually come grab me from the A&E."

I chuckled and shook my head as I watched her trying to make sense of my room. "Well, don't you worry your pretty little head about it, okay? I know where everything is in here."

Crossing her arms in front of her chest, Ara narrowed her eyes at me. "Really? Okay, so where's the Elips mineral samples from last week?"

I pointed to a bin pushed behind a lamp on the floor. "Right there."

"Okay, how about the fossils we found on H'atula?"

Walking to one of the shelves, I pulled down a large, black bin and set it in front of her. "There. Still doubting me?"

"Sure," Ara said, keeping her arms crossed. "But, when we have a day off together, we're coming back here, and I'm going to help you put this place in order."

Groaning, I shook my head as I pulled a binder from the bottom of a pile on my desk. "Okay, mom!"

Flipping it open, I found the tab I needed and turned to the page titled Shard Containment for Rift Travel. I quickly read through it, refamiliarizing myself with the bulky technology. "Alright, seems pretty standard. I just need to take into account the extra mass for the jump, and we should be good to go!"

Clearing her throat, Ara cocked an eyebrow at me. I looked at her, confused about what she was doing. She was hinting at something, but I couldn't understand what. After several seconds of us staring at each other, Ara sighed and shook her head.

"Forgetting something? Or rather, *someone*?"

It finally clicked, and I rolled my eyes and threw my head back in frustration. "Damn it! Why does Chet have to suck so much?"

Laughing, Ara turned and walked out of the room, leaving me no choice but to follow. "Come on. It's not that bad. And remember, I'll be there to hold your hand."

I laughed as we made our way down the hall toward the one place we knew Chet would be. Sure enough, the second I turned the corner to the gym, we heard the loud crash of weights slamming to the ground, followed by a man roaring out and people cheering him on. Yeah, like I said before, he's a tool. I strapped the containment case to my back and reached for the door handle.

"I bet you ten bucks he's going to scream 'For Destiny!' before we leave," I whispered to Ara, causing her to cover her mouth to stifle a laugh.

"Ah! My Rifter and Healer have finally arrived!" Chet yelled to the crowd gathered around, watching him work out.

Now, I might be a big dude, but Chet was ridiculous. I never knew him before either of the Rift Events, so I'm not sure if he was always a freak of nature or if he got his size from his abilities. He stood well over seven feet tall and was five hundred pounds of pure, solid muscle. It was one more reason I hated being paired with him. One Chet was equal to three ordinary people when it came to jumps.

"Hey, Chet, you about ready?" I asked, looking at my watch, which now glowed with the coordinates we were being sent to.

"Of course, sir Rifter!" Chet said with a boisterous laugh. "Give me but a moment, and I shall be with you, post haste!"

I sighed and shook my head as he turned and left the gym, followed by his groupies. "I hate him. So. Much."

"Oh, stop," Ara said, touching my arm. "I think it's funny. He's like one of those blokes who like dressing up, attending Renaissance fairs, and pretending to be a knight. He's a bit of a muppet, but he's got a good heart."

I gave her a weary look, trying to express my annoyance as best I could. "Yeah, it's not his heart I have issues with, though."

We waited almost thirty minutes before the doors swung open, and Chet walked back out wearing precisely what I feared. Heavy plate armor covered his entire torso, arms, and legs. Every piece had been perfectly polished and buffed, causing the overhead fluorescence to shimmer off brilliantly. Most people saw a brave hero ready to fight the good fight against the forces of darkness. I saw another two hundred pounds of useless metal I'd have to drag across the Realms.

"For Destiny!" Chet yelled, pumping his fist high as the group following him cheered his name.

"Told you," I whispered to Ara, who once again tried to cover her mouth to hide her laugh.

Chet stopped in front of me and offered his gauntleted hand. I sighed and grabbed it, ensuring I had a firm grip. Before I could reach for Ara, I felt her fingers slip in between mine, gripping firmly. It was something she'd done since her very first jump with me. I initially thought it was strange, but now I find it incredibly endearing. I gave her a reassuring smile to let her know I had her no matter what.

I closed my eyes and opened myself to the pull I felt deep inside. It was always there, just below the surface. Dr. Saph said it was the energy of the Rift calling to itself. It yearned to return to the Pathways, so it was up to me to keep it in check. I couldn't just let it go where it wanted, though; otherwise, it would tear me apart. I needed to guide it along the edges, letting the pull of the Rift take me to where I wanted.

Keeping the coordinates in my mind, I felt the pull of the Rift, and then we were off. Everyone felt something different when they jumped. Some people said it felt like they were falling, and others said it was like the cosmos were ripping at them. To me, it felt calming. Yes, it was chaotic and scary. But at the same time, it felt familiar, like I belonged in the tornado of energy that flowed throughout the universe.

After five consecutive jumps, I finally felt our destination approach. Slowly, I began pulling back the energy drawn from my core to ease our way into the Realm. At that moment, for the first time ever, my power didn't obey me. Instead, I felt an even stronger pull that almost ripped Chet and Ara out of my hands. I gripped tighter, trying to pull the energy back once again. Another violent tug pulled me backward, and I felt like I was free-falling from a great height.

My heart raced as I searched for which direction I needed to go. I was lost in the rapid currents, unsure which way was right. Cursing under my breath, I fought down a rancid pit that formed in my gut. I felt Ara's fingers squeezing between mine, and a cooling relief washed through me. She was using her power to calm my mind while I battled through the Rift, and it was exactly what I needed.

With one final push, I found our location. Gritting my teeth, I strained every muscle and pulled away from the Rift. Seconds felt like hours as I waited to see if it was finished. I realized we were out when I felt Ara rubbing my finger with her thumb.

I opened my eyes just as I collapsed to my knees, feeling every bit of energy drain from my body. Ara yelped and stepped forward, steadying me before I fell completely over. I briefly stared at nothing before my vision finally cleared. A warm pair of emerald green eyes stared deep into me. I gave her a weary smile and nodded my thanks.

"Sorry about that," my voice was weak and hoarse. It felt like I'd spent an hour screaming at the top of my lungs.

"You're good," Ara said quietly, running her hand over my face to wipe away the sweat pouring down. "That was . . ."

I nodded, closing my eyes once again. "Yeah. That was a new one for me. I've never had that happen before."

Looking around, I noticed we were in a sort of glade in the middle of a large forest. The trees around us were at least twice as thick and tall as the old redwood trees in our world. It was night, but this Realm had two moons sitting high above, illuminating the forest around us. I looked around in confusion, realizing we were missing someone.

"Where's Chet?"

Ara closed her eyes and placed her hands on my temples. I felt the familiar cooling rush, and my heart began to slow back to normal. "As soon as we got here, he took off, telling me to stay with you until you came around."

"Really? How long was I out?"

Opening her eyes, Ara gave me a warm smile as she shrugged one shoulder. "Just a couple of minutes. And it looks like you're all good now. But your official orders are to rest. So you just sit here with me, and we'll let Chet do the initial scout."

I wanted to argue with her that the sooner we completed the scouting, the sooner we could leave. But I knew she was right. I wasn't feeling that great and could use a bit of a rest. I sat back, holding either side of my head as I thought about what happened. Never had I felt so out of control in the Rift. There had been times when it was a bit on the rough side. Especially when I had large groups or had already jumped multiple times that day. But even then, my power had never disobeyed me.

We sat silently for several minutes, listening to the strange calls of this world's wildlife sing out into the night. The cool breeze wisped around us, drying the last bits of sweat rolling down my neck. I closed my eyes and focused on breathing, ensuring I could still feel the gentle pull of power that usually resides just below the surface. I know it sounds weird coming from someone who looks like a stereotypical meathead, but yoga and meditation work wonders when it comes to jumping. It helps you regain your energy faster and makes the jumps easier when you're not having to fight to keep your balance every time.

"So," Ara said, breaking the silence. "I've never done a new point jump before. How do they . . ."

"Know we're not going to die instantly on a planet with no sustainable atmosphere?" I finished for her with a chuckle. "It's usually the first question people ask during one of these. I don't know the specifics, but the brains much higher up on the ladder figure it out beforehand. They do some kind of calculations with probabilities and quantum physics, and a bunch of other words my high school diploma didn't teach me. I've heard of them finding a point before where the calculations determined it wasn't hospitable for humans, so we never went. Or maybe they passed the info on to one of the other Realms better suited for it. Not really sure."

Nodding acceptance, Ara looked around the clearing again. "Have you done many of these kinds of jumps before?"

Shrugging, I tried to think about all the new points I'd jumped to over the years. "I think a couple hundred?"

Ara spun and looked at me in shock. "A couple hundred? You've been to hundreds of different worlds?!"

I laughed loudly, shaking my head and giving her a cocky grin. I'd almost forgotten that Ara didn't come with us on every jump since most were mundane. They're just glorified errands like supply runs for embassies, for the most part. "I've been to thousands. I meant *new* point jumps. For some reason, they tend to send me when they pop up."

Taken by surprise, I watched as Ara stared at me in amazement. "So why did you ask me to come with you on this one? Your note made it seem . . ."

Her question caught me off-guard. "Huh? What do you mean? What note—"

Before I could finish, a terrible howl shattered the calm night air. Without a second thought, Ara and I shot to our feet, scanning the clearing for danger. A massive explosion boomed from somewhere in the distance, causing the ground to shake under our feet. More howls began to fill the air, coming from every direction through the trees.

"What's going on?!" Ara yelled, pressing herself closer to me as she frantically looked around.

"I don't know, but we need to leave!" I shouted, tapping my watch to pull up Chet's GPS tracker.

Three concussive booms broke through the forest, each closer than the last. The force of the explosions rocked the ground, causing Ara to lose balance and fall into me. Steadying her with one hand, I cursed as the small watch screen showed only mine and Ara's tracker. Less than a hundred feet away, a heavy limb from one of the trees cracked and fell hard to the ground just as another explosion sent a new tremor through the earth.

"Where is he?!" I screamed, trying once again to find Chet's ping.

"Turtle," Ara gasped, gripping my arm tightly in fear.

I looked down to reassure her but saw she wasn't looking at me. Her eyes were wide in terror as she stared across the clearing. I quickly turned and saw what had caused her reaction. My stomach lurched, and my knees grew weak when my eyes landed on the creature stepping into the glade.

I'd never seen anything like it before, and the only word I could come up with was monster. It stood over eight feet tall and was covered in what looked to be matted gray fur. Massive arms as thick as my torso hung low, with clawed fingers almost dragging the ground beside it. It had a long snout with sharp, jagged teeth sticking out in several directions. Its eyes glowed a dim yellow as it glared at us across the clearing.

"ACA VIMATO LINASIT!" The creature yelled before tilting its head back and letting out another terrible howl into the night sky.

The language didn't register with our chips, which meant this creature wasn't in the RRS Database. That was somewhat comforting, knowing that we weren't the only ones in the dark here. Except, we *were* the ones in the *actual* dark with that thing.

"FUCK!" I screamed, grabbing Ara by the hand and yanking her behind me.

I took off through the thick trees, trying to put some kind of distance between us and that creature. I felt Ara trying to keep up, but my legs were much longer than hers. Cursing again, I stopped and turned, wrapping one arm under her knees and the other behind her back.

"Wait, What?" Ara tried to protest as I began to run again, carrying her in my arms.

"LOOK FOR CHET!" I yelled, just as another howl came from beside us, followed by more explosions.

I felt Ara shuffling in my arms as I turned and pushed away from the last explosion. "I . . . I can't find him!"

"Shit!" I yelled, just as the ground behind me erupted, shooting sharp pieces of rock into my body.

I fell forward but tucked at the last moment so I didn't crush Ara underneath my heavy frame. She flew from my arms as I rolled almost a dozen yards before finally coming to a stop. My head was foggy from the concussive force of the explosion, and I had a sharp pain stabbing my left hamstring. I blinked several times, trying to clear my vision to find Ara. My heart froze when I finally saw her.

Less than ten feet away stood the monster. Well, at least it was *a* monster. It was about the same height as the other one, but its fur was a fiery red. But that didn't matter. What did was the woman he held hanging in the air by her throat.

"Ara!" I yelled, trying to force myself to stand back up.

You know how they say your adrenaline kicks up so high in the heat of battle that you can even ignore pain? I'm telling you right now, that's bull shit. I felt every bit of that pain as I slowly stood back up. The monster kept its back to me, either not having heard me scream or just thinking I wasn't a threat.

Ara clawed at the monstrous hand that was wrapped tightly around her throat. Her legs dangled several feet in the air as she flailed in a feeble attempt to breathe. I saw her eyes, wide in terror, turn to look for me, begging for help. Something inside snapped, and a rage I hadn't felt in years boiled over.

I yelled out, not sure if it was in pain or anger, and charged. Tilting down slightly, I drove my shoulder hard into the creature's back, slamming my entire body weight into it. The monster didn't even move an inch. I, on the other hand, felt like I'd just slammed shoulder-first into a solid concrete pillar.

"Fuck!" I screamed but didn't let the failed attack stop me.

I pulled back my fist and swung as hard as possible to where I thought its kidney would be. My fist hit what felt like solid rock, and three fingers broke instantly. I screamed and cursed but continued trying to find a way to break Ara from the monster's grip. I stepped in front of the creature, hoping to get it to focus on me instead. I swung my uninjured hand, punching it in its gut. Again, my attack did nothing.

The monster kept its eyes focused on Ara, whose face had started turning blue as her movements grew weaker. I knew I was out of time. There had to be a weakness to this thing, right? Growing desperate, I frantically looked around and noticed something that gave me hope. This creature was a male. And all men know one universal truth: Balls are sensitive no matter where you're from.

Taking a quick step back, I slammed my size fifteen, steel-toed leather boot as hard as I could directly into the monster's groin. One of its testicles instantly burst, while the other rocketed deep into the creature's body. Based on what I learned in my eighth-grade health class, I knew its blood vessels and nerves had most likely twisted, cutting off the appendage's circulation. It was a condition every man had learned to fear, known as testicular torsion.

But that wasn't the only damage done to the monster, though. The tip of its penis had caught between my boot and the creature's tough skin, severing the head from the root. Ara fell to the ground as the monster released a horrible cry of pain. Its knees buckled, and it fell, clawing at its now ruined genitals.

I rushed to Ara, who lay coughing furiously on the ground, trying to refill her lungs. "Are you alright? Can you stand?"

After several more coughs, Ara shakily nodded, and I helped her to her feet. The monster continued to writhe in agony on the ground, howling unintelligible sounds into the night. Just then, another explosion boomed only a few feet to our left. I cursed, looking at my watch one last time but still only seeing our two dots.

"We have to go!" I said, grabbing Ara with both of my hands.

"What about—"

"We can't wait for him! We have to go now!" I said, not even waiting for her to respond.

I closed my eyes and opened my core, letting the energy of the Rift yank us from the realm. The exit was much harder than the entry. I felt extreme pressure as countless invisible strands pulled from every angle. The pain radiating through my body was magnified a hundred times as we barreled through the chaos that was the Rift. I tried to return to the RRS, but something was blocking me.

I knew which way to go, but every time I tried, it felt like I was slammed into a brick wall. I gritted my teeth as more pain shot through my body, but I kept pushing forward. In one last desperate attempt, I flung myself at the invisible wall blocking us from returning and finally broke through.

Chapter 5
The Long Road Of Recovery

Hospitals suck. The food, the air, the constant beeping sounds. Especially those damn beeping sounds. It's too much like an alarm clock if you ask me. Either way, I'm sure everyone here can agree with me that hospitals are just the worst.

One of the best things to come out of the SRE was all the Healers that gained their powers. In a single day, the need for hospitals around the world plummeted. Why go to one when there's a good chance one of your neighbors was a Healer? Just a bit of energy here, a touch of the hand there, and *boom*! You're all taken care of!

Unfortunately, Healers weren't all-powerful, all-knowing Gods. Unlike the rest of us, their abilities were somehow linked to their knowledge of healing. I don't know; I'm not a Healer. Go ask one of them if you want to find out more. I just know that Healers tended to be doctors and nurses, which made their powers even stronger. Ara was a nurse practitioner and one of the best around, if I say so myself.

Hospitals still exist, though. Sometimes, a Healer can't handle a situation on their own, or whatever's wrong with the person is so horrible that special teams are needed to deal with it. They can't do things like replace missing limbs, cure cancer, or anything like that. So nowadays, hospitals are mainly used for severe cases and people needing surgery or whatnot. Since the FRE, I've tried to avoid them at all costs. But sometimes we just don't get a choice, do we?

The soft beeping of the heart monitor was the first thing I heard as my mind returned to reality. The sterile plastic smell of the oxygen tube up my nose caused my stomach to flip, bringing back horrible memories from the past. Slowly, I cracked open my eyes, letting the slightest bit of light in.

Big mistake. It felt like someone took a burning hot ice pick and shoved it directly into my eyeball. I groaned in protest, cursing whoever thought it was a good idea to put fluorescent lights in a hospital room. A gentle cooling sensation flowed through my body, and the pain in my head faded as I felt soft fingers brush through my hair.

"Hush now," Ara whispered, her voice calming as I felt her energy bleed away the worst of the pain. "It's okay, Turtle. You're okay."

Turning my head toward her voice took so much energy. It felt like every muscle in my body had been flushed with battery acid. I'd run marathons before without feeling anywhere close to this sore. I opened my eyes and tried to put on the best smile I could for the woman leaning over me.

Ara was wearing a pair of light blue scrubs, with her fiery red hair tied in a high bun. Her emerald gaze stared intently into my eyes, searching for something deep within. It took me far too long to realize she was sitting on the edge of my bed, with her hand resting gently on my cheek. My face flushed, and I forced myself to break eye contact with her.

"What happened?" I asked; my voice was raspy, barely above a whisper.

"You saved me, that's what," Ara said, trembling.

Slowly, I shook my head as I replayed the last few minutes of the escape. "I didn't—"

"Yes, you did," Ara said, leaning closer and grabbing my hand. "If not for you, I would've died back there. You saved me *and* got us back home."

My mind raced as I thought about those monsters and how I'd never heard of anything like them before. I've seen things most would never think possible. I've met beings that, until ten years ago, we thought were only make-believe. Yet, those monsters were on a whole other level.

Flicking my eyes up to meet Ara's, I tried to focus on what I wanted to ask. It was still hard to talk, and I could feel myself rapidly losing energy. "Chet?"

Ara took a deep breath before slowly shaking her head. "The official reports say he was KIA, but they're not releasing who he was with or where. The truth is, they're just not sending anyone back to find him. At least, not anytime soon. So, if he isn't dead already . . ."

She let the implication hang in the air. I nodded, a lump forming in my throat. Chet was a self-righteous, arrogant prick who took his cosplay too seriously. He was a giant pain in my ass almost every time I worked with him. But he didn't deserve to be abandoned like that. Even with all his faults, he wasn't a bad guy. Just annoying. Yet, if the RRS didn't want to send another team to look for him, there wasn't anything I could do about it.

I felt Ara's soft hands slowly rubbing my fingers as I tried to look around. There wasn't anything extraordinary about the room—the same mundane wall paint and crappy motel art that you find in any hospital. When my eyes landed on Ara, I noticed the fading marks from bruises around her neck. Something inside me churned, and I felt my deep-set rage rise once again. That monster hurt her. More than that, he tried to kill her! *Her*!

Ara was the sweetest, funniest, kindest person I've ever met. And that creature tried to kill her. I made a silent vow right then and there that if I ever came across that beast again, I'd do so much worse than just kick him in the nuts. Next time, I'd take its head off.

Noticing my eyes on her neck, Ara flushed and ran her fingers over the fading marks. "Whatever those creatures were . . . the wounds they inflict can't be healed with our abilities. I've had several of the best Healers try, and they're all confused by it. But it's okay. It's much better now that I've had some time to heal."

Furrowing my brow, I shook my head as much as I could. "Time? How long has it been?"

"About two weeks?"

My mouth dropped open as I stared in disbelief. "Two weeks?! What . . . How?"

Tears formed at the edge of Ara's eyes as she quickly turned away, trying not to let me see. "When we came out of the jump, it was bad. I'd never seen someone lose that much blood and still be alive. Your aim was impeccable, though. You dropped us into the A&E right in front of Dr. Astin. He's the best Healer I've ever met and had you on a gurney before I could even stand up."

Her voice trembled as she continued to stare out into the hall. I wasn't sure what she was looking at, but something deep inside urged me to comfort her. I reached out and placed my hand on her thigh. She jumped slightly before looking down and seeing it was only my hand. Giving me a strained smile, she gripped my fingers and squeezed.

"You had severe internal hemorrhaging. Blood was pouring from every orifice that I could see. Your hamstring had been all but severed in half, several broken bones, a dislocated shoulder, and countless pieces of stone shrapnel sticking out from your back, legs, and arms. If it wasn't for Dr. Astin . . ."

Well, shit. Everything was such a blur there towards the end that I still couldn't make sense of what happened. But after hearing all that, I had no idea how I was still breathing. Part of me wanted to ask if there'd been another miracle, but then I just shook that away. I didn't really care how I was alive. I was still here, and that's all that matters.

A soft buzz sounded, causing Ara and I to look at the small table beside the bed. My phone's screen lit up as it buzzed again with the incoming call. Ara reached over and picked it up, smiling as she handed it to me. "Honey's been checking in almost every hour since I told her you'd most likely be waking up today."

I raised an eyebrow, looking cautiously at the phone. "She's going to be pissed."

Ara snorted a quick laugh before standing from the bed and walking to the door. "I'm sure you can handle whatever she throws at you."

I swiped up on the phone just as Ara left. "Hey, Honey Bear. Miss me?"

"T-Turtle? Is that you?" Honey's voice shook, and I could tell she was crying.

I grimaced, hating that I made her worry about me yet again. "You mean you've already forgotten my sexy voice?"

"Fucking asshole!" Honey screamed before promptly breaking down into uncontrollable sobbing. "How can you do this to me again? How?!"

"Hey, I'm sorry. I promise I—"

"NO!" Honey shouted, cutting me off. "Which hospital are you at? If they let you have your phone, you're not at the RRS anymore. Where are you?"

I sighed, knowing there was no sense in arguing with her. "Can't say for sure. But since Ara's in scrubs, most likely at Central."

"I'll be there in ten minutes!"

Before I could say anything, the call ended, and the screen went black. Well, that was lovely. There's nothing like a good haranguing right after waking up from a medically induced coma.

I forced myself to sit higher in the bed and immediately regretted that decision. A wave of nausea washed over me, and the world felt like it was about to spin off its axis. I gripped the bed's railing and closed my eyes, hoping the vertigo would pass quickly. It took several minutes of deep, focused breathing before I could open my eyes again.

I leaned back and looked up at the ceiling, wondering what in the hell happened during the return jump. I remembered reaching our Realm, but something was blocking me from exiting the Rift. I beat at it repeatedly, but whatever it was wouldn't budge. It felt like my body had been trapped between crashing waves and a massive stone cliff.

The door slowly opened, and Ara walked back inside, bringing me a cup of water. She grinned as she forced the drink into my hand. "Healers orders."

I took a long sip of the water; the cool liquid felt good going down my sore throat. I leaned forward to place the cup on the table just as Ara stepped toward me. Her hand rested on my own, and I felt an almost static electricity between us. Looking up, I stared into her eyes as she gazed intently back. I'm not sure if it was the drugs in my system or if I was still delirious from what happened, but something overrode my common sense.

I grabbed her hand and pulled her closer, wrapping my other arm around her waist. Before I realized what I was doing, our lips met. Ara stiffened for barely a second before letting out a long breath, opening her lips slightly to let her tongue meet mine. I was lost in that moment. Nothing I'd ever felt before compared to the soft warmth of her lips. Ara released a subtle moan as she pressed herself further into me, and I could feel both of our hearts racing as the kiss grew more passionate.

"Yes, Ma'am, Room 503," a voice from the hallway broke in, causing Ara and I to snap back to reality.

Faster than I thought possible, Ara darted to the opposite side of the room just as the door opened, and Honey stormed inside. I was torn between looking at her and Ara, who was now trying to make herself invisible behind her. Honey's eyes were rimmed red, and it looked like she hadn't slept more than a couple of hours for the past two weeks. She all but ran to my bed and threw herself on top of me, causing a new wave of pain to shoot through me.

"Ah! Watch it, woman! Remember, you don't get my life insurance if you're the one who kills me."

"Shut up!" Honey cried, her tears soaking into the chest of my hospital gown. "Just . . . Shut up."

I sighed and wrapped my arms around her, holding her tightly. "It's okay, I promise. I'm fine. Ara got me all patched up, and I'll be good as new before you know it."

I looked over to where Ara had been standing but was surprised to see she was gone. Honey pulled back, glaring at me with fierce determination behind her eyes. "I'm taking you home."

"Honey, I'm—"

"I said I'm taking you home!" She snapped, her anger mixed with sadness and fear. "You don't get it, Turtle. I won't lose you. Not again. Never again."

"What do you mean, again? I didn't go anywhere."

Honey sobbed once again, pushing her face into my chest. "Yes, you did. First, Sal tried to take you from me. And then that . . . *thing* during the FRE. You were gone. I felt it. It killed you, and I was left all alone. I can't go through that again! You can't . . . You promised me! You promised!"

I stroked her hair as she continued to cry, hoping it would help bring her some comfort. It's funny how we can spend so much time and energy trying to bury things in our past just for something to bring them crashing back around us. As Honey cried on my chest and I combed my fingers through her thick, curly hair, I remembered when she and I were kids. Looking back now, it was obvious what was happening. But kids don't know what signs to look for, do they?

Honey was one of those kids who always wore big, baggy clothes, trying to slouch and do whatever it took to get people not to notice her. I remember thinking it was strange that she constantly seemed scared when I accidentally touched her arm or leaned too close to talk to her. Yet, she always wanted to hang out with me, never wanting to go home, especially at night. Thinking about it after the fact, I hated my parents even more because they knew what was going on and did nothing to stop it.

It was when I was about fifteen that I finally realized. I'd gone to surprise her with something one night when I ran into her piece of shit stepfather coming out of her room, drunk. I saw Honey lying naked on the floor, curled into a ball, silently crying with a bloody lip, and the smell of her stepfather still on her. I couldn't even think; the entire world just went . . . red. The next thing I remembered was holding the asshole by the throat while blood poured from his ruined face. I told him if he ever laid another finger on Honey again, I'd kill him.

Come the end of it, he had a broken jaw, shattered nose, fractured orbital, and more than a dozen broken ribs and fingers combined. He had to stay in the hospital for over a week after that. I got lucky, and they didn't call the cops on me. I guess they were more worried about people finding out what he'd been doing. Her shitty mother blamed Honey for it all, though. But with me living next door, neither one touched her again. After that, any time Honey would have a panic attack or get scared about anything, she'd always come lay on top of me. I'd stroke her hair to reassure her that I would always be there and would protect her no matter what.

That was when Mr. Jackson took me under his wing and began teaching me how to fight properly. And it wasn't just how to punch, either. It was about how to control the urge to use violence for everything. He taught me anger management so that I wouldn't become victim of that rage again. He never once said I was in the wrong for doing what I did, and neither did Honey. And it was because of the two of them that I was able to avoid going down a darker path in life.

We lay like that for an hour before an orderly came in with my discharge papers and a wheelchair. One of the best things about having Healers run the hospitals is that there's a lot less wait time when it comes to being discharged. I remember, before the Rift Events, having my appendix out and the hospital taking seven hours to release me. And that was after I had to let them watch me pee. I mean, I don't kink shame but do it on someone else's dime.

As Honey wheeled me out to the garage, I looked around for Ara but didn't see her anywhere. I figured she just got busy and we'd talk later. I wasn't sure what that kiss meant or if it even *needed* to have a meaning. I'm not the best when it comes to the whole 'feelings' thing. But it had been a very long day for me, so I figured I could think about it more clearly after resting a bit.

I'm not the type of guy who likes to just sit around all day with my thumb up my ass, doing nothing. My ADHD won't allow that. Take time off to rest and recover from a near-fatal, super traumatic event? Nah! Why do that when you could be hiking across rocky terrain while trying to practice foraging skills you learned from a Wiki article that you read at three in the morning?

Besides, a whole week of lying in bed, having Honey and Sara consistently checking in every ten minutes to see if I needed any-thing, was just overkill. I love them both, believe me. But I didn't even get enough privacy for any kind of 'me time,' if you know what I mean. I love that they have each other, but I've been single for a *long* time now and haven't had anything even resembling sex for longer than I'd like to admit. So, having them pop into my room every time I barely sighed heavily didn't make it a great place to relieve some tension.

So, after a week of bed rest and against some very loud protests from Honey and Sara, I decided enough was enough. I needed to get out for a while. I felt my muscles atrophying, lying there all day, and I wanted to move. So, I started heading to Frelling State Park, just outside Krayden. I spent a few hours there each day, working on building my endurance back up and enjoying being by myself for a while.

I looked around the dry creek bed, taking a big drink from my water bottle. On days like this, I really missed Champion. It had been about four years since he'd escaped our backyard at the new house, and we were never able to find him after that. Honey, Sara, and I searched for months, but nothing ever came of it. It was one of the lowest points in my life, and I hadn't dared to own another pet since.

Just as I was about to turn around, I felt a slight buzzing in my pocket. I sighed and shook my head as I pulled out my phone and answered the call. "I've barely been gone an hour."

"Be careful in that creek bed, love," Honey warned from the other end of the line. "There's been an increase in scorpions out there."

"Really? I haven't seen . . . Wait a minute. How do you know where I am?"

"That's . . . not important," she tried to deflect my question. "Are you about to head home?"

"No, no, no! How do you know where I am?" I asked, looking all around to see if she had followed me.

"I ... might of ... putagpstrackerinyourshoe ..." Honey quietly mumbled.

"You chipped me? What the hell?! Not cool," I shouted, though I had difficulty keeping a smile off my face. Honey was very protective, and I wasn't surprised she did something like that.

"HEY! I wouldn't have to if you'd just stay home and rest like I told you to. What if you fainted or something out there? You know how big that place is. We'd never find you. Then, you'd end up dying and having your dead anus eaten by wolves. Is that what you want? To be wolf shit? You should be thanking me!"

"I'm taking the GPS out of my shoe," I sighed as I began walking back down the trail to the parking area.

"Go for it," Honey snickered. "They're on sale right now and I have nineteen more ready to go. You'll never find them all."

Shaking my head, I let out a loud laugh at her ridiculousness. "Oh, I'll find them; just wait and see."

"Turtle, I have a Costco membership and two disposable incomes. Try me."

"Okay, okay. And to answer your question, yes, I'm heading back." I laughed, turning down another trail looping to the ridge's top.

"Good! Meet us at Xander's," Honey said, the smile audible over the phone. "We never got to celebrate the adoption news last month, and now we need to celebrate you getting cleared for work tomorrow, too."

Reaching my car, I pulled out my keys, flicking the clicker. "Xander's? Really?"

"Oh, come on," Honey whined. "We haven't gone in forever. Besides, it's Thirsty Thursdays."

I grimaced. Fucking Thirsty Thursdays. I felt like I was having PTSD flashbacks of douchey frat boys and lukewarm piss beer. Honey must've known what I was thinking because she laughed even harder.

"We were thinking . . . why don't you invite Ara to join us?"

My heart felt like it skipped a beat with the mention of Ara. It had been almost two weeks since I was released from the hospital, and things between us had gotten weird. She'd come over once or twice to check on me right after I got home but never came further than my bedroom door. And she only stayed for a few minutes before saying she had to leave for one reason or another. I'd barely get to say a word to her before she was gone.

I noticed she also refused to look me in the eye, which made me feel even more like shit. It was clear that I crossed a major line with her in the hospital. I'd obviously misread things between us and made her uncomfortable. This is what I was afraid of most and why I never tried pursuing anything in the past. I replayed that kiss over and over in my mind, and each time, I wanted to go back and slap myself for trying to make a move on her. There was a pretty good chance that I permanently ruined our friendship.

"Uh . . . I don't know," I said, rubbing the back of my neck as I looked around the empty parking area. "She's been pretty busy lately, and I don't want to—"

"She's free tonight," Honey interrupted me. "I already checked."

"What? Why would you do that?" I asked, worried that it might make Ara even more uncomfortable that my roommate asked about her plans. "And how do you even have her number?"

Honey laughed, making my concern grow even more. "She and I've been texting since you were in the hospital. She seems like a really nice person. We'd love to get to know her better. Besides, I think she has a crush on you."

It was my turn to laugh. "Yeah, right! Someone like her wouldn't be caught dead with a guy like me. She's way too smart for something like that."

I expected Honey to laugh and make some kind of smart-ass response, but she didn't. It was quiet over the line for a long minute, making me pull the phone away from my ear to make sure the call hadn't dropped. "You're an amazing man, love. And people other than Sara and I see it. Trust me, invite her tonight."

The line clicked before I could say anything. I furrowed my brows as I looked at the blank screen. It's strange for Honey to get serious like that, especially regarding me and women. She'd usually be the first to mess with me about how I had to live with them forever, and they weren't going to let another woman take me away.

Sara and Honey liked to joke around and pretend to be into me. They act overly affectionate and possessive, even calling me things like love and stud. They'd do it even more so in front of other women. I knew it was just them giving me a hard time and fucking with me. But this was the first time either of them had encouraged me to hang out with another woman.

I sighed and swiped on my contacts list. 'Arabella Anderson' was the first name on the list. I got in my car and turned it on, letting the AC start to cool the hot interior while I just looked at the picture I had for Ara's contact. I'd taken it just after her first jump.

Her hair was frazzled, and her skin had taken on a slightly greenish hue from motion sickness. Yet, she still had the biggest smile on her face, proud that she'd actually done it. She told me she'd previously backed out of over ten jumps at the UK branch before her transfer. She said it was something about not having anyone she felt safe with.

Yet, not even two days after starting at the Krayden facility, she came directly to me and asked if I'd take her on my next jump. It surprised me because most Healers liked to stay here, close to either their hospital or the RRS infirmary. So, I took her on a quick trip to Taritia to deliver supplies to the embassy. It was a nothing jump—the equivalent of dropping a letter at the post office. Yet, when we returned, she had the biggest smile for days and wouldn't stop thanking me.

She officially requested to join my team that week and has done countless jumps with me since. I chuckled as I remembered that first time, though. She was so nervous that when I reached for her hand to make the jump, she interlocked our fingers instead of just holding our palms like everyone else. It's a habit that continues to this day and is one of the many reasons I started falling for her.

I hit the call button and listened to the line ring. One. Two. Three. I sighed, slightly disappointed but not surprised that she didn't answer. I kicked myself again for my stupid lack of judgment in the hospital.

"Hello?" Ara's voice came from the receiver just as I was about to hang up. "Turtle?"

The sudden sound of her voice made me jump, causing me to drop my phone on the ground. "Shit! Hang on! I dropped the phone!"

I struggled to bend enough to grab the small plastic contraption and pulled it back up, gasping for air from the sudden workout. "Hey! Ara? You still there?"

Ara chuckled, obviously having heard my fumble. "Yeah, I'm here. What's going on? You need something?"

"No," I said with a smile. I bet if anyone were around, I'd look like a giant idiot right then. "I mean, yeah. Sort of. I was just wondering, are you free right now?"

Silence. Great. I spooked her again. If there were an award for the most awkward jackass, I'd for sure be a finalist.

"Ara?"

"Uh . . . yeah! Sorry! Yeah, I'm free; what's up?" her voice sounded shaky, as if she were nervous about something.

"Well, I'm heading to Xander's and was wondering if you'd like to meet me there and grab some drinks? It's Thirsty Thursday . . ." I sounded like such a tool. If the rational part of me could step outside right now, I'd slap myself back into the coma.

"Xander's? Uh, yeah! That sounds like fun. There's some stuff I've wanted to talk with you about anyway."

Her words stabbed me right in the chest. I didn't want to make anything awkward for her or ruin a fun night by bringing up my stupidity. I'd hoped we could just pretend that nothing happened and everything would return to normal. I hate uncomfortable situations, especially when I'm the cause.

"Sure, but I should let you know that Honey and Sara are going to be there too," I quickly added, hoping that would help make her feel more comfortable.

"O-Oh? Okay, so it's not a . . . never mind! Okay, yeah, that sounds like fun. I'll see you all there in a few."

She quickly hung up, and I stared at the black screen. Letting out another loud exhale, I slammed my head onto the steering wheel and cursed my name for being such an idiot.

Chapter 6

Thirsty Thursdays

Thirsty Thursdays. Oh, how I hate thee? Let me count the ways! I don't know; maybe I'm biased. I just *really* hate Thursdays. But I've yet to meet anyone who shares the same sentiment.

It took me about twenty minutes to get back to Krayden and head to the pub a few blocks from the RRS known as Xander's. That wasn't its real name, just to be clear. It's something like Rift Ranger Tavern, but no one actually calls it that. They opened it shortly after the Krayden facility was completed, back when the PR team from the RRS tried to give us the name Rift Rangers-like we were some kind of Wild West lawmen or something.

The Ranger name didn't last more than a few commercial stints and a random billboard for recruitment. No, this was Xander's. And I don't think anyone knows why. The owner's name is Wayne. I've never heard of anyone named Xander even working there. It's not the name of the street it's on. Just for whatever reason, every single person knows it as Xander's.

Everything in that place was themed around the Rift. Menu items, drink specials. Hell, even the decor. I'm ashamed to admit that I contributed a few things from my jumps in the past for free drinks or to impress a woman enough to take me home for the night. Hey, I never said that I wasn't a tool, too. I'm just less of one than the others.

I walked in and instantly regretted agreeing to this as the bar was packed, and I could barely hear my thoughts. I scanned the room until I saw Honey waving me over to a small corner with four chairs surrounding a table that was obviously a Yondirian design. It looked like a square gray rock with thin gold lines etched throughout. It might look fancy, but it was actually that Realm's equivalent of Ikea.

I waved back to show that I saw her, then turned to the bar, forcing myself through a group of Healers who looked like they'd just finished a shift from hell. Waving at the bartender, some poor guy in his early twenties, I ordered four 'Rifter Specials.' I understand the owner tries to have a theme for the place, but all it really did was make us sound even more like pretentious assholes when we ordered. Xander's was also a pain in the ass because they required you to work for the RRS to order anything, which I'm sure played *no* part in why Honey wanted to come here. Looks like drinks are on me tonight. At least with them requiring our watches to order, we didn't have to deal with the crowds of the college bars around town. But considering how many people the agency employed, it's still a cluster fuck most nights.

With a quick scan of my watch, the tab was made. I walked back to the girls, who'd been hunched together, talking like a pair of conspiring wenches. "All right, what's this all about?"

Honey and Sara sat back, both with giant smiles plastered on to play innocent. "We don't know what you mean. We just wanted to grab some drinks to celebrate, that's all!"

"Uh-huh," I said, narrowing my eyes at them. "If that were the case, we'd have gone to Hugo's or even that fancy wine place y'all have wanted to try. I know y'all are up to something, and I *will* get to the bottom of it."

I reached into my pocket and pulled out the GPS tracker I'd found in my shoe when I got to my car. I held it up, along with one that was in my glovebox and another from inside my gas cap. "I also found these, too."

Honey's face turned dark red as Sara shot her a look of surprise. I thought she was about to get on to Honey for overstepping, but I was wrong. Sara started laughing hysterically as she placed a hand on Honey's leg and squeezed. "I told you he'd find them!"

"I gave him clues," Honey grumbled, crossing her arms in front of her chest in mock upset. "He won't find the next ones."

I laughed and shook my head, pointing to my watch. "Don't you think I get tracked enough?"

Shrugging one shoulder, Honey grinned wolfishly at me. "That's them. Not me."

I sighed, seeing the futility of arguing with her. I didn't really care. If it made her feel more comfortable, then so be it. "Just don't be putting any in my work clothes, okay? I've got scanners I have to go through, and I'm not sure I'll be able to justify a foreign GPS with a simple 'Sorry, boss, I got this yandere roommate, you see?'"

Honey huffed but continued to smirk at me. I felt a movement from behind and turned, expecting to see our drinks being delivered. But to my surprise, Ara was standing barely a foot behind me, smiling sheepishly. I was stunned as I looked her over, amazed by how hot she was right then. She wore a pair of daisy dukes that accentuated her firm ass and a white button-down shirt tied into a bow just above her flat midsection. Her ample chest strained at the few buttons she had done up, and a neon pink bra peaked out in a few places. Her curly red hair was let down, framing her freckled face perfectly and ending just about her mid-back.

Okay, let's get one thing straight. I respect all women. Every woman has the right to wear whatever they want for whatever reason they want, and no one should have any right to tell them otherwise. I'm also one of the first to admit that there's a rather large portion of men who ogle women to the point of making them uncomfortable, which is utterly unacceptable. But at that very moment, I couldn't tear my eyes away from Ara even if you'd told me another Rift Event was happening.

I wasn't sure how long I was staring at her with my mouth open since most of the blood in my body had stopped heading to my brain and was instead causing my pants to grow extra tight. A slap from behind brought me back to reality, and I quickly looked around to regain my bearings. Honey had slapped me before stepping forward and wrapping Ara in a giant hug. That surprised me, considering Honey didn't like anyone touching her except Sara and me. Well, I guess her other play partners when she has them, but still, no one else.

"It's so good to see you again," Honey said, rocking Ara back and forth.

Ara laughed, returning the hug, but I saw her eyes flick toward me. "Thank you for inviting me! I was getting so bored working on those charts."

Sara walked up and hugged Ara as well, causing me to question even more just how much these three actually knew each other. Honey and Sara stepped aside, leaving Ara and me in front of each other. I smiled and half bent, half leaned forward to awkwardly hug her with my butt pushed back. I didn't want to draw her attention to my cock, which was now at half-mast from seeing her in that outfit. Ara laughed and tried to hug me tighter, but I wouldn't let myself slip again.

I knew she was just being polite in front of the others, so I'd make sure not to do anything to make the night awkward for her. "Thanks for coming. Here, take a seat. I already ordered some drinks for us."

Ara chuckled and sat beside me while Honey and Sara returned to their seats across the table. Honey rolled her eyes and gave me a skeptical look. "Let me guess, Rifter Specials?"

I shot her a glare, cocking my eyebrow in challenge. "So? It's the best one!"

"It's literally *just* whiskey on the rocks. Some people might not like straight alcohol, you know. Ever consider that?" she asked, cocking her eyebrow at me but quickly flicking her eyes toward Ara.

Ara must've seen it because she laughed and shook her head. "Oh, I like whiskey. I enjoy the burn, if you know what I mean?"

Sara laughed and nodded along. "For sure! Honey, on the other hand, likes the sweet stuff. The sweeter, the better."

"Why do you think I got the Rifter Special?" I asked, giving Honey a wicked smile. "Revenge for chipping me."

Everyone laughed, but Ara shot me a quizzical look, hoping I'd explain. I leaned closer to her and showed her the failed GPS trackers. "Honey's afraid I'm going to run away or something. So, she's been putting GPS trackers all in my clothes and car. I found these today."

Ara's eyes widened in shock briefly before she began to laugh much harder than I expected. She turned toward Honey while wiping a tear from the corner of her eye. "I can't believe you *actually* did it! I thought you were just joking around. That's bloody hilarious!"

Honey chuckled and shook her head. "I don't joke when it comes to protecting my Turtle."

A server brought our drinks and set them on the small table between us. We all grabbed a glass and held it up in the air. I don't know why we do it. Again, it's just one of those things everyone does, and no one knows who started it. "To Destiny!"

I cringed, the words making me think about Chet. There hadn't been a day since I woke up that I hadn't thought about him. I constantly played the night over and over in my mind, wondering what I could've done differently. If I hadn't messed up the jump, we would've done the scout together. If I'd been stronger, I would've been able to fight that monster, and Ara wouldn't have been hurt. So many regrets, not enough hours to fixate on them.

I sipped the whiskey, letting the burn flow down my throat. Pointing between Honey and Sara, I tried to bring the focus back to happier things. "So, have y'all heard back from any agencies yet?"

"Oh, that's right! You've been approved for an adoption license. Congratulations!" Ara said excitedly.

Sara and Honey laughed and looked at each other, reaching to hold each other's hands. Sara shook her head and squeezed Honey's hand before looking back at us. "Not yet. But we're expecting to soon. We needed some time to finish making the last few preparations. Plus, we've had to help a certain stud muffin get back on his feet again."

I gasped, placing my hand on my chest in mock indignation. "Well, I never! I'm perfectly capable of taking care of myself, thank you very much."

Sara smirked and narrowed her eyes at me. "Uh-huh. So, tell me, where do we keep the extra toilet paper?"

I stopped to think. I went over every inch of the house in my mind, drawing a blank. I narrowed my eyes at her as she grinned even wider. I mouthed the words 'Fuck You' at her before taking another drink.

"So," Ara said, taking over the conversation to my relief. "How did you two meet? You're just adorable together!"

Honey blushed as Sara laughed, squeezing her hand even tighter. "Actually, we met because of Turtle."

That took me by surprise. I shot straight in my seat, tilting my head in confusion. "What? No, you didn't. Y'all met at your coffeehouse."

Sara laughed, and Honey gave me an exasperated look. "Seriously? You don't remember?"

"Remember what?"

Honey sighed before shaking her head. She turned back to look at Ara and smiled once again. "Sara and I met because she wanted to fuck Turtle."

Now, that was news to me. I spit out the bit of whiskey I'd just sipped, coughing furiously as I beat on my chest. "W-What?!"

Sara laughed as my face heated to a deep crimson. "Turtle used to come into my coffeehouse almost every day to read. I later found out it was because he'd just been dumped and didn't have anywhere else to go after she kicked him out."

"He didn't tell me he was living in his car for three weeks," Honey shot an angry look at me, daring me to speak. That was not a trap I wished to set off, so I kept my mouth shut.

"Anyway," Sara said, continuing her story. "He'd come in and sit there for hours reading, not bothering anyone. At first, I didn't even bat an eye since a lot of college kids wanted a place away from their dorms and roommates just to exist. Hell, that was one of the reasons I didn't go to college—too many people. But anyway, after a couple of days of Turtle coming in, I noticed the sitting area had started looking much cleaner, especially when I'd come back from doing inventory or something. It turns out that Turtle was cleaning up when he thought I wasn't looking. Stuff like picking up trash and wiping tables, that kind of thing. But he never said anything to me about it. I already thought he was hot, and that really got the engine going, you know? Then I started noticing the books he was reading were all in my wheelhouse. And man, can he read! He'd go through a book a day, if not more!"

Ara shot me a surprised look. "Really? I know you like to read, but that much?"

I shrugged and tried to hide my embarrassment. "Eh. It's a way for me to escape reality for a bit, you know? That's why I'm so big into fantasy."

"I understand that," Ara said, nodding. "You'll have to tell me some of your favorites, though. I'm dying for a new read! Sorry, go on, Sara."

"Well, I tried flirting with him several times. You know, offering him free drinks, bending slowly to pick things up in front of him, leaning over with no bra and the girls on full display, stuff like that. But he never made any kind of move on me. Then, Honey started coming in and meeting him, and I have to admit, I was a little upset," Sara said with a chuckle. "I figured, of course, the stud muffin who loves to read is taken. Though, to be honest, that made me want him even more. A man around my age who *actually* respected his relationship and didn't so much as look at the hot piece of ass flashing him every time he looked at her? It's unheard of! But then I noticed they didn't act like other couples. So, one day, I decided to bite the bullet and ask Honey about him. She made it *very* clear that I should back off!"

"What?" Honey scoffed, her face turning red. "I . . . I did not! All I said was that he was my best friend and had just gone through a nasty breakup and that it probably wasn't a great time for someone to try to start something with him right then."

Sara arched her eyebrows and stared her wife down. "Really? That's the story you're going with?"

Honey turned even more red and looked away, her hands fidgeting in her lap. "I might've been a little . . . harsher than I should've been. But I was in protection mode! My Turtle had been hurt, and I'd just found out he'd been sleeping in his car for almost a month!"

Letting out a chuckle, Sara reached over and squeezed Honey's hand. "Babe, you told me that you weren't going to let a 'blonde country bimbo' take him away from you, even if I had a perfect ass."

We all turned our attention to Honey, who was staring hard at the wall beside us. "Well . . . at the very least, I complimented your ass."

Sara laughed again and brought Honey's hand up and kissed it. She looked back at us, her smile genuine. "Soon after that, Turtle got his place in Krayden and didn't come out as much. But Honey did. She came back and apologized, letting me know a bit about their history. I was honestly shocked by it all. At first, I was just going to say it was fine and move on. But Honey started coming almost every day, and . . . just one thing led to another, I guess you could say."

"So, you're not fully lesbian?" Ara asked, tilting her head. "I mean, I'm not trying to label you or anything; I just assumed since you two are married . . ."

Both Honey and Sara laughed and shook their heads. "No, it's fine. We know how it looks. But no, neither of us are. Honey's bi and I'm pansexual. We're also polyamorous with an open marriage."

"Pardon my ignorance," Ara said with a slight blush. "I just didn't know there was a difference between Bi and Pan. And that's awesome about being poly! I am, too. Bi and poly, I mean. Though, I've never had a partner who was okay with it."

Sara smiled warmly as she reached out and touched Ara's leg. "I understand the struggle, for sure. Luckily, Honey and I have had great communication about other partners and all of that entails. We even recently came to a pretty big decision about something regarding that aspect of our lives, which we're both *really* hoping will pan out. And it's fine about not knowing the difference between bi and pan. Really. There is one, but for the sake of this conversation, let's just say they're close enough. I'm always happy to discuss it later if you have questions. If we aren't willing to teach, how can we expect people to know, am I right?"

Ara smiled, obviously glad she hadn't upset either of the women. "I couldn't agree more! My father used to say something very similar. He was a professor at a Uni outside of London. He loved to teach and loved it even more when he had students who wanted to learn."

"That's amazing," Honey said, finishing her drink with a grimace. "What about your mother? What does she do?"

Ara's face fell slightly as she looked down for a moment. She quickly recovered her smile and shook her head. "She's . . . retired. But we're not that close. She wasn't around much when I was growing up. Work always came first for her, you see. And even though she's retired now, we haven't really spoken since I transferred to Krayden."

"I'm sorry to hear that," Honey said but nodded understandingly. "But hey, I'm sure both your parents are proud of you! You're a Healer with the RRS. You've been to other worlds and have seen things no one ever thought possible until ten years ago."

Laughing, Ara nodded and shot me a warm smile. "Well, I have Turtle to thank for that. I'd never would've been able to do any of it without him there with me."

"Nah," I said, shaking my head. "You're a natural. You've saved my ass so many times over the past couple of years; I don't think I'd survive without you by my side."

Ara's face fell again, and she looked down at the floor. Well, shit. There I go, messing it up already. Here we are, having a great time getting to know each other, and I have to bring up one of the most traumatic things she's ever had to deal with. I really need to keep my foot out of my mouth. I looked at Honey, hoping she'd take pity on me. Luckily, she gave me a wink and stood, offering her hand to Ara.

"Hey, why don't you come with me to get more drinks? Real ones, this time. And don't worry, Turtle already started the tab."

Ara allowed Honey to pull her from the chair and toward the bar. I watched them disappear into the crowd before turning to see Sara staring at me with a wide grin. "You look like the damn Cheshire Cat, you know that?"

Sara laughed before hopping over to the seat Ara had just left. She leaned close to me, lowering her voice enough that I had to strain just to hear her. "She really likes you, Turtle. You see that, right?"

I sighed and shook my head, leaning back in my chair. "Not you, too."

Sara tilted her head, giving me a pointed look. "Listen here, you big doofus. You're not very good when it comes to people dropping hints. So, take it from us. Make your move."

I smirked, poking my finger into her ribs, making her yelp and pull back. "Sure. Like the hints you claim to have given me? What was that bull? You never wanted me. You've always been all over Honey."

Sara looked behind me and smiled wide before standing up and leaning beside my ear. "Not only would I have let you fuck me senseless back then, but I'd let you bend me in half and break me with that giant cock of yours tonight. In fact, I'm pretty sure we all would. And all you'd have to do is ask."

My throat went dry as I stared at her in shock. Sara stood with an evil chuckle and slowly returned to her seat. Of course, she's just fucking with me again. Honey and Ara reappeared before I could say anything, carrying four frozen margaritas. Honey passed out the drinks and raised hers in the air in celebration. "Now, it's a party!"

From that point on, the night got better and better. We all joked and told stories. The drinks kept coming, and soon, I had a decent buzz going. I constantly looked at Ara, who seemed to blush more as she stole glances at me. At one point, our knees touched, and I was afraid she would pull away. But to my surprise, she didn't. I felt her finger slowly stroke my leg as Sara told a story about a guy who tried to buy coffee with a cat.

"Are you telling me that's where Beans came from?" I asked in shocked amusement.

Sara laughed and nodded. "Why do you think he was named Beans? Cause I got him for some Coffee beans!"

We all laughed, and I put my hand down on my leg, wondering if I was just imagining things. But to my surprise. I felt Ara's finger start to rub against mine, and a warm sensation began to fill me. I looked at her, and she looked directly back at me for the first time that night. Her cheeks were red from drinking and laughing, but her eyes held something more.

I was locked onto her gaze, and just like at the hospital, I felt something deep inside yelling at me to go for it. I saw Ara blush, and her breathing quickened as I leaned toward her. Her beautiful eyes glistened as I got closer, and I thought I saw the slight crack of a smile on her lips.

"Shit!" Honey's voice broke through my trance, instantly causing me to spin to look at her in confusion. I saw her glaring at something behind me, and whatever it was, she was not happy about it.

"What's *she* doing here?!" Honey growled, clenching her fist just as Sara gripped her arm, holding her in place.

I looked between them, dumbfounded about who could make their moods shift so quickly. The answer didn't take long to reveal itself. "Hello, *lover*."

The words simultaneously sent a chill down my spine and made my stomach lurch into my throat. That voice was one I, unfortunately, knew all too well. I closed my eyes, praying that if there were a God somewhere out there, they'd burn this entire place to the ground at that very moment.

"Sal!" Honey all but yelled, shooting to her feet with her fists clenched. "You have *no* right to be here. Get out, now!"

"Aww," the woman's sultry voice purred in vicious pleasure. "Don't be like that, *Honey Bear*. We're all friends, aren't we?"

Sara stood, wrapping an arm around Honey's shoulders to stop her from attacking the woman behind me. "Sal, you're not welcome here. Go find someone else to torment."

Sal chuckled just as I felt a thin hand rest on my shoulder, making every nerve ending in my body scream. "Oh, Sara. I just wanted to say hello to *my* little Turtle, that's all. I'm sure *he* wants to see me, don't you, lover?"

I felt sick to my stomach as the memories of the woman who utterly destroyed me flashed through my mind. I loved Sal more than I thought a person could, giving her everything I had and then some. She used it all to torment me, cheat on me, ruin me financially/emotionally/mentally, and then mock me to everyone who would listen. And do you know how stupid I was? I let her do it over and over for years. Every time we'd break up, I'd swear she wouldn't fool me again. But then she'd show up out of the blue, and I'd somehow fall right back into her toxicity yet again. As I've now said countless times, I'm not the most intelligent man.

"Leave him alone!" Honey yelled, taking a step forward before Sara could pull her back.

"I don't think we've met," Ara said, standing to face Sal with a less-than-happy smile. "Who are you?"

I continued to stay seated with my back to Sal, not daring to look at her. From the brief silence, I knew Sal was sizing Ara up to see if she was a threat. "Hm. And who are you? Another one of Honey and Sara's playthings? I'm not sure why they even got married if they're just going to keep bringing other people into their bed."

"Actually," Ara said, touching my shoulder. "I'm here with Turtle."

The warmth of her hand and the steadiness of her words snapped me out of the shock Sal's sudden appearance put me in. I stood and turned, looking down at the familiar woman who smirked at me. Sal was just under six feet tall and had an athletic build. Her chocolate hair was styled perfectly to frame her face, and her thick red lips matched her form-fitting dress.

"Sal, I think you should go," I said, hoping my voice came out more confident than it sounded in my mind.

Sal pouted her lips before smiling at me once again. "Oh, lover. I've missed you. You're looking good."

"This is an RRS bar," Ara said, wrapping her arm around my own, making it a point to press her chest close to me while she did so. "You're not an RRS employee, are you?"

Sal sneered at Ara for a brief moment before collecting herself. She smiled again, turning to wave someone over. "I'm not, but my date is."

I looked up just in time to see a massive figure push through the crowd to stand beside Sal. Of, fucking, course that's her date. Kyle. Fuck Kyle. All Kyles. Okay, maybe not all of them. But definitely this one.

Kyle was the Head of the Swords. Whereas Shields like Chet go to protect and defend, Kyle and the Swords are sent to 'handle' problems. They have extremely powerful but volatile abilities. These guys would throw a fireball in a room the size of a closet, even if their team would get caught in the blast. They didn't care about the safety of anyone except themselves. I know from very personal experience.

"Well, well, well," Kyle said, sneering at me.

It takes a lot to look down at me, but as Kyle's more than a foot taller than I am, he can do it easily. Seeing him standing next to the thin-framed Sal, I couldn't help but wonder how he hadn't snapped her in half. There were plenty of times when we were together that I thought I was going to seriously hurt her with as rough as she liked sex. And I'm a quarter of Kyle's body mass.

I felt Ara's arm slip away, and I turned to see her staring in disbelief at the Sword. "What are you doing here?"

Kyle laughed and wrapped an arm around Sal's shoulder. "I'm on a date. What about you? I thought you said you had charts to file tonight?"

I furrowed my brows in confusion as I looked at Ara, who was struggling to form words. "I-I did. I finished and wanted to get out for a bit."

"And you just so happen to run into this coward?" Kyle sneered, his glare finding its way back to me.

"What did you just call me?" I growled, the anger in my chest rising.

Removing his arm from around Sal, Kyle took a step forward and violently jabbed a finger into my chest. I bet he expected me to fall backward or maybe wince in pain. But bullies like him were nothing new to me. And I wasn't some weak little kid who could be shoved around. I stood my ground and gritted my teeth at him.

"You're a coward," Kyle growled. "You got Chet killed and left him to rot in an unknown Realm all because you were too chicken shit and weak to do anything."

I was shocked he knew anything about it. The report filed said Chet fell to an unknown combatant—no names of his team, no mention of what Realm, and nothing about his body not being recovered. Yet, Kyle seemed to know it all.

"You don't know what you're talking about," I said, trying to keep the surprise out of my voice.

Kyle poked me even harder in the chest, trying to provoke me further. "I know everything, coward. How you fucked up your jump and had to sit around while Chet did all the heavy lifting.

How you tried to run away when those creatures showed up. You even failed to protect your Healer, almost getting her killed in the process."

"Kyle! Enough!" Ara yelled, taking a step toward the man. "Stop it right now!"

Kyle shot her a toothy grin but didn't move from in front of me. "That's what you told me, isn't it?"

His words hit me in the stomach like a sledgehammer. Every ounce of air was ripped from my lungs as I turned to look at Ara. Her face had gone pale, her eyes wide in disbelief. She tried shaking her head, but no words left her mouth.

"You're such a pathetic excuse for a Rifter, you know that?" Kyle asked, turning back to me. "You couldn't protect her, so she came running to me the very night you got back. How does that make you feel? While you were wasting the Hospital's time healing your sorry ass, your Healer was in my arms, crying about how scared she was. No wonder she requested the transfer off your team."

The world spun, and I felt my knees tremble. I looked back at Ara, who was viciously shaking her head, tears rolling down her cheeks. "NO! That's not it. Turtle, don't—"

"Aw," Kyle laughed, stepping back beside Sal, who now beamed with sick enjoyment. "Why don't you do everyone a favor, *Rifter*, and just disappear? Go find a Realm where no one knows you and just stay gone. You're no good to anyone here."

I couldn't stop staring at Ara. The pit in my stomach filled my throat, and I felt completely numb. She continued to shake her head as tears ran down her face. "Turtle, please! It's not like that. I swear!"

I couldn't anymore. Everything had gone quiet, and I felt like someone had ripped me out of my own body. I turned and walked out of the bar. The warm breeze of the night air whipped around me as I walked through the parking lot. It sounded like someone was calling me from somewhere far off, but I just couldn't deal with that. I was done.

A hand gripped my arm and pulled, spinning me around to see Ara's crying eyes looking up at me. "Turtle, please. Let me explain. I can explain."

"I-It's okay," I said, all emotion gone from my voice. I didn't trust myself with emotions anymore. Despite what I just learned, I didn't want to hurt her. "I understand; you don't have to say anything."

"NO!" Ara yelled, squeezing my hand. "Please, just let me explain!"

"I hope your new Rifter does a better job for you in the future," I said before seeing Honey and Sara standing right behind her. "Guys, please make sure Healer Anderson gets home safe."

With that, I turned and walked down the street, not really sure where I was going. I couldn't drive, and I sure as hell couldn't stay at the bar. The inner turmoil raged inside, and for a brief moment, I felt as if my power tried to rip out of my body. I stumbled before catching myself, shaking my head in confusion. Looking up, I was surprised to find I was in the small park next door to my old apartment.

I looked at my watch and then back around the empty park. This was more than eight miles from Xander's, yet I'd only been walking for a few minutes. My mind was racing with too many thoughts. I clenched my fists before letting out a scream of frustration and anger. I poured all my emotions into that yell, forcing every bit I could out of my body. Dropping to my knees, I hung my head.

I. Hate. Thursdays.

Chapter 7

The Troublesome Neko

Ever had one of those moments when you're just so done that you genuinely don't care what happens to you anymore? It's not like you want to harm yourself, but hey, if you just stopped existing, that wouldn't be too bad. It's a shitty state of mind to be in. And what sucks most is that a majority of people are afraid of ever admitting they've had those feelings, so they hide it and try to pretend everything's okay.

All that does is make it rear up again and again, each time getting worse. But because you didn't talk about it before, it's clearly too late to try now, right? And since no one admits to feeling it, everyone thinks they're completely alone. It's a vicious cycle and one of the worst feelings to have. So, if you're reading this and have felt like that before, this is your sign you're not alone. We're out there. Trust me, you're not alone.

I, on the other hand, was alone- at least in the sense of being alone in the middle of a park in an abandoned neighborhood. After the FRE, most of the buildings in this area had gotten damaged beyond repair. The people who owned properties sold them to the RRS, which promised to revitalize the community. Yeah, that never happened.

I tried to keep up with the other residents from my old building after Honey moved me in with her and Sara. But between training with the RRS, traveling to new worlds, dealing with Honey and Sara's crazy antics, and everything else, I lost contact with most of them. However, each year, on the anniversary of the FRE, I still leave flowers on the corner where Mrs. Atkin died. She didn't have any family, so Honey and I got her cremated and spread her ashes out at sea after it was all said and done.

But I digress. Here I was now, alone, feeling betrayed and hurt by someone I'd realized I cared a lot about. The old me would've simply washed my hands of her. I'd done it countless times before. When I thought someone was trying to hurt me, *boom*, instant disconnect. For some reason only God knows; the only one I hadn't been able to do that with is Sal. But for anyone else, I was usually a 'one strike and you're out' kind of guy.

I don't know why I was hurting so much hearing about Ara. We hadn't been dating. Hell, we barely kissed once. But, for some reason, I felt a deep ache in my chest, like it had been a long-time partner who betrayed me. We'd been on the same team for years, and I'd had a crush on her almost the entire time. For fuck's sake, I purposefully hadn't tried hooking up with anyone the past few years, all because I wanted to be with her. But I think it hurt most because I knew Kyle was right about me.

I was a failure. I was a coward. I abandoned Chet, and I got Ara hurt.

I was at my lowest and decided to do something I never thought I'd be cliché enough to do. I looked up at the sky, staring directly into the softly pulsing light of the Rift, and screamed. "Why?! Why did you waste a miracle on a coward like me? A weak, pathetic coward. Why?"

Of course, silence was my only answer. I felt like such a dumbass, but at least it felt good to scream for a few minutes. I sighed, dropping my head in defeat. I didn't know what the answers were, but I knew I wouldn't find them on my knees in an abandoned park at night. That's how you find *other* things that I just wasn't in the mood to deal with at the moment.

As I was about to stand, I heard the creaking of metal coming from behind me, causing me to jump and spin. I *really* didn't want to find out what someone on their knees in an abandoned park at night would typically be looking for. To my surprise, a woman in her early 20s sat on the swing a few yards away, staring at me.

She couldn't have been more than five feet tall and wore sheer blue fabric draped in a strange design across her chest and hips. Her eyes were what drew my attention the most, though. They glowed slightly yellow in the dark, reminding me of a cat's eyes. She even had one of those headbands with two orange cat ears pointing up. Her flowing orange hair fell in waves behind her back as she leaned forward just enough to expose her cleavage to me.

"Hello?" I called out, looking around the park to see where she'd come from.

The girl just stared, slowly blinking her eyes as she tilted her head to the side. "What are you doing, Daddy?"

I didn't know who this girl was or why she called me Daddy, but her tone made it sound like we knew each other. I looked around again but still didn't see anyone else. Cautiously, I stepped closer, hoping to get a better look to see if I could recognize her. She was pretty cute, most likely in one of the sororities at the college. Maybe I met her at the bar before?

"Nothing," I said cautiously. "I'm sorry if I bothered you."

I turned and began walking back toward Xander's, hoping to get there before they towed my car. The girl let out a soft giggle, and I heard the creak of the metal chains as she slowly began to swing her legs. "What's the rush, Daddy? Why not come and play with me?"

I stopped and spun around, my nerves already on edge from the night. "Stop calling me that! I don't know you, and I'm not in the mood for games right now."

The girl pouted, giving me the same look a spoiled brat would when not getting their way. "Boo, you're no fun. But I guess you had a rough night, so I can't blame you too much."

I shook my head, trying to figure out what this girl's problem was. "How . . . I . . . Bah, what would you know about it?"

The girl tilted her head slightly, giving me a strange smirk. "I know many things. Some happened long ago. Some are happening right now. Others, I don't know if they'll ever happen. Time's funny that way."

This woman was freaking me out. I whipped around again to see if someone was trying to prank me. But no one else was in sight. "Okay, crazy lady. I'm going to go now. Have a nice . . . whatever this is."

I spun and began walking even faster, hoping to put as much distance between me and this girl as possible. She let out another soft chuckle before calling out to me. "Chet's still alive, you know."

Her words hit like a brick wall, stopping me instantly. My heart pounded as I turned back to her. I didn't know who this woman was, but I was just about at the end of my rope. I stormed back toward her, finally letting some anger out from behind the dam. "What the fuck did you just say to me? What do you know about it?"

The girl didn't move as I approached. I got within a few feet of her and stopped, hoping my size would scare some sense into her. She just looked up at me with that same bratty smirk. A shallow movement from the top of her head surprised me, and I almost jumped back. That wasn't a headband with fake cat ears on her head. They were real! One of the ears twitched just as I noticed a previously unseen tail flicking playfully behind her back.

"What are you?" I asked, astounded by the creature.

I'd known what Nekos were from anime, but I never heard of an *actual* race of human/cat hybrids before. I briefly wondered if another of the Realms had sent an emissary but quickly dismissed that idea. There were proper channels for that to happen. They wouldn't just show up in some random neighborhood in the middle of the night.

The girl looked up to the sky, her yellow eyes glimmering in the light of the Rift. She turned back to me with an even bigger grin as her tail flicked excitedly behind her. "I'm RUI, Daddy!"

I waited for more, but she obviously thought that was a full explanation. I thought about all the Realms I'd heard of, but none had the name Rui. "Will you please stop calling me that?! And Is Rui your name or your species? What are you? Where are you from?"

Rui shrugged one shoulder and continued to swing back and forth. "I'm just RUI. There are none like me, and I'm like no other. I was alone, but now I'm with you. I'm from here and from there. From everywhere but also nowhere. I've always been and will continue to be when all things come to an end."

I sighed and shook my head. This girl was *really* starting to annoy me. I'm not sure what was wrong with her, but she needed to either be on some kind of drug or off it. I looked toward the parking garage but remembered my car was more than eight miles away. Groaning, I shook my head in frustration. I knew I could call the RRS, and they'd send a team to get her. That was technically protocol if we encountered any unknown species in our world.

"Listen, I'm going to make a quick call, okay? There are some nice people I want you to meet. They'd love to hear all about you."

A flash of orange fur whipped as I pulled my phone from my pocket. Rui's tail slapped my phone out of my hand, shattering it on the ground. "Jesus Christ! What was that for?"

"Time's almost up, Daddy," Rui said, swinging harder. "You have to go back."

"What are you talking about?!" I yelled, pointing down at my ruined phone. "Do you know how expensive those things are?!"

"You have to go back," Rui repeated, her grin seeming plastered to her face.

I gritted my teeth and growled at the woman. "Go back where?! What are you talking about?"

"Destiny awaits," Rui said, looking back toward the Rift. "She's waiting for you, even if she doesn't know it yet. Save her before it's too late."

Just as I was about to open my mouth to yell at her again, Rui swung forward and touched my chest. An explosion of energy went off inside me, and I felt my core open to the Rift without my guidance. I was torn away from my Realm, cast into the hurricane of energy that made up the cosmos. I spun to gain my bearings, but everything was moving too fast. I'd never jumped without coordinates before and had nothing to orient myself to.

The currents ripped me in every direction as I fought, trying to gain control over my power once again. I didn't know how long I'd been lost in the storm, but eventually, I felt a slight resonance in the distance. I couldn't place it, but it felt familiar. I focused with every fiber of my being, trying to wrestle my power back into submission. It took several more minutes, or maybe hours, before I could finally start guiding myself with any kind of control.

I brought the familiar feeling back into focus and pushed my way there. I felt so tired, and my head throbbed with the effort. But I was soon rewarded with solid ground under my feet. I quickly closed off my core and dropped to my hands and knees, gasping for air. It took several more minutes before I could stand and look around to see where I had ended up.

My stomach lurched, and I felt like I was about to lose every bit of food I'd eaten that day. I knew exactly where I was. Two moons shone brightly overhead, and the tall trees of the new Realm lined the same glade I'd come to during the last jump. And just like that night, the terrible howls of those creatures rang out into the night sky.

Fuck! Double fuck! Double fuck covered in burning shit!

I searched around the clearing, looking for a place to hide until I could muster the energy to make another jump. It usually took at least five minutes after entering a Realm before I could jump again, and it would be a very short one at that. It was one of the reasons we tried to make our jumps consecutive inside the Rift rather than coming out into a different Realm and trying again. It took much less energy to do it like that. I also had yet to determine where the next closest jump point would be, so I needed time to figure it out.

The howls echoed, seeming to grow louder by the second. I cursed and ran, hoping I was picking a direction away from the monsters. I felt a soft buzz on my wrist as I broke through the tree line. Looking at it in utter disbelief, I saw a dot flashing from up ahead. It was Chet's SOS signal. He *was* alive!

The monsters roared, getting ever closer. I heard the first explosion and felt the tremor as I turned and ran in the direction that Chet's signal was coming from. I just needed to keep the monsters behind me and Chet in front. How hard could that be while navigating an alien forest in the dark?

More explosions and howls echoed, and I pushed harder. My body was reaching its limit, but I wouldn't stop. I wasn't going to abandon Chet again. We'd both be coming home this time.

The buzz on my watch slowly grew in strength the closer I got to the signal. In the distance, I saw the faint glow of a fire from behind another group of trees. I looked at my watch, and sure enough, Chet's signal was coming from right over there. I ran harder as an explosion erupted so close that pieces of dirt pelted my limbs. I broke through the tree line, just to be met with a horrific sight.

Suppression cages of various sizes lined a clearing with a large fire pit in the middle. I'd only ever heard about these types of cages before, so seeing them in person sent a cold shiver down my spine. They were made of some kind of metal found in the Unatilak Realm that had a way of suppressing someone's abilities they got from the Rift. But it wasn't the cages that made me sick to my stomach; it was what was inside. Or should I say *who* was inside.

Beings from at least ten other Realms had been crammed in each one. Several were so full the occupants couldn't even sit down properly. I stared in horror as countless eyes turned to me, and soon, the pleas for help began. There were several from Winly, a few Taritians, and even some imps, along with several others I recognized. Each turned and started calling out for me to release them. I think what surprised me most was that everyone in the cages was female.

I knew for a fact that Winly females don't ever leave their world, as the Rift causes them to go barren. It was also required that Taritian females keep at least three male guards with them when out of their Realm for fear of slavers. And that's when it hit me. These monsters that attacked us weren't simply natives defending their homes. They were slavers collecting stock for sale!

I'd never come across any before, but I'd heard some of the Swords talking about them in the past. I think they called them the Marrog or something like that. But very little was known about them, so they weren't in our Database yet. What we did know was that they were supposed to be tough as hell and had many of the same abilities as the Swords and Shields. Any time a new encampment of Marrog was found, it usually took a dozen or more Swords to wipe them out. Yet, from what I understood, they were usually only found in established Realms. This jump point was supposed to be new, so how did the slavers already have an encampment of this size?

I ran to the first cage, which held seven of the Winly, looking for a way to open it. "Where's the key?"

One of the women pointed to a stack of chests on the other side of the encampment. I rushed over and tore open the first one. At first, I only found some strange pieces of fabric and a bunch of silver and gold discs that I could only assume were currency of some kind, but no key. Just as I was about to give up and move to the next one, something dropped beside my foot. It was a small, silver key that looked to be a fit for the cage locks. Strange, it must've been wrapped in one of the pieces of fabric and fallen when I was moving things around.

I grabbed the key and rushed over to the cages, opening them one by one. "I need your help! I'm looking for a man like me.

A human. He's much larger than I am and would've probably sounded like a giant tool. His name's Chet. Has anyone seen him?"

None of the prisoners answered, each looking around at the others as they piled out of the cages. After emptying the last one, I pointed away from where the Marrog would be coming from. "Go that way! I'll try to lead them off in the other direction. Can anyone jump?"

They all looked around at each other before one of the Taritians stepped forward. "I can, but my energy is low. I can't take many with me, and I only know the coordinate's to my home."

I nodded and pulled off my watch, setting my pin and clicking the SOS. I handed it to the Taritian and closed its feathered fist around it. "Take as many as possible, and then get this to my embassy in your Realm. Do you know where it is? Good. Take it there, tell them Rifter TTL sent you, and then tell them everything. Got it?"

The Taritian bobbed her long neck before turning and grabbing seven of the weakest-looking captives in her arms. Within a blink of an eye, they were gone. I looked at the remaining prisoners and motioned for them to start running. "GO! I'll do what I can, but you have to go!"

They all began running away, and I turned to look back around the camp. Chet's signal had come from here, but I saw no sign of him. I heard a loud horn blow somewhere in the distance, and then the night erupted into pure chaos. Several explosions rocked the ground, and countless howls of the Marrog echoed, all making their way back to the encampment. I cursed, knowing I was out of time.

I ran to the opposite side of the clearing when something landed on the ground a few feet away. It took me by surprise, and I stopped, looking for where it had come from. Yet I didn't see anything or anyone around. I reached down and picked up the strange object.

It looked like a scimitar with strange markings all over the blade. Whatever metal it was made of glowed a soft blue, and didn't seem to reflect the firelight nor the moonlight from above. No sooner had I gripped the weapon did the first Marrog break through the trees. It saw me and then the empty cages, causing it to let out a vicious roar as it charged.

The monster was massive, even bigger than the two I'd previously encountered during my first jump. Its fur was almost pitch-black, and the bulging muscles of its arms and legs pulsed as it sprinted toward me, pointed teeth bared. Luckily for me, my adrenaline was pumping into overdrive, and I didn't instantly freeze as the living nightmare closed the distance.

Now, I like to use an old saying about this kind of situation. Fool me once; shame on you. Fool me twice; I'm going to cut your fucking head off. The Marrog ran straight at me, but I wouldn't try to go toe-to-toe with it like before. I learned that excruciating lesson the last time. Just as it reached me, I jumped and rolled out of the way, swinging the weapon out as I passed it.

I don't know what metal this weird thing is made of, but I want *all* of it for Christmas. The blade easily sliced through the rock-hard muscle and bone of the monster, amputating its thick leg completely. It fell heavily to the ground; this time, its howls were of pain and confusion. One thing I learned growing up hunting in Texas is that you don't let your kill suffer. Even if it's a dick that deserves it. I spun quickly, and the blade sliced through the monster's neck, decapitating it.

God, I love this thing! Before I could appreciate the fantastic weapon more, six Marrog rushed out of the forest. They took one look at me and didn't even hesitate. I let out a curse and turned, deciding now would be a good time for a strategic retreat. I ran into the forest, trying to keep the slavers at my back. Unfortunately, after several close calls and almost skewering myself a dozen times, I had to ditch the badass sword. You don't run with scissors, and that goes the same with big-ass swords made of metal that could cut stone, okay?

I had been out there for over an hour, barely staying ahead of the pack. I ran in a zig-zag pattern for a while, trying to confuse them. When that didn't work, I decided to double back, hoping to get a few more minutes to recheck their encampment. If Chet was somehow there, that big SOB would really come in handy when dealing with these assholes. I reached the edge of the camp and was relieved to see the suppression cages were still empty. I looked around as quickly as I could, trying to see if I could find any clue as to where Chet was.

Just as I was about to give up again and try to find the remaining prisoners, something caught the corner of my eye in the distance. Just beyond the trees, there looked to be a small shack tucked away in the shadows. I quickly ran over to it and saw it was also locked with the same kind of lock as the cages. Luckily, I kept the key from earlier.

To my relief, the tumbler turned and opened, and I rushed inside, closing the door behind me. The room was almost pitch black, with only a tiny sliver of light coming from a crack in the window high on the wall. I closed my eyes briefly, trying to get them accustomed to the darkness. I could see better when I opened them again, but not by much.

The shack had nothing besides a few blankets, a table with half-eaten food, and a pile of fabric on the floor. I sighed and shook my head; it was just another waste of time. But as I reached for the door handle to leave, a soft moan broke the silence, causing me to spin and look around again. I still couldn't see anything until the pile of fabric moved, catching my full attention.

I dropped to my knees and touched the mound, only to kick myself for not realizing someone was underneath. A person was curled into a ball under layers of fabric. My heart raced as I pulled on their arm, flipping them over. Well, it definitely wasn't Chet.

It was a woman, maybe six feet tall, with fair skin and long, blonde hair. Her face was dirty and bruised, and her lips were swollen and cracked from dehydration. She wore a wool shirt caked in blood and dirt, with skin-tight leather pants, and her bare feet were bloodied and cut in many places. But what took me by surprise were her ears. They were slightly elongated and had a sharp point to them. My heart pounded in my chest. I was looking at an actual Elf!

Well, I'm not sure that's what she is, but that's what every story, movie, and video game ever depicted them as. I'd never heard of Elves being real, nor had their Rift equivalent been discovered. A loud horn bellowed from outside, and the howls of the Marrog grew louder. I knew it was only a matter of time before they found us.

"Hey," I whispered, shaking the woman as hard as I could. "Hey! Get up. We got to go!"

The woman let out an audible moan, but her eyes remained closed.

"FUCK!"

I stood up and ran to the door, cracking it just enough to see the encampment in the distance. The horn blew again, and I saw three Marrog enter the clearing, looking around intently for my tracks.

"Damn it," I whispered before turning back to the woman on the ground. "*Hey! We need to go!*"

Again, she didn't move. There were more howls outside, and I knew I was out of time. They'd found my tracks. I cursed, preparing to do something that went against every instinct in my body. I grabbed the woman and lifted her into my arms, cradling her as tightly as possible. I heard something hard hit the floor and looked down. Considering the woman didn't have any kind of pockets, I wasn't sure where anything could have fallen from. It was at that very moment the entire world stopped.

Laying on the ground where the woman had just been was a piece of shining . . . something. It was about half the size of my pinky but didn't look to have an actual shape at first. The more I stared at it, the more I realized the edges of it seemed to bend and move as the brilliant light inside radiated a warmth that made me feel . . . at peace. I felt a deep pull from inside as if my entire core was yearning for the object. I'd never seen anything like it before, yet it felt familiar as I reached down and picked it up.

A roar so loud the window rattled broke me from my stupor. That was it. I couldn't wait a second longer. I closed my eyes and opened my core to the Rift, letting the currents rip me and the woman into the waves. Yet, something felt different this time. As we were drawn further away from that Realm, the usual tornado of energy that made up the Rift was. . . calm.

What normally felt like roaring rapids pulling in every direction now felt more like a gentle stream. I could even stand still, which had never been done before. I felt a strange warmth radiating through my entire body as I suddenly became aware of jump point after jump point all around me. Places I'd been and others I hadn't yet. I somehow knew exactly where each one led and what I'd find there.

The woman shifted in my arms, bringing me back to the task at hand. I felt for home and instinctively knew right where to find it. As I reached the edge of the Rift, a buzzing sensation filled my chest, getting stronger the closer I got to exiting. Just as I was about to step out of the Rift, the buzzing was replaced with a massive jolt of electricity, and I was thrown violently back into my world, unconscious.

Chapter 8

New Phone, Who Dis?

Have you ever had one of those nights? You know the ones I'm talking about. Where you get such fantastic, out-of-this-world amazing sleep that everything is absolutely perfect when you wake up? When you feel like you can face the day with a smile and a pep in your step, no matter what the universe wants to throw at you? I don't know what that's like, but I heard others do.

Yet, when I opened my eyes the following day, I could tell something was different. For one, no alarm! I got to do what I've only ever heard other people talk about— wake up naturally. On my own. Without any beeping! In hindsight, that should've set off some major warning bells, but screw it. I would enjoy every second of my alarm-free existence while I could.

The sun's bright rays poured through my windows, and in the distance, I heard some birds chirping and a lawnmower further down the street. I slowly opened my eyes, cursing for the umpteenth millionth time my bedroom window faced East. And then I cursed myself for being a massive procrastinator who kept putting off buying blackout curtains. But let's be honest, we all know whose fault it *really* is: Honey's. That's my story, and I'm sticking to it.

Grabbing a pillow, I shoved it over my head, trying to block out every bit of light and sound in a vain attempt to fall back asleep. The softness of my bed wrapped around me like a cloud, and for a few minutes, I drifted into that wondrous space between consciousness and sleep. It felt like floating in a gentle pool without a care, just like the Rift felt last night. With that thought, my eyes shot open, and I sat up, looking around my room in a panic.

I was in my bedroom, and nothing was amiss as far as I could tell. My heart raced as I searched all over, looking for the woman I'd saved the night before. Yet, there was nothing. I was alone. I took a deep breath and slowly let it out, calming my heartbeat as I tried to recall what happened when we left the jump point.

Something had been strange with the currents of the Rift. It was like nothing I'd ever experienced before. Even though I'd always felt comfortable traveling the Pathways, it was the definition of utter chaos every single time. But last night, it felt so calm, and I could've sworn I was able to see thousands of jump points all around me.

I let out a long sigh and shook my head. Maybe it was all just a dream? I mean, I did wake up in bed. I might be the Head Rifter, but not even I could land with that kind of precision. I usually got within a fifty-yard radius of where I was aiming for. Last night, I was trying to return to the RRS so the Healers could help that woman. There was just no way I'd have been able to jump straight into my bed. The odds of that were *literally* incalculable. Okay, maybe not, but definitely for me. I'm sure Lana could give me a number if I asked. Either way, it had to have been a dream. Everything about last night was just too bat-shit crazy to have actually happened.

A real-life Neko knew intimate details about me, then activated my power to send me flying through the Rift back to a monster-infested hellscape. Then, after freeing dozens of captives from slavers, I found an actual, in-the-flesh elf with a weird, glowing thing that seemed to defy the logic of physics itself. And on top of it all, the chaotic torrent of the Rift somehow bent to my will and allowed me to jump straight into the comfort of my bed? God, I'm never drinking tequila again.

I decided it was time to get up, so I stretched and placed my feet on the floor. I tapped my watch for notifications like usual, but it was missing. I stared blankly at my bare wrist in confusion for the briefest moment before the memory of giving it to the Taritian came rushing back.

"No. It can't be."

I whipped around, searching my room once again. Whether I was looking for the elf or my watch, I wasn't sure. I just needed something to clear things up for me. I looked at the nightstand and saw my phone wasn't on its charger, either. Then, I remembered that Rui girl breaking it in the park. Maybe *that* was the proof I needed.

I grabbed my laptop and opened the program that linked to my phone. Don't judge me, okay? Sometimes, I get caught up watching something and don't want to take the time to look for my phone. I guarantee countless of you out there are guilty of the same.

The second the program finished loading, I was assaulted by ding after ding, showing dozens of missed calls and texts. My heart sank, knowing this wasn't going to be good.

Message: Honey Badger

"Turtle! Come back! That guy was a fucking asshole. Don't let him get to you. Come back, please? Ara's really upset."

"Okay, I'm getting pissed off now. Why are you letting someone like him get to you like this? You're twenty times the man he could ever be!"

"Why aren't you answering me?!"

"Hello? Turtle! ANSWER ME!"

"This is why I GPS you, you know that, right? I'm going to start putting it in your food from now on if you don't answer me!"

"TURTLE! Seriously! This isn't funny. We're all worried about you, and Ara hasn't stopped crying. Don't blow this! She's an amazing person who really cares about you; just come talk to her!"

"Turtle, I'm freaking out. You've been gone for like two hours. Where are you?"

"Seriously! Answer me!"

"Ara's home; I'm in the car, driving alone. So, you can answer me now, okay Love? We can talk about it. Just us. Like it's always been. You and me forever, remember?"

"If you don't answer me in the next three minutes, I'm using find my phone, and then I'm going to shove it up your ass when I get there! Stop being such an asshole and answer me!"
"Why are you at the park by your old place? I'll be there in five minutes; STAY THERE!"
"Where are you? It's pitch black out here."
"TURTLE! Please, don't do this. Please don't leave. I'm sorry. I'm sorry, please, just come home. Please."
"Please, Love. I can't lose you. I love you."

Well, fuck. My heart tore seeing just how upset I made Honey. She's going to be so far past pissed when she sees me. But I deserve it. I shouldn't have just stormed away like that. It's a bad habit that I just take off when I get upset. I need space, you know? Feelings are hard.

And it's not like I give two shits what Kyle thinks. But he wasn't the reason I left. It was Ara. Knowing that she thought those things about me and even requested a transfer from my team without so much as giving me a heads-up? I felt a stabbing in my chest again, thinking about it all.

Message: Sara-dipity

"Hey, Sweetie, where'd you go? Come back, okay? You know Honey and I have your back."
"Turtle, Honey and Ara are worried about you. I know you can take care of yourself, but can you at least send a quick text so they know you're okay?"
"Hey, Stud. Now I'm starting to get worried. Can you call me? Honey took Ara home and said she'd drive around looking for you. If you

want, I can be an ear. Come home, please? I'll let you put your head in my lap if you do ;)"

"I'm sorry, I'm barely staying awake. I love you, Sweetie. We both do. Please know that no matter what Sal or whoever that giant troll dick was says, WE LOVE YOU. Come home to us."

Double fuck. Sara doesn't get emotional very often, but when she does, it's rough. I hated myself even more now. I was just a giant walking dildo.

Message: Arabella Anderson

"Turtle, please come back. I can explain everything. Kyle's an asshole, and I swear this is just a big misunderstanding. I promise I can explain if you give me a chance?"

"Please, I know it sounds bad. I really do. I should've come to you a lot sooner. But please, I promise I can explain."

"Turtle, I'm scared I ruined things between us. I don't want that. Please message me when you're ready. I won't push any further. I can't tell you how sorry I am about all this."

I sighed, not sure what to think. She didn't deny saying any of it. In fact, she *had* to be the one to tell Kyle, as we were the only two to know the full scope of what happened. I wasn't sure if I was angry at her or myself. I know what she went through was horrible, and she probably was just looking for someone to give her some kind of comfort. But why did it have to be Kyle?! Why couldn't she have come to me?

Message: Unknown Number

"Hey, Lover. Why'd you run off so fast? Want some company? ;)
Give me a call soon. Maybe we can 'catch up' over at my place later.
Kisses."

I felt a load of bile wretch up to my throat. Sal was evil; no ifs, ands, or buts about it. She gets physical pleasure from other people's suffering. I wasn't sure if I felt more sorry for her having to deal with Kyle or vice versa. Either way, those two deserved each other.

Message: Restricted

"It's about time you woke up."

I stared in confusion at the text. Who sent me that? I tried to look up the number, but all it had was an emoji of a cat paw and nothing else. Looking back at the time stamp, I was surprised to see that it had been sent just now while I was reading the others. Before I could do anything else, another one came through.

Message: Restricted

"Open your door."

I stared between the computer screen and my bedroom door. My heart raced as I slowly walked over and turned the handle. Clenching my jaw, I swung the door open, expecting someone to be there waiting. But the hallway was empty. I looked up and down either side, but there was no one. I sighed and was about to close the door when something at my feet caught my attention.

A small package about the size of a loaf of bread was sitting on the floor. It was wrapped in what looked to be just plain butcher paper, with no indication of its contents. I reached down and picked it up, feeling something inside shift. I closed the door and sat back on my bed, staring at the package for several minutes.

I shook my head again and opened the box, my breath catching when I saw what was inside. Lying at the bottom was my watch and a new smartphone. I picked up my watch and studied it carefully. Maybe it wasn't mine? All RRS employees had the same standard-issue watch. They stored each person's clearances, orders, and personal information inside. It was the agency's proprietary equipment, made with parts from another Realm. It never needed to be charged and was practically indestructible as well.

I clicked through it, and sure enough, it was mine. But the strange part was that the previous night's data had been wiped completely. I'm not the greatest regarding tech, but I remember them telling us that there was a better chance of ice water in hell than these things ever getting hacked. I'm paraphrasing, obviously.

Clasping the watch back around my wrist, I felt a strange sense of relief wash over me. That was surprising, to say the least. I usually do nothing but complain about having to wear it 24/7 and have everything I do get tracked by the government. But I guess after so many years, I just felt naked without it. Is that a sign of Stockholm Syndrome? I need to look it up.

The only thing left was the phone at the bottom of the box. I picked it up and turned it over in my hand, noticing it was considerably heavier than any other phone I'd ever had. Instead of the typical fruit logo on the back, there was a cat's paw print. I hit the power button, and the image of an orange cat face with glowing yellow eyes greeted me as the screen booted on. Something about it tickled the back of my brain, but it quickly disappeared as the home screen popped up.

My jaw dropped as I saw the sheer number of apps already installed on the phone. The UI was almost identical to my old one, which made looking through it relatively easy. But there were hundreds, if not thousands, of apps installed. I'd never heard of most of them, and it also looked like a majority were grayed out as if they weren't available. I stopped on one that was softly blinking orange. It was just a picture of a small pot of honey.

Shrugging, I clicked it and almost dropped my phone when I saw Honey staring right at me, her eyes red with heavy bags underneath. She seemed to be looking directly at me, but her eyes moved slightly back and forth like she was reading something. Judging by the art in the background, it looked like she was sitting in the coffeehouse. Just as I was about to say something, Honey turned to look at someone to her side.

"Hm?" she asked, before quickly shaking her head. "No, Lana hasn't heard from him either. I was just looking up his credit card activity."

I was shocked that she so freely admitted to hacking into my accounts. Well, I guess she wasn't actually hacking me. I gave her all that info years ago so she could help me take care of bills and things when I was going on longer jumps. But still!

"Yes, I know he wouldn't like it!" Honey snapped but then quickly bowed her head in apology. "I'm sorry. I'm just . . . so worried."

"I know, Babe," Sara's voice came from off-screen. I saw her peak slightly into the frame as she kissed the top of Honey's head. "We'll find him. I promise. He loves you and wouldn't just disappear like that. I'm sure we'll all be laughing about this over drinks soon. And, if he tries to give you any attitude, you know how good my shibari is. I'll tie him up for you so he can't get away again."

Honey chuckled and slapped at Sara's retreating ass. I hit the back button, and the screen returned to the list of apps. What in the actual fuck is going on? Before I could tap on another, a notification popped up.

<u>System Notification</u>

"Time's almost up. Don't trust the RRS. Destiny awaits."

I stared blankly at the notification. What. The. Fuck.

Chapter 9

Insert Cliché Villain Threat Here

I've seen plenty of movies, okay? Nothing good happens when technology becomes sentient and has access to the Internet. This is the start of a terrible timeline; I can feel it.

I stared at the notification for several minutes, unsure what to think. Why did those words sound so familiar? I mean, despite working for them, I already don't trust the RRS. I can't name a single government agency that should be trusted fully. I've been with them for a decade already, and there was definitely some shady shit going on that I just couldn't put my finger on. So that little bit of a warning didn't mean much.

But what does it mean 'time's almost up'? And why does every goddamn thing have to always be about destiny?! A person can't take a dump these days without it being attributed to destiny.

Shaking my head, I cleared the notification. Looking over the screen again, I sighed and put the phone away. I quickly jumped into the shower to wash away the layer of dried sweat, and what I could only hope was dirt from the other Realm. My watch buzzed, and a cold stab filled my stomach as I read the words across the screen.

"RifterTTL- report to Director Wallace Administration Wing Corridor Seven 0900."

"Well, that can only be good news," I grumbled, turning off the water before drying off and brushing my teeth.

If the Director wanted to meet with me, I could only assume word had finally gotten back from the Taritian Embassy. The events from last night had been so ridiculous I'd already expected difficulty getting anyone to believe me. Even more so now that I had my watch back and all the data had been cleared. But considering I'd *literally* just gotten a warning from a weird, seemingly conscious off-brand smartphone, I began to feel like maybe I should keep these particular cards close to the chest for the time being.

I finished getting dressed, grabbed my new phone, and headed to the door. It was after 8:30, so I was already running late, and dealing with all the security at the RRS would only make me more so. I opened my messaging app, which, thankfully, looked the same, and all my texts were still there. Hopping into the group chat with Honey and Sara, I sent them a quick message apologizing and telling them that my phone had broken and I would explain everything that evening. Just as I locked the door, my phone buzzed, causing me to stop to read the new message.

<u>System Notification</u>

"It appears as if you're traveling. Would you like to use the maps feature?"

I went to click 'no' but realized there wasn't one. There was only 'Accept.' Lovely. The sentient phone already had a glitch. That can only lead to great things down the line, right?

Hitting 'Accept,' a strange map with a detailed image of my neighborhood popped up. A 'Favorites' button at the top was highlighted in orange. I clicked it and almost dropped the phone yet again. It listed all the places I frequented: Sara's Coffeehouse, Xander's, the RRS, and even Frelling State Park. But underneath all of that was a box that said: REALM 924.

Hesitantly, I touched that box, and a new list came up, all with REALM followed by a set of numbers. Randomly, I clicked on one just to see, and sure enough, the map changed. REALM 826 looked very similar to Winly—large rock formations around with the earth barren of any plant life. I looked at the 'Favorites' list and bit my cheek to stop from screaming when I saw 'REALM 924 EMBASSY' listed, along with one of my favorite places to visit in the Winly Realm: Fargog's Tavern.

I shook my head furiously. There just wasn't any way something like this was possible. Even with all the tech we traded with the other Realms, there wasn't anything close to this in development. Hell, we still relied on pin-drop proximity GPS! Let me give you a quick comparison here.

Imagine you need to find a place. We currently have the equivalent of a person drawing a picture of that place on a used napkin and pointing you in a general direction with a compass from the 1700s. But this thing was offering the equivalent of direct access to state-of-the-art satellites with 800k resolution. It was simply impossible!

REALM 924 popped back up, and the RRS button was highlighted. I sighed, not sure why the phone was insistent that I used my GPS to find the same place I walked to daily for years. But I guess I shouldn't piss off what's probably going to be our new computer overlord. I hit the button, and another list appeared. It was the entire facility registry.

Okay, this had to be bullshit. The RRS kept such a strict seal on its inner workings that this information was impossible for anyone to find. I scrolled down the list until I saw Wallace, G. highlighted in orange. With a sigh, I began walking as I touched the Director's name.

It happened faster than I could even comprehend. Before my foot landed on the sidewalk, I felt my core open and the all-too-familiar pull of the Rift. My eyes widened, and I cursed as I readied myself for the yank. But it didn't happen. Just like last night, the pull was subdued, gentle even. And I didn't get taken into the Rift and spun to God knows where. In the blink of an eye, my core closed again, and I stood outside the Director's office.

I stared wide-eyed at the door and then frantically looked around the hall. A few people were walking around, but no one noticed that I just happened to appear out of nowhere. I've been saying this a lot lately, but this right here was *literally impossible*! Everything we've ever known about jumping tells us you can't jump in-realm.

If you wanted to jump to another place in your own world, you had to jump out to another first and then return with the new destination set as your coordinates. At a minimum, it should take me 8 minutes to jump from here to the next closest Realm and then back again. It was nearly double that time for most other Rifters because they would have to make multiple jumps. Yet, there was no denying it.

I jumped in-realm and even did it without triggering any of the agency's alarms! There were sensors everywhere to detect anyone entering or leaving the Rift. If someone jumped without permission, all kinds of alarms would go off, and everyone would be on high alert. But as I looked up at the small puck-shaped sensor on the wall, it was clear that it hadn't detected my jump. *How the hell did a phone do that?!*

Before I could question it further, the door to the Director's office suddenly swung open, and I was face-to-face with Director Wallace and . . . Ara. They'd obviously not been expecting me to be there—I mean, neither was I. I took a giant step back as they quickly stopped, trying to avoid slamming into me.

"Ah, Rifter," Director Wallace said, quickly recomposing himself. "You're a tad early. I like that! Good man."

I couldn't help but glance at Ara, who looked just as professional as ever, wearing light green scrubs and having her hair pulled back in a tight bun. Her face flushed red as she saw me looking at her, and she opened her mouth as if to say something, but I couldn't let her do that. I'd already made this an uncomfortable work environment and couldn't keep doing that to her.

I quickly turned to the Director and gave him a large smile, offering him my hand. "Hello, sir. Yes, I was in the area already. I hope it's okay, but if you need time, I can return later."

Wallace gripped my hand briefly before shaking his head. He turned toward Ara and gave her a slight bow. "I'm sorry to cut this short, Healer Anderson. I'll reach out soon to discuss final preparations. Is that alright?"

Ara's face fell as she nodded. Looking back up, she gave Wallace a tight smile. "Thank you, Director. I look forward to it. But would it be possible for me to borrow Tur- ah, Rifter TTL for just a moment? I need to go over his clearance very quickly."

"There's no need for that," I said, holding up my hand, trying my best to put on a fake smile. "I was already cleared by Healer Lindemen yesterday. Also, Director Wallace, I've come to understand that my team needs a new Healer. I wanted to let you know that I'd be happy to talk to Healer Lindemen about the position this afternoon. I'm sure he'd be fine with the transfer."

Ara's face fell even more as she stared at me. It took everything in me to keep that fake smile going. I wouldn't be the reason things were made more challenging for her. She'd be ruined if the Director or anyone else learned she broke confidentiality. I wouldn't let that happen. So, the easier I made her transfer, the better it would be for her.

"Oh?" Wallace's eyebrows raised in a high arc. "So, you already know about the Healer's request?"

I clenched my jaw and nodded my head once. "Yes, sir. I was informed about it yesterday. I appreciate all the hard work and dedication of the Healer and wish her only the best in her next venture. But, as you're aware, a Rifter must always look forward, never back."

Letting out a short laugh, Wallace nodded in agreement. "True, true. That's why you're in charge of your department. You know exactly where your head needs to be. Now, please come in."

I smiled again, keeping my eyes focused in front of me. I knew my facade might break if I stole even a glance at Ara. As I stepped between the two to enter the office, I felt soft fingers touch my arm, and the familiar cool sensation of Ara's power flushed through my entire body. I hesitated for just a second before continuing inside.

"Well, I guess that's good news for you, Healer," Wallace said as he stepped back into his office. "As it appears the Rifter has anticipated his team's coming needs already, I'll begin preparing for your transfer immediately."

"T-thank you, sir," Ara said, her voice so low I almost didn't hear her.

Before the door closed, I broke my resolve and turned to take one last look at her. Her eyes were wide and glistening as if she were fighting to hold back tears. She bit her lip, staring intensely at me until the door shut between us. That was a mistake. I felt the lump in my throat form as I turned my head and closed my eyes, trying to refocus.

"I'm sorry about this, Rifter," Wallace said, returning to the chair behind his desk while offering the seat opposite him to me. "I know Healer Anderson was a part of your team for a while. In fact, I believe she's been with you longer than the rest of your team combined. I'm sure it's not easy to lose a member so valued this abruptly."

I nodded again, trying to force a casual smile onto my face. "You're not wrong, sir. But I truly believe Healer Anderson is meant for great things. As with most others, being on my team was probably not her final goal in life. It's one reason I usually recommend those from the Rifting teams switch things up every year or so. It allows people to gain experience without risking burnout or limiting their potential. In all honesty, I probably should've insisted she transfer years ago so her career path wouldn't stagnate. If I may, sir, I'd like to leave a formal standing letter of recommendation for her files. No matter if she's transferring to another Rifters team or if she'll be stationed in a hospital, she deserves the highest praise for all the work she's done with me and my team."

Wallace smiled and nodded, making a few taps on the tablet that sat atop his desk. "That's most gracious of you, Rifter. I'm sure she'll greatly appreciate your kindness. The recommendation of a Rifter, especially one of your prestige, can go a long way in propelling someone's career."

I simply nodded and then braced for what was to come next.

"So, Rifter TTL," Wallace said, looking at something on his tablet. "The reason I called you in today was because we received . . . some interesting reports this morning."

"Oh?" I asked, raising my eyebrow, trying to play it as cool as possible.

Looking up from the tablet, Wallace set it on the table and leaned back in his chair. "Word reached the Taritian Embassy that a group of civilians had been rescued from slavers by one of *our* Rifters last night. Would you happen to know anything about that?"

I made a show to look confused, trying to study the man who was scrutinizing me. "Last night? Slavers on Taritia? I'm shocked! They have some of the best security I've encountered in the civilized Realms."

"Well, no, it wasn't actually *on* Taritia," Wallace said, maintaining his intense eye contact. "It was the new jump point you and Healer Anderson were just sent to survey."

I raised my eyebrows in mock surprise. "Oh really? That's strange. I wasn't aware that anyone else had the coordinates yet."

"They don't," Wallace confirmed. "We thought it best to . . . limit exposure until we could better determine the threat level of the Realm. Either way, someone rescued more than three dozen captives and even killed the leader of that tribe of Marrog. When the Swords were sent in, they found the creatures frenzied without their leader and . . . dispatched a majority of them. The remainder were successfully captured, which will greatly help further peace in the Realms. It was actually very fortunate for those involved. This is the first time we've been able to take any of those beasts alive. If their leader had still been around, they'd have all fought until the bitter end. Now, we can finally add them to our Database and hopefully learn some much-needed information about how their kind operates."

Now, that was a surprise to me. I didn't realize the one I killed was their leader. "Oh, wow. That seems pretty intense, for sure. But I'm a bit lost, sir. Why are you telling me all of this?"

"Because one of the rescued captives went to our Embassy on Taritia and said that 'Rifter TTL' saved them."

I had to fight back the cocky grin that I felt starting to form. "Me? But that doesn't make any sense, sir. Today's my first day back, and I was under strict orders not to jump until I reported in."

Wallace slowly nodded before standing up and walking to a counter at the side of the room. He pulled the top off a crystal whiskey decanter and poured a finger into two glasses. He returned and offered me one of the drinks, making it clear it wasn't optional. I grinned as I took the glass, but on the inside, I had to fight hard not to roll my eyes at the man.

Seriously? He just pulled the absolute, most stereotypically cliché villain moves ever. If I hadn't already suspected he was a bad guy, this would've put that nail in the coffin. I mean, it's 9:00 in the damn morning!

"With what we gathered," Wallace continued, leaning against his desk as he sipped his drink. "It's been reported someone was being held there that was . . . unlike any of the others. A woman from a Realm that none have ever seen before. The witnesses said she had a beauty rivaling that of the Gods."

By this point, it's taking everything in me to stop from audibly groaning. I mean, yeah, the elf was cute. But a 'beauty to rival the Gods?' Who does this guy think he's kidding right now? The woman's face flashed in my mind, and something deep inside stirred, causing me to feel an intense longing for her. Shaking my head, I cleared the feeling away. What the hell was that?

"But it's not who or what she is that's important," Wallace said, and I could see the evil little twinkle in the back of his eye. "It's what she carried with her—an artifact of great importance. We're not entirely sure what it is or what it does. But it is undoubtedly crucial that it doesn't . . . fall into the wrong hands."

The . . . *thing*, whatever it was, definitely seemed important. I remembered how everything in me was drawn to it the moment I saw it. But, just like with the woman, it was also missing when I woke up this morning. I searched all over my room and found nothing.

"Our sensors picked up an unauthorized jump in and out of our Realm last night, both taking place within the city of Krayden. Now, I'm quite certain if someone were to say . . . find said woman or object and bring her or it into the RRS for protection, they would be entitled to major, well-deserved rewards. Promotions, accolades, bonuses . . . really, I'm sure just about anything that person desired would be a fitting reward for doing their job to help protect the Realm. And it goes without saying that trivial things such as breaking protocols and jumping to a quarantined world would all be forgotten with impunity."

This son of a bitch. His little song and dance was such a cliché veiled villain threat it wouldn't even make the cut in a straight-to-streaming b-flick spin-off. I bit my tongue and continued smiling at him as if I was taking it all in. I knew I just needed to keep playing the part. Right now, they have no kind of proof other than the word of some scared prisoners who saw me for a whole four minutes in a dark forest. They don't even have my watch, which had the data wiped anyway. So, let him try to threaten me all he wants.

"That does sound like an amazing opportunity, sir," I said, nodding but trying to keep a look of ignorance on my face. "Unfortunately, I don't know how I can help. If you want, I could coordinate between my team and some of the Swords to head back to the jump point to look around?"

Wallace's face soured, and his eyes grew harder as he looked down at me. "The Realm is still under quarantine and cannot be entered."

I nodded my acceptance as I stood, placing my untouched glass of whiskey on his desk. "I understand, sir. Well, if there's any other way I can be of assistance, please let me know."

I turned and quickly made my way back to the door, hoping to get out of there before Wallace tried to push any further. I wasn't so lucky. Just as I gripped the door handle, Wallace cleared his throat, and I heard him tapping something on his tablet.

"Oh, Rifter," he said, causing me to turn back to look at him. He was reading something on his tablet before gazing up at me with a fake look of sadness. "I do apologize for this, but it appears as if the paperwork for your clearance wasn't filed correctly. I'm afraid we can't let you return to active status today. Don't worry; I'll take care of it personally, so it shouldn't take too long to clear up. Why don't you spend the next day or so with your friends and family? Like your niece, Lana? She's enrolled in our RRS programs at UCLA, isn't she? Those programs are challenging to get into, and students fail out of them almost every day, you know. Or how about your friends Honey and Sara? I heard the great news about the happy couple being approved for an adoption license. They're so hard to come by, and I've heard horrible stories about couples having them revoked, sometimes for no apparent reason. It also appears that you and Healer Anderson greatly admire each other. It would benefit you both to enjoy time together before her transfer. While I can request that she stay here locally, there is always a chance the powers that be might need her at one of the outlying embassies. I heard they're in desperate need of Healers out in Plexata. Have you ever been? It's a terrible place, ravaged by war, and a disease just killed all their women, leaving nothing but those lonely men to fight with no kind of companionship... So, please, take this time to enjoy them all, and we can talk again when this whole paperwork situation clears up in a day or two. All right?"

My rage flared, and I clenched my jaw, doing everything I could not to lunge at the fat little man. If he thought for one second I would stand there and let him threaten all the people I loved and cared about, he had another thing coming. I knew I could rip him from this Realm and stick him somewhere the RRS would never find him. Maybe that would wipe that smug smile off his face.

"And send transcription," he said into his tablet, shooting me another smile. "I apologize—new policies. I've started recording all of my meetings. Just as a failsafe in case I cannot perform my duties for whatever reason. My replacement would then be caught up with what's happening around the RRS. Efficient, don't you think?"

Fuck this guy with a two-by-four wrapped in barbed wire. Sideways. Set on fire. I couldn't touch him, at least not with how things were now. He held the cards for the moment. I just needed to buy some time to think.

I gave a slight smile and nod before turning and leaving the room. The door had barely shut behind me when a massive figure stopped me from taking another step. I looked up and groaned as black eyes stared down at me.

"Hey, Gregg," I said just before the security guard gripped me by the front of my shirt and pulled me off my feet to look him in the eyes.

"NOT GREGG!" He shouted as he turned and dragged me through the halls until he was able to literally throw me out of the security gate.

I landed hard on the pavement, the air rushing from my lungs as I rolled. "Fuck you too, Gregg!"

I stood and tried to dust myself off as a few people quickly rushed past, whispering while shooting me strange glances. Oh, yeah. This is going to be great for my reputation.

Sighing, I turned and walked down the street, heading home. It wasn't even 10 in the morning, and I was already getting a migraine from all this bullshit. My phone buzzed, and I pulled it out, answering without even looking to see who it was.

"Hel—"

"TURTLE!" Honey's voice screamed from the other end, causing me to yank the phone away from my ear. "WHERE THE FUCK ARE YOU?!"

"Ah, hey, Hon—"

"NO!" Honey yelled again. "No, no, no! Where are you, RIGHT NOW?!"

I sighed and shook my head. "I'm heading home. I should be there in like five—"

"STAY THERE! DO YOU UNDERSTAND?!"

"Jeeze! Lower your voice! You keep yelling like that, and I won't need the phone; I'll be able to hear you from across town just fine."

The line went dead, and I knew I was in for the chewing out of a lifetime. To be fair, I do deserve it. I was a complete ass. Again. God, I might just be a bad person after all. Good guys don't hurt their friends as much as I do, right? It seems like that's all I've been doing lately: hurting people I care about.

I made it home and went to my room to lie down. I didn't even bother getting undressed. I didn't care. Pulling out my phone, I decided to try playing with a few of the new apps to see what they did. While scrolling, I noticed a small cat paw icon at the bottom of the screen, usually where a phone's assistant program would be.

Figuring it was worth a shot, I swiped on it and was shocked to be greeted with familiar yellow cat eyes looking back at me. Rui, the woman from the park, was on my screen, looking at me with the same bratty smirk she had last night. I almost dropped my phone as I jumped at the girl's sudden appearance. "What the hell?!"

"This isn't hell, Daddy, You're currently at 25—"

"I know where I am," I yelled, staring intently at the phone. "And what did I tell you about calling me that?! I meant, what are you doing on my phone? Did you send this to me? Who the hell are you?!"

Rui rolled her feline eyes and scoffed like I just asked the stupidest questions in the world. I noticed her left ear twitch as she looked back at me, seemingly annoyed. "I'm on the phone because it helps me assist you better. Yes, I did give it to you, since you complained about your other one being broken. Besides, it was insufficient for what you need, anyway. And like I told you last night, I. AM. RUI."

I gritted my teeth in frustration as I glared at the girl. "That doesn't tell me anything! Why can't you just speak straight?"

Rui's right ear twitched as she tilted her head to the side. "I don't know what you expect from me, Daddy. I'm not fully operational yet. I'm doing the best I can."

That caught me by surprise. Dots began to click in my brain, and I looked at the girl anew. Too many things started to make sense with that one phrase. "Operational? Like, a program? Are you a computer program or like an AI or something?"

Rui scoffed again and crossed her arms underneath her ample chest. Was her chest that big last night? I honestly couldn't remember. "I'm not a computer, Daddy! I'm just . . . not . . . fully operational yet."

"So, how can you become fully operational?" I asked, sitting up in my bed.

"Only you can do that, of course!" Rui smiled at me, a glint in her eyes.

I blinked, trying to figure out what that meant. "Me? I don't know anything about computers!"

"I told you I'm not a computer!" Rui's demeanor changed, and she scowled at me with her fists clenched at her sides. "I'm RUI! And you're the only one who can do it, Daddy!"

"Jesus, we're going to be stuck in a loop," I sighed, shaking my head. "For the love of all things good and holy in the world, will you please stop calling me that? It makes me feel very weird."

Rui smirked and put a hand on one of her hips, sticking her tongue out at me. "Make me."

I sighed and shook my head. I don't know what I did to deserve this. "Okay, whatever! Just . . . can you at least tell me what you do?"

Rui gave me a bright smile, and I saw the sparkle in her eyes as she almost jumped up and down. "Of course! I'm your Rift User Interface. This means I'm your girl for anything you need help with involving the Rift! Want to check in on friends and family? Easy. Want more precise and smoother entry and exit from the Pathways? No problem! And like you saw last night, I can even take a physical form to help you in *any* way you need."

Information overload. I felt like my mind was about to burst. Everything Rui said was more impossible than the last, yet she never flinched. I was afraid if I poked too much at it all, I'd have a massive aneurysm trying to make it make sense.

I rubbed my eyes furiously, feeling the migraine that was coming on. "Okay, I'm going to need a little bit to . . . process this. It's just . . . a lot."

"Your blood pressure is spiking, and your cortisol levels are out of balance," Rui said, a hint of concern in her voice. "Do you want my help with some tension relief?"

I stopped rubbing my eyes and stared back at the phone. "What's that now?"

The phone screen went black, and I started to freak out, thinking I'd broken it. "Rui?!"

"Right here, Daddy," her voice came from just beside me, causing me to nearly jump out of the bed.

"JESUS CHRIST!" I screamed, clutching my chest. "DON'T DO THAT!"

Rui giggled and covered her mouth with one hand as her tail flicked the air behind her. She was sitting cross-legged on my bed, the fabric of her dress riding high up her smooth, porcelain thighs. "Do you want me to stay like this? I can always switch things up for you too, Daddy."

I studied her carefully, trying to figure out what she was talking about. I didn't have to wait long as her body shifted before my eyes. My jaw dropped in complete shock as I saw a perfect replica of Honey sitting on the bed with me, just wearing Rui's sheer blue fabric that now barely covered her massive breasts and the top of her hips.

"How's this?" Rui asked, using Honey's voice. "You produce more serotonin when looking at this form, and I can feel your sexual desire for her. I've also noticed the same with this one."

Rui's body shifted again, this time into Sara. Her chest got quite a bit smaller, but the thin fabric of her skirt barely covered her perfect ass. "I can recreate anyone you've had previous interactions with to perform *any* task you desire."

Shifting again, Ara was now sitting beside me, her green eyes peering right into mine. "Hmm, it seems your body reacts the strongest to this one. It's common to relieve stress and tension through sexual acts, isn't it? I'm more than happy to suck your cock until you explode your hot cum down my throat, sir!"

"NO!" I yelled, jumping off the bed. "I don't want to have sex with you, or . . . any of the others! I think I might just take a vow of celibacy right now after seeing that. Please, go change back to . . . you."

The woman tilted her head and pouted at me, shifting back into her original Neko form. "I don't understand. I'm here to assist you and offer companionship."

"I don't need that kind of companionship from you," I tried to explain as my heart continued to pound in my chest. "I just want answers."

Rui stared at me, her tail flicking several times in the air. "Fine . . . but, you know the offer's always on the table. I give you full consent for anything your dirty mind can come up with. Any day, any time."

I let out a long sigh, thanking whatever God I could that I dodged the massive shitstorm that would've come from Honey barging into my room to see a half-naked version of either herself or Sara blowing me. "Now, with you out here, does my phone still work? Or do you have to be in there?"

"I'm in there, *and* out here," Rui said with a single nod, smiling as if that explained everything.

I rubbed my eyes in frustration yet again. "Of course you are. Why wouldn't you be? I can't just get a simple explanation for anything, can I?"

Rui rolled her eyes and let out a long sigh. Looking at me directly in the eyes, she slowed down her speech as if she were talking to a child. "All functions of your phone will continue to work, and I'll still be able to monitor you. However, while I'm not in the Rift, our interactions over your device will be limited until I return to it. Do you understand, Daddy?"

I heard the front door slam open, causing the walls to shake violently. "TURTLE!"

"Fuck me," I said, shaking my head. I looked at Rui and waved her away. "Hide or return or . . . change into something that's not a human woman! Honey can't know about you."

The door to my room burst open, and Honey stared at me with a mixed look of anger and relief. I raised my hands to try to stop her, but she wasn't having it. She ran inside and launched herself at me, tackling me to the ground.

"ASSHOLE!"

Chapter 10
Cracking The Shell

I know what most of you are thinking right now. Honey's crazy, and it's an unhealthy relationship and all that. I can totally see where you're coming from and why you might think that, too. But you haven't known her as long as I have. You didn't have to go through the shit with us. You've gotten a small portion of the big picture. And while I agree she shoule *absolutely* turn that yandere knob down about eleven notches, I don't blame her for it.

For most of our lives, it was us—together against the world, often literally. And she's saved me *way* more than I've ever saved her. To have that kind of bond with someone is a fantastic experience that most won't get. But at the same time, others also don't have to worry about getting tackled to the ground and punched in the crotch for not responding to some text messages. So, I guess it's a . . . take the good with the bad kind of situation?

Honey lay entirely on top of me, her ear pressed into my chest, listening to my heartbeat. After about a solid hour of screaming, crying, and slapping at me for being so selfish, she calmed down, and we just lay together. I stroked her hair, and she used her finger to draw random designs on my chest.

The first time Sara saw us like that, she almost stormed out of the house, thinking she was being cheated on. While they are polyamorous, they have rules that keep their relationship strong. One is that you always tell the other about a new partner; otherwise, it's viewed as if you're trying to hide something and associated with cheating. It took a lot of reassurances and several more instances where she witnessed how innocent it was before Sara got comfortable with it.

The funny thing is that *she* started doing the same after about a year of us living together. Sara would come home after having a stressful day, or something would've happened, and she'd be upset. Without saying anything, she'd just lay on top of me and wait for me to start stroking her hair. It threw me off the first few times, too. But now, it just is what it is. And who am I kidding? Having two hot women lying on top of me almost daily wasn't what I'd consider a bad home life.

"I'm not saying what you did was right," Honey said, staring into space. "But I can see your side of things now. I'm sorry about the stuff I said, Love. I didn't realize just how bad that jump affected you. I should've seen it sooner."

"Hush," I said, looking up at the ceiling as my fingers continued to comb through her thick locks. "It's not on you to try to fix me. I knew I was taking it hard, but I thought it was something I could handle. And for the record, I don't give two shits about what Kyle or any of the others have to say. I got upset because it was Ara who thought those things about me. I don't know why; I just . . . really care about what she thinks of me."

Honey looked up, resting her chin on my chest. "She really does like you, Turtle. Like, a *lot*. You should've heard some of what she said after you left."

"Like what?" I asked, trying to look down at her.

Shaking her head, Honey turned to the side again to continue drawing with her finger. "I promised I wouldn't say. But I'll tell you that I think it's more than just a crush. A lot more."

I sighed and shook my head. "I think you're just grasping at straws there. Ara's an amazing woman. But I seriously failed her. She deserves someone who isn't going to let her get hurt. Someone she can feel safe with. That's not me. It's why she's transferring off my team."

Honey shot up, a fire in her eyes I'd rarely seen before. "You listen to me, and you listen good. That woman has gone through some shit. And I'm not even talking about your last jump. She has history, just like we all do. Do you know *why* she went to Kyle that night? Did you even give her the chance to explain anything?"

I clenched my jaw, refusing to meet Honey's glare. "It doesn't matter."

Pushing off of me, Honey stood. Before I could react, she kicked me in the ribs, causing me to scream out in pain. "Hey! That hurt!"

"Good!" She yelled, kicking me again. "Let this remind you that you're not an *actual* turtle. All those years ago, when your brother and his friends used to beat the shit out of you and mock you, calling you a turtle, what did you do? You became one to protect yourself from people, creating this hard exterior so no one could ever hurt you again. You've hidden behind that for so long you seem to have forgotten you're a human! You're allowed to feel things! Pain sucks, but it's a part of life!"

She kicked me twice more before I finally rolled away and sat up on my knees, keeping my face down. Honey grabbed either side of my head and forced me to look up at her. Tears had started streaming down her face as she gazed deep into my eyes.

"I love you more than I even have words to describe," she said, her voice cracking with emotion. "But I can't keep watching you armor yourself like this. After the FRE, I thought you'd realize that life was too short to lock yourself away like that. We got you to open back up with us, and both Sara and I fell even more in love with you. But now, you're doing it again. And this time, you're locking out a woman who I genuinely think loves you, too. You didn't see the pain I did last night. Pain like that can only be caused by someone you love. For once in your goddamn life, I'm begging you. Crack that shell of yours and let her in. Don't be Turtle, be Tom again."

Her words stung. It had been over twenty years since she used my real name, and hearing her say it sounded strange. She was right, though. I wanted to protect myself from all the pain back then. So, I leaned into it when they called me turtle as an insult. I made it so they could never use it to hurt me again. I became the Turtle whose hard shell would protect him against anything the world tried to throw at him.

"I . . . I don't know how to do that," I said, looking back toward the ground.

Honey wrapped her arms around my neck and squeezed my face into her chest. She hugged me for several minutes, and I soon became uncomfortably aware that she was not wearing a bra. I tried to pull my face away, but she squeezed tighter, shoving my face deeper into her large, soft breasts. "Don't push me away, Love. Let me help you."

"Let us both help you," a voice came from the doorway.

Before I could try to move, I felt another set of arms around my neck and a smaller pair of firm breasts press into my head. Sara had apparently come home and witnessed some of what was happening. The women both squeezed me, and I decided that if that was the way I died, so be it. Being smothered by the breasts of two beautiful women was definitely not the worst way to go.

After another minute, the women broke the embrace. I was finally able to take a deep breath of air, not realizing just how close I'd come to legitimately passing out. I looked up at Honey and then Sara. Both women had tear-stained faces but were also smiling at me.

"I didn't hear a lot," Sara said, looking between Honey and me. "But if there's anything I can do to help, you know I will. I love you so much, Sweetie. I'm here for you just as much as Honey is, understand?"

I chuckled and nodded. "Thank you. I mean that."

The girls grinned and hugged me once more. We stayed like that for a few minutes before Sara got a call from the Coffeehouse and had to step out. Honey pulled out her phone and started texting furiously. I looked at her, trying to see who she was messaging. The second I moved closer, she yanked her phone away and shot me a dirty scowl.

"Mind your own business," she said, quickly turning and leaving my room, shutting the door as she did.

I was alone again, sitting on the floor, letting everything sink in. See what I mean? Honey has some issues, but it all comes from a place of love. And I really wouldn't trade that for anything else in the world. So, if I have to deal with some GPS trackers and an occasional haranguing or two to have her in my life, I'll take it.

"Aww, that was cute," Rui's playful voice said, inches behind my ear.

I jumped and let out a very non-masculine scream in surprise. I shot around to see Rui standing just behind where I was sitting, staring at me with her bratty grin. Holding my chest, I took several deep breaths in an attempt to calm my now-racing heart.

"Jesus Christ! Stop doing that, or I'm going to put a bell around your goddamn neck!"

Tilting her head back, a strip of pink leather slowly materialized and wrapped around Rui's neck. A small golden bell appeared right in the middle, dangling just in front of her throat. She looked back down at me with an almost evil smile. Tracing the collar around her neck, she let her fingers rest on the bell, giving it a slight flick to hear it chime.

"Is this to your satisfaction, Daddy?"

My mouth gaped open as I stared at the woman, losing all words. I let out a long breath and shook my head in defeat. "Sure, yeah, why not?"

"Thank you, Daddy," Rui said, hopping up and down like a little kid who just got a gift from Santa.

I squinted at her suspiciously, studying every move she made. "What's wrong with you? Seriously."

Rui tilted her head to the side, giving me a quizzical look. "What? Don't you like it, Daddy?"

I opened my mouth to respond, but the sound of my door opening caused me to turn around, eyes wide as Honey stood in the doorway. She furrowed her brow, looking behind me to where Rui was standing, and I tried everything I could to come up with any kind of explanation for the troublesome Neko. "Honey, I . . . uh . . . it's not—"

"What the hell?" she asked as she crossed her arms under her chest. "What is that?"

"She's . . ." I turned to gesture at Rui, but the girl was gone.

The empty space threw me off until a slight motion on the floor drew my attention. A short orange tabby cat wearing a pink collar was now sitting where Rui had just been. I was shocked to see familiar yellow eyes looking back at me as the kitten slowly blinked and let out a soft meow.

"You got us a kitty?!" Honey excitedly rushed in with a giant smile. She picked up the now cat Rui and held her close, rubbing her face against the kitten's soft fur. "Turtle! When did you get us a kitty?"

"Uh . . ." was about the only thing I could say as I watched Honey dance with Rui in her arms. The kitten let out another meow, which only made Honey squeal with happiness. "Baby! Come, look. Turtle got us a kitty!"

Shaking my head, I tried to quiet Honey down, but she was already too invested. She giggled and held Rui up high to get a better look at her. "What's your name, you little cutie? Aren't you the sweetest little girl? Aww, you're so soft!"

Sara rounded the corner and crossed her arms in front of her chest, smirking at Honey and then shooting me a look. "Really? You couldn't warn me first?"

"I . . ."

"AH!" Honey squealed again, beaming a massive smile at us as Rui began to purr in her arms. "She likes me!"

Sara sighed and shook her head, turning to leave my room. "We still should have some of the stuff from Beans in the garage. Luckily, I packed it up instead of donating it after he passed."

Honey bounded after Sara, holding Rui tightly as they went down the hall. I stared after them, dumbfounded, not exactly sure what just happened. I looked around my now-empty room and then back out the door. I still had so many questions for Rui, but it was painfully obvious that Honey wouldn't be letting the poor cat go any time soon.

I heard a soft buzz from my bed and saw my phone screen lighting up with a new message notification.

<u>Message: Arabella Anderson</u>

"Hey, can you please meet me at Gus's Cafe? It's about work. We don't have to discuss other things, but this is important. Please."

I sighed and shook my head. Everything in me wanted to delete the text and go about my day. I was only going to open myself up to even more pain if I saw Ara again. But Honey's words echoed through my mind. I can be an adult about all of this. Two former colleagues can get together for coffee without it being weird. Right?

I sent my confirmation before grabbing my wallet and sunglasses and headed toward the door. As I passed through the living room, I saw Honey holding a plastic stick with a feather attached to a string. She dragged it in front of Rui, who looked overwhelmingly unimpressed by the toy. Honey beamed up at me, having the time of her life with the new addition to the house.

"Where are you heading?"

"I need to meet someone at Gus'," I said, grabbing my keys off the hook and opening the door. "I'll be back soon. Be careful with Rui, okay?"

"Rui?" Honey asked, looking back down at the cat. "What kind of name is that?"

I just chuckled and left them to have their fun. Climbing in my car, I turned on the AC to start cooling it down. It was late spring, and the days were getting hotter and hotter. I looked in my rearview mirror, and a flash of movement caught my eye near the side of the house. I quickly turned around but didn't see anything out of the ordinary. I thought it looked like someone had been watching me from just around the corner. But as I checked again, there was no one in sight.

The image of the elf woman from last night flashed in my head. She'd been on my mind a lot since waking up. I'd wondered where she'd gone, but figured she was most likely whatever her Realm's version of a Rifter was and probably went back home. Yet, a part of me somehow knew she was still around. I couldn't explain it even if I tried. I'd get to see her again, and the thought made me happy for some reason.

I sighed and chalked it up to just my imagination. I mean, can you blame me for seeing weird stuff at this point? Even I think I needed to check myself into the psych ward with all the unbelievable crap that's happened in the past twenty-four hours. I pulled out of the driveway and turned into town, making my way to the small cafe that was one of the few in the entire city that wasn't themed around the Rift.

As I pulled into the parking lot, I realized how strange it was that Ara wanted to meet there. It was on the opposite side of town as the RRS and more than a twenty-minute drive from the central hospital where she worked when she wasn't at the facility. She also lived much closer to the RRS, so why pick this place?

Taking a deep breath, I slowly got out of my car. My mind raced at what I was going to say. The pain I had felt hearing what Ara really thought about me was still fresh in my mind. The old me would've liked to do something to lash out. Yet, I couldn't do that to her. Despite everything, I still had strong feelings for her and wanted her to be happy.

I saw her sitting in a booth in the back corner, far from anyone else. She looked deep in thought, staring into nothing, not noticing me at first. I know I'd seen her earlier at the agency, but I still couldn't help but think about how good she looked. The voice that was the old me screamed, telling me to turn around and leave before the pain happened. But I couldn't do that.

Finally, Ara's eyes focused on me, and I saw her demeanor shift. The hint of a smile formed on her lips as she waved me over. Casually, I walked to the booth and sat down, folding my hands on my lap. I gave her a soft smile and nod, causing her to blush.

Ara looked down at her half-drunk coffee and bit her lip, obviously trying to think about what to say. "Thank you for coming. I was worried—"

"You said it was important," I cut her off, trying to keep my voice as calm as possible. "I've known you a long time. If you think something's important, I trust you. So, what's up?"

Ara's face flashed a brighter red, but she cleared her throat and looked me in the eyes. "Something's going on at the RRS. Something big."

I sighed and nodded. I figured something was going to happen. If that elf and whatever she carried is as important as Wallace said, they'll do whatever they can to find them. "Do you know what?"

Shaking her head, Ara looked down at her coffee again. "Not really. There are some rumors. But all the big guns are being called in, and everyone's been put on standby."

A server approached and asked if I wanted anything to drink, to which I politely declined. They topped off Ara's coffee and left us alone again. Ara looked at me, her eyes filled with unasked questions. She bit her lower lip nervously, a little tick I noticed she had when she was working herself up to say something. I sat quietly, waiting, letting her take the lead.

"Th-There's another rumor going around that you were suspended," she said, studying my face. "That you stole something from the RRS? And when the Director confronted you about it, you got violent, and security had to throw you out."

I scoffed and rolled my eyes, shaking my head at the absurdity of it. So much for their little act. I guess they don't have patience for the long game. I saw the confusion on Ara's face and gave her a soft smile. "Don't worry. You should know not to listen to the rumors of that place. People gossip because they don't have anything better to do."

"So, why aren't you there right now?"

Sighing, I looked out the window before turning back to her. "There was a mistake in my clearance forms. It's as simple as that. It'll get cleared up in a few days."

Ara furrowed her brows as she stared hard at me. "I checked your clearance forms this morning after they'd been submitted. Everything's perfect with them. Now, why are you lying?"

Clenching my jaw, I fought an internal battle. I didn't want to lie to her. She was the last person I'd ever want to do that to. But I couldn't take the chance of her getting drawn into this more than she already had.

"That's the exact reason Wallace gave me," I said. While technically not a lie, it still wasn't the whole truth. I had to live in the gray for as long as I could. "I'll be back soon enough."

We sat in silence for several minutes, neither of us knowing what to say next. I felt a stabbing in my chest as I studied the soft curves of Ara's face and the cute cluster of freckles that lined her cheeks. Thinking about it, I didn't know when I started noticing those little things about her. At some point in our years working together, I realized I had feelings for her. And now those feelings were coming to kick me in the ass.

"Well," I said, placing my hand on the table to stand up.

Before I could move, Ara grabbed my hand, squeezing as tightly as she could. The suddenness of it took me by surprise, and I stopped, seeing her stare intently at me. There was a fire in her eyes that I'd never seen before.

"Turtle, please don't go," she said, her voice hiding a slight tremor. "I need to say something. Please. After I'm done, if you never want to see me again, I'll respect that. But please, give me five minutes."

I felt the ache in my chest building, knowing that if I stayed, the pain would be inevitable. Swallowing the lump that had formed in my throat, I gave her a slight nod before settling back in my chair. Ara let out a low sigh of relief, seeing I was staying. She took a deep breath, obviously trying to settle her nerves.

"I know; I made a huge mistake by talking to Kyle," she started, and I already knew I wouldn't like what I was about to hear. "I have no excuse for it. When we got back from that jump, and I saw just how badly you were injured, something inside me broke. I was so scared. They separated us so fast that I didn't know if you were alive or dead. Even after my debriefing, they *still* wouldn't tell me anything. I was going crazy. Kyle was a friend . . . or so I thought. He'd done some jobs with my old station before I transferred here. I figured since he's the new Head Sword, he might be able to get me some answers. I guess the toll from it all just got to me, and I broke down, telling him everything that happened. But I never once said I didn't feel safe with you or that you were a coward. He took everything I said and twisted it. I never would say something like that about you. Turtle, you're the *only* one I feel safe with."

She squeezed my hand tighter, leaning forward as she tried to stress her point. "I've known I've had feelings for you for a long time. At first, I thought it was just one of those stupid workplace crushes you hear about. That, eventually, it would go away. But the more time we spent together, the more I saw what kind of person you are, and the harder I fell. You're passionate, funny, kind, and fiercely loyal to those you care about. And when I saw you take on that monster, throwing away your own safety to save me, I knew what I felt was real. I know how daft that sounds. Who can fall in love with someone they've never even been on a date with? But that's the truth. I called in every favor I could to have you taken to my hospital once you were stable enough. I sat by your bed each day, holding your hand and infusing as much of my power into you as I could. Even though you were in a coma, I wanted you to know that I was there and I wasn't ever going to leave."

Yup, all the pain. My heart felt like someone was stabbing me over and over with every word she said. Clearing my throat, I looked out the window so she wouldn't see my moment of weakness.

"And then you requested to transfer off my team," I said, my voice betraying my feelings by cracking.

Ara's face fell, and she looked down at the table in shame. She slowly nodded before looking back up at me. "Yes, but it's not what you think. The day you woke up and we shared that amazing kiss, I made up my mind. I wanted to be with you. But, since I was on your team, there was no way the agency would allow it. I know I was an idiot and should've approached you first. Hell, I don't even know how you really feel about me. But I knew if I tried to broach the subject while on your team, you would've instantly rejected me, even if only to protect my career. Honey confirmed that when I talked to her last night. She said you'd give up any bit of happiness for yourself if it meant protecting those you care about. I figured it would be better to seek forgiveness than ask for permission. I put in the transfer and waited for it to push through before I told you. That's why I didn't come over much when you were released. I didn't trust myself not to spill everything right then and there."

I was at a complete loss. I'll freely admit I'm a giant asshole. 100% grade-A prime asshole. Here I had one of the smartest, kindest, most beautiful women I've ever met willing to completely change her entire career path just to be with me, and I acted like a toddler who got his feelings hurt and took off without a word when she tried to explain.

Ara stared at me, her eyes wide with anticipation as she studied my face for any reaction. I didn't know what to do or say. Feelings aren't really my wheelhouse, okay? I usually have Honey or Sara around to tell me what to do. With a long sigh, I turned my hand over and gripped Ara's in return.

I saw her eyes light up as a smile grew on her face. I returned the smile and felt the cooling rush of her power filling me. She studied my face carefully as if trying to confirm my intentions. "Does that mean . . ."

Chuckling and giving her a slight nod, I squeezed her hand a bit firmer. "It means we *really* need to work on our communication. But I've had those same kind of feelings for you. I've wanted to be with you for years, Ara. Hell, I haven't even been on a date in years because I wanted to spend whatever free time I had with you. I just didn't want to make you uncomfortable or jeopardize your future with the RRS."

Ara half laughed, half sobbed as she jumped up and threw herself at me, wrapping her arms tightly around my neck. I laughed as I tried to return her embrace at the awkward angle the booth had us in. Before I knew it, her lips were pressed firmly into mine, and the same feeling of pure electricity I felt the first time we kissed radiated through me.

Ara broke our kiss but stayed wrapped around my neck, her eyes gazing hard into mine. I could see the redness of her cheeks growing and could feel her breasts press hard into me as she smiled affectionately. Her voice was soft but heavy with desire as she leaned forward to whisper in my ear. "Do you maybe want to—"

Before she could finish, a high-pitched alarm rang out from her watch, causing both of us to jump in surprise. She looked down in shock as she read the flashing message. Her face contorted in increasing confusion the more she read. Shaking her head, she stood up and looked around the Cafe.

"What's going on?" I asked, noticing my watch didn't get the message.

"Bloody Hell. Sorry, I have to go," Ara said, putting a ten-dollar bill on the table. She leaned in and gave me another passionate kiss before she turned toward the door. "I promise I'll come over later, and we can pick this up, okay?"

Before I could respond, she was out the door, and I was left alone in the booth. I looked at my watch, waiting to see if anything would happen, but it didn't. Sighing, I pulled out my phone and noticed I had two notifications.

Message: Honey Badger

"Rui is such a weird name for a cat! Can I please rename her Princess Fluffy Butt?"

I chuckled and swiped to the following notification.

System Notification

"DON'T LET HER CALL ME THAT, DADDY!"

Chapter 11

The Elf And The Thief

When you spend your days using strange magic powers to travel chaotic energy currents to fantastical worlds, you can forget what driving places feels like. I've had the same beat-up Pontiac since I was a freshman in college. I got it for $300 and a carton of cigarettes— and I'm not joking in the slightest. Honey and Sara have been on me for years to buy another car since I make good money as a Rifter. I can't blame them too much because this one's been a rolling turd fire the entire time I've owned it, but I've been able to keep it going this far.

It's probably because I drive it maybe once every other month, and even that's just to head to Frelling or maybe to grab a bite to eat somewhere too far to walk. I work less than a mile from where I live and have two amazing roommates who do most of the shopping. Plus, my favorite place to hang out is only a couple blocks from my house. There really isn't much reason for me to get behind the wheel.

But on days like today, when I have nothing going on and don't have to work, I remember how relaxing it can be to simply go for a drive. After leaving the Cafe, I didn't have anywhere I *had* to be. Honey and Sara were still home, so I couldn't talk to Rui for a while. Ara was busy with whatever that notification was. And I didn't have the mental strength to try to figure out where that elf woman went or what that object she carried was.

The image of her face flashed in my mind again, and I felt a strange tugging inside my chest. Seriously, where could someone like her go without being noticed? I knew I needed to find her before the RRS, but I didn't even know where to start looking.

So, instead, I just drove around town for a bit. It's incredible how much can change over a decade without you noticing. Whole neighborhoods had been developed, while others were all but abandoned. New restaurants and boutiques filled one area, and the next had commercial warehouses that were a massive eyesore. Whoever set up this town did a crappy job.

My phone buzzed as a notification window popped on my screen. I sighed as I opened the message, wondering what new hell awaited me.

Message: Honey Badger

"HEY! They had an opening at the clinic to get the kitty her shots. We didn't see any tags, so we figured we might as well get her checked out. We'll be back in a bit!"

Poor Rui. I don't think she knew what she was signing up for. I chuckled and shook my head as I visualized this seemingly all-powerful entity that can manipulate the energies of the cosmos, being forced to take a shot in the ass. I'm sure nothing bad will come of that, right?

I decided to stop at a small mom-and-pop pizza place to get a couple of slices for lunch. They'd just opened for the day and weren't busy, so I could take some time to read an actual newspaper while I ate. Yes, I'm weird. I like physical forms of media over digital. Of course, having everything streaming directly on your phone is more convenient, but there's just something about holding a book or newspaper that makes you feel more accomplished when you finish reading it. It's probably why, my entire life, books were the only possessions I ever really cared about. My room was lined almost floor to ceiling with shelf after shelf of books I've collected over the years.

One of the reasons I liked this pizza place was that it was next door to a secondhand indie bookstore. The Bookery was known for two things: having some of the strangest, most eclectic selection of books and the absolute *best* lemon bars you'll ever eat. The owner's wife was a baker, making them all fresh daily. Eating one is like having an orgasm with your mouth. It was my next stop after lunch.

Leisurely, I strolled through the stacks of bookshelves, perusing the worn titles as I went. Stopping to look at an old fantasy novel, I got one of those strange feelings, as if someone was watching me. I looked around, but there was no one there. I shook my head, playing it off as the stress of everything making me paranoid. Besides the bored-looking girl behind the counter, I was the only one in the store.

I didn't have anything I was looking for, so I just walked the cramped aisles, letting my eyes graze over book after book. A shift in the air caused me to spin, just to be greeted with nothing but more books. I could've sworn it felt like someone had just walked past me. Looking around intently, an uneasy feeling began to creep down my spine. Something was off, but for the life of me, I just couldn't figure out what.

Shaking my head, I tried to brush it off once again. Finishing the last bite of the pastry I'd bought when I first came in, I wiped my hands with the napkin and turned to leave. Nothing was catching my attention, and besides, I really needed to get back home to get more information out of Rui. Just as I started walking, a sudden thud behind me caused me to jump and spin.

At first, I saw nothing, just the empty aisle stretching to the back of the store. I shook my head and let out a long breath, chastising myself for being so jumpy. As I was about to turn back to the exit, something on the floor caught my eye. A book had fallen off the shelf and now lay at my feet. Curious, I reached down and picked it up, reading the faded cover.

<u>The Unknown Realms by Annabella Saph, Ph.D.</u>

What the hell is this? As I studied the cover, many questions began racing through my mind. Was this the same Dr. Saph who recruited me for the RRS? She'd given me one of the best blowjobs of my life that day, and we'd even casually hooked up several times over the years before her retirement. But now that I think about it, I never actually learned her first name. Listen, I already feel you judging me, and you can keep that to yourself.

I opened the copyright page, and even more questions popped up. The book had been published over twenty years ago, well before the FRE and formation of the Rift. I remembered Dr. Saph saying she'd been with the RRS for a while, but it was mainly all just theoretical studies. At least, that's what I assumed. Back then, there was no way for them to know anything about Realms or the Rift. How could she have written an entire book about the subject over a decade before any of it was proven to exist?

Walking back to the front, I set the book on the counter and smiled at the cashier. The girl seemed annoyed that she needed to put down her phone to check me out. I kept it simple and made my purchase. A whole $3.87 later, I was back in my car heading home. Even if I couldn't talk to Rui yet, I now had something that might help me learn more about what's going on.

As I pulled into the driveway, I noticed Sara's SUV was gone and figured they might still be at the vet. I opened the door to the house and decided to double-check and make sure no one was home. "Hello?"

No answer.

"Honey? Sara?"

Nothing.

"Rui?"

I went back to my room and closed the door. It was mid-afternoon, and I had nothing else to do for the day. That meant it was a perfect time to kick back and enjoy my new book. I quickly changed out of my uniform and put on a pair of old scrub pants and one of my novelty t-shirts that Honey constantly complains about. She hated when I'd wear one out in public, calling me an overgrown man-child. But, come on. 'Silence is gold, but duct tape is silver' is hilarious.

I stretched out on my bed, opened the book, and soon found myself bored to tears. While this looked like an old fantasy paperback, it read more like a thesis paper. Now, I'm a very proficient reader. I've read some pretty complicated books in the past. You have to be able to keep up with tons of details and intricate plots if you want to read anything with decent world-building. Saying all of that, I didn't understand about two-thirds of what was written in this book.

I know I'm not the most intelligent man out there, but come on! I'm relatively sure she just made up some of these words. I was about to give up and switch to an old favorite of mine when a line caught my attention.

"With a substantial energy influx, the ability to create a proximate node for incursion can be obtained. This would allow us to permanently access the Pathways and better predict and possibly even create core altering events."

I stared for a long time, letting the words sink in. I'd heard Dr. Saph use the term 'node' before when referring to a jump point. And many of the higher-ups often referred to the SRE as a 'core-altering event.' When we first started working with the RRS, none of us questioned how Dr. Saph knew half of the stuff she did. I'm pretty sure most of us were still in shock after the Rift Events. We were so overwhelmed by magic being brought into our world it never occurred to us to question any of it.

I tried to read on—I *really* did—but it was *so boring!* I couldn't understand most of the jargon, and what I could made little sense. Whoever greenlit this book for publication should be banned from reading forever.

Despite my best efforts, my eyes started getting heavy, and I soon found myself drifting off into the no-man's land of sleep. God, I missed naps. As adults, we rarely ever get to take the time just to shut off and let the crapshoot that is reality disappear for a bit. I wish I could go back in time and tell the younger me to enjoy naps while I could.

A sound from outside broke through the darkness, and I shot up in bed. It took several seconds for my brain to catch up as I stared wildly into my pitch-black room. I must've been asleep for a while, as night had claimed the sky outside. Taking a few deep breaths to calm my racing heart, I reached for my phone.

Message: Honey Badger

"Hey, Love. You were passed out when we got home, so we didn't want to wake you. Sara and I are going to meet up with Ara at Xander's again. Girls only tonight! Don't worry. We won't bash you too much ;)"

Great. Just what I needed right now. While I wasn't worried about Honey or Sara saying anything negative, I was concerned that they might overstep Ara's boundaries. But there wasn't anything I could do about it other than hope that Sara would be the voice of reason like always and reign in Honey if she got too crazy.

Message: Arabella Anderson

"Sorry about earlier, but something came up at the agency. Good news! I've been given a few days off while they're taking care of my transfer, so maybe we can spend some time together? I know we still have a lot to talk about, but I'd love to see you tomorrow. Honey and Sara said they wanted to grab drinks tonight, though. So, I hope you're having a good day. And thank you again for letting me explain things. I can't even begin to tell you how much that meant to me. Okay, I should stop blathering on. Text me later?"

I chuckled and shook my head as I read her message. Ara tends to keep talking when she has a lot on her mind. I've gotten texts from her that could fill an entire novella. Some find it strange, but I find it endearing.

System Notification

"I'm not a real cat! I don't need shots!"

I sighed before swiping up on the small paw print at the bottom of the screen. Rui's face appeared, scowling at me. She was cute, even if she was massively annoying. I saw her tail flick the air behind her, and I couldn't help but smile. Her scowl deepened as she narrowed her eyes at me.

"I'm aware you don't need shots," I stated, rubbing the sleep from my eyes. "But it wasn't my fault. You're the one who decided to pretend to be a house cat."

"You told me to change into something *other* than a *human female*," Rui stated, stomping her foot down to stress her point. "You told me that!"

Chuckling, I nodded. "Yeah, well, I'm sure one shot isn't going to hurt you. I mean, can you even feel pain?"

Rui's ear twitched, and she looked like I just said the most offensive thing possible. "How dare you?! I can feel lots of things. That's rude!"

I sighed but held up a hand in mock surrender. "I'm sorry. I didn't mean anything by it. But can you blame me for not knowing? I don't even know *what* you are."

"DADDY!"

"And please, I'm begging you, stop calling me that," I groaned.

Rui crossed her arms under her chest and stared at me. Okay, I know her breasts weren't that big before. Was she making them bigger every time? When we first met, she was a decent B-cup like Sara. The next time, she went to at least a C-cup, like Ara. Now, she was giving Honey a run for her money with her D's. I shook my head, trying to push the thought out.

"That's it," Rui said, turning her back to me. Her tail snapped in the air angrily toward the screen. "I don't want to talk to you right now."

Before I could say anything, the phone went black. I stared in shock, though I don't know why. I mean, after everything, a bratty Neko being upset with me is low on my priority list at the moment. I put the phone on my bedside table and stood up. Stretching, I twisted around until I heard the satisfying crack from several places along my spine. It freaked Sara out whenever I did that, but it felt so good!

Stepping out of my room, I stopped to listen for just a moment. The house was silent, save for the low hum of the AC. Considering it was Friday night, I'm sure Xander's was packed, and the girls would be out late. While I was a little disappointed that I wouldn't see Ara this evening, I knew it was probably best that she blow off steam with the others. Honey and Sara had always been the life of the party and could get even the most introverted person to come out of their shell.

I went to the bathroom and stripped down as I waited for the shower to heat up. My muscles were sore from the jump last night, but I was too big to soak in the tub. Thankfully, I was able to have one of those tankless water heaters installed when the house was built. So now I can take as long of a shower as I want without worrying about it too much.

A noise from somewhere down the hall caught my attention. I stopped just before stepping into the shower and listened. "Honey? Sara?"

There was no answer. I shrugged and stepped into the flowing hot water. Is there anything that feels better than a hot shower with good water pressure? It's a rhetorical question. Of course, there's not.

The steaming water flowed over my aching muscles, and I let my mind wander. Too much had happened recently that I just hadn't been able to deal with properly. I thought about Chet and then the Marrog attacking Ara. I thought about Rui and all the absolute craziness that came with her. And then, for some reason, I thought about the elf woman.

Wallace said the other prisoners described her as a beauty to rival the Gods, which was ridiculous. That shack was dim, so I hadn't gotten the best look at her. But, I mean, come on! She was pretty in that whole 'damsel in distress' kind of way. But definitely not Helen of Troy, that's for sure. I just wondered where she was. I figured I could ask Rui, but I'd have to wait until she's in a better mood.

Another sound from outside the bathroom broke into my thoughts. I strained to hear, but nothing else happened. I looked at my watch and saw it was just after eleven, so I knew it wasn't the girls getting home yet. If they left the bar before midnight, I'd buy a lottery ticket.

I turned off the water, grabbed my towel and dried off. Wrapping a slightly larger towel around my waist, I opened the door and stepped out into the dark hallway, listening for any sound of movement—still, nothing.

I shook my head, chastising myself for being paranoid. There was nothing there. I was just stressed, and my mind was playing tricks on me.

I walked back to my room and reached over to turn on the lamp next to my bed. The light barely flickered on just in time to see a fist flying into my jaw. The blow hit hard, and my head spun, knocking me off balance. Another struck my stomach, causing all the air to rush from my lungs. Before I realized it, a boot hit me in the chest, knocking me backward onto my ass.

I barely saw a shadow move when thin arms wrapped around my neck from behind, squeezing hard. "Where is it, thief?!"

It was a woman's voice, but not one I recognized. She squeezed tighter as I tried to pull at her arms. Her grip was firm, but I had a lot more muscle mass than she did. I was able to pull her arm away just enough for me to turn slightly and slam my elbow back into her stomach. The attacker yelped and broke away, allowing me to suck in some much-needed air.

She didn't give me time to gain my bearings, though. I rolled onto my hands and knees to push myself up, just to feel her heavy boot crash into my ribs. The familiar feeling of bone cracking caused me to curse as I tried to roll away, just to be stopped by my bed frame.

The assailant kicked me again, directly in the same spot. I yelled out in pain and anger as the woman took a swing at my face. This time, I was able to reach up and catch her wrist, pulling her off balance. She was fast and flexible, though, twisting out of my grip and recovering her footing before I could stand.

Jabbing forward, she struck me in the jaw and then the throat, sending me into a massive coughing fit. She leaped onto my back, wrapping her arms around my neck again.

"Give it to me, thief!" She yelled, squeezing as hard as she could. "Give it to me now!"

I don't know what I did to deserve being a magnet for the crazies. Seriously. How is it that they all just seem to find me? What did I do in a previous life to deem this necessary?

Unfortunately for this woman, she was a bit outclassed when it came to street fighting. I very obviously had the weight on her and also spent years not only training with my neighbor but also having to keep rowdy jocks and pompous frat boys under control. This wasn't the first time someone's tried to choke me out.

I forced myself up to my feet, much to the dismay of my attacker. I felt her squeeze even harder, grunting with the effort. To be fair, she wasn't half bad. Her form was pretty good. It just wasn't good enough.

I spun and slammed back into my wall as hard as I could. My aim was a bit off, and I was met with a loud crack, and an avalanche of books crashed around as a shelf broke. But it got the job done. The woman let go, falling to the ground in a heap. I saw her trying to stand and knew I couldn't just let her keep attacking me.

Reaching down, I gripped her collar tightly. But to my surprise, she ducked her head and pulled back, slipping entirely out of her shirt. I stared in shock as she stood before me, raising her fists again. With the light of my small lamp, I realized two things.

First, I found the elf woman from last night. Second, she was now topless and about to attack me.

Her long, golden hair was tied back in a simple ponytail, and her crystal blue eyes stared at me in pure rage. I was stunned, not knowing what to do, as I watched her large chest bounce ever so slightly with her movements. Her perky pink nipples stood in contrast to the creamy tone of her breasts. Listen, I wasn't trying to look, okay? And I paid for it, believe me.

She struck forward, punching me in the stomach again, right beside where her boot had cracked my ribs. I yelled out, dropping her shirt and moving away as I tried to protect my injury. She was so fast I could barely see her fists as she began to land strike after strike. This woman was pissing me off.

"Give it to me!" She yelled again. "Give it back, you thief!"

I was done. I knew if I didn't do something quick, this woman might actually try to kill me. As she came in for another strike, I surprised her by rushing forward, tackling her onto my bed.

She slapped and snarled to get me off, but I knew this was my only chance. I grabbed her wrists and pinned them above her head, using my lower half to secure her legs.

"Stop!" I yelled, my anger beginning to boil over. "I didn't steal anything from you! I don't know what you're talking about. Stop hitting me!"

The woman screamed and thrashed, the fury in her eyes clear as day. "You're a liar and a thief! Give it to me! It's *my* destiny!"

It took everything in me not to roll my eyes. "What the fuck are you talking about? I didn't take anything from you!"

"You stole my destiny! Give it back, thief!"

My frustration reached its boiling point, and I yelled as loud as I could, causing the woman to freeze in my grip. I was taken by surprise at the quick shift in her demeanor. She stared wide-eyed; the fiery anger that filled her glare a second earlier dulled, overtaken by a look of genuine fear. Well, that made me feel like a dick. I don't like it when women are afraid of me. I've done everything I could to be a safe person for them. But I mean, come on! I can only get punched so much.

"Listen," I growled, gripping her wrists tighter. "I didn't steal anything from you. In fact, I'm the one that saved you from those dickheads last night! If it weren't for me, you'd probably be up for auction to be some rich asshole's new sex toy. You should be thanking me, not attacking me!"

"I'm Princess Lynriel Galdihorn of Ellyssia. I needed no help from a thief like you," she said sternly, but I could hear a modicum of doubt behind her words. "Now, unhand me this instant and give me back my destiny!"

This time, I *did* roll my eyes. "What the fuck is up with everything having to be about destiny? Listen, lady, I didn't take anything from you. I don't know what you're talking about. And to be honest, my limit for bullshit has just about been maxed out. Now, for the last time, stop attacking me!"

Lynriel stopped trying to struggle but continued to glare at me. "Then why can I sense it? It's here, you have it, thief. You can't lie to me!"

"I don't know what you're talking about," I said, shaking my head. "Now, will you please just calm down? If you promise to behave, I'll let you go, and we can sit down to talk about all of this, okay?"

Lynriel glared, studying me. I knew she was looking for some kind of sign I was lying. I finally got a good look at her face and was stunned. She was by far one of the most beautiful women I've ever seen, not going to lie. I'm not sure what exactly it was, but there was something about her that made my heart ache as I looked deep into her eyes. The tips of her ears suddenly began to turn a shade red, and she turned her face away from me.

"Unhand me, and I'll think about it," she growled. "But just know I won't leave here until you return it to me, thief."

I gritted my teeth in frustration. "I told you, I'm *not* a thief! I don't have whatever you're looking for."

She strained against my hold, her glare quickly shifting back to one of anger and contempt. "I said, give it to me! Give it to me right now!"

My door smashing open caused Lynriel and me to look up in surprise. There, in my doorway, stood Honey, Sara, and Ara. All three stared at us in a mixture of shock and anger. That was when I became all too aware that my towel had fallen off during the fight. So not only was I naked, but a topless woman was lying underneath me, screaming 'Give it to me' at the top of her lungs.

Fuck. My. Life.

Chapter 12
Spilling The Beans

Mistakes were made, okay? I understand that. But, in the heat of the moment, when you're in the middle of getting the living shit kicked out of you, worrying about keeping a towel on isn't high on your priority list. It was a perfect storm of Murphy's Law, with me at the epicenter.

For the longest second of my life, no one moved. It was like someone had hit the pause button on the universe as Ara stared at me in horror. Then, everything began to move much faster. Ara shook her head and spun on her heels, taking off down the hallway.

"I-I should go," I heard her say as her footsteps echoed off the floor, Sara following right behind.

"Ara!" I called out but didn't move. I wasn't sure if Lynriel would attack me or the girls if I let her go. "Ara, come back!"

"What the fuck is this?" Honey yelled, storming into the room. "Turtle! What the shit?!"

"Ara!" I tried to call out again but was answered with the front door slamming shut. "Fuck! Will you please go after her for me?"

"Why would I do that?" Honey asked, pointing to Lynriel, whose face had turned an even deeper shade of red. "It looks like you already got someone to have fun with."

"It's not . . . FUCK!" I growled in frustration, glaring down at Lynriel. "If I let you go, you better *not* attack me or my friends, understand? I'm *not* in the mood to be tested, you hear me?!"

I don't know if it was her embarrassment with the situation or if maybe my tone made it clear I was serious, but Lynriel lowered her eyes and bobbed her head in acceptance. I stood up and began to run down the hall, just to be stopped by Sara, who was coming from the front door. She blocked the door with fists on her hips, glaring daggers at me.

"No, Turtle! You can't go after her like that."

"I just—" I tried to say, but Sara put her hand on my chest and pushed.

"I said no! You know I love you and would do anything for you. But believe me when I say if you take one more step toward that door, I'm kicking you in that giant cock of yours."

That was when I remembered I was still naked. I quickly tried to cover myself with my hands, turning my back to her. Now that I faced down the hall, I saw Honey staring at me from in front of my room with her arms crossed.

"Can y'all just turn around until I get dressed?" I asked, slightly embarrassed they were seeing me like that.

Don't get me wrong, after so long of living with one another, we've all seen more than our fair share. I've lost count of how many times we've seen each other naked before. In fact, it seems to happen on a weekly basis lately. It's usually little stuff like them forgetting I'm home and walking around the house without a top on, not closing the bathroom door when they're showering or coming into my room when I'm changing; stuff like that. But, I mean, come on! Those are accidents. Give a guy at least the illusion of privacy, for God's sake!

"Why?" Honey asked, the anger evident in her voice. "You had no problem showing everything to some random floozy just two minutes ago."

I cursed and walked back to my room, stepping past Honey to go inside. Lynriel sat on my bed, wearing her shirt once again. She tried to stare defiantly at me, but I wasn't in the mood. I ripped open my dresser drawer and put on a pair of running shorts and a new shirt. Turning, I threw my hands in the air as Honey and Sara entered my room.

"There, now, can I go after her?"

"No," Honey said, trying to block the door as best she could. "Explain this to us, now."

I sighed and rubbed my eyes. I felt like my head was about to explode from how fast everything got so fucked up. I didn't want to drag any of them into this mess. The less they knew, the better. But, at this point, they'd been thrown in the deep end with me. So, I guess they deserve to know what was happening.

I knew there was no way I could go into detail about everything, but there were some things I could at least try to explain. "Something happened last night I didn't tell y'all about."

Trying to walk the line between telling them just enough while dancing around other things like Rui and the strange way the Rift acted was a pain and a half. But I told them about getting sucked into the Pathways and sent back to the new Realm. They were horrified when I told them about the Marrog and their captives. I then explained how I found Lynriel unconscious and had to jump without any coordinates to save both of our lives.

"Wait, that really *was* you?" Lynriel asked, her brows furrowed as she stared at me. "In the darkness, I'd all but given up. My only hope was my destiny, but even that was fading with time. The Marrog kept me drugged, so I couldn't complete the binding or even enter the Pathways to escape. But then I felt a warmth wrap around me, and my mind felt at ease for the first time in ages. The next thing I knew, I was waking up on the floor of this room, my strength and vitality restored, and all my injuries healed."

I cocked my eyebrow, giving her a pointed look. "You weren't here when I woke up this morning, though."

Lynriel scoffed and shook her head, looking at me like I was an idiot. "Did you expect me to sit around and wait for you to wake up and try to imprison me again? I was free for the first time in weeks and intended to stay that way. It wasn't until I was far from here that I realized you'd stolen it from me. I've been following you all day, waiting for you to reveal it."

I sighed and shook my head. "I didn't take anything from you!"

Scoffing again, Lynriel crossed her arms and clenched her jaw. "We'll see about that."

"Wait, if this happened last night, why didn't you tell us?" Honey asked.

I sighed again and motioned out the window of my room. "Because the RRS, that's why."

"What?" Honey asked. "They told you not to tell anyone? Why? It sounds like you're a hero! You should be getting awards and medals and all that."

I had to stifle the sick laugh that bubbled up. "The RRS isn't what it seems, okay? You know how I've always thought it could've been an evil, soulless government agency? Well, it turns out I was right. Since I was forbidden to jump, especially to that particular Realm, I decided to keep what happened to myself. The prisoners didn't get a good look at me, and . . . due to technical errors, my watch data had gotten wiped. So, there wasn't anything linking me to it. I just figured I'd keep my head low, and it would all blow over. I was very wrong. Wallace knows it was me; he just can't prove it. But that didn't stop him from going full villain mode on me this morning. Seriously. He couldn't have gotten more cliché if he tried."

Sara smirked and let out a short huff. "Did he do the whole 'offer a drink and pretend to be your friend' thing?"

I enthusiastically threw both my hands toward her as I nodded furiously. "YES! I mean, how can they *not* know that's the most basic bitch bad guy move anyone can make?! Anyways, he started with the offers of rewards and money and yadda yadda yadda. Then, the veiled threat of possible repercussions for jumping into the quarantined Realm. I wasn't worried about any of it. But then, he crossed the line by threatening everyone I love."

"Wait, what do you mean?" Honey asked, her concern growing.

"He threatened Lana and her schooling. Both of you, too. He made it clear he'd have your adoption license taken away. He even went after Ara. There's a world called Plexata that's been at war for . . . well, forever. And a disease recently killed all of their women. He pretty much guaranteed that if I didn't play ball, Ara would be sent there to . . . keep the soldiers company."

I saw the pain and anger cross the girls' faces. I knew what they were feeling. Boy, did I know. Even now, just recounting the story, my rage was pounding at me to kick Wallace's ass.

"Why would he do that?" Sara asked, her eyes starting to water. "We didn't do anything! We just want a family."

"Hush, now. It's okay," Honey whispered, wrapping Sara in a tight hug. "It'll all be okay. I promise."

I let them take a few minutes to calm down. It was hard news to swallow for anyone. Sara had always wanted a family. It took years for her to convince Honey to agree. Honey isn't necessarily against children; she's just still hung up with her own shitty childhood. But she loved Sara and wanted to help make her dreams come true. They'd started seeing a therapist both as a couple and individually, and Honey finally came around to the idea of children.

"What exactly do they want from you?" Honey asked, finally turning back to look at me.

I pressed my lips together, waving my hand at Lynriel. "They want her."

"Me?" Lynriel gasped, surprised by my response.

"Her?" Sara and Honey looked between the two of us, not sure what to think.

I nodded and dropped my eyes to the ground. "Yeah. I don't know why, but it's definitely not to give her a welcome party. No one's ever seen her kind before. And . . . they think she's carrying something really important. I'm not sure what, but I have a feeling it's this 'Destiny' thing she keeps accusing me of stealing. WHICH I DIDN'T!"

Making it a point to stare at Lynriel with those last words, I cut off the rising retort she was obviously about to say.

"Well, if all they want is her, why not give her to them?" Sara asked, tears streaming down her face. "I mean, you don't know it's something bad, right? They could just want to ask her questions or something."

I shook my head, knowing it was going to be much worse. "You know how rare Rifters are, especially one like me. If they're willing to lose me by going after the ones I love, I have no doubt they're willing to do some horrible things to her. At the very least, she'd be locked in a cage to be studied. But most likely, she'll be interrogated and tortured for information."

"I'd like to see them try," Lynriel growled, her fists clenched in rage. "I'm Princess Lynriel Galdihorn of Ellyssia. Protector of the Pathways. Vessel of the One. No one shall dare lay a hand on me!"

I'd be lying if I said Lynriel wasn't damn sexy when she got angry. I know I shouldn't be thinking that, but I'm only human. Sue me.

"What is this *thing* they want?" Honey asked, turning her attention to Lynriel.

The elf crossed her arms under her chest and narrowed her eyes at Honey. "That doesn't concern you!"

"We can't help you find it if we don't know what it is," I pointed out, trying to make her see reason.

Lynriel clenched her jaw as she was obviously struggling with an internal debate. It was a solid minute of painful silence before she exhaled loudly and looked away from us. "It's known as the Sh'landriel. It's part of the One, and it's my destiny to find them and fuse them into my core."

"Yeah, none of that makes sense," I said, shaking my head.

Lynriel huffed and rolled her eyes. "Well, I don't know how else to explain it to you. Even a lowly bata-rat knows about the Sh'landriel. Don't blame me for your ignorance."

Honey growled and took a step toward Lynriel. "Listen here, you pretentious little—"

"Hey!" I stepped between the two women before they started swinging at each other. "Let's just, everyone calm down. There's been enough violence today. Trust me."

Sara pulled Honey back closer and hugged her tightly from behind. "Turtle, what do we do?"

I sighed and shook my head, looking between my best friends and the elf princess sitting on my bed. Jesus Christ. I *actually* referred to her as an elf princess. What is wrong with my brain?

"Honestly, I don't know," I said, shrugging my shoulder. "My whole plan was to keep denying it all, and eventually, they'd have to accept it. There wasn't proof I was there. Lynriel was nowhere to be found. I hadn't told anyone, and nothing else linked me to it. But, now she's here, and you two know just about everything."

"Three," a voice said from the hallway.

I jumped as Ara stepped into view, tears streaming down her face. I stared at her in shock, trying to come up with something to say. But before I could, she rushed toward me and jumped. Without thinking, I caught her as she began to kiss me over and over. I was so confused.

After a solid minute of her basically attacking my lips with hers, Ara pulled back just a little to look me in the eyes, smiling. "I knew you were an amazing man. I knew it!"

I was at a loss. I stared dumbfounded at her as she laughed and kissed me again. Like, I mean, I'm not complaining or anything. But after earlier, this was *not* how I thought things would be going with her.

"Ara," I tried to say between kisses. "Ara, hang on."

She pulled back, her smile wide as tears ran down her cheeks.

"How much did you hear?" I asked, setting her down on the ground.

"Everything," Ara said, wiping her face. "Sara told me they'd figure out what was going on and asked me to wait outside for a few minutes to calm down. I came back in so we could talk, and I heard what happened to you last night—being ripped away like that? I can't imagine how frightening that was! And then what you did for Lynriel and dozens of others, risking yourself over and over again . . . What kind of man does that?"

"A stupid one?" Honey commented, but I saw the hint of a smile on her face.

"An amazing one," Ara said, still focused on me. "Even now, it looks like you're trying to do whatever you can to protect everyone around you."

My face burned red as she continued to praise me. I wasn't used to that kind of attention and didn't know how to accept compliments or admiration. In fact, it made me very uncomfortable when people said nice things about me. Yes, we've already established I have issues, okay?

"But I'm putting all of you at risk now," I said, my frustration with the situation growing.

"Hey," Ara said, reaching up and holding either side of my face. "You're not doing anything. It's them, not you. And you don't have to be alone in this! Let us help you, and I'm sure we can find a way, right?"

She turned to look at Honey and Sara, a hopeful glint in her eyes. "We just talked about this, didn't we? It would be us three—"

"Ara!" Honey rushed forward and put her hand over Ara's mouth. "Shush! He doesn't need to know anything about what we decided."

I cocked my eyebrow and gave Honey and Sara a curious stare. "I'm sorry, you did what now? What have you decided for me this time?"

I knew I shouldn't have left them alone together. Who knows what those two talked Ara into. And they know I'd probably just go along with it no matter what if it was the three of them coming at me. This better not be some elaborate ruse to get me into therapy or something. I ain't got no time for that!

Ara laughed and pulled Honey's hand away from her mouth, squeezing it tightly. "I'm just saying, we already agreed we would be there for him, right? This, right here, is something he needs us all for."

Sara smiled, but I could tell there was still sadness behind her eyes. She wrapped one arm around Honey's waist and the other around Ara. "Ara's right. We're here for you, Sweetie. Just tell us what you need."

"I hate to break up this . . . touching harem moment," Lynriel said, standing from the bed. "But, you still haven't told me why I can sense the Sh'landriel here if you claim not to have stolen it."

I shot her an irritated look. "We're not a hare—"

"What does it look like?" Ara interrupted me, turning to face Lynriel. "How can we help you find it if we don't know what it looks like?"

Lynriel sighed and rolled her eyes again. "If it were such a simple thing that could be easily described, it wouldn't be a Sh'landriel, would it?"

"You have to give us something to go off of," Honey said, the irritation for the elf still apparent.

Sighing, Lynriel held up her little finger to give perspective. "It's about this big. But sometimes it's bigger, and other times smaller. At times, it has every shape imaginable; others, it has none. But there's always the light of the One radiating from within. When you look upon it, it's like—"

"A sense of peace like no other washes over you," I finished for her, remembering the object and how it made me feel.

"Yes!" Lynriel shouted, rushing to me and gripping my hand excitedly. "You've seen it?! Where?"

I shook my head and shrugged my shoulders. "I saw it lying on the ground in the shack I found you in. I thought I was holding on to it when we jumped, but it was gone when I woke up, just like you."

Lynriel's eyes grew wide, and her mouth gaped open as she stared at me in disbelief and horror. "Y-You traveled th-the P-Pathways with it . . . uncontained?"

"Uh, yeah? I mean, it was just lying there, and it looked important. I figured you had it when you left this morning."

"Wait!" Ara shouted, drawing my attention. Her eyes were almost as wide as Lynriel's as she stared at me. "Could she be talking about a shard?"

I furrowed my brows and shook my head. "No! It wasn't a shard. I mean . . . what do shards look like anyway?"

"No one knows," Ara said. "Each Realm claims they look like different things. However, one of the most consistent descriptions mentions that they glow with a pure white light. If you did your *training* like you're *supposed* to, you'd know that!"

I shook my head before returning to Lynriel, who continued staring at me. "Y-You t-t-raveled the Pathways with it, UNCONTAINED?!"

Shaking my head even faster, my mind raced, trying to come up with a different explanation. "No, no, no. A shard . . . It can't . . . I mean, I wouldn't . . . Are you *sure* that's what it was?!"

"YOU TRAVELED THE PATHWAYS WITH IT, UNCON-TAINED?!"

Chapter 13

What Are Rules Made For Anyway?

Rule Number One: You never jump with an uncontained shard. They made that *painfully* clear during training. You *never* jump with an uncontained shard. Ever. Period.

Yet, never once did they think to tell us *what a shard actually looked like!* I'd always assumed it was like some kind of broken metal . . . thing. Not a glowing piece of *whatever* that seemed to defy all sense of logic and wasn't bigger than my damn pinky! What kind of all-powerful object is so small it could get lost in the couch cushions?!

"Okay, what does this mean?" I asked, staring between Ara and Lynriel.

"I . . . I don't know," Ara said, shaking her head. "Nothing like this has ever happened before."

"YOU TRAVELED THE PATHWAYS WITH IT, UNCON-TAINED!" Lynriel was almost hysterical at this point. I held up my hands to try to calm her down and quickly learned that was the wrong thing to do. Lynriel shoved me, causing me to take a step backward to keep my balance. "I knew you were a thief! All your talk about wanting to save me, but that was just a lie. You stole my destiny away from me!"

She shoved again, making me take another step backward.

"HEY!" I yelled, puffing out my chest in an attempt to get her to stop. "I didn't steal anything! I didn't even know what it was. I grabbed it in case it was something of yours. I had no idea it was a shar-lali or whatever you call it. Besides, we were surrounded, and it was either jump or let us both be captured. I'm not sure if you enjoyed being their prisoner, but I sure as shit knew that was going to be a hard pass for me."

"Um," Sara looked confused between Lynriel, Ara, and me. "What's the big deal? Why does it matter?"

Ara turned and shrugged her shoulders. "None of us knows. It's just the absolute number one rule when jumping through the Rift. Technically, we're all supposed to always carry containment cases with us. But almost no one does. They're big and cumbersome. And no one's ever actually found a shard before."

Just before Lynriel tried to push me again, I held up both hands and stopped her. "HEY! STOP! Use your words, not your hands. Why is it so bad that I jumped with it? If this Sh'ladida thing *is* a shard, no one's ever told us the consequences of jumping with one out of containment."

Lynriel gritted her teeth and balled her fists so tight I wouldn't have been surprised if she broke the skin of her palms with her fingernails. "You Gods damned, good for nothing, kruff-muncher!

There's no way to know the consequences because no one's ever been stupid enough to try! Some of Ellyssia's greatest scholars postulated that the Pathways might absorb them to be reformed in a new Realm. But that's just a theory! Besides, there's no way to know when or where that might happen if that *is* the case. The *Sh'landriel* are fragments of the One, the entity that expands all time and space. The power of all things comes from her and cannot exist without her. It's my destiny to find the Sh'landriel and reunite them. Only then can the Pathways be fully tamed."

I sighed and shook my head in confusion. "That's nice and all, but fairytales don't really help us right now."

"Watch your tongue," Lynriel almost spat at me. "This isn't just any tale. It's the known history of the Realms. How can your kind be so oblivious? I've met civilizations that had barely crawled out of the primordial sludge who knows all of this."

Throwing my hands up in the air, I gave an exacerbated huff. "I don't know what to tell you, Lady. There are thousands of religions out there in our world alone, and I don't give a flying fuck about any of them. What I care about is what happens when someone jumps with a shard."

Covering her face with both of her hands, Lynriel slowly shook her head. "This is my fate now? Having my destiny stolen from me by a moron?"

I rolled my eyes and sighed. Looking over at Honey and Sara, I saw they had the same dumbfounded look on their faces that I'm sure I had most of the night. "I don't think we're going to get much further tonight. It's late. I'm sure no one's in the best headspace, and I'm completely exhausted after everything. Can we put a pin in all of this right now? Maybe some sleep can help us think better in the morning."

They nodded but then looked warily at Lynriel and then Ara. I looked at the still-shocked Healer and put my hands on either side of her shoulders, turning her toward me. I gave her a reassuring smile, causing her cheeks to flush as she looked up at me. "Are you okay to drive home? Or would you like me to take you?"

Her face scrunched in confusion briefly before looking back at Honey and Sara. They both nodded at her, and she turned back, a shy grin on her face. "Well, I talked to Honey and Sara about maybe just staying over tonight. I don't really feel safe at my flat right now."

Alarms went off in the back of my mind, and I tensed with her words. "What? Why? What's wrong?"

"Oh," Ara said, shaking her head and trying to smile at me. "It's nothing to worry about too much. It's just . . . Kyle lives in my building. And after last night, he tried a few times to get me to come to his place to 'cheer me up.' And today, after the rumors about you being suspended went around, he started following me, saying he was trying to keep me safe. I told him several times to leave me alone, but then he said he'd be checking in on me throughout the night. That was too much. So, is it okay if I stay here? Just until I can get him to back off."

My blood boiled. I wanted to kill Kyle. Not hurt. Not teach a lesson. I wanted to kill him. I forced a smile and nodded, bringing her in for a tight hug.

"You can stay for as long as you need, no questions asked."

I felt her body sink as if a great weight had been taken off her shoulders. Ara squeezed me tighter, thanking me once again. I looked at Honey, who gave me a wicked smirk, causing me to narrow my eyes at her. "Is the bed even set up in the guest room? I thought everything was getting taken out for the nursery."

"We pulled a few things out, but the bed and dresser are still in there," Sara responded. "I figured tomorrow, one or more of us can go with her to pick up some clothes and whatnot so she can just stay here for a bit."

Nodding, I smiled at my two best friends. I was so lucky they were in my life. I could always count on them to think clearly, even when I can't. I was about to start heading to the guest room to help set up the bed when someone clearing their throat caught my attention.

Lynriel stood a few feet away, arms crossed under her chest, glaring at me. That's when it hit me: she had nowhere to go either. The entire RRS was probably out looking for her, so it wouldn't be the smartest idea to send her to a motel or something. I let out a long sigh and cursed under my breath.

Looking over the warrior elf princess, I realized her clothes were beyond filthy. Dirt, mud, and what I assumed was blood stained her torn shirt and trousers. I'm not sure where she got the boots from, but they appeared to be two sizes too big and had seen better days. Her hair had also been matted in a few places, and I kicked myself for not realizing sooner that they probably weren't allowing her to bathe regularly as a prisoner. I sighed and shook my head. This house was about to get cramped.

"Can one of you take Lynriel to the bathroom and show her how a shower works? She's still covered in dirt and whatever else from that shack. Maybe lend her some clothes, too? I'll figure out . . . something by the time she's done."

Begrudgingly, Honey motioned for Lynriel to follow her into the hallway. The princess tried to protest but was silenced by Sara coming up from behind and pushing her out of the room. I sat on my bed with my head in my hands, trying to make sense of the insane amount of information I just received. I felt a soft hand rest on my neck and squeeze gently, followed by the cooling relief of Ara's power flowing into me. Within seconds, the ache in my ribs subsided, and I knew they'd been healed.

I looked up and gave her a tight smile. "Thanks. I needed that. Now, if I can just get my head to stop feeling like it's going to explode, that'd be great."

Ara smiled warmly at me and nodded. "Yeah, I can imagine. But, as you said, it's been a long day, especially for you. You need to rest so your mind can start to process things. That's what REM sleep is for. After we get everything settled, I can try to help you fall asleep if you want?"

I cocked my head in confusion. "Really? I didn't know you had that kind of power."

Chuckling, Ara shook her head before leaning in close to my ear. "I never said I'd use my power."

She stepped back, giving me a wink. I felt the heat in my face grow and knew I'd probably turned a few shades darker. Let's get one thing straight. I am not embarrassed about sex. Like, ever. I've had a very good sex life over the years with my share of women. But this was different. This was Ara.

Before I could say anything, I heard a commotion down the hall, followed by Honey yelling. "Will you just get in the damned shower?! I swear it's perfectly safe!"

I sighed and shook my head again. "I better go try to help them."

Before I stood, Ara leaned down and kissed me. Unlike earlier, when she was all but attacking me with her mouth, this time was soft and gentle. I felt tenderness behind it, and a primal urge deep inside stirred. Pulling back, she smiled at me one last time. "Thank you for everything. I can't even begin to tell you how full my heart feels right now. But you should stay here and let us deal with your new guest. I doubt she'd be very appreciative of you seeing her naked *again*."

My face flushed as I thought about Lynriel lying topless underneath me. I nodded my appreciation as Ara left and walked to the bathroom. I heard more of a scuffle and a surprised scream echo out. "That's hot! What is this sorcery?!"

I got up and closed my door, allowing myself a quiet moment. Shaking my head, I tried to figure out what to do next. My phone buzzed with a new notification.

<u>System Notification</u>

"Well, that looked like fun."

I gritted my teeth as I sat back on my bed and swiped up on the cat paw. Rui's eyes almost sparkled with glee as she beamed at me. Her ears pointed straight up, and her tail flicked excitedly behind her. If she weren't so frustrating, she'd look adorable.

"Are you shitting me?!" I almost yelled, staring down at the Neko. "You saw all of it and never once thought you should try to help?"

Rui shrugged while giving me a playful smirk. "I mean, you didn't ask for help, did you? Besides, I'm still mad at you for what you said earlier."

I groaned and rubbed my eyes. What cosmic deity did I piss off so much to be cursed with this woman? There had to be worse people more deserving of this aggravation. Looking back at the phone, I made eye contact with the Neko.

"Whatever. Can you just give me some insight into any of this?"

Rui tilted her head, making a big show of trying to think about something. It lasted about ten seconds before another wide smile crossed her face, and she nodded. "I think I can help with some answers. What you call shards and Lynriel's Sh'landriel are the same. Though, I'm pretty sure that was obvious from the start."

I rolled my eyes and sighed. "I could do without the sass."

Rui smirked at me again, this time winking as well. "Oh, shush. You love me. Anyways . . . the pieces of the Sh'landriel are composed of the very energy that makes up what you call the Rift. It's chaos in its purest form. The Ellyssians believe it's their destiny to collect all its pieces. In doing so, they feel they can fully control the Pathways and bring peace to the Realms."

I sighed and shook my head. "And let me guess; there's some big bad guy out there who wants to collect them to kill everyone or something like that. Why is this turning more and more into a bad comic book movie adaptation?"

Rui shrugged and shook her head as well. "I don't know about all that. But I can tell you that Lynriel has been searching the Realms for a long time, looking for the Sh'landriel. The one she carried was actually seven pieces combined and took her over three thousand years to find."

My eyes felt like they were going to pop out of my head. "Three *thousand* years?! She doesn't look older than 25! And that small little thing was seven pieces together? How many are out there?"

Rui made a show of trying to count on her fingers. "Hmm, I'm not sure, exactly. But if the legends most races believe are true, there should be 42."

"Fuck my life," I exhaled, feeling the enormity of it all start to bear down on me. "Okay, so other than them possibly being a part of some cosmic entity, can they do anything else? Is there any other reason they're so valuable?"

"Well, of course! Most beings can't handle the power from a Sh'landriel and would die immediately if they tried to fuse with one. But for those rare few who can do it and survive, it increases their gift a hundredfold. They'd be able to do things others could never even dream of. You're a prime example! Why do you think you're the only one who can jump as far and as long as you can?"

"Are you serious?!" I shouted, shocked by her revelation. "I have a shard inside me?"

Rui nodded and smiled wide. "Yup! You're one of the very few who've successfully fused with the Sh'landriel. So, back during the SRE, those who survived direct contact with the Rift during the First Event had their gifts awakened and became the Swords, Shields, Healers, and Rifters. You, on the other hand, were different. Your core opened and absorbed a piece of the Sh'landriel during that time, and it gave you that strong connection to the Pathways and magnified your gift! It also has other effects as well. Have you noticed that others who have an attachment to the Rift tend to be drawn toward you? That's because of the Sh'landriel. Some find its power welcoming and want to be close to you. Others perceive it as a threat and want to destroy it."

"Jesus Christ, why didn't that tentacle monster just kill me?" I groaned, rubbing my face in frustration. "I don't even know how to respond to any of that right now. I . . . No, I'll worry about that later. For now, do you at least know where Lynriel's shards went?"

Rui squinted her eyes at me, her face adopting a look of concern. "Are you sure you weren't struck in the head at any point today?"

I gave her a hard stare in return. "No, why?"

Sighing, Rui disappeared from my phone, and my heart skipped a beat. I searched the screen, tapping the cat paw icon repeatedly. "Rui? Rui!"

"I'm right here, geez," Rui's voice came from beside me, causing me to jump in surprise.

"AH! Fuck! What did I tell you about doing that?!"

Rui smirked, her tail coming forward and bopping me on the nose. "Silly, Daddy."

I growled, looking back down at my phone. "There has to be a setting or something that I can turn change to get you to stop calling me that, right?"

Rui giggled and swatted at me softly with her tail once again. "Nope!"

Sighing, I gave her a pointed look, trying to express I wasn't in the mood to play around. "Well, then, can you please answer my question? Where are Lynriel's shards?"

Rui studied me carefully before reaching out her hand and placing it on my chest. A warm shock rushed through my body, and everything around me felt like it had come alive. I could feel the push and pull of objects against each other and even gravity. I could sense the subtle waves of energy coming out of the Rift that seemed to lay just under the surface of everything else. I even sensed time and understood that it might not be as linear as we thought.

As Rui removed her hand, everything returned to normal, and I gasped, feeling like I'd just come up for air from deep underwater. I stared at the Neko wide-eyed as it finally clicked, and I felt like an idiot. "They're . . . in me?"

Rui's smile turned to one of genuine warmth. "They're not just *in* you. They're a part of you now. They've fused into your core. It's why you've had better control over the Rift and can now jump within the same Realm as easily as you can walk. The Sh'landriel also gives you your connection to me!"

"Wait, you? But I saw you before I ever met Lynriel. In fact, you're the one who sent me there!"

Rui giggled and nodded. "Yes, but that was because you'd already been infused with a piece of the Sh'landriel that had me inside. During your first time in that Realm, when the Marrog were chasing you, an explosion sent a bunch debris into your body. Mixed in there was a piece of the Sh'landriel. It embedded into one of your wounds and was absorbed into your core when you entered the Pathways to come back home. That was me!"

I stared, dumbfounded. All of this was just too crazy. "Wait . . . I . . . What?"

Rui laughed and flashed me her toothy grin. "I was the Sh'landriel you were hit with when trying to protect Ara. It took me a while to become . . . me. You see, I haven't been me in a long time. But because of you, I've gotten so much more back!"

"So, is that why you said only I can help make you complete?" I asked, cocking my eyebrow at her.

Rui bobbed her head up and down excitedly. "YES! You now have more pieces of the Sh'landriel inside your core than anyone has ever managed to hold! Of the natural beings who can fuse with them, the most anyone's been able to have in the past is three. That's why the Sh'landriel are supposed to be contained when traveling the Pathways."

"Wait, what? What does jumping with it contained have to do with this?"

"You really are clueless sometimes, Daddy," Rui said with a smirk. "Think about how you're able to jump using the Rift. Essentially, you're turning your body into the same energy that makes up the Pathways, which is exactly what the Sh'landriel are also composed of. Let me see if I can explain it a bit easier for you . . . Oh! Okay, think about it like this. You're cupping your hands and holding some water in them. Now, what would happen if you yourself turned into water as well? The water you were holding becomes a part of you!"

I rubbed my eyes and shook my head, the throbbing in my temples growing with every word the Neko was saying. "This still doesn't make sense! If that was the case, wouldn't they want all of us Rifters to fuse with the shards? Why make us use contaminants?"

"There's an excellent reason why," Rui explained. "The Sh'landriel are too powerful for most people. There's only a rare few who can handle one. And of those, if any try to fuse with more than what they can hold, they essentially become walking fusion bombs that destroy entire worlds. There's also a very specific way to fuse with one to make sure it doesn't kill you. That's the ritual you heard Lynriel mention. Entering the Pathways with one uncontained is like injecting the energy of an atomic bomb directly into your veins. Your body has to adapt to that new power *very* quickly, or it'll overload you. If the Sh'landriel fails to fuse or the person isn't compatible, the best scenario is that it's lost back into the Realms, and the person dies. In the worst case, an entire Realm would be wiped out of existence."

That instantly made my asshole tighten, and I stared hard at the Neko, who was acting as if this was simply a hypothetical scenario and not one that I just experienced. "I'm sorry, but did you just say that I could've died or become a FUCKING BOMB AND DESTROYED THE WORLD?!"

"But that didn't happen to you! You're special. You now have twelve Sh'landriel inside your core, and you're stronger than ever. I'd expect nothing less from the man powerful enough to claim me!"

"Twelve?!" I blurted out. "How?"

Rui studied me for a moment, a puzzled look crossing her face. "I . . . I don't know. But I can promise you that there are twelve. That's including the seven you stole from Lynriel."

"I didn't steal anything!"

"Bullshit!" Lynriel's voice yelled as she slammed my bedroom door open.

Her angry glare was belittled by the attire the girls had given her to wear. Her hair was combed silky smooth, hanging well past her waist, and her fair skin was still pink from the hot shower. She wore a white 'Hello Kitty' shirt with pink sleeves that strained against her massive breasts and a pair of hot pink sleep shorts that barely covered her firm ass. Honey's PJs, no doubt about it.

"You did steal it," she said, storming up to me, pointing a finger in my chest. "You're a thief, and I won't rest until—"

"Hey!" Honey shouted from the doorway, her anger directed at Lynriel. "Enough of that right now! It's late, and we all want to get some sleep. If you want to keep yelling, do it in the morning."

Lynriel huffed and rolled her eyes, but she did seem to deflate some. Turning back to look at Honey, Lynriel watched Sara and

Ara enter my room. All three girls had changed into similar night clothes, with Ara wearing a light green Care bear shirt and shorts.

"So, how does this work, then?" Lynriel asked, placing her hands on her hips.

"How does what work?" Sara asked, genuinely confused.

Scoffing, Lynriel motioned first to me and then to the girls. "The sleeping arrangements. I'm quite familiar with the harem dynamic. Is there a hierarchy I need to know about? Who beds him first each night? Is it all together, or do we go separately? I warn you now, I won't be bred by him, so one of you must be close by to take his seed."

We were all stunned. I had no words. I tried to move my mouth several times, but nothing would come out. Thankfully, I was saved by Sara, who began to laugh hysterically. At first, I was relieved that she hadn't gotten upset. But when she doubled over with her face turning red from laughing so hard, I started to think that maybe I was the one who should be offended.

"No," Honey said, closing her eyes and shaking her head. "That's not going to happen tonight. We have our own rooms. Ara will be using our guest room. *You* can take the couch."

The look of righteous indignation that swept over Lynriel would've been comical if I hadn't known how hard her fists were. "HOW DARE YOU?! I am a Princess of Ellyssia! I don't sleep on . . . on . . ."

"It's fine," I said, standing up and walking toward the door. "Don't worry, *Your Highness*. You can have my bed. I'll take the couch."

I could tell the girls didn't like that answer. I saw Ara's eyes widen, and she began to open her mouth, but I put up a hand to stop her offer. "It's okay, really. Everyone needs sleep tonight. I'm running on fumes right now. Let's just go to bed, and we can all talk again in the morning."

Everyone nodded and began to clear out of my room. A flash of orange fur flew between my feet, and I saw Rui in her cat form trotting down the hallway to Sara and Honey's room. Honey's eyes widened, and a huge smile broke across her face. "AWW! The kitty wants to sleep with me!"

I sighed, giving Rui a warning look to be on her best behavior. Soon, everyone was in their rooms, and I lay on the couch that was not made for someone my size. I stared at the ceiling, thinking about all the revelations today. Closing my eyes, I tried to force it out of my mind. I wanted to think of Ara, but for some reason, I could only picture the icy blue of Lynriel's eyes. Soon, I began to drift as I thought about the mysterious elf, a sunny beach, and the perfect margarita.

Chapter 14
Wake-Up Call

Once, when I was younger, I tried to run away from home. I'd had enough of all the fighting, the screaming, the broken dishes, holes in the walls, and not-so-quiet crying in the middle of the night. I was only a kid, yet I knew that wasn't how it was supposed to be. Families were supposed to love each other, yet all I'd ever gotten was contempt from my father, my brother's anger, and my mother pretending I didn't exist to appease the other two.

So, one night, I grabbed my backpack and filled it with a few changes of clothes, my toothbrush, and my favorite book. I waited until my father had drunk himself unconscious, and my mother was busy cleaning up yet another set of broken dishes in the kitchen. I swiped the cash off their dresser, a whole $27, and took off. I had no destination or plan in mind. It was just me and the open road.

I had felt so overwhelmed with everything that I didn't know what else to do. I was helpless to fix any of it, yet the weight of it all was crushing me. Now, obviously, I didn't get too far. Honey saw me sneak out and followed me. She found me sitting at a bus stop about a mile away, even though the buses stopped running hours before. She was still jumpy with physical touch, but somehow, she gathered the courage to wrap her arms around me, letting me know I wasn't alone.

My emotions had grown so big that I didn't know how anyone could feel such things and keep living. But, with the arms of my best friend squeezing me tight, I felt something inside start to crack. Soon, I was crying uncontrollably, and Honey just let me. She didn't have to say anything. Knowing she was there supporting and loving me allowed me to release the Hoover Dam worth of emotions I'd built up.

These days, I'm a lot better at dealing with my emotions—well, not necessarily dealing with them so much as being able to keep them contained easier. I still felt the crushing weight of everything around me, but now I use sarcasm and dark humor as a more appropriate outlet. Being mature and dealing with emotions just doesn't seem like a good time to me.

I only bring this up because, until this point, I've only admitted to not being good with feelings. So, at least now you can have a bit of insight into why I am the way I am, and maybe cut me a little slack, okay? I'm doing the best I can with what I've got to work with.

The weight of everything that happened over the past day felt like it was crushing my chest. Everything I thought I knew had once again been turned upside down, and the careful control I thought I had on things was slipping through my fingers. I was brought back to being that same little kid who couldn't do any-thing to help the people around him.

"You shouldn't be thinking about all of that right now, Daddy," Rui said with a giggle while using her tail to trace a line down my bare chest.

I chuckled and looked over at her lying beside me on the beach's warm sand. "And how do you know what I'm thinking, kitten?"

Rui gave me a mischievous grin before disappearing. A heavy weight sank on my hips, and I looked up and saw the playful Neko sitting on me. To my surprise and joy, we were both completely naked. Her perfectly pink nipples grew stiff with excitement as she began to slowly grind her smooth slit along my already erect cock. I could feel the juices of her pussy coating me with each tilt, and her breath became more jagged as she increased her speed.

"Because I'm inside you," she said, a purr in her voice that was only there when she was happy. "I know you better than you know yourself. Why do you think I call you Daddy? I know you love it, no matter how much you try to say otherwise."

Her pace increased along with the wetness of her slit. It was like nothing I'd ever felt before. My cock throbbed, aching to slip inside her slick opening. Her swollen clit rubbed against my shaft, sending waves of pleasure through her body that I could see with each thrust of her hips. I tried to grab her ass but found my wrists bound with ropes to something out of sight. When the hell did she do that?

"Don't worry, *Daddy*," she said that last word with an evil chuckle. "Our time will come . . . Get it?!"

She laughed at her own joke as she ground harder and faster. Sweat covered her body as she edged closer and closer to her orgasm. "Ah, shit! Right there! Yes! Yes! Your cock feels so good!"

Rui threw her head back to let out a scream of pleasure, and I felt her entire body shake with wave after wave of orgasmic bliss. I thought she'd stop, but after that brief pause, she began grinding again, this time even harder and faster.

"Don't worry, Daddy," she said, gasping for air as my cock grew even harder underneath her. "I'll always take care of you."

The world around me went black, and I felt like I was falling from a great height. I should've been scared, but I wasn't. I just felt sore. As I began to wake up on the extremely uncomfortable couch in the living room, I realized that it had all been just a dream.

I felt the familiar weight of either Honey or Sara lying on top of me, so I reached up and stroked their hair, hoping to wake them up gently. As my fingers worked through the soft locks, I felt something curious toward the top of their head. A soft pair of furry ears twitched as I gently touched them with my fingertips, causing the woman to let out a soft giggle. "That tickles, Daddy."

I shot my head up and looked down to see familiar yellow eyes staring at me. Rui was lying on top of me, completely naked. Her bare chest started to rumble, and I realized she was actually purring. She smiled and lazily blinked at me.

"This feels nice," she said, opening her mouth in a big yawn. "Now I know why the others like to do it so much."

"What are you doing?" I hissed at her, quickly looking around the room to make sure we were alone. "Why are you on top of me, *naked*?!"

Rui chuckled, and her tail playfully flicked my nose. "Silly, man. Kitties don't wear clothes."

I sat up, causing Rui to squeal and pout at being dislodged from her spot. "You can't just . . . do that! What if one of the others walked in? I'm pretty sure I'm already on very thin ice with Ara as it is!"

Rui snorted a short laugh before standing up to stretch. She made sure to pose right in front of me to show off her very feminine physique. "Oh, don't worry about her. I heard their entire conversation last night. She's good with a lot more than you think. Besides, they're all still asleep."

My heart was pounding in my chest, but I couldn't help but notice that Rui's body now matched that of Ara's. They had the same breast size, the same flat stomach leading down to perfect heart-shaped hips, and the same round, firm ass. The sight of her perfectly smooth pussy made me wonder if that matched Ara's as well. I shook my head and slapped myself in the face. Don't be a dirtbag, Turtle!

"Rui! Please, for the love of all things good in this world, put some clothes on! You're going to make my heart explode!"

Rui smirked as her tail began to stroke my rock-hard erection through my shorts. "I can help make something else explode if you want, *Daddy*."

Her voice was soft, with a bit of a purr as she emphasized the honorific. I groaned and slapped my hands over my face. This woman will literally be the death of me, I just know it. She's either going to do something to give me a heart attack, or she's going to cause one of the girls to straight-up murder me.

"Please, stop calling me that! Especially when you're naked."

"Remember what I told you, Daddy. I know deep down you like it," she said with a giggle, and I heard the rustling of fabric as she put her clothes back on. "Like I said, I'm a part of you just as much as the Rift. There's nothing you can hide from me. When sexual partners have called you that in the past, you became 47% more aroused and climaxed 28% harder."

I groaned again but looked up in relief to see she was back in her sheer blue fabric cover. "That's different! First off, we're *not* sexual partners. Second, that was in the bedroom, in the heat of the moment. Not all day, every day. And, again, *we're not sexual partners!*"

Rui chuckled and approached me, leaning in less than an inch from my face. Her large cat eyes stared hard into mine, and I was actually at a loss. "Then explain that mind-blowing orgasm you just gave me on our beach."

She gently kissed the tip of my nose before standing and walking down the hallway. The only thing I could do was stare in shock at her swaying hips and perfect ass. Yep. This girl was absolutely going to be the death of me.

I shook my head to clear my mind, hoping it would help bring the blood flow back in that direction. I looked at my watch and saw it was just after eight, so the girls should be waking up any time now. It was Saturday, which meant Sara and Honey were both off work. Usually, they'd try to drag me to some farmers market or a craft . . . thing. But after everything that happened last night, I figured we'd be spending most of the day discussing it.

When I was sufficiently satisfied that I could stand up without knocking over any lamps with the Rui-induced erection, I went to the kitchen and started a pot of coffee. Rummaging around the cabinets, I found all the ingredients I needed to make my famous Captain Crunch-encrusted French Toast for everyone. After turning on some of my 90s rock, I got to work. I wasn't sure if Ara liked French Toast and didn't know what kind of food Lynriel ate. But beggars can't be choosers.

I took a sip of my coffee and flipped over another piece of toast when I felt thin arms wrap around my torso and a set of firm breasts press into my back. I held my breath, praying to whoever I could that it wasn't Rui again. Turning to look over my shoulder, I was relieved to see curly red locks and no cat ears.

"Good morning. How was your night?"

"Hmm," Ara hummed, squeezing me a bit tighter. "It was alright, I guess. My head's not feeling the greatest, though. Not sure if it's from the shots at the pub or the massive information overload when we got back here."

I chuckled and nodded my understanding. "I bet. I put two ibuprofen in that small cup by the water bottle. That's for you. The girls should be out in just—"

"We're here," Honey's sleepy voice came from the hallway. "And can you please turn down the music? My head's killing me."

It took everything in me not to laugh even harder as I turned down the music. I pulled the last piece of French Toast off the pan before turning to give Sara and Honey a bottle of water and their pills. They all grumbled their thanks before chugging it down. "Go, sit. I'm just about done. Wait, can one of you go get Lynriel, please?"

Sara and Honey gave each other a look before turning back to me. "What do you mean? She wasn't in your room. We looked there and in the bathroom when we first got up. We figured she was out here with you."

I tried to think if I'd heard anyone leave the house this morning. But the only thing that came to mind was Rui's bare chest pressing into me. My face flushed, and I coughed to cover up the reaction. "That's strange. Maybe she's . . ."

As I struggled to think about where she could be, Lynriel turned the corner of the hallway, crossing her arms as she shot me a scowl. "Maybe I'm what?"

I tried to smile at her, but I could tell we were already off to a bad start. "Hey, how'd you like the bed?"

Lynriel shifted uncomfortably, breaking her stare. "It . . was adequate, I suppose. It's a far cry from my bed in Ellyssia, but still better than the floor of that shack they were keeping me in."

"I can imagine," I said, motioning for her to sit at the table beside Ara. "Come have some breakfast. I made my special French Toast."

Lynriel furrowed her brows as she slowly made her way to the table. "What is frenched toast?"

I set a plate in front of her, dusting it with powdered sugar and leaving the syrup to the side. "It's a type of sweet bread. Just trust me."

As they all started to eat, I watched Lynriel study the plate. She picked up the fork, poked at the bread, and then looked at Ara to see how she was eating it. To my relief, Ara was chowing down, taking a large forkful with a massive smile. Lynriel cut off a piece and took a nibble.

Her eyes widened in amazement, and soon, she took large bites along with the others. I grinned, happy that everyone was enjoying it. Because of work, I rarely got to cook anymore, so this was also a nice treat for me.

Ara sat back in her chair, rubbing her stomach with a satisfied smile. "That was bloody amazing! And this coffee is the best I've ever had! Is this what you use at your cafe, Sara?"

Sara beamed with pride as she nodded. "Yup! My family actually sponsors a few local plantations in Central America. It was a bitch and a half to come up with the funding, but we were able to secure three plantations and ensure their workers were getting paid fairly and working conditions were being held to the highest standards. Our coffeehouse was just the beginning. We're moving into wholesale distribution, and I'm talking with a few local grocers about starting to carry our products."

"Wow," Ara gasped. "That's unbelievable. Cheers to that!"

Sara blushed, and Honey smiled lovingly at her. "Yeah, we're so proud of her. Aren't we, Turtle?"

I lifted my second cup of coffee with a smile. "Damn straight! And if they end up shit-canning me from the RRS, at least I know I have a job helping with distribution. Maybe we could get this stuff on Taritia. We could be the first inter-realm coffee roaster."

We all laughed, but I saw that something I said caught Sara's attention. Before I could follow up, Lynriel cleared her throat and stared at me. "We need to talk."

I sighed and nodded. "I was hoping to at least wake up a bit more first, but I know you're anxious about things."

"I know the Sh'landriel are not gone because I can feel them," Lynriel said, narrowing her eyes at me. "Tell me, have you noticed anything . . . strange lately?"

I scoffed and motioned wildly around the room. "Were you not paying attention last night? It's been nothing but strange the last two days!"

Lynriel looked at the other three women, sighing before returning to me. "Can we discuss this in a more . . . private setting?"

"Anything you have to say to him, you can say in front of us," Honey responded, shooting Lynriel a stern look. "Don't think that we've forgotten you attacked him last night."

Lynriel gritted her teeth and returned Honey's heated look. "I was trying to reclaim what was stolen from me! And you have no right to speak to me in such a way. I'm Princ—"

"Hey!" I yelled, cutting her off. Holding up a hand, I looked them both in the eyes. "Enough of this already! Both of you. If we're going to get through . . . whatever this is, we all need to work together. Okay?"

To my shock, Honey and Lynriel's faces fell, and they both looked down. It was like they were children that a parent had just scolded. They each muttered an apology but continued to avoid eye contact. I shook my head, wondering just what in the hell was going on. Honey was never one to be cowed so easily. And Lynriel didn't seem like the type to let just anyone speak to her like that.

"Now, Lynriel," I said, having her look back at me. "I trust everyone in this room. You can, too. What do you want to ask me?"

Lynriel bit her lip, and I saw her ears growing redder by the second. "I-I was just going to ask if you wouldn't mind removing your shirt for me again."

I stared in disbelief at the elf, trying to ensure I'd heard her right. The shocked look on Ara and Sara's faces and the growing look of anger on Honey's confirmed I had. I set down my coffee and nodded my head toward the hallway. "Actually, maybe we should talk about things in private."

"Like hell you are," Honey said, staring angrily at me. "If I'm not mistaken, you have a brand new, amazing girlfriend who just happens to be sitting *right here*, correct? And you're wanting to go strip for this woman again?"

"That's not what this is!" Lynriel shouted, her cheeks starting to match the redness of her ears.

"Then what is it?" Honey shot back, narrowing her eyes at the blushing woman.

Lynriel scrunched up her face, trying to think of the words, before loudly exhaling, pointing angrily at me. "I know it's impossible. It's *absolutely* impossible. But I don't have any other ideas. I have to see if the Sh'landriel are inside him."

"And just how do you plan on doing that?" Sara asked.

Scoffing, Lynriel crossed her arms under her chest and stared back. "I have my ways."

Before Honey could react, Ara spoke up for the first time, taking us all by surprise. "It's okay. I don't mind."

Now, it was our turn to stare at *her* in disbelief. I cocked my eyebrow, making sure I'd heard that right. "I'm sorry, what was that?"

Ara chuckled and shook her head as she smiled at me. "It's okay. I trust you, Turtle. And you already know I'm not a jealous person. I know it's still really early for this kind of conversation, but I'm about as open as you can be. Just don't lie or try to hide anything, and you can do whatever you like with whoever you like. Within reason, of course. So, if Lynriel thinks she can get us answers by getting you naked again, I say do it."

I saw Lynriel's face flush even deeper crimson, but she didn't say anything in response. I smiled and approached Ara, leaning down and kissing her head. "You're an amazing woman, you know that, right?"

"And don't you forget it," Ara laughed.

I stood up and took off my shirt, turning to Lynriel. "Alright, what do you need me to do."

Lynriel blushed furiously but slowly stood and approached me. Her eyes traced my chest and stomach, and I suddenly became very grateful that I hadn't skipped abs at the gym this week. She gingerly touched my stomach with the tips of her fingers, slowly drawing them in strange patterns.

I wasn't sure if she was intentionally trying to trace my scars or if it was purely a coincidence. But her fingertips grazed over the large stretches of scar tissue, and for the first time, I wasn't self-conscious about them. I'm not going to lie. Between the softness of her fingers and the sensitive areas she touched, I had difficulty keeping things from happening.

Turning slightly, Lynriel pressed her ear to my chest, and her arms naturally wrapped around my midsection. I stood with my hands out to the side to show the other girls I wasn't trying any funny business. Lynriel took several deep breaths with her eyes closed, and the silence in the room grew almost palpable. Something deep inside seemed to stir, and I had an overpowering urge to be as close to the princess as possible.

Suddenly, Lynriel shot back and stared at me in disbelief. "H-How?"

I shook my head in confusion, even though I already had an idea of what she was referring to. "What did you hear?"

"You . . . You shouldn't be alive. It's *impossible*!"

This put the other three girls on edge, and each became more apprehensive. "What do you mean he shouldn't be alive?"

Not taking her eyes off me, Lynriel just shook her head repeatedly. "This can't be. It's impossible."

"Okay, start talking, pointy ears, or I'll make you," Honey said, half standing from her chair.

The insult seemed to jolt Lynriel back, and she shot an angry scowl at Honey. "If you ever call me that again, I'll—"

"What did you hear, Lyn?" I interrupted, bringing her attention to me as I put my shirt back on. Surprisingly, the elf princess didn't admonish me for shortening her name.

Instead, she just shook her head again, staring me directly in the eyes. "The Sh'landriel . . . they're inside your core. But it's not even just mine. I counted at least twelve! No one person can survive with that many. I have five in my core, but my body was specifically made to hold them!"

Well, at least now I knew what Rui told me last night was correct. Whether that was a relief or not, I still wasn't sure. As I stood there, letting it fully sink in, Lynriel did something I never expected. She unceremoniously dropped to her knees, tears streaming down her face. Instinctively, I knelt and reached out to hold her shoulders.

"Why? Why you?" she cried, shaking her head. "It was *my* destiny!"

"Hey," I spoke softly, trying to keep my voice calm for her. "Listen, I'm sorry. I didn't—"

"It was supposed to be ME!" Lynriel cried out even louder.

I looked up to see if any of the other girls could help. They all sat motionless, not knowing what to do. They might not understand what was going on exactly, but they knew nothing they could say would make this better for the poor woman.

"And now, to add insult to injury," Lynriel said, slowly looking up to meet my eyes. "I have to be bound to an idiot who doesn't even know what the Sh'landriel are."

That caught my attention, and I tilted my head at her. "What do you mean, bound to me?"

Scoffing, Lynriel rolled her eyes and wiped the tears off her cheeks. "I told you already! I'm the Protector of the Pathways and the Vessel of the One. Those pieces were already bound to me, but the ritual wasn't completed."

I stared blankly at her, trying to connect the dots. She scowled, making her irritation of my ignorance very clear. "Don't act like you haven't felt it, too! The constant draw toward each other, the undeniable urge to be closer for reasons you can't explain. It'll only grow stronger over time, too. The Sh'landriel have fused into your core but are bound to mine, meaning our souls are now forever linked. We're bound to each other until all the Sh'landriel are gathered and our cores merge to bring the One back into the universe."

"I'm sorry, but WHAT THE ACTUAL FUCK?!"

Chapter 15

Commitment Issues

When you grow up in an environment like I did, you don't really have the greatest views on things like love and marriage. My brother used to say my mother cheated on our father, and I was the son of some random guy, and that's why they fought so much. It was why my father hated me, and my mother refused to even acknowledge me. Now, if that was true or not, who knows? My brother's a grade-A dick, and I wouldn't trust him as far as I could throw him.

Yet because of all that, not to mention my oh-so-fun on-again-off-again toxic relationship with Sal, I haven't thought something like forever was in the cards for me. I had plenty of hook-ups and 'relationships' that lasted about a month or two, but nothing I ever saw as forever. It wasn't until I met and fell for Ara that I even started considering the possibility of a long-term relationship.

Now, to hear Lynriel say that we're bound together, *forever*, until our cores merge into one? That's an entirely new level of commitment I was *not* ready for. I began to feel a bit like a trapped rat on a sinking ship. If I had to rip each one of these damn shards out of my chest with my bare hands, I would. There was no way I would let something like a shiny rock determine my entire existence like that.

"Hold the fuck up," I said, shooting to my feet and shaking my head furiously. "I did *not* sign up for that!"

Lynriel scoffed and crossed her arms under her chest. "And you think I *did*?! It was supposed to be *my* destiny. *Me. Alone.* I'm not supposed to be bound to . . . to . . . someone like *you*!"

I know I should've probably taken offense to that, but I had other things going through my mind. "No, no, no. This isn't right. How do we fix it?"

Lynriel rose to her feet and took an angry step forward, jabbing me in the chest with her finger. "There *is* no fixing it! Once a Sh'landriel merges with someone's core, it's there until the person dies. So, unless you're saying you want to die—"

"NO!" The three other women yelled, almost in sync.

Rolling her eyes, Lynriel shot them an irritated look. "I didn't say I was going to kill him. I don't want to kill anyone, especially not him. Don't you understand? The Sh'landriel he fused with are bound to me! So that means if he dies, so do I. That's why I'm saying we're stuck sharing a life that's linked together. And that's how it'll be until either the One is reformed or someone finds a way to remove Sh'landriel from a person's core without death. But considering my people have been trying to do that since the formation of the Pathways, I doubt it can be done."

Yeah, the walls were closing in now. I looked at Ara, who surprisingly didn't appear as distraught as I was. I guess the shock hadn't fully sunk in for her yet. I tried to take a few deep breaths, but I felt like my chest was getting tighter by the second. Not knowing what else to do, I quickly turned and walked out of the front door.

Now, I had no idea where I was going or what I was going to do. Hell, I was still only wearing running shorts and a stained 'No Fear' shirt I found at a thrift store a few years ago. I didn't even have shoes or my wallet. Luckily, though, my phone was in my pocket. Pulling it out, I repeatedly hit the cat paw button, waiting for Rui to appear.

Nothing. Shit, she must still be in her physical form. How exactly does she work, anyway?! What kind of all-powerful entity couldn't be in two places simultaneously? The logic isn't logic-ing!

My mind was racing as I tried to figure out what to do. This was *way* past my pay grade. I never wanted this! I always dreamed of a simple life, you know? Before the FRE and having the world flipped upside down, I wanted to find a place to live out in the country somewhere. Maybe find a job that lets me use my hands and enjoy the quiet life.

But no! Instead, I get flattened by a giant tentacle monster and then coerced into working for a government thief agency that may or may not be evil, which makes me travel cosmic pathways to see strange worlds and deal with assholes like Kyle. And just when I think I have a chance of finding some happiness with my extremely hot English coworker, I get told I'm now bound to a bipolar elf warrior princess who thinks it's our duty to merge our very beings together just to bring back some God I'd never heard of before! WHAT THE FUCK, UNIVERSE?!

As I roamed the streets of Krayden, I wondered who could help me figure this out. I highly doubt anyone would believe 98% of what happened in the past two days, though. I was essentially fucked. Just then, I felt my phone buzz in my pocket.

System Notification

"It appears as if you're traveling. Would you like to open maps?"

Just like yesterday, 'No' wasn't an option. Apparently, Rui was trying to tell me something. Sighing, I hit 'Yes,' and my neighborhood appeared on the screen. At the top, the 'Contacts' button was highlighted in orange. Tapping it, I scrolled down, trying to figure out what that mangy Neko was trying to do. I stopped when I came across the name she highlighted.

Lana-Banana

I stared hard, wondering what Lana had to do with this. She was just a student at UCLA, not someone who'd know anything about ... well, any of this bullshit. I tried to close the app, but the phone buzzed, and Lana's name began to flash orange. I turned the screen off, and the phone buzzed even harder at me.

"FINE!" I yelled, pressing Lana's highlighted name.

Like before, I felt my core open very slightly, and the pull of the Rift blurred the world around me. Within the blink of an eye, I stood outside Lana's apartment door. I'd only been here once to help her move in, but this was no doubt her place. I quickly looked around, still shocked that I could jump like that. I wondered if I could do it anywhere or only to places I'd been before. Making a mental note to check that later, I looked at my watch to see the time.

9:57. Which means it's just before 8 in the morning in California. It was Saturday, so I doubted Lana had any classes, and I didn't want to be the jackass to knock on her door this early on the weekend. I remember what I was like at that age, and I wasn't sure if I was ready to see my innocent little niece hungover or, god-forbid, with some hook-up. That was an image I couldn't handle with everything else going on.

I turned to leave, figuring I'd come back in a few hours when Lana had time to wake up. I would just text her and tell her I was in town for something and wanted to drop by for a few. But, just before I could step away, Lana's door opened, and she started walking out. Her eyes were only half open, and she was carrying a giant steel coffee mug. Her short, brown hair was pulled back in a tight ponytail, and her thin-framed glasses seemed to slide down her nose.

It took her several seconds to register me standing there. I saw the realization in her eyes as she bolted straight in surprise. "U-Uncle T? What are you doing here?"

"Hey, kiddo," I tried to play it cool, smiling at her. "I . . . I was just in the area doing something for work and thought I'd come to see my favorite niece!"

Lana's eyes narrowed as she looked me up and down. "Right . . . I'm your only niece. And do you always work in outdated graphic tees . . . with no shoes on?"

Shit. I really didn't think this through. Hey, I've admitted I'm not the smartest, okay? Leave me alone.

"Uh . . ." I stammered, trying to think of something. Anything. "Well, I . . . uh . . . actually got here last night. Yeah. I stayed at that motel down the street. And I'm trying that barefoot running thing everyone's been raving about!"

Lana pressed her lips tightly together, giving me a look that made it clear she wasn't buying it. Of course, she wasn't buying it. She's the most intelligent person I know! I mean, that was probably why Rui thought I should come here.

"People don't actually run barefoot," Lana said, shaking her head at me. "The shoes they wear are thin to simulate being barefoot. And they don't do it in downtown LA . . . at 7 in the morning. What's going on?"

I sighed and shook my head, realizing there wasn't any reason to lie. This girl was too observant and smart for any excuse I might try to think of. I knew I needed to come clean about everything; I just wasn't sure how she'd take it. I mean, even *I* think I needed a trip to the loony bin, given how crazy it all sounded.

"Listen, do you have a few to talk?" I asked, motioning to her apartment. "But If you've got somewhere to be, I can just come back."

Lana looked me over again before shaking her head and opening her door. "No, I was just going to study at the library before it got busy later. But it's not something that can't wait."

I followed her into the small, one-bedroom apartment. Looking around, I realized this girl was either *really* type-A, or she had a condition we'd never discussed. Everything in the condo was immaculate. There wasn't a single thing that didn't have a designated place. And talk about clean! There wasn't a piece of dirt or dust anywhere.

Lana put her keys on a hook by the door, and I noticed she adjusted them so they hung a specific way. She motioned for me to take a seat on her couch; honestly, I was afraid to. It was all so neat and clean that I was scared she might have some kind of meltdown the second I messed something up. She sat in a small armchair opposite the couch, giving me a quizzical look.

I sighed and sat as gently as possible, trying not to leave any wrinkles on the fabric. Lana noticed and smiled, letting out a soft chuckle. "It's okay, Uncle T. Just relax. I'm not the type to freak out over stuff like that. I just like things neat when possible. Now, tell me why you're here. In California. At 8 am."

Taking a deep breath, I settled back into the soft cushions and gave her a serious look. "Listen, I know that this is going to sound completely batshit crazy. Just, please, let me explain everything before you call the men in white coats to come get me, okay?"

What happened next was an hour and a half of me telling Lana everything. The term 'word vomit' doesn't even come close to what I was doing. I didn't hold back, either. Starting with the first jump all those weeks ago, the Marrog, my injuries, Ara, meeting Rui in the park, getting sent back, finding Lynriel and the shard, jumping back and how the Rift acted, the phone, in-realm jumping, the RRS, Wallace's threats, the suspension, Rui again, Ara again, Rui again again, Lynriel's attack, the Sh'landriel, Rui for the fourth time, Lynriel's declaration about being bound, and then my in-realm jump to her place . . . because of Rui.

I have to give Lana credit. She kept her composure through the entire thing. Besides her eyes going wide a few times and an occasional sharp inhale, she stayed calm as a cucumber. When I finished, I sunk back into the couch, feeling like a giant weight had been lifted off my chest. It felt good to finally tell someone everything. Is this what therapy feels like? Should I actually find a therapist? Nah, I'm sure I'm fine.

"Uh . . ." Lana said, looking out her window at the brick wall of the building across the street. "That's . . . wow."

"Yeah," I said, shaking my head. "I don't know what to do, who to talk to, or how to even begin figuring out the next step."

Lana nodded softly, her focus still out the window. I could tell she was deep in thought. She had the habit of spacing out when lost in her head. It was a trait that we both shared, apparently. Considering I had nowhere to go, I let her have as much time as she needed.

After about five minutes of silence, she turned back to me with a curious look. "You said that this Rui can materialize in a physical form?"

"Yeah," I nodded, holding up my phone. "I mean, when she wants to, I guess. It's impossible to determine just what she's going to do. She's like a bratty sorority girl who only does what she wants, no matter what."

Lana chuckled and gave me a slight smile. "I know those types. There are plenty of them in my classes. But . . . do you think you could have her come here? I'd love to meet her and maybe pick her brain."

I shrugged and swiped up on the cat paw icon. Nothing. I sighed and shook my head. "Sorry, kiddo. It looks like she might—"

"Hi, Daddy," Rui said from just beside me on the couch, causing me to jump and throw my phone up in the air.

"JESUS CHRIST! WHAT DID I TELL YOU ABOUT DOING THAT?!"

Rui chuckled, swiping her tail at my face while flicking the little bell on the collar around her neck. "Hey, I'm wearing that bell you wanted."

I clutched my chest, feeling my heart pound furiously inside. I looked at Lana, who was staring in shocked fascination at Rui. "I-It's true! You're . . . real?"

Rui smiled at Lana as she crossed her legs underneath herself on the couch. "Of course I am!"

Lana began to smile as she studied the Neko. "This . . . this is unbelievable. Nothing in the research suggests . . . I mean, anything like you! I have so many questions."

Rui tilted her head to the side, one of her ears twitching slightly. "I don't know how much I can answer. I'm only here to help Daddy."

I groaned and leaned my head back to look at the ceiling. "Please, for the millionth time, stop calling me that! At the very least, don't do it in front of my niece."

"Oh, I don't care about that," Lana said, swiping her hand to dismiss my complaint. "Trust me, it's more common than you think hearing girls call their boyfriends 'Daddy' around campus."

"But—" I tried to protest but was quickly stopped by a furry tail to the face.

"Shush," Rui said, giving me a playful smile before looking back at Lana. "We don't have very long, so we need to hurry."

I cocked my head at her, staring hard at the irritating Neko. "What do you mean?"

"Everything he told you was the truth," Rui said, ignoring my question completely. "I figured out of everyone he knew, you'd be the best to try to point him in some kind of direction."

Lana tapped her bottom lip with her fingernail. "But if everything he's said is true, then *you're* the best one for that job."

Rui shook her head, pouting her lip slightly. "I can't. I'm not fully operational yet. My understanding of most things happens in the moment. Daddy usually does or says something, and the information just . . . makes itself clear to me. It's like it's always there, just hidden by a thick fog."

"Fascinating," Lana said with a smile. She leaned forward in her chair, staring deep into Rui's eyes. "You're part of the Rift? Or, these Sh'landriel?"

Rui tilted her head, and one of her ears twitched several times. I'd started to make the connection she did that when she was thinking about something. "Yes and no. I'm of the One, but not the only one. I'm me, or at least part of me I used to be. The pathways run through me, but they're not me. Yet, they came from me, or at least a me I was another time."

"That makes no sense at all," I grumbled, shaking my head.

Rui scoffed and rolled her eyes at me. "I don't know how to make it any more clear than that!"

"I think I understand," Lana said, nodding thoughtfully. "The One was everything before it was broken by the Rift or Pathways as you call it. But it only exists because it also came from the One? So, since you're a part of the One, that same energy connects you to the Rift, but it's different than what you are. Am I somewhat close?"

Rui's eyes sparkled as she gave Lana the biggest smile I'd ever seen. "YES! I knew you were the right person for this."

"Hm," Lana hummed as she sat back in her chair, tapping her lip again. "I really wish I could take you to meet some of my professors. Everything we thought we knew about the Rift will be thrown out the window when this gets out."

"Except, it's *not* going to get out," I said, glaring at my niece. "The RRS *can't* know about this, Lana. That includes your professors, classmates, or anyone else. They're threatening not just your future but Sara and Honey as well. Not to mention threatening to essentially send Ara to become a human sex toy. I don't care what they do to me, but I won't give them more reasons to look harder at any of you."

Lana narrowed her eyes, pointing at my wrist. "You say that, yet you're still wearing their watch. Correct me if I'm wrong, but they use that to track you, right? And, do you honestly think they don't have mics on them, listening in to every word we've already said?"

My heart froze in my chest, and I cursed myself. How can I be *so* stupid?! Lynriel was right. I'm a fucking moron. I'd given them every piece of information they could want and more. All because I'm too stuck in my ways to not take off my damn watch!

I instantly ripped at the watch band, as if somehow taking it off now would do any good. As I fought with the buckle, a slender hand rested gently on my own. I looked up to see Rui giving me a warm smile. "It's okay; I took care of it already, remember?"

I blinked several times, trying to think back. "Wait, you ... erased the data from the night of the jump ..."

Rui chuckled and swatted at me with her tail. "I did more than that, silly. I blocked them from being able to track you or listen to any conversations we've had. I did it with Ara's watch, too. Hopefully, she won't mind."

I stared in stunned silence as Rui slowly blinked her large yellow eyes at me. "That ... I ... Thank you. I don't know what else to say. You really are amazing, you know that?"

For the first time, I saw Rui actually blush and turn away. Her tail flicked happily behind her back as she picked at an invisible thread on the couch. "It wasn't anything. I told you I'd always take care of you. Just like you'll always take care of me, right?"

Another first, I found myself genuinely smiling at the blushing Neko. Despite how incredibly, unbelievably, *astronomically* annoying she's been, she did what was right by me and mine. I cursed inwardly. *I'm going to have to let her keep calling me Daddy, aren't I? Damn it.*

Before we could say anything else, both of Rui's ears pointed straight up. Quickly looking around the room, she gave Lana a big smile, clasping her hands in gratitude. "Time's up! It was so nice to meet you in person, Lana. I can't wait to see what you come up with. Until next time!"

Before we could say anything, Rui vanished into thin air. Lana and I stared at the spot she'd been in, dumbfounded at her abrupt departure. Yet, we didn't get to think about it too long. Within five seconds of Rui leaving, I felt a strange pressure coming from somewhere around me. It wasn't my core opening again, but it did feel similar. That feeling vanished point three seconds before a massive pounding on Lana's door made us both jump.

"I KNOW YOU'RE IN THERE!" Lynriel shouted from the hallway. "IF YOU THINK YOU CAN HIDE FROM ME, YOU'VE GOT ANOTHER THING COMING!"

"Who's that?" Lana asked, a look of fear washing over her.

I sighed and stood from the couch. "A very pissed-off elf princess."

I barely had the door cracked open when Lynriel pushed her way inside; her face twisted in obvious anger. Honey must've given her more clothes because she now wore a purple silk button-down and black yoga pants with running shoes. I had to admit, if I weren't in genuine fear for my safety at that very moment, I probably would've considered her hot. In that 'I can rip you apart with my bare hands, and I have the six-pack to prove it' kind of way. She demonstrated that strength by shoving me back further into the apartment.

"Hey!"

"Don't 'Hey' me," Lynriel growled. "I bore my soul to you, allowed you to see a moment of weakness, and you just . . . run away?! To what, yet another woman? Just how many are in your harem anyway?"

I slammed my hands over my face as I heard Lana stifle a snort of laughter. "I DON'T HAVE A HAREM! This is my niece, Lana. She's by far one of the smartest people I've ever known, and I thought she might be able to help us with this whole . . . whatever it is."

Lynriel scoffed and gave Lana a dismissive look. "Her? She's barely a toddler."

"Hey!" Lana shouted, crossing her arms in front of her chest. "I'm twenty-one, thank you very much. And I'm at the top of my class in all RRS courses. I even found the jump point that led to the Realm Uncle T found you in."

Lynriel's eyes widened, and she stared in disbelief at Lana and then me. "Twenty-one? How long do you people live? I wasn't even able to walk at that age!"

"It depends, but definitely not as long as you," I grumbled. "But age doesn't matter. She's beyond smart, and if anyone can help us figure something out, it'll be her."

My phone began to buzz, so I looked down at it sitting on the couch and saw that Honey was calling. I hit 'Decline' and turned back to Lynriel. Whatever chewing out I was going to get from

Honey could wait. "How did you find me, anyway? Did Honey put another GPS on me?"

Lynriel looked confused as she narrowed her eyes at me. "What in all the Realms is a gee pee esse? Never mind, it doesn't matter. I told you we're bound. I can sense you when I need to."

"Wait," I said, shaking my head, chastising myself for only realizing it at that moment. "You jumped here! The RRS has sensors that detect when someone enters or leaves the realm. You just led them straight to us!"

Scoffing, Lynriel rolled her eyes. "Why would I leave your Realm when you're still here?"

Confused, I cocked my head at her. "Huh? Then how did you . . . wait, can you jump in-realm too?!"

Lynriel gave me a look that made it clear she thought I was an idiot. "Of course I can. Do you think you have to leave your Realm first just to go somewhere else in the same world? That's . . . the stupidest thing I've ever heard."

"Hey! Until yesterday, I was always told the Rift is too unpredictable to jump in-realm. The currents are too strong. No one's been able to jump with that kind of precision before. Well, until I did it yesterday by accident."

"By . . . accident?" Lynriel scrunched up her face in a strange mix of frustration and disbelief. "How . . . No, never mind. I'm just going to assume it has something to do with stupid. I mean, how have your people survived for so long not having the most basic understanding of anything?"

Once again, my phone started buzzing as Honey tried to call. I hit 'Decline,' knowing I was only making the haranguing worse for myself later. But I just couldn't deal with that right now. I rubbed my eyes in frustration and motioned for Lynriel to sit on the couch.

"Listen, just . . . come take a seat," I said, sitting heavily back on the soft cushion. "As I've said, Lana might be our best bet to figure any of this out."

Grumbling, Lynriel walked over and sat cautiously on the couch beside me. For some reason, she sat a lot closer than anyone should. She had a solid foot of space on her other side, yet she sat with her leg almost pressing into mine. I shook my head, figuring she wasn't used to our ways, and hadn't known she didn't have to be so close.

Lana sat down and cleared her throat, studying Lynriel carefully. As far as I knew, Ellyssians had yet to be discovered. So Lana was seeing the physical embodiment of what we've always known as elves from stories and movies. Being as big into fantasy as I was, I can only imagine the thoughts running through her mind.

Just as Lana opened her mouth to say something, her cell phone rang, startling her with the sudden loud noise. She looked down and furrowed her brows as she read the name. "Why is Honey calling me?"

I sighed and shook my head. "It's probably because I just ignored two of her calls."

"But," Lana said, giving me a confused look. "How does she know you're here? You said you just happened to pop over after you left your house."

Rolling my eyes, I gave her a slight shrug. "She probably *did* put another GPS on me."

Shaking her head in disbelief, Lana answered the call. "Hello? Honey?"

Lynriel turned to me and narrowed her eyes again. "What is this thing you keep saying? And why does she need to know your location? If you're supposedly not in a harem, like you claim, that's weird."

"Wait, slow down," Lana said with an urgency that made me turn back to her. "They did what?"

"What's going on?" I asked, sitting forward, my anxiety causing my heart to race.

Lana looked up at me, clearly in disbelief at what she was hearing. She tapped her screen and turned on the speakerphone so we could hear Honey ourselves. "The RRS just showed up and kicked in the door. They were looking for your uncle, and they took Ara away in handcuffs!"

Chapter 16

The Waiting Game

Nothing has ever filled me with rage more than when someone hurts a person I love. Granted, I haven't had many in my life that I actually cared about, but the ones I do mean everything to me. Honey, Sara, Lana, and Ara are all precious to me, and I would do whatever it takes to keep them safe. And yes, I know what you're going to say. Ara and I haven't even gone on a date yet, nor have we been able to sit down and talk about anything regarding our relationship.

The thing is, we've known each other for years, and I felt an immediate connection with her from the beginning. Sometimes you just know, you know? I'd thought a lot about it over the years. We shared the same interests and sense of humor. We're usually in perfect sync when out on a jump, and let's not forget just how drop-dead gorgeous she is. I've known for a long time that I wanted something more with her; I just never pursued anything because of all the reasons I've already mentioned countless times. Things were different now that we could finally give 'us' a chance.

But now, the RRS has come in and taken her away. None of this was even about her. They wanted me! Or, more specifically, they wanted Lynriel and her shard. But they were trying to get them through me.

I shot to my feet, my heart pounding in my chest. This was all my fault. I could've stopped them from taking her if I'd only been there. My mind was racing, and I felt like I couldn't think straight. The only thing that kept coming to mind was jumping straight to the facility, grabbing Wallace by the balls, and leaving him out in the middle of the Rift.

"I have to get back," I said, my mind focused solely on getting to Ara.

"Hey," Lynriel said, grabbing my arm and spinning me to face her. I expected her to be angry that I was taking off again, but I was surprised to see a look of concern on her face. "I know you must be spiraling right now. I'm not sure what your relationship is with that woman, but you can't just rush into things without thinking them through."

I shook my head, clenching my jaw. "There's no time! If I don't get there soon, who knows what they'll do to her."

"And what about the rest of us?" Lynriel asked, squeezing my arm tightly. "What will happen to the others if you go rushing in there, getting yourself killed because you didn't take a few minutes to formulate a plan? Not to mention, that would also kill me. Is my life worth that little?"

I knew she was right. Charging into situations head-on without thinking ahead got me into a lot of trouble in the past. I couldn't do that this time. I wasn't the only one affected by my actions anymore. That point was driven home as I saw the slight look of fear behind Lynriel's eyes.

"We can figure this out together," she said, squeezing my arm in support.

I took a deep breath and closed my eyes to try and shut out the screaming voice in my head. The rage burned hot in my chest, but I was able to keep it from exploding out. After some controlled breathing, I opened my eyes and gave Lynriel a slight nod. The relief was apparent as I saw her shoulders slightly relax and her face soften.

Looking back to Lana, I gave her a nod and motioned toward the door. "Tell her we're heading back."

"Lana, if you hear from your uncle, tell him they're waiting for him outside the house," Honey said in a very measured tone.

That made me take another pause. I was sure Honey had heard me, so why was she acting like I wasn't there? Then it hit me; she was putting on an act in case the RRS was listening to the line. Those bastards wouldn't think twice about illegally listening to a person's private calls.

I gritted my teeth harder. These assholes were thoroughly testing my anger management skills. My mind raced as I thought about what to do. An idea came to me, and I knew where we could go. I just needed to relay it to Honey in a way the RRS wouldn't know. Lowering my voice, I whispered my message to Lana so the phone mic wouldn't pick up what I was saying. "Tell her I mentioned visiting Mrs. Atkin, okay?"

Lana relayed the information, and there was a brief silence on the line. After a few seconds, Honey cleared her throat, and I heard shuffling in the background. "Okay. We'll wait to visit her, then. No use in all of us piling into her tiny place. Thanks for letting us know."

Nodding, I gave Lana the all-clear to hang up. I walked up to my niece, who was now shaking from nerves, and hugged her. "We're going to get this figured out, I promise. Until then, maybe take a few days off from class, okay? In the meantime, there's a book that might make more sense to you than it did to me. It was written by the former Director of the RRS, Annabella Saph. It's called 'The Unknown Realms.' Maybe give that a quick read and let me know what you think?"

Lana nodded as she returned my embrace. "Please be careful, Uncle T."

I smiled and squeezed her tight before letting go. "Eh, don't worry about me. If a goddamn tentacle monster from another Realm couldn't kill me, I doubt some bureaucrat pencil pusher will."

Pulling up the maps on my phone, I instinctively offered my hand to Lynriel. She gave me a quizzical look before reaching out for it. I was surprised when she did the same thing as Ara and interlocked our fingers. Chuckling, I hit the 'Rui's Park' location button under my 'Favorites' tab. I guess the Neko thought, since I didn't remember the name of the actual park, it would be the easiest way for me to know what it was.

My core opened for a split second before closing back. Lynriel and I now stood in the middle of the small neighborhood park where I'd first met Rui. It was right beside my old apartment building in the all-but-deserted neighborhood. I didn't even worry about looking around to see if anyone saw us, as no one came there anymore. Hell, not even the homeless took refuge in the abandoned buildings for some reason.

As we walked to my old apartment, I was struck by how quiet the neighborhood was. Other than the distant sound of traffic coming from the main street of the college and random bird calls, it was dead silent. That made it even creepier if you ask me. Lynriel and I were probably the only people within a mile radius, and it felt weird.

As we made our way up the steps to the old building, I felt a slight squeeze around my fingers. I looked down in surprise, not realizing I was still holding Lynriel's hand. Giving an awkward smile, I released her. "Sorry about that."

Lynriel quickly averted her eyes and shook her head. "N-No, it's fine. I understand you're a bit preoccupied at the moment."

I nodded my gratitude before turning back to the door. I tried the handle, but of course, it was locked. Why wouldn't it be? We didn't have time to figure out another way in, though. The RRS was on the move, and the longer we're in the open, the more chance they'll have of finding us. Rearing back, I slammed the bottom of my foot hard into the door, shattering the old wood into countless pieces as it flew open.

That was a mistake. In my infinite wisdom, I failed to consider that I was still barefoot. Biting my tongue hard, I tried to keep any show of pain off my face. I just performed a perfect, one-kick door breach; I couldn't let Lynriel know how excruciating it was.

I looked at the stairs leading up to my old apartment but decided against going up. This building hadn't had power in years, and I didn't want to take the chance of stepping on something while fumbling around in the dark. Instead, I walked over to Mrs. Atkin's old door. I placed my hand on the knob but froze.

It'd been nine years since I was last in the building. A little over a year after the FRE, the three of us had come to gather Mrs. Atkin's belongings to donate to a local nursing facility. The building had been shut down, and the former landlord said anything left would be thrown away or sold. I knew Mrs. Atkin would want her stuff to help others rather than line the pockets of that prick anymore.

A soft touch brought me back to the present as Lynriel gently placed her hand on top of mine. She'd gotten extremely close and stared intently at me with crystal blue eyes. I didn't know why, but something deep inside was compelling me to kiss her. Shaking the intrusive thoughts out of my mind, I gave her a small smile and tried the door. Luckily, it was unlocked, so I didn't need to subject my foot to another splinter-fest.

The apartment looked exactly as I remembered, only now with more dust and a not-so-subtle scent of mold. The two things we left all those years ago were Mrs. Atkin's small couch and the bed, which technically belonged to the landlord. Yet, it appeared he hadn't been too worried about coming to sell the stuff, as both were still there.

I hit the couch cushions a few times, sending a cloud of dust into the air. That wasn't the smartest idea on my part. Lynriel and I erupted in a massive coughing fit and had to step into the bedroom to catch our breath. The irritated princess shot me a dirty look, making it clear she thought I was an idiot.

"Sorry," I grumbled, my throat scratchy from the dust.

Sighing, Lynriel walked over to the bed and softly sat on the edge. "Whatever. Now, should we start to come up with your plan?"

I sighed and shook my head, motioning back toward the door. "No, you were right back there. My actions have consequences for more than just me right now. Let's wait until Honey and Sara get here so we can figure it out together. The sucky thing is we don't know how long the agency plans on camping out in front of the house. Guess it just depends on how bad they want us."

"Me," Lynriel said, giving me a sharp look. "They want me, not you."

I nodded and did my best to sit as softly as she had on the bed beside her. "Yeah, well, if they want you, they'll have to go through me first."

We sat in silence for a long while, each of us lost in our thoughts. Eventually, Lynriel turned to look at me, her voice barely above a whisper. "Why are you doing this?"

Her question caught me off-guard. I turned and tried to study her face in the dim light. "What do you mean?"

Letting out a long exhale, Lynriel fully turned on the bed and crossed her legs underneath herself. My eyes quickly flicked down to her breasts straining against her blouse. They were large like Honeys and looked firm even without a bra on. I couldn't help but appreciate the view.

"Why are you helping me like this?" Lynriel asked, her voice soft, as if she were afraid of the answer. "Even before learning about us being bound together, you seemed ready to fight this battle on my behalf. You were willing to risk yourself and the people you care about for a stranger. You didn't know me. It's not your destiny to reunite the Sh'landriel. I mean, why did you even rescue me in the first place? I was no one to you."

I'd been trying to figure that out myself this whole time. "I'd love to say it's because of some valiant sense of honor or whatever. But honestly, I wasn't even thinking when I did it. I saw a pretty girl in trouble, and I wanted to help. And as far as why I'm helping you now . . . it's one part because it's the right thing to do, and another part I want to do whatever I can to stick it to those bastards. The fact we're bound or whatever isn't even a factor, really."

Lynriel studied me carefully, probably trying to see if I was being serious. "That's . . . that's it? You just thought I was pretty and wanted to help?"

Shrugging, I lay down to look up at the ceiling. "What can I say? I'm a sucker for blondes, I guess."

I expected her to slap me or, at the very least, tell me that I was being vulgar or distasteful. But instead, there was only silence. Tilting my head slightly to look at her, I saw her ears had grown a deep shade of red, and she seemed lost in thought once again. I smiled and looked back up at the ceiling.

As I went over everything that happened the past few days, I remembered something Lynriel had mentioned after breakfast. "Hey, earlier, you said your body was made to hold the shar—Sh'landriel. What did you mean by that?"

I looked over and saw Lynriel biting her lower lip. I couldn't tell if she was trying to think about how to answer or chastising herself for saying something she shouldn't have. With a long sigh, her shoulders slumped forward in resignation. "I . . . I wasn't born like most people. I was created."

That made me prop myself up on my elbows, looking her over in disbelief. "What? Like, you're a robot or something?"

Scoffing, Lynriel rolled her eyes and crossed her arms under her chest. "No, I'm not a robot! I'm a living, breathing, conscious Ellyssian. I'm just as alive as you or any of the others. I just . . . wasn't born. My people are much older than yours. We're the first race ever to gain sentience. We were the first to travel the Pathways and the first to master the powers of the One. It's always been our duty to bring the One back into existence. But one person cannot handle more than a few pieces of the Sh'landriel. So, my father, the King, decided to create a vessel to house them in. They created me using his DNA along with his three wives and fourteen concubines, who were also powerful in their own rights."

"Wow," I said, shaking my head. "That's . . . unbelievable. So, did you grow up in a castle or something?"

Lynriel seemed to deflate even more, and I saw a familiar sadness behind her eyes. "No. Our people's greatest scholars, magi, and warriors raised me in a facility. Because of my purpose, they didn't want me to become attached to any one person. So, I was kept alone and only saw my father or one of my mothers every few years. And I was only allowed to meet my brothers and sisters once. The day I was sent out into the Pathways to search for the Sh'landriel. There was a feast, I was given the court's blessings, and then I left my Realm for the last time. I haven't seen my home in longer than I can remember. My father and mothers have all long since passed away. The same goes for my siblings and their children. I would bet that if I were to go back to Ellyssia right now, the records of my creation and mission are probably only remembered by the historians."

"Really?" I asked, trying to find a way to delicately ask the question no man is supposed to ask. "So, how long have you been gone? And how long do your people normally live?"

Lynriel looked at her palm, and I wondered what she could be staring at. After a silent minute, she sighed and shook her head. "Ellyssians typically live a thousand years, give or take. My father was already over six hundred years old when they created me, and it took a little over two centuries to finish my training. But I've been traveling the Pathways for almost five millennia now."

My eyes bulged as I looked her over again. She didn't look a day over 25, yet she's saying that she's more than five thousand years old?! The longest-living species I'd heard about before today was the Kalori, who lived seven hundred years on average. The people of Ellyssia were fascinating, to say the least. Lynriel's shoulders slumped, and I saw a distant stare that I was all too familiar with.

"You'd think after all this time of being alive, it wouldn't bother me," Lynriel said, her words soft as her mind drifted to a far-off place. "My purpose is the most noble anyone could ever hope for. Yet the thing I've wished for most was for even just one of them to have some kind of compassion towards me. To show me that they cared about who I was rather than what I was meant to do. It's funny . . . you've known me for a day and have already shown me more kindness than any of my own family ever has."

I was starting to realize that the beautiful elf princess was broken on the inside, just like me. Neither of us knew the love of any parental figure. I'd had the shit beat out of me on a regular basis, and she was kept in near-total isolation throughout her childhood. The only life she knew was one of servitude and sacrifice.

"You said you have five shar—Sh'landriel inside your core right now?"

Lynriel nodded, placing a hand over her heart. "Yes. My people had collected only three over countless millennia. I was fused with those from the moment of my creation. I was incredibly lucky to find two in the same Realm about four hundred years after I started my journey, and I immediately fused them to my core. But the process of doing so debilitates me for far too long, and I'm all but defenseless during the process. So, I decided not to fuse with anymore until I could find a safe place to perform the ritual. I had seven saved when the Marrog found me. I'd been surrounded and couldn't let them get a hold of the Sh'landriel. So, I began to bind them to me, but the ritual was interrupted, and I was knocked unconscious. Although they hadn't fused with my core, they had embedded into my body, so they weren't found when I was taken. And as you know, I was kept drugged . . . until you saved me. I'm not sure how they came undone from my body, but I'm glad it wasn't the Marrog who found them."

"I'm sorry," I said, laying back down. "I don't think I've said it yet. But I swear, I wasn't trying to take anything from you."

"I know," she said, and I felt her shift to lay beside me on the mattress. "I'm upset at myself more than anything. It took me thousands of years to find them, and I lost them all in the blink of an eye. I understand you were only doing what you thought was right. I've noticed that about you. Even at the risk of your own safety, you do what's right for those around you. And now that we're bonded, I can feel your spirit and sense what kind of person you truly are. You . . . you're actually a pretty amazing man."

"Oh, yeah," I chuckled, nudging her with my arm. "I'm the best. Don't you forget it."

Instead of chastising me, Lynriel let out a soft laugh as well. We continued to lay in silence, just staring up at the ceiling. There's not much to do in an almost empty apartment without electricity. Soon, my eyelids grew heavy, and I eventually dozed off.

My sleep was uneasy, to say the least. For some reason, I had a nightmare where all the people I loved were in separate cages, just out of my reach. Yet, I knew they'd all be lost if I tried to save any one of them. It made my anxiety kick up hard, and I jolted awake.

I stared up at a dark ceiling, not fully coherent yet. A familiar pressure lay on my chest, and instinctively, I stroked Honey's head. I felt something strange as my fingers passed through her silky, straight hair. Honey's ears felt weird, and I softly pinched them to figure out what it was. The woman inhaled sharply and let out a soft moan. I squeezed and rubbed the strange, pointed tip, trying to understand what I was touching. I felt something hot and moist begin to rub my leg, causing my eyes to shoot open in surprise.

Lynriel had fallen asleep on top of me, just like the other girls had come to do. As I softly pinched the tips of her elongated ear, a shudder coursed through her body, and she squealed as she tried to bury her face into my chest. Her leg had been crossed over mine, and she'd been grinding herself on my thigh as I explored her ear. She seemed to convulse twice more before falling completely limp against me, and I felt a warmth soak into the crotch of her pants. Wait a second . . . did she. . .?

Almost as if she'd read my mind, Lynriel shot up and rolled, sitting as far away from me as she could on the bed. I sat up on my elbows, trying to study her in the dim light. Her face had turned a deep crimson, and I saw her glaring daggers back at me.

"Y-You . . . How dare . . . What makes you . . . I didn't . . ." Lynriel started and trailed off several times, her emotions so high she couldn't figure out what she wanted to say.

"Did you just . . . cum?" I asked, figuring I couldn't get into worse trouble anyway.

"N-NO!" Lynriel shouted but quickly looked away as she bit her lower lip. "Why would . . . I mean . . . You . . . NO!"

I studied her more and saw a large wet spot on her yoga pants. Her nipples had grown so stiff they could probably cut glass. She saw me looking at her sensitive areas and quickly covered her breasts with one arm and crossed her legs, giving me another stern glare. "You can't just . . . do that! It's improper for a Princess to . . ."

Smiling, I gave her a slight chuckle as I sat up. "Listen, it was an accident. I'm sorry if I did something improper. I don't want you to think I did it on purpose or that I'm the kind of guy who'd take advantage like that. But I will say that just because you're a Princess doesn't mean you shouldn't be able to enjoy pleasurable experiences."

Lynriel seemed to drop some of her guard, and her arm fell away from her chest. "I . . . I know. That you wouldn't do something like that without permission, that is. I'm sorry for reacting like that. It's just been . . . a long time since something like that's happened."

"You mean your panty-soaking orgasm?" I joked, causing Lynriel's face and ears to turn a darker shade of crimson.

"Will you just . . . not talk about it?" she huffed, refusing to look me in the eyes. "And It's not my fault, okay? An Ellyssian's ears are . . . extremely sensitive. It's actually an erogenous zone. I've been so focused on finding the Sh'landriel I'd given up all carnal desires. It's been countless years since . . . *that* has happened. Even then, it's only ever been by my own hand."

That piqued my curiosity, and I raised an eyebrow as I looked her over again. "Wait, are you saying that you're a virgin?"

Lynriel scowled at me, but I also saw a bit of fear behind her eyes. "S-So what? I'm destined for things more important than the pleasures of the flesh. It's just . . . damn it! This is so embarrassing!"

"Hey! It's okay," I tried to reassure her. "There's nothing to be embarrassed about. Really. Especially with me. I'm just surprised, that's all. I mean, you seemed all too ready to jump in bed with me last night thinking I was in a harem."

"That's . . . I . . ." Lynriel scoffed and shook her head, not knowing what to say.

With a long sigh, Lynriel pouted her bottom lip. Damn, she really was sexy. But, no! Bad Turtle! I have Ara. I shouldn't be thinking like this about someone else.

I reached over, touched her knee, and squeezed softly, hoping it would convey my sincerity. "I know how important it is for you to find the Sh'landriel. But if you're eventually going to be giving up your life for the sake of bringing back the One, you shouldn't deny yourself at least a bit of worldly pleasure, right? I mean, what's the point of fighting to save all of this if you don't get to have any fun along the way?"

Lynriel looked down at my hand, and I saw a glimpse of what could only be considered lust filling her eyes. Shit. I'm sending her mixed signals, which she doesn't need right now. I pulled my hand away, causing her to look up in disappointment.

"I'm sorry, I should've clarified," I said, standing up from the bed. "You should be allowed to have fun, just . . . not with me. I'm with Ara. Kind of. I think, at least. We haven't really had a chance to discuss it with everything going on."

Lynriel cocked her head to the side and squinted her eyes at me. "But . . . we're bound together. I can't be with anyone but you now."

That made my heart freeze, and my stomach feel like it was trying to make a quick exit out of my ass. "I'm sorry, what's that?"

Furrowing her brows at me like I just asked the stupidest question in the world, Lynriel crawled to the edge of the bed and got up on her knees, coming almost eye-level with me. She placed her hand on my chest, and I felt a warmth radiate through my body as the primal urge to ravage the princess nearly overwhelmed my sense of reason. Staring hard into her eyes, I felt a powerful connection to the woman, and it took everything in me not to pull her in for a kiss.

"You feel it, don't you?" Lynriel whispered, her voice soft but heavy with desire. "The Sh'landriel pulls us toward each other. They call to the ones inside me as mine do to yours. This is the most intimate connection anyone could have to another person. This is what I meant when I say we're bound. I'm yours, and you're mine, and nothing can stop our cores from being drawn together. We can deny and try to fight it, but it'll always bring us back together. No one else will share a bond as deep as we have because of this."

I had a maelstrom of emotions rushing through me at that moment—passion, guilt, love, anger, desire, and more. I wanted Lynriel. Every fiber in me wanted to throw her down on that dusty mattress and ravish her body until neither of us could walk again. But, deep inside, I couldn't stop thinking about Ara. No, I couldn't do this to her.

I stepped back, breaking Lynriel's touch, and the overwhelming sensations quickly diminished to a dull roar. "I can't. Ara . . ."

Lynriel smiled, and I could see a fire of determination in her eyes. She wanted this and would fight for it any way she could. "I know I mentioned that I was familiar with the harem dynamic last night. But there's actually more to it than that. You see, on Ellyssia, women outnumber men nearly a dozen to one. So, forming harems became the common practice in our Realm. A strong male like yourself could have as many lovers as he desires. My father had three wives and fourteen concubines and was considered conservative by Ellyssian standards. I accept that you already have other paramours, and I'm happy to share you with them. Besides, your Ara mentioned earlier that she was fine with us being together. Your harem can be complete with me as your bounded partner."

I slapped my hand over my face and groaned. "I told you I *don't* have a harem! And, yes, polyamory is relatively common these days. But what Ara said earlier could've meant several different things. I can't just—"

My phone buzzed, cutting off what I was about to say. Lynriel's face fell, and I kicked myself for putting us in this position. I'm a giant walking dildo. At least, that's how I felt seeing the hurt behind the princess's eyes.

I looked at my phone, and my heart froze once again.

Message: Arabella Anderson

"HELP"

I quickly looked around the empty room, thinking about what to do. Lynriel must have seen the panic on my face and stood from the bed. "What's wrong?"

"It's . . . It's Ara," I said, clenching my fist as I thought about what they were doing to her. It was just after one, which meant she'd been in their custody for a couple of hours, going through God knows what. "I can't just wait here anymore. I have to do something!"

Lynriel shook her head, and I knew she was only trying to get me to think straight. But at that moment, I just couldn't. Before she could speak, I placed both hands on her shoulders, forcing her to look into my eyes.

"Wait here for Honey and Sara," I said. "Do *not* leave this apartment unless it's an emergency. I'll be back as soon as I can.'

"No! You can't—"

I didn't hear what she said, as I'd already hit the map button on my phone and clicked on Ara's name. My core opened and pulled me from the old building and away from Lynriel. Before I could even blink, I was standing in a hallway somewhere in the RRS, looking at a solid metal door with a sign that read "Wing E- Interrogation Room 3." Gritting my teeth, I reached for the door. I was taken by surprise as it swung open and was greeted with the beady eyes of Director Gram Wallace staring back at me.

"Oh, hello there," Wallace said, the hint of a smile cracking his lips. "I'm so happy to see you. Come, let's have a little chat, shall we?"

Chapter 17
Final Ultimatum

There are few things I truly hate in this world. Don't get me wrong, there are *tons* of things I don't like. Things like slow internet speeds or orange juice with pulp. I mean, what's the point? Just eat a damn orange if you want pulp!

No, there are only a select few things I genuinely hate. Alarm clocks, Thursdays, Kyles, onions, and Gram fucking Wallace. And right now, he was topping that list. It took every ounce of self-control I had not to break the pudgy little man's nose right then and there.

"Follow me, Rifter," Wallace said, motioning as he walked to the next interrogation room.

Swallowing my rage, I followed, pushing past him as he opened the door. I knew what he was wanting, so there wasn't any reason to put on an act. By the expression on his face, I could tell he was surprised. He probably thought I'd make a big scene or try to feign ignorance.

But I wasn't stupid. As he'd led me to the room, I'd seen the five security guards rounding the corner down the hall. They'd probably been on standby in case I showed up. Yet, since I could see the jump alarms hadn't gone off, they most likely didn't expect me to suddenly appear right in the middle of the facility.

The interrogation room was simple, with a large metal desk in the middle and two chairs set across from one another. I guess they got their decorating advice from a bad TV cop show. I sat heavily in the uncomfortable metal chair, crossing my arms in front of my chest. I was still only wearing my running shorts and a stained T-shirt with no shoes on. It was doubtful Wallace would believe I walked in the front door. Lynriel might've been right. I should've thought about this more.

Before the door closed, I saw Wallace smile and wave for someone to enter. That was when my day went even more down the shitter. Kyle stepped into view, sneering at me from the hallway. The asshole was so big he had to duck and turn sideways to get in the door. Glaring me down, he slowly walked around until he stood behind me. Did he think that was intimidating? I swear these guys watch too much Law and Order.

Wallace shut the door and walked around to sit in the chair on the other side of the cold, metal desk. His eyes were glued to his tablet as he scrolled through, intently reading something. I continued staring at him, not giving either of them the satisfaction of thinking I was scared. I swear to God, I could hear an old analog clock somewhere ticking away the seconds as we sat in complete silence.

After what felt like forever, Wallace finally tapped his screen a few more times and set it down. He looked up with his usual fake smile, interlocking his fingers as he leaned forward. "I apologize for this, Rifter. I know this isn't how someone of your prestige is used to being received."

From behind me, Kyle scoffed. Wallace sent the behemoth of a man a scowl before smiling back at me. "I would love nothing more than for us to be able to get past all of this . . . unpleasantness and get things back to the way they should be. Don't you agree?"

The struggle is real. Trust me when I say it took every fiber in my being not to lunge over that table and beat the man to death with that damned tablet of his. Gritting my teeth so hard I could hear bone creaking, I gave him a nod. Wallace took this as a good sign as his smile grew, and he picked up his tablet again to read something.

"Before we get started," the director said, scrolling through the screen. "Can I ask how you got here this morning? Our logs don't show you going through any of our security checkpoints."

He set down the tablet again and gave me an expectant look. I sighed and shook my head. Not because of the game he was playing but because I was about to try something I never thought I'd be desperate enough to do. I was going to put my trust in an irritating Neko.

"Something's wrong with your tablet, *sir*," I said, saying that last part as sarcastically as I could. "I went through the checkpoints the entire way."

Shaking his head, I saw Wallace's smile grow ever so slightly. He obviously thought he had me. He picked up the tablet again and swiped up, handing it to me to show the logs. "You see that, Rifter? Our system is *never* wrong."

My heart pounded, and I held my breath as I looked at the screen. Yet, when I read the list, I couldn't help but smile. "Sir, I'm not sure what you mean. My name and ID number's right there."

Wallace ripped back the tablet and scoured the list, his eyes bulging when he saw my name. I wanted to laugh as I watched the plump man's face grow red with anger. Rui was on it, and I knew I'd owe her big time after this.

"Well . . ." Wallace grumbled, angrily tapping the screen several times. "This . . . I don't . . . I mean . . ."

"Sir?" Kyle asked, finally noticing something was amiss.

Wallace glared at me before looking up at Kyle. "The Rifter is correct. Apparently, he *did* go through security."

"Ain't no way!" Kyle yelled, stepping forward so that he towered over me. "My men were at every entrance! They'd never let this coward in without my say-so."

Wallace now glared at the hulk of a man. "Well, obviously *some-one* dropped the ball. But, I'll address that later."

Turning his attention back to me, the director did his best to compose himself again. Rui threw a wrench in his carefully planned interrogation, which made his mask crack slightly. But he was far from being done.

"Well, I'm glad that little *misunderstanding* was cleared up," he said, hitting a few places on the tablet again. "But, there's also the inconsistencies with your watch."

"My watch?" I asked innocently, raising my wrist to show him I was wearing it. "I always keep it on, like I've been instructed, sir."

I saw the same arrogant smile forming as he scrolled further down his screen. "Yet, your watch shows that you haven't . . ."

His words trailed off as I saw his eyes grow wide in disbelief again. "No, this . . . this can't be right."

"What can't, sir?" I asked, trying hard not to laugh as the director's face grew a deeper crimson.

"I-I was assured that your watch had you at home this morning, yet you . . . you weren't there when the Swords showed up," Wallace stammered.

I shook my head, acting confused again. "I was out for a jog. I'm trying that whole barefoot running thing my niece has been raving about. I also visited an old family friend while I was out. When I got home, I'd heard about what happened and came straight here to figure out why Healer Anderson was taken into custody."

"His watch had him there!" Kyle bellowed, grabbing me by the back of my neck and squeezing hard. "He's lying!"

"Sword KIA, stand down!" Wallace yelled, standing from his chair. "Our technology is *never* wrong, do you understand me? Release the Rifter at once!"

Kyle growled his frustration but pushed me forward, releasing my neck. That was definitely going to leave a mark. I wondered if Sal was still alive after a night with him. She liked things rough, but I highly doubted her tiny frame could take even a tenth of Kyle's brutality.

"There's no way!" Kyle bellowed again, and I could feel the rage radiating from him. Like, literally.

Kyle's ability was fire manipulation. Remember what I said earlier about jackasses throwing a fireball in an enclosed space? Yeah, that's Kyle. He can produce and manipulate fire and is immune to being burned. So, he has no problem using his power whenever. Even if it risks others on his team, he'll do whatever he wants if it means getting the job done.

"Can I ask *why* Healer Anderson was brought in?" I interrupted Kyle's incoming tirade.

Wallace glared daggers at Kyle a moment longer before returning to me. He didn't try to put back on the fake smile this time. "She's been accused of tampering with her device to provide false information to the RRS."

I tilted my head, narrowing my eyes at the director. "Tampering with her device? I was always told they are impossible to tamper with. Who accused her, and what proof is there?"

Scrolling on his tablet again, Wallace grumbled as he shook his head. I held my breath, hoping Rui wouldn't let me down now. I was rewarded with seeing all the blood draining from Wallace's face as he read something on the screen. He looked up at Kyle standing behind me, and his color quickly returned. I've never seen a man do a better impression of a tomato in my life.

"YOU IMBECILE!" Wallace shouted, pointing his finger at Kyle. "YOU TOLD ME HER DATA HAD HER AT HOME!"

"It . . . It did," Kyle protested, obviously on the defensive now. "I went into her apartment like, nine times throughout the night. She wasn't there. But her watch said she was!"

"I just looked at the logs *myself*, and it shows she hadn't returned to her residence since yesterday morning. Do you have any idea what you've done? Do you have *any* idea *who her mother is*?!"

Now, that caught my attention. Was Ara related to someone important? Since I've known her, she never liked to talk about her mom. The only thing I could remember was that she was retired, and they weren't close. I need to ask Ara more about it later.

"I SWEAR!" Kyle shouted, obviously not liking being talked to in such a way. "Of course, I know who she is! You think I'd waste my time with a piece of ass that doesn't put out if I didn't?!"

You know what? A douche is too nice of a term for this prick. He's an enema. Plain and simple.

"This is all *his* fault!" Kyle yelled, and I felt his heat get closer to my back.

My skin felt like I was standing too close to a raging fire, and all the tiny hairs on the back of my neck burned off. Yet before the agitated man grabbed me again, Wallace pointed furiously toward the door. "Sword KIA, that's enough! Go to my office and wait for me there."

"But—"

"I said go!" Wallace yelled, staring hard at the man.

I didn't dare turn around, but I can imagine the expression on Kyle's face had to look like he tasted ass. The room was deathly quiet for some of the longest seconds of my life. Wallace's glare was the only thing keeping me from being turned into a smoldering pile of ash. I thought there was no way someone like Kyle would listen to the round little man.

Yet, to my surprise, Kyle eventually growled something unintelligible before I heard the door open and then slammed shut. Thank God the glass viewing window was from the Winly realm and could handle extreme force. Wallace stared at the door for several more seconds before slowly sitting down with a deep exhale. He deflated a bit as he sat back, and for the briefest of moments, I thought I saw a glimpse of the man behind the curtain, so to speak.

"I apologize for that, Rifter," Wallace said, a weariness in his voice that wasn't there before. "With this new information coming to light, I'll have Healer Anderson released immediately."

I gave a slight nod of appreciation and got ready to stand from my chair. "Thank you, sir. I'll make sure she knows that it was the Swords' error, not the agency itself."

Before I could finish standing, Wallace motioned for me to sit back down. "Unfortunately, we're not done here."

I groaned internally, knowing it wouldn't have been that easy. Sitting again, I sighed and waited for the director to continue. Wallace stared at the dark tablet on the desk for a moment as if he were lost in deep thought.

"Your name is Tom, correct?" he asked, returning his focus to me.

That took me by surprise. It wasn't the question I thought he'd be asking, that's for sure. "Uh . . . Yes, sir."

Nodding, Wallace leaned forward and lowered his voice as if trying to tell me some secret. "Listen, Tom. I don't like having to be the bad guy here. Do you think I signed up to threaten my employees and their loved ones? No! But apparently, it's in the fine print that they don't tell you about until after you get the job."

I studied him, wondering if he really thought I'd buy the buddy act now. Villains are so dumb sometimes. Wallace made a few taps on his tablet before sliding it over. I was shocked to see a picture of Lynriel staring back at me.

"I'm not going to ask you anything right now. I'm simply going to tell you some things that you may or may not already know," Wallace said with a long sigh. "All of this is extremely confidential. But you can forget about simply losing your job or going to jail if it gets out. If *anyone* finds out I told you this, not only will they kill us both, but most likely everyone we've ever loved or cared about as well. And I'm not speaking figuratively here, either. Understand? Now, this woman is from a race called the Ellyssian. They're thought to be the first race ever to discover how to travel the Rift and use its energy to gain abilities such as the Swords and Shields. They believe the shards are fragments of their God."

So far, everything he'd told me was old news. Granted, it was only a couple of hours old, but still nothing that I hadn't already known. So, I pretended to listen to everything so he wouldn't catch on that I was several steps ahead of them.

"However, this woman is more than she appears," Wallace said, pointing to Lynriel's picture. "She was sent out into the Rift by the Ellyssians to collect the shards. They don't believe anyone except themselves has the right to use them. She's their top assassin and has been confirmed by hundreds of Realms to have killed thousands, if not more."

Okay, that's new. I stared in shock at the stern-looking picture of the woman who, not even an hour ago, had been sleeping on my chest. There just wasn't any way that was true. What kind of game was this guy up to now?

"I can imagine what's going through your mind right now, Tom," Wallace said, leaning back in his chair. "And listen, she's a gorgeous woman. I can absolutely understand the urge to want to protect her. But she's not as innocent as I'm sure she's making herself out to be. I'm not sure what happened or how you got to that jump point and back without your watch and coordinates. But from what the witnesses have said, you're a damn hero, son. You should be getting rewarded, not threatened."

I stayed quiet, just looking down at the picture. That couldn't be the real Lynriel. I saw how she acted when we fought. She wasn't trying to kill me; she just wanted the Sh'landriel back.

"I don't want to hurt anyone," Wallace continued, rubbing his face in frustration. "And that includes her. I can give you my word: if you help bring her in, she won't be harmed in any way while in our custody. She'll be given every courtesy we have. We only need to find out what she knows, and we need that shard. I guarantee if I can get it for the higher-ups, they're not going to give two craps about her crimes in the other Realms. She hasn't done anything here. They'll warn her to stay away from us and let her go. No one knows the true power of Ellyssia, and believe me, no one's eager to pick a fight with them to find out."

I sat back, looking up to study Wallace. Now, I know this man is so full of shit he needs a bidet to brush his teeth. But, if there was even the smallest fragment of truth to what he was saying, I couldn't completely ignore it. If he was actually willing to let Lynriel go after she told him everything she knew, wouldn't that be worth it? Especially if it saved the rest of the people that I loved.

But then the little hamster wheel started spinning in my head again, and I realized what that meant. If she told them about the shard, they'd turn their focus on me. The walking shard container. Who knows what they'd do when they discovered I had so many inside my core? And if they do anything to me, who knows how it'll affect Lynriel since we're bound.

I shook my head, letting out a deep exhale. I couldn't make any kind of decision right now. I had more questions for Lynriel and Rui before I threw myself into the jaws of the beast. "Sir, I—"

"Stop right there, Tom," Wallace said, holding up a hand. "I've just given you a lot of information. It's only fair that I give you time to think about things. So let me tell you what's going to happen next. First, you and I are going to walk out of here, and you're getting a new watch assigned to you. The same goes for Healer Anderson. You'll take her home and have a long chat with her and your other friends. I want you to think hard about everything and take tonight to consider if their lives are worth all of this. I told you I don't want to have to hurt anyone, but my hands will be tied if I don't have results by tomorrow. If you don't have the shard or the Ellyssian here by noon, the RRS will come after you and everyone you love."

I clenched my jaw, the rage that burned so bright earlier beginning to return. "Is that a threat, sir?"

"No," Wallace said with a soft shake of his head. "It's just the facts. Make the right decision, Tom. You don't owe this woman anything. She's a murderer. An assassin. Bring her in peacefully, and we'll have options. Don't, and . . . well, I'm sure you can imagine what."

Wallace stood and walked back to the door without waiting for me to respond. He opened it and moved aside for me to leave ahead of him. As I stepped into the hallway, I saw two security guards escort Ara out of the other interrogation room. She looked so defeated, her eyes red and puffy as they were taking the handcuffs off her wrists. Looking towards us, Ara's eyes met mine, and I saw hope come back. The cuffs were barely off when she ran down the hall, jumping directly into my arms.

Ara buried her face in my chest as she tried to squeeze her arms around me. I returned her embrace and held her as close as I could. "Hey, it's okay. Everything's going to be okay."

I felt hot tears soak into my shirt as she pressed herself even more into me. "I was so scared! I . . . I didn't know what to do."

"It's okay," I said as calmly as possible, stroking her hair just as I did with the other girls. For some reason, they all seem to like it. "We're leaving together right now."

As we turned to walk toward the exit, Wallace stepped in front of us, blocking our path. He held up two new watches, handing them to us with an expectant look. I rolled my eyes but gave him my old watch and put on the new one along with Ara. "Remember what I said, Rifter. Noon."

I grunted my acknowledgment and pushed past the portly man, holding Ara's hand the entire way out of the building. We passed several Swords and Shields, all giving us glaring hard at us. I guess word spread fast. Oh well, fuck all of them.

We didn't speak until we were out of sight of the RRS. As we turned the corner to the street I lived on, Ara stopped and pulled at my hand. I turned and looked down, knowing she'd been through something downright traumatic today. Her big green eyes studied my face for a long minute as if she were searching for something.

"Turtle," she said, her voice barely a whisper. "I—"

"Hey," I smiled, hoping to calm her nerves. "Listen, don't worry about any of this, okay? I'm so sorry you got caught up in my mess. I never meant to bring this kind of drama into your life. But I'll fix it, okay? I'll have Sara take you home, and you can rest for a bit. We can talk in a few days when the dust settles."

A look of shocked anger crossed Ara's face as her brows furrowed. "What? What are you saying right now? I know you're not trying to take all this on yourself!"

"Well, I—"

"No!" She yelled, stomping her foot at me. "I told you I wanted to be with you. I don't feel safe without you. You've always been there for me since I transferred here. I don't know what Wallace said to you back there, but there's no way in hell I'm letting you deal with it all on your own. Now, stop this nonsense, and let's go home to talk about everything. Together."

Without waiting for me to answer, Ara stomped down the sidewalk back toward my house. God, she was so cute when she got mad like that. I had an overwhelming desire to rush up behind her and swoop her into my arms. And that's precisely what I did.

She let out a squeal of curses laced with laughter as I cradled her in my arms, carrying her down the street. "Put me down you . . . you . . . giant oaf! You can't just—"

"Oh, but I think I can," I grinned at her, turning up the path to my front door.

There was no surveillance van sitting outside the house, which meant Wallace probably called them off already. I also didn't see Sara's SUV in the driveway. Cursing on the inside, I realized I hadn't told them not to head to the old apartment when we got out of the RRS. Oh well. Lynriel was still there, so they could pick her up for me. Besides, I felt like Ara and I deserved a little alone time.

I sat her on the porch and typed my code on the door lock. But before I could open it, Ara grabbed my arm again and turned me to face her. I saw a fire in her eyes that I recognized all too well. Reaching up, she gripped a handful of my shirt and pulled my face down, pressing our lips together. Her kiss felt like heaven. Her lips were soft and full, warm and just perfect in every way.

Pulling her in, I wrapped my arms around and lifted her, never breaking the kiss. She locked her legs around my waist and held the back of my head, our kissing growing more intense with each passing second. Instinctively, I reached down and opened the door, walking blindly into the house. All I cared about at that moment was Ara and how amazing she tasted.

I slammed the door shut behind me and tried my best to walk down the hallway, all while Ara's tongue was dancing inside my mouth. There might've been a couple of accidental wall bumps, but eventually, we made it to my room. Gripping her waist, I pulled her off me and tossed her onto the bed. She laughed, her cheeks glowing bright. Biting her lower lip, she propped herself onto her elbows and beckoned me with one finger to join her. She didn't have to ask twice.

I know we'd both just had a pretty rough morning— Ara even more so. But, this was years of built-up sexual tension between us that was finally permitted to be released. There was no way either of us could've stopped it now.

Lowering myself on top of her, we kissed again. I felt her rapid breaths blow hot against my skin, and I could feel the tips of her hardened nipples pressing through the thin nightshirt she was still wearing. I couldn't believe this was finally happening. Everything just felt so perfect at that moment.

Her thin fingers reached down and pulled my shirt over my head. We broke our kiss so she could sit up, ripping her shirt off as well. This wasn't going to be gentle or slow lovemaking. No. We were both ravenous for each other. This was going to be hard, intense, passionate fucking.

I stared in amazement at her perfectly freckled breasts. Her nipples were a dark shade of pink and expressed her arousal beautifully. I couldn't wait. I leaned down, grabbed one breast in my hand, and took the other one in my mouth. I let my tongue slide over and then flick her nipple, gently biting it while I squeezed the other.

Ara let out a deep moan as her head tilted back. She ran her fingers through my hair as she pulled me harder into her chest. "More!"

I obliged and began pinching her other nipple, causing her to inhale sharply. She was perfect; I wanted to spend every minute of the day exploring her body. There was a deep need to give her as much pleasure as I possibly could. The fact that it had been years since the last time I had sex sure wasn't helping the situation either.

After several minutes of Ara writhing and moaning from her nipples being stimulated, she pushed me back ever so slightly. I looked into her eyes, worried I'd done something wrong. But that fear was forgotten when I saw her thumbs hook under the waistband of her sleep shorts as she pushed them down her legs.

To tell you I was hard is an understatement. My cock was so full; I wasn't sure how I had any blood left to keep me conscious. I licked my lips as she took off the shorts and threw them across the room. In the back of my mind, I realized her pussy was as smooth as Rui had mimicked that morning.

The thought barely crossed my mind when I felt a rush of air. Ara yelped in fright as her eyes widened, looking at something behind me. My heart froze in my chest as I prayed to anyone I could that it wasn't what I thought it was. Then, I felt something soft touch the back of my leg.

"Hi, Daddy!"

Chapter 18
Cat's Out Of The Bag

I'm not sure if I've made this very well-known yet, but I *hate* surprises. Like, with a passion. On a Kyle level, *hate*! So please tell me, why does an all-powerful, seemingly omniscient entity that's also a part of me enjoy jump-scaring me?! And, of course, it's at the very definition of wrong place, wrong time.

I nearly jumped out of my skin at Rui's voice behind me. Spinning, I stared in disbelief at the frustrating Neko, who, knowing how much she just scared me, smiled innocently back. On the one hand, I was thankful she was wearing clothes this time. But on the other, I now had a very frightened and confused Ara pressing her bare chest into my back.

"STOP DOING THAT!" I bellowed, clutching my chest in a vain attempt to calm my racing heart. "What are you doing here?!"

Rui tilted her head slightly, looking me up and down before flicking her eyes toward Ara. The Neko smiled wider and crossed her arms behind her back, pressing her chest out even further. It didn't slip my notice that she was still imitating Ara's body, with her breasts pressed against the thin blue fabric of her wraps. It was a strange mixture of sexuality and innocence as she leaned forward, pouting her lip slightly.

"Aww, don't be like that, Daddy! I wanted to ask if I did good earlier. That *was* what you wanted me to do when you were talking to the director, right?"

I took several deep breaths and closed my eyes for a few seconds, trying to stop myself from snapping at her again. The anger from earlier came back and was now mixing with the sexual desire I was experiencing with Ara and the new frustration with Rui's sudden appearance. But I knew I owed the troublesome Neko big time. Without her help, who knows how that all would have ended?

"Yes, thank you," I said, looking back at her. "I was going to thank you later. In private. Without anyone else around."

Rui's eyes widened, and I could physically see her smile change from one of happiness to one filled with dirty intentions. That was when I realized how what I just said could've been interpreted. I violently shook my head and waved my hands as if I could wipe away the words. "No! Not like that, Rui. I meant so I didn't have to explain you to anyone else. Everyone already thinks I'm crazy as it is!"

"What are you talking about?" Ara finally spoke up from behind me, and I could feel the tips of her nails starting to press into my sides. "What's going on? Who is she? And why does she keep calling you Daddy?"

I sighed and dropped my head in defeat. God damn it. I knew Rui would get me in hot water at some point, but this was literally the worst possible time for her to pull something like this. I'm pretty sure I've gone past blue balls and entered dark indigo with as much pent-up sexual tension I've experienced lately.

"It's . . . It's a long story," I grumbled, turning to face Ara. I was surprised to see the look she was giving me wasn't one of anger or even fear. It looked more like simple curiosity. "This . . . is Rui. Don't worry; she's friendly. Overly so, in fact. She's very . . . damn it. In all honesty, she's a fucking menace. But she *is* very helpful. When she wants to be. She's my Rift User Interface."

"Wait," Ara said, shaking her head and giving me a skeptical look. "A Rift User Interface? I've never heard of that before. Do all Rifters have them?"

"Nope! Only Daddy!" Rui answered for me, a sense of pride in her voice.

"I think it would be better to let her try to explain it," I said, motioning toward Rui. "You're smarter than I am. Maybe you can make better sense of what she's saying than I could."

Ara arched one eyebrow at me in confusion but then turned her focus on Rui. I looked around the floor to find Ara's clothes but couldn't see them anywhere. Though, to her credit, it appeared she wasn't worried about being naked in front of the curious Neko anymore. Leaning back onto her hands, Ara freely exposed her perky nipples without even a second thought. Wait a second. Could she be a closet exhibitionist? This was a side of her I never knew existed. And I'd be lying if I said I didn't think it was hot.

Rui hopped over to the bed and climbed beside Ara, sitting on her knees. The Neko's smile was enormous as she looked the naked woman up and down. "Wow, you're so sexy! Now I know why all three of them want to be with you. Can I join in, too?"

"RUI!" I yelled, my face growing hotter from embarrassment. "This isn't the time, place, or anything else! For the love of all things good in the world, will you please behave for five minutes?"

Rui's face dropped, and she looked down at the mattress. Even her ears drooped, and her tail lay still behind her. The sight sent a bolt of guilt through my chest, and I had an uncontrollable urge to apologize and try to make it up to the eccentric Neko.

I felt a slap on my arm from behind, and Ara shot me a stern glare. "Don't be mean, Turtle! She isn't hurting anyone. It's not like I didn't already know about you three. I mean, I'm lying naked in your bed. Besides, Honey, Sara, and I've already discussed the arrangements for the three of us. And after hearing what she said this morning, I'm sure Lynriel will be getting in on it soon, too. So it's fine if Rui wants to join. I've already told you I'm good with it as long as you're honest with me. Now be nice and let her talk."

"Wait, what?" I asked, turning to see her more fully. "What do you mean Honey, Sara, and you already—"

"Thank you, Ara," Rui interrupted me. Her smile had returned, and her ears pointed back up. "I know how he gets, so it's okay!"

I sighed and shook my head, feeling my blood pressure rising even higher. That's just what I needed. Honey and Sara are already a handful with their joking around and Honey's yandere tendencies. Now I have Lynriel and this deep connection we seem to share through the Sh'landriel and all *that* entails. Then, adding Rui in was like having pure, unfiltered chaos poured into the mix.

I mainly just want to make sure that Ara knows she isn't going to get lost in the mess all of the others are sure to cause.

"So, as Daddy said, I'm his Rift User Interface," Rui began, slightly bouncing up and down as she spent the next hour explaining things to Ara.

I'm not going to lie to you. I might've zoned out there for a little bit. In my defense, though, I've been living through it all in real-time. I didn't need reminders about any of it. It wasn't like she was saying anything I didn't already know.

By the end of the explanation and the few questions Ara was able to ask, she looked utterly overwhelmed. She leaned back against the headboard of my bed and stared out into nothingness as it all sank in. While she was processing, I turned my attention to Rui, who was focused on me now.

"Why did you show up right now?" I asked, trying to piece it together. "Why didn't you wait until I was alone? You know I was trying to keep some things secret. Particularly you."

Rolling her eyes, Rui crossed her arms under her chest as she huffed. "That's something every girl wants to hear."

"That's not . . . I didn't mean . . ." I sputtered, instantly feeling the need to try to clarify myself. "You know what I meant!"

Rui smirked and winked at me, her tail flicking playfully behind her back. "I know. I'm just teasing! But, a lot of stuff is about to happen, and like I've told you before, time's almost up."

"But what does that even mean?" I asked, throwing my arm out to gesture toward the window. "Time's almost up for what?

What's about to happen, and how do you expect me to do anything about it? I'm basically on house arrest right now!"

"Oh, ye of little faith," Rui said, using her tail to boop me on the nose. "I've already fixed both of your new watches. That one was on me the first time. I didn't think to monitor Ara's apartment to ensure no one was checking on her. But now that they know she's here, that'll be easy to deal with. The bad news is, she'll have to be a bigger part of this than you wanted."

I gritted my teeth and rubbed my eyes. Nothing could ever be simple, could it? "Part of what? You still haven't even told me what any of . . . *this* is!"

I saw Rui's shoulders drop slightly, and her smile faded. But it was different than when I scolded her. It looked more like she was tired. A heavy weight that I couldn't see was resting on her shoulders, and she'd been keeping me from noticing.

"I . . . I don't know," Rui said quietly. "I just know something big is about to happen, and you're the only one that can do anything about it. I'm sorry. I really want to help, honestly! I just . . . don't know."

I stared at the now stoic Neko, studying her every move. This could be another trick for her to mess with me. But I didn't think that was the case. She was annoying and frustrating and tap danced all over my last nerve, but she didn't seem like the type to outright lie to me. Maybe it was the soft spot I had for pretty girls in trouble, or perhaps it was because she was a part of me. Something just told me she was telling the truth.

I sighed and rested my hand on her head, gently scratching between the two orange cat ears sticking up. Rui seemed to melt, and a soft purring came from her chest. Her tail flicked contentedly behind her back as she looked up at me with large, yellow eyes. I smiled as I pulled my hand away, trying to think about what to do next.

"So, wait," Ara said, finally rejoining the conversation. "You're able to change our watches and even the logs in the RRS system, right?"

Turning to give Ara her attention, Rui nodded. Her soft orange tail snaked around and rested on my lap as she looked at the naked woman. "Yes, that stuff was simple."

"Can you go back and look into their files? Maybe see what missions they have coming up?" Ara asked, an excitement in her voice. "I'm sure whatever's going on, they're going to have something to do with it."

Rui tilted her head slightly as her ear twitched several times. Besides that subtle movement, she remained utterly motionless. It was a bit unnerving to see someone be that still. Not even her chest moved to indicate that she was breathing. Wait, does she breathe? Would a physical representation of an other-worldly being that existed outside of time and space need to breathe? I really should pay more attention when I interact with her.

After another full minute of complete silence, Rui slowly blinked, a confused look crossing her face. "That's . . . strange."

"What's strange?" I asked, an uneasy feeling beginning to fill my stomach.

"Yesterday, I discovered something odd about the RRS," Rui explained, her eyes still unfocused. "Despite being one of the youngest Realms *and* being so far behind others in development, almost all the known Realms report to the RRS. But that isn't the strangest thing. For me, accessing this world's technology takes nothing more than a quick thought. But just now, I found some files I can't get into. This Realm shouldn't have anything that could stop me from accessing it. Everything from nuclear codes to entire nations' defense systems is as easy to read as a book at the library. But . . . the RRS has some files I can't even access."

I let out a deep sigh and shook my head. "Of course they have technology so advanced a literal Goddess can't even open it."

Rui smiled, and her eyes widened as she looked at me. "Aww, Daddy! You think I'm a Goddess?"

I inwardly slapped myself for that. She wouldn't let me live that one down for a while. But I mean, technically, if what Lynriel said was right, Rui is part of the One, who was their God. So, that makes sense, right? Jesus, my head's hurting from all of this.

"Okay," Ara said, focusing back on what Rui mentioned. "That's obviously what we're looking for, right? I mean, if movies ever taught us anything, it's that the evil government agency is usually hiding something world-ending."

I stared at her for a long minute, feeling my attraction for the sassy British woman grow even more. "This is why we work."

Ara blushed and tried to hide her smile, but otherwise didn't stop her train of thought. "Well, what do we do now? It's not like they'll let us back in with open arms to pick through their secured database."

Rui's ears stood straight up, and I saw her back stiffen. I'd already seen it once that day and knew what it probably meant. The Neko smiled sheepishly as she flicked her tail at me one last time. "Do what you need to; just know that whatever's happening will happen soon. *Very* soon. Let Lynriel teach you how to control your jumping better. You know you can't always rely on your phone, right? Not that I mind being so close to your—"

"Rui!" I cut her off just as I felt the all-too-familiar pressure of the Rift opening.

In the blink of an eye, the overly sexual Neko was replaced with an ordinary-looking orange tabby sitting on my bed. Ara's mouth fell open as she stared into familiar yellow eyes. The pressure increased for less than a heartbeat before disappearing altogether, leaving Lynriel in the middle of my room, looking none too pleased.

"You absolute, idiotic, thick-headed—"

"Hey! Easy now; just calm down," I said, standing and raising my hands toward her in an attempt to calm the storm.

I know I'll sound like a broken record when I say this, but I think it bears repeating. I. Am. Not. A. Smart. Man. I just don't learn, do I?

Lynriel lunged forward and punched me in the stomach, causing all the air to rush from my body. I doubled over in pain, my mind going fuzzy from the strike. I tried to breathe, but my lungs decided to stay on vacation for a bit longer. A small hand gripped my chin and forced me to look up as I coughed violently.

Lynriel glared hard into my eyes, her crystal blue gaze boring deep into me. If I hadn't known better, I would have thought she'd been crying. The edges of her eyes looked red and puffy, but that could've been all in my head, as I couldn't make sense of the world at that particular moment.

"Don't you *ever* do something like that again!" Lynriel said through a clenched jaw. "Your life is no longer your own, don't you understand?! You have the single largest concentration of Sh'landriel I've ever seen fused inside your core. But more than that, we're bound together now! Do you have any idea how worried . . ."

Her words failed her as I saw the pain creep into her eyes. Well, if I didn't feel like a prolapsed anus before, I sure did now. Seeing the hurt she felt made me realize a couple of things. First, this whole 'bound' thing must make someone's emotions go *way* overboard. Second, something deep inside me wanted me to do whatever it took to make it up to her.

Before she could continue scolding me, I wrapped my arms around her. I hugged her tightly and felt her body tense momentarily before relaxing as she returned the embrace. That strange feeling I had since fusing with her Sh'landriel calmed, and warmth radiated through me. It's hard to explain, but I felt like I was home for the first time as we hugged, which was beyond inappropriate as my girlfriend was sitting naked on the bed just behind me.

That thought made me stiffen and quickly pull out of the embrace. I turned to look back at Ara, expecting her to be upset. Yet, the look she was giving me was one of love and happiness. It threw me off as I held my breath, waiting for the shoe to drop.

Ara chuckled and shook her head as she sat up, walking on her knees to the edge of the bed in front of me. She wrapped her arms around my neck and pulled me in for another passionate kiss. The points of her stiffening nipples pressed into my chest as our tongues danced with each other. I was lost in that kiss until she pulled back to look me in the eyes again.

"Don't worry so much, Turtle," Ara said, her voice playful as she gave me a toothy grin. "I told you, I'm okay with it. I know we need to discuss things more formally and set what each of our boundaries are. But I promise, I don't mind. Just don't fuck her before me, okay? After, though, go to town on all of them."

I heard her words, and her actions backed up everything she said. Yet, somewhere deep in my mind, Admiral Ackbar was screaming, "IT'S A TRAP!"

"Where are your clothes?" Lynriel asked, breaking into our shared moment.

"Bloody Hell," Ara gasped as if suddenly realizing she was still naked.

She tried her best to cover her breasts with one arm as she searched the floor for her discarded PJs. Neither of us could find them, so instead, she grabbed my shirt and put it on. Ara wasn't as small as Sara but was pretty close to it. So, seeing my 4XL shirt on her petite body was almost comical.

"Did you leave me in that rat-infested garbage pile just to come get your dick wet?" Lynriel asked, a new fire in her eyes.

"No," I said, shaking my head furiously. I did *not* want to get punched again. "I went to the facility and got Ara out. Swear to whatever God you want me to! We just got back here about an hour ago."

"An hour?" Lynriel scoffed and crossed her arms. "You've been here for an hour while I waited in that dank, dismal room, wondering if you were being tortured or worse?"

I sighed and dropped my shoulders in defeat. She got me on that one. My brain wasn't exactly doing the thinking by the time we'd gotten home. So, I had no one else to blame but myself.

"I'm sorry," I said, not knowing what else to do. "If it makes you feel any better, I ended up getting blue-balled."

Narrowing her eyes at me, Lynriel took a step closer. "What is 'blue-balled' and why would that make me feel better?"

"It means I got him all worked up, but he didn't get to pull his cock out yet," Ara said with a smile, winking at me as she started walking out of the room. "I'll call Honey and Sara and let them know we're here."

Great. Just what I needed. Another woman who thought it was funny to tease me to the point of exploding in my pants. Yay me!

"Oh," Lynriel said, the irritation in her voice gone as the slightest of smiles cracked her lips. "Well, then, that actually *does* make me feel a bit better."

"Lovely," I grumbled, sitting back on the bed. "So now that we're all done with that, I needed to talk to you about something."

Lynriel arched an eyebrow but stayed quiet as I continued.

"Something big is about to happen," I started. "I don't know what, and I don't know when. I don't even know where or why. But something big is about to happen, and I need to be prepared for it. You have the best understanding of the abilities given by the Rift I've ever seen. Can you teach me how to control mine better?"

Lynriel studied me for a long moment. I felt her eyes boring into me as she obviously debated whether she should help me or not. I'm sure she wasn't thrilled I might be throwing myself back into danger. But if Rui was right, I needed to be better prepared for whatever was coming.

"You want me to . . . teach you how to control the gifts from the One?" Lynriel asked, almost as if she was trying to make the words make sense. "What am I supposed to even teach you?"

I shrugged one shoulder and gave her as cocky of a grin as I could muster. "Well, I know I'm pretty awesome as it is, but anything new you can show me would be great."

"And what do I get out of this?" she asked, clearly already having something in mind.

Shrugging again, I motioned around the room aimlessly. "I mean, if there's something you want, just—"

"You'll owe me a favor, no questions asked," she said, interrupting me. "No talking back. No fighting me. Nothing. I call in this favor, and you oblige immediately."

I studied her, trying to gauge what she was thinking. In the back of my mind, Wallace's voice echoed the warning about Lynriel being an assassin and having already killed thousands of people.

I know he's utterly full of horseshit, but still, I couldn't be too careful.

"I won't hurt anyone," I said warily, tensing my muscles to flee if she took that poorly.

Lynriel shrugged one shoulder but kept her eyes locked on mine. To her credit, it didn't seem like my response insulted her in any kind of way. "I don't need you to. If I want to hurt someone, I can do it myself. Or would you like a demonstration?"

"Nope," I quickly answered with a shake of my head. "All good there. Okay. You have a deal. You teach me how to control this stuff better; I'll owe you a blank check."

Narrowing her eyes again, Lynriel placed her hands on her hips in irritation. "I don't want a 'blank check,' whatever that is. I want a favor of my choosing later on."

"That's . . ." I began to explain but decided just to let it go. "Okay, deal."

Lynriel smiled; this time, it looked much more sinister than before. "Good! But before we get started, I need you to tell me something. And I want *complete* honesty."

My heart suddenly stopped as a cold sweat formed on the back of my neck. It's never good when a woman says that. "Okay . . . What's that?"

Taking a few steps forward, Lynriel pressed herself into me, leaning barely an inch away from my face. I could smell a subtle sweetness on her breath as I gazed into her crystal blue eyes. "Who's that girl sitting on your bed pretending to be a cat?"

Chapter 19

This Is Making My Head Hurt

I would like to go on record right now and say I don't like lying. I don't like keeping secrets, nor do I like intentionally being deceitful. But, as an adult in the real world, I know that sometimes the truth should be filtered and kept close to the chest.

Rui was a secret that I knew eventually would have to come out. But, with everything that's been going on lately, I didn't think it was the best time to tell everyone about her. I mean, she's *really* hard to explain. And keep in mind, most of the stuff you've heard about so far has all happened in a two-day time frame. *It's a lot* to deal with.

My heart was frozen as I stared deep into Lynriel's eyes. I want to think I was playing it pretty cool, but deep down, I know I probably looked like a teenager who was just caught with his first porno magazine. I did everything in my power not to look at Rui, but the intensity of Lynriel's gaze made it impossible to keep eye contact with her.

Turning my head, I saw Rui was still in her cat form, staring at Lynriel. Her feline face was hard to read, but I could've sworn the cat also looked confused. I looked back at Lynriel and tried to smile as I shrugged my shoulders. "I don't know what you're talking about. It's just a cat."

Lynriel's eyes narrowed, and I felt an overpowering urge to cover my balls. "I said be honest with me. You want me to teach you, correct? That means you need to be able to trust me in all things. The same goes for me with you. So, who is she?"

I felt droplets of sweat bead down my neck as my mind raced to think of an answer. The decision was taken out of my hands when I felt the familiar shift in the air and heard the bed squeak slightly from the added weight. "How did you know? I was so careful!"

Lynriel turned and studied the pouting Neko sitting on my bed. I looked between the two, entirely at a loss for what to say. This was *not* how I wanted things to go. But I guess there wasn't any way for me to keep hiding it forever.

"Well," Lynriel began, crossing her arms under her chest as she smiled smugly at Rui. "First, I've seen your cat form at least four times, and your stripes changed every time. Second, I can sense the Sh'landriel in you. Though it does feel different than any I've encountered in the past. And finally, this morning, I watched your . . . let's call it a wake-up call?"

I got to witness something I'd never imagined I'd see. Rui was speechless. Her jaw hung as she stared at Lynriel. "But . . . I . . . You were . . ."

"I'm a Princess of Ellyssia and the destined vessel of the One," Lynriel smirked. "I've been at this for a *very* long time. I can see through such . . . childish antics."

Rui narrowed her eyes, and she glared at the woman. "It's only because I'm not fully operational yet. Just wait. I'll wipe that smile right off your face!"

"Hey," I said, stepping in between the two. "Rui, don't hurt our friends. And Lyn, you don't have to be so smug about everything."

Rui's ears dropped, and she looked down at the floor. It's not surprising, as the Neko didn't like being scolded. What surprised me, however, was when Lynriel did almost the same thing. Her eyes dropped to the ground, and I could see a look of what I assume was . . . shame? What the hell is up with these women lately?

"Sorry, Daddy," Rui mumbled as she flicked an invisible thread on the mattress.

I sighed and shook my head. There wasn't enough aspirin in the world to deal with the headache that had been building up over the past few days. Placing my hand on Rui's head again, I scratched between her ears. As before, that seemed to cheer her up, and she began to purr slightly.

"Listen, you told me that I need to be prepared for what's coming up, and I need Lyn's help. This is the exact opposite of how I wanted to approach this, but we can't help that now. I'm going to check on Ara, and you can be the broken record again. Try to explain everything before I get back."

Rui's ears drooped again, but she didn't put up any resistance. Instead, she just nodded as she continued looking down at the mattress. Then I turned to Lynriel, who'd been watching my interaction with Rui with a curious stare.

"And you, *Princess*, don't act like you always know everything. You're not on your own anymore. There *will* be things you don't know or need help with. And that's okay. Listen to Rui and see if y'all can't maybe learn a thing or two from each other. We're all on the same team in the end."

Trying to regain some of her pride, Lynriel tilted her chin up and put on a look of subtle boredom. "Fine. Whatever. I doubt she'll tell me anything I don't already know. But I guess there's no harm in hearing what the kitten has to say."

"DADDY!" Rui growled in irritation.

I decided it was time for me to step out. If they wanted to go after each other, I highly doubted someone like me could stand between them. "Behave, you two!"

"You're okay letting her call you that?" Lynriel asked as I reached for the door.

I let out a long sigh and shook my head. "I've reached the acceptance stage of grief at this point."

Walking out into the hallway, I closed the door loudly behind me to press my point that I was done. I heard voices coming from the living room, so I went down the narrow hall until the three women sitting on the sofa came into view. Honey and Sara sat on either side of Ara, who was still wearing only my discarded T-shirt. The women each had an arm around Ara's shoulders as they discussed what had happened at the RRS. As I came into view, though, their attention turned to me.

From two, I saw looks of love and kindness. One, however, was glaring at me so hard I'm sure I would've burst into flames if she had the ability. "Honey, I can explain."

"Explain?" Honey asked, her teeth clenched behind a tight smile. "Oh, you mean about how you thought it would be a good idea to jump *directly* into the middle of the corrupt government agency that's not only coming after you but all of us as well? Or maybe how you somehow got out of there over *an hour ago* and just failed to tell us anything about it? Is that what you wanted to explain?"

Nothing will make me clench my sphincter as tight as seeing that look Honey was giving me. I would bet hard money that if Ara weren't sitting right there, I'd probably already be on the ground holding a certain appendage while I writhed in agony. Thank all the Gods for Ara!

"Babe, we talked about this. . ." Sara said softly, stroking Honey's arm that rested around Ara's shoulders. "If we want this to work—"

"I know, I know," Honey huffed. She closed her eyes and took a deep breath. And then another. And another. Several more later, she reopened her eyes, and I saw the anger behind her gaze had dulled into mild irritation. "I'm sorry, Turtle. I *know* you had your reasons. I *know* you're doing what you feel is best. But, please, for all of us. Remember, you're not alone. We're in this together, okay?"

There's nothing like having the same sentiments I *just* stressed to Lynriel get thrown back into my face. The universe is a bit of a bitch that way. Listen here, I don't need my own advice, thank you very much! I'm perfectly fine being a hypocrite. Damn universe or destiny or whatever you are.

I let out a long sigh and slumped down into my recliner beside the girls. "You're right. I'm sorry. But when I got that text from Ara, I just couldn't—"

"What text?" Ara interrupted, looking confused. "I haven't texted you at all today."

That took me by surprise. "What? Right before I went to the facility, you texted me, 'Help.' I jumped straight there as soon as I got it."

Ara shook her head, her brows furrowing even more in confusion. "Turtle, I didn't have my phone. It was here the whole time."

What in the hell is going on? I pulled out my phone and opened the messages app. Sure enough, right at the top was Ara's plea for help. I turned my screen around and showed them the text. Ara reached her hand under Sara, who squealed and squirmed playfully. Pulling out her phone from under the woman, Ara opened it and scrolled through her messages.

"What the . . . I . . . I didn't send this!"

Honey and Sara looked at her phone, noting the time stamp. "We were here, but I didn't send that. Did you, babe?"

Honey shook her head, also trying to figure out the mystery. "No. And even still, it was locked. Didn't you see she just used her fingerprint to open it? There's no way we could've sent anything."

We all sat in silence, thinking about who could have done something like that. I only knew of one person, and she was currently too preoccupied for me to ask. But it didn't seem like something Rui would do either. She was relatively direct, all things considered. Don't get me wrong, she's still confusing as hell and talks in riddles sometimes, but she hasn't lied to me or tried to deceive me like that. If she had wanted me at the RRS, she would've had no problem telling me through another system notification.

"Okay, what's go—"

"Finished," Lynriel interrupted as she walked from the hallway, stopping directly in front of my chair.

I was honestly shocked that she was done already. There's no way they covered everything so quickly. It took Rui over an hour to explain things to Ara. On top of that, I've been living through it all, yet *I* still don't fully understand a good chunk of what was happening. How could they have covered all of it in the span of . . . five minutes?!

Lynriel crossed her arms under her chest as she stared at me expectantly. I tried to subtly look at her hands to see if they had any blood on them. She might not have talked about everything in five minutes, but she could've tried to kill Rui in that time. As if reading my mind, Lynriel rolled her eyes and let out a long sigh.

"No, I didn't kill her," she said with a huff.

"Kill? Kill who?!" Honey shot up, fear filling her voice as she looked around.

"I said I *didn't* kill her," Lynriel said, motioning toward the hall just as an orange tabby cat slowly walked into the living room.

Honey gasped and ran over to scoop up Rui into a tight hug. "I swear to God, if you lay a hand on my—"

"Sara," I said, giving the blonde a quick look.

"On it," Sara said, standing and wrapping her arm around Honey. "Babe, remember . . . we breathe out the bad thoughts, and . . . we don't give them a voice."

Grumbling under her breath, Honey took a few deep breaths before kissing Rui several times on the head and whispering something into her ear. I can only imagine what she said had to be something negative about Lynriel because Rui began to purr louder and nuzzle her cheek. These women are going to be the death of me: each and every one of them.

"Girls, Lyn and I need to talk and then do some . . . training of sorts," I said, slowly standing from my chair.

Honey narrowed her eyes at me and then Lynriel. "What kind of training? You going to strip naked and pin her down again?"

"That'll come later," Lynriel said, shooting her a wicked grin. "If the rest of his harem is going to leave him with blue balls, it's only natural that I, as the one he's bound to, should alleviate them. Don't you think?"

Jesus, she learned the phrase not even ten minutes ago, and she's already using it. But at this point, I've had my ass thoroughly handed to me by the elf princess a few different times. And I could honestly say I didn't know who I should be more scared of. Lynriel had experience and training. Honey had that Latina temper and enough crazy to fill the entire Rift. The look Honey gave Lynriel made it clear no breathing exercises were about to fix this.

"HOW *DARE* YOU?!" Honey shouted, dropping Rui and stepping toward the princess. "You're the *last* one he'll be sleeping with! If anyone's going to do that, it'll be Ara or m—"

"AND ON THAT NOTE," Sara yelled, pulling Honey away and down the hall. "We're going to go talk about some things back here if you need us! Ara, you're welcome to join unless you need to do that . . . training or whatever with them."

As Sara dragged her down the hallway, Honey pointed at me while making eye contact. "AND YOU! I'M GPS-ING YOUR ASS AGAIN TONIGHT!"

Ara looked at me, a bemused look on her face. She arched an eyebrow, which I took as her asking if she needed to stay. I shook my head and let out a deep breath. "Why don't you go with them? You're not going to be able to do . . . well, whatever I'm about to do."

Standing, Ara approached me and stood on her tiptoes, planting a sweet kiss on my lips. "I'll talk to Honey more, too. If this is going to work for all of us, she'll need to get that jealousy in check. Now, you two don't have too much fun. And if you do, cold water works best to clean it up."

Before I could respond, she disappeared down the hallway, followed by a streaking orange ball of fluff. Cold water? What did she mean by . . . oh. OH! God damn it, Ara. Not you, too!

"Why do you have to antagonize Honey so much?" I asked, retaking my seat. "We're all on the same side here."

Lynriel's face twisted in irritation as she motioned back down the hallway. "*Me*?! It's *her*! She's been nothing but hostile towards me."

"Well, in her defense, her first impression of you is you attacking me in the nude," I said with a shrug.

Lynriel's cheeks turned a deep crimson. "That . . . I-I wasn't . . . I was only topless. *You* were the nude one!"

"I was nude because you attacked me right after I got out of the shower," I said with a slight smile. "I mean, if you wanted to see my dick that bad, all you had to do was ask."

It took about ten seconds before Lynriel couldn't hold my gaze any longer, and she turned in a huff. "Pervert."

I laughed and shook my head. I knew this conversation wasn't going to go anywhere. But it felt good to have some banter between us. Everything was getting too serious, so being able to poke fun a bit made it slightly more bearable.

"I find it hard to believe that you got through everything with Rui in such a short time," I said, trying to bring the focus back to the task at hand. "It took her over an hour with Ara."

"Well, most of what she had to say, I already knew," Lynriel said with a shrug as she sat on the edge of the couch. "But I'll admit, she did have *some* useful information. And now, I think I know where to begin with your training."

I arched an eyebrow in surprise, and I felt genuine excitement. I don't think I'd ever been actually happy to learn something before. This was very new to me. "Awesome! Where do we begin?"

"I think I'm going to have to teach you some fundamentals first," Lynriel said with an exacerbated sigh. "Your race doesn't seem to teach you *how* to navigate the currents of the Pathways. You simply allow them to rip you out into nothingness and rely on your technology to guide you where you're going."

"There's another way?" I asked, genuinely surprised. "I've talked to those even in the other Realms who can ju— I mean, travel the Pathways, and they all seem to be doing the same thing."

Slowly nodding, Lynriel pinched the bridge of her nose in frustration. "That's what I gathered from the kitten. By the way, *what* is she? I've never seen a race like that before. I mean, I understand she's a part of the One. But when her Sh'landriel attached to your desire, you shaped her into that. What race is she?"

I blinked several times as I let that nugget of information sink in. "I'm sorry, I did what now? She's attached to where?"

Lynriel gave me a blank stare, probably wondering if I was messing with her. But this was all brand new information to me. "You *are* aware that when someone is able to fuse with a Sh'landriel, it latches onto one of their emotions, don't you? It's how you access the power of the One. You only need to tap into and open yourself to its power. The downside is that it can make that emotion a bit . . . overactive? That Rui-girl told me her Sh'landriel was fused into your desire. That's why she's so . . . sexual with you? That's also why she seems to always know exactly what you want. Probably even better than yourself. When you desire something, she's the first to know. Did she not tell you this? She said she explained it to

Ara after getting permission to join your . . . wait, did she really not tell you?"

I kicked myself hard. This is what I get for not paying attention while they were talking. I knew I shouldn't have zoned out so much. Stupid Turtle!

"No," I said with a long sigh. "But, that . . . makes a lot of sense now that you're saying it. She does seem to instantly know the second I'm wanting something. And It's been really weird having her be so sexual and calling me . . . well, you know. Yet, somewhere deep inside, it kind of felt . . . right? Natural? And I have to admit, ever since the day I fused with her Sh'landriel, I've had some pretty intense . . . thoughts and urges. So if having one attached to an emotion makes it overactive, that would explain why I'm having a hard time controlling myself."

I thought about it for a minute. If Rui is attached to my desire, what does that mean for me in the long run? While I was glad for the new information, it made a pit in the bottom of my stomach. I wasn't the most 'innocent' person out there, to say the least. And now an all-powerful entity shares my . . . oh, God help us all!

"Wait," I said, arching an eyebrow at her. "What emotions are yours attached to?"

Lynriel's face and ears turned a bright red, and she quickly looked away. "It's . . . inappropriate to ask someone that."

"Come on," I said, grinning at her blushing cheeks. "You know mine. Besides, aren't we bound now? Shouldn't you be able to trust the person you're bound to?"

I watched Lynriel's jaw clench several times as she obviously fought an inner battle. After a solid minute of silence, she let out a long huff of air before turning back to look at me. "Fine. But I'm only telling you this because it affects you as well. Mine is connected to anger. It's why I tend to lose my temper so quickly. I'm not proud of it, but I can't do anything about it, either. Saying that . . . the most recent Sh'landriel that fused into your core were originally bound to me. This means that our emotions are now linked as well. At least as far as I can tell. Ever since you saved me and we became bound together, I've been having difficulties controlling certain . . . desires."

"Wait, so—"

"Yes," Lynriel scoffed again. "I've never had these kinds of urges before. The binding already makes us want to be as close to each other as possible. But what I'm feeling now is much more . . . primal than that. I know you sense it, too, so don't lie and say you don't. Our desires will only grow, fueled even more so by the binding of the Sh'landriel. I'm sure that's why what happened earlier . . . happened. The more Sh'landriel attached to an emotion, the stronger it'll become."

I shook my head and rubbed my eyes, trying to let that sink in. "Why are they all on that one emotion? Wouldn't they get attached to different ones?"

"No," Lynriel said. "Whatever emotion your first one attaches to, the others will too. They're constantly trying to fuse back together, after all. Your first one must've been fused into your core during a time of great desire. Do you remember when it happened and what you were doing?"

I thought back and tried to remember the SRE. Honey and Sara had left to do something, so I was home alone and on bed rest. I remembered being excited that I could finally have some alone time to . . . wait. Seriously?! That's why it's attached to my desire?!

"Anyway," I said, clearing my throat as I changed the subject. "To answer your original question about Rui, as far as I know, it's not a *real* race. We call what she is either a cat girl or Neko. It's an imaginary being from another country in our world. Usually found in comics, video games, and cartoons."

"And what are those?" Lynriel asked, sitting forward on the seat of the couch.

I keep forgetting she's not from around here. Of course, a five-millennia-old elf warrior princess wouldn't know what anime is. I mean, if it weren't for the translator chip, she and I probably wouldn't even be able to talk to each other. That thought made me think of something else.

Before coming across Lynriel, I'd never heard of her kind before. I didn't think anyone had. Yet, Wallace seemed to know a lot about her and her Realm. And now that I'm thinking about it, my translator chip has been working with her, meaning her language is in our Database. The same Database that not even Rui could break into now.

"It's not important," I said, waving off her question. "I'll show you later if you want. But now that you talked to Rui, you know everything I know. So, where should we begin our training? I don't think we have very much time."

Lynriel smiled, cracking her neck in a very menacing way as she stood from the couch. "A test of strength! Let's see if those big muscles of yours are just for show or if they're actually good for something."

Chapter 20
Cue Training Montage!

I want to start by saying I'm not out of shape. I run six to ten miles a couple times a week and go to the gym with Sara every other day when possible. I even came in fourth in a weightlifting competition last year. I'm not a meathead, but I stay enough in shape that I can take care of myself in a fight if I ever need to. And when I was a bouncer, I needed to pretty frequently.

So when I tell you that Lynriel's 'test' made me feel like my heart would explode and every muscle fiber in my body was being torn to shreds, know I'm serious about it! After two hours, I was lying in a heap on the ground in our backyard, gasping for air as I felt the blood being shot through my arteries at mock-Jesus speeds. I'd long torn off the replacement shirt I'd put on right before we began and now lay shirtless on the grass, staring into the afternoon sky.

Lynriel appeared above me, looking down at my broken body with a smirk on her face. "Not too bad for a non-Ellyssian. You were actually able to make it through my warm-up routine. I'm impressed."

"Warm . . ." I gasped out as I tried to focus on her. "Up? I . . . nearly . . . died!"

To her credit, Lynriel had barely begun to sweat. That was impressive, considering she'd been doing everything right alongside me the entire time. If she was able to do all of that and more, how the fuck was I able to get the upper hand on her during our fight?

Snorting a small laugh, Lynriel sat on the grass beside me, pulling my head into her lap. It was a bit of an awkward angle, but her thighs were soft, and something about it made me feel extremely relaxed. To my surprise, she raked her fingers through my hair as she looked deep into my eyes.

"You should be proud," she said with a smile. Her voice was gentle, and there was even a hint of laughter behind her words. "No one else has been able to keep up with me like that—not even my trainers toward the end. I've never met a man who could do even half of that without quitting or complaining in some way. Not you, though. You did it all."

I tried to give her my cocky grin, but I was still breathing too damn hard to pull it off. "That's . . . right. I'm . . . awesome like that!"

Lynriel snorted again and shook her head as she looked around the yard. I could tell she was thinking about something, but it felt wrong to ask her about it. She'd been through even more than I had lately. Just two days ago, she was a prisoner about to be sold into a life of slavery or worse. Not to mention thousands of years traveling through the Rift alone, trying to complete an all-but-impossible task. All to eventually give up her own life to resurrect some God. Or, I guess, if she's the vessel . . . Goddess?

But now I'm in the mix, and we're bound. Even though I'm still not 100% sure what that entailed, I got the point that she and I would fuse to become the One. So, let's just go with the term gender-neutral deity. That way, all bases are covered.

"Does the One have a name?" I asked, finally able to breathe somewhat normally. "Like the different religions here, all their Gods have names. Or is it just the One?"

Lynriel thought for a moment before looking down at me. I could see some uncertainty behind her eyes as she studied my face. "Yes . . . but it's forbidden to say to any who are not from Ellyssia."

"Oh, no worries," I said with a nod of acknowledgment. "I understand. I just wanted to learn more about you and your people."

Narrowing her eyes slightly, Lynriel seemed to go on guard. That was when I remembered what Wallace said about not knowing much about their Realm. There was likely a good reason for that.

"Why?"

I shook my head and tried to give her a reassuring smile. "No reason. I just think you're fascinating. You're the embodiment of what I've always fantasized about. You're a badass, drop-dead sexy, elven warrior princess!"

Lynriel's ears and cheeks burned a bright red as she blushed and looked away. "O-Oh. Thank you. But I'm not that sexy. You should've seen my sisters—the true princesses. Their beauty was unmatched throughout all the Realms. Compared to them, I'm incredibly ordinary."

"Hey," I said, raising my hand and awkwardly touching her cheek. "You're gorgeous. Do you know the description they gave me when asking about you? They said that your beauty rivaled all the Gods. And I actually agree with them on that. But don't get me wrong, that isn't what defines you. You're talented, cunning, incredibly intelligent, and by far the best fighter I've ever seen! And do you know how brave you are just for going up against Honey as brazenly as you have?! Don't disparage yourself!"

Lynriel's face grew even more crimson, and she refused to look me in the eye. It was sweet, even if it felt weird compared to her normal personality. I felt like I was getting to see the real Lynriel. The one no one else had ever met before.

"Hey!" Sara's voice rang out from behind Lynriel, where I couldn't see. "We're going to take Ara to grab some stuff from her apartment and then head to the store to get things for dinner. Are you guys going to eat with us?"

"What are you making?" I called back, my mouth watering at the thought of Sara's home cooking.

"She's making what she's making," Honey responded. "You're going to eat it no matter what it is."

Half shrugging, I looked up at Lynriel with a sly grin. "Well, she's not wrong."

Before I could say anything, I heard the door close and knew they'd already left. I decided it was probably best to get up so we could keep training. Slowly, I stood, my legs feeling like rubber as

I did. Lynriel offered me her hand for support, but I declined. I needed to be able to do this on my own. I just had to push through the pain first.

"Okay, what's next?" I asked, stretching out my arms to bring them back to life.

"You should rest," Lynriel said, shaking her head. "You don't need to push yourself so hard."

Waving off her concern, I cracked my neck and was rewarded with three loud pops. "Nah, I'm good. I seriously don't know how much time we have until . . . whatever's going to happen, happens. I need to be stronger to protect you and the others."

Lynriel stared, looking at me like I'd just grown another head. "W-What? I don't need you to protect me! I'm a Princess of—"

"Yeah, yeah, yeah," I said with another wave of my hand. "I'm *beyond* aware that you can take care of yourself. That doesn't mean I can't try to protect you. We're bound, remember? I'm not just going to sit back and watch as someone tries to hurt you. If they want you, they'll have to go through me first. And I fight dirty. I told you about when I saved Ara from the Marrog, right?"

Lynriel stared at me as if she had difficulty understanding what I was saying. I even began to question if my translator chip was jacking up. It's supposed to seamlessly translate anything I say into the person's native language. But then again, Ellyssia has been kept a secret from most people, so who knows if the Database is complete.

But as I saw a single tear form at the edge of her eye, I understood she was just surprised someone was willing to do that for her. She'd been trained to be a warrior her entire life. It hadn't sounded like she'd been shown much love or compassion as a child *or* adult. Before I could say anything about it, though, Lynriel wiped her eye and looked away.

"Well," she said as she cleared her throat. "If you're so stubborn that you want to risk injuring yourself further, I better go slow. If I anger Honey again, you might have to prove those words and protect me from her."

I winced at the thought. Don't get me wrong; Honey is small enough that I could easily throw her over my shoulder with one arm. But I would *not* be coming away from that without making some sacrifices.

"Alright," Lynriel said, refocusing herself. "Let's start with precision . . . jumping? I think that's the word you keep using. How have you been doing it the past few days?"

"Rui's phone," I said with a shrug.

Narrowing her eyes, Lynriel looked me up and down. "What is a phone?"

I sighed and shook my head. There had to be a better way to explain things. Maybe I could have Sara or Ara give her some kind of technology and idioms class? Either way, it wasn't going to happen tonight.

"It's a piece of technology," I said, motioning to my phone lying on the patio's step. "But there's going to be plenty of times I won't be able to rely on it."

Lynriel looked at the phone and then back at me with a sigh. "Alright, well, close your eyes."

I followed her instructions. Without my vision, I leaned on my other senses to track my surroundings. I felt the heat from the slowly setting sun bathing my skin. The warm breeze dried some of the sweat from my workout. The sound of birds and insects filled the air around me, and I felt the ever-present pulsing of the Rift high above.

"Everything is connected through the Pathways," Lynriel said, her voice taking the tone of a teacher instructing a class. "There's a push and pull of energy that will either draw you near or propel you away. Do you feel it?"

I tried my best, but at the moment, the only thing I felt like that was coming directly from the Rift. "Not really. Other than coming from above us, I don't . . ."

My words trailed off as Lynriel placed a hand on my chest, and I felt her body press close to me. I kept my eyes closed, but I could feel the heat radiating off her skin and a strum of energy connecting us even deeper than our physical touch. "Do you feel that?"

"Yes," I said, my voice soft as the urge to pull her closer grew.

"Focus on this," Lynriel's voice was thick, heavy with intent. "Your Sh'landriel are fused into your desire, so feel it build deep within. Want it with every fiber in your being. Desire is associated with many other feelings like passion, lust, and even fear. All will cause you to desire something. You need to want to feel the connection to all things."

At that moment, the only thing I desired was to take Lynriel inside and fuck her until neither of us could walk straight, even though I knew that was wrong. Ara made it clear she was okay with Lynriel and me being physical with each other, which made things easier. However, one of the boundaries set was that I didn't do anything until after Ara and I had been together. So, I needed to fight my baser urges a bit longer.

I forced myself to turn my attention to the world around me. I tried to think about how much I wanted to feel what Lynriel was describing, but nothing was happening. It all still felt the same. We stood there for long minutes while I struggled to get any kind of push or pull. Nothing. Nada. Zip.

Sighing in frustration, I finally opened my eyes. I was greeted with the crystal blue of Lynriel's irises only a few inches from me. They reminded me of those almost unnaturally clear pools of water you'd find in glaciers. And just like with those pools, I could fall into Lynriel's eyes and drown if I wasn't careful.

I stepped back and cleared my throat, motioning broadly around us. "I don't feel anything other than what's coming from the Rift."

Lynriel looked slightly disappointed that I stepped away, but she quickly regained her composure. "Well, it normally takes years to perfect, and you want to learn it in an afternoon? Give us both some slack here."

I nodded, knowing she was right. I couldn't expect to learn the secrets of the universe in a single day. It'll take at least a long weekend—five to seven business days max.

We stayed in the yard for another three hours. Lynriel talked to me about the relationship matter had to space, the Pathways, and on and on. I might've zoned out a time or two there. Hey, I'm not perfect! This is why I didn't finish college, okay?

The smell of Sara's cooking reached us before much longer, and our stomachs growled simultaneously. I cocked an eyebrow at Lynriel as I motioned toward the house. "How about we call it a night and get something to eat?"

Nodding, Lynriel turned and headed back. I followed right behind, doing my best not to stare at her perfectly toned ass in the yoga pants she'd borrowed from Honey. The struggle is real!

As we entered the house, we were greeted with the most fantastic smell anyone could walk into. *Fajitas*! And not just any fajitas, but *Sara's fajitas*! She was searing the steak as we walked past, and my mouth watered, seeing the pile of freshly made tortillas sitting on the counter. Honey was putting her guacamole on the table while Ara finished setting out the beans and rice.

Looking up as I walked into the room, Ara smiled and bounded up to me. She'd changed and was now wearing a white shirt and extremely short running shorts that barely covered her backside. "So? How'd it go?"

"He has some of the best stamina I've ever seen," Lynriel answered, walking past Ara and grabbing the water bottle Honey was trying to hand me. "In all the Realms, no one has come close to keeping up with me like that. I look forward to what else his endurance can do."

That last bit was said with an evil grin toward Honey. I inwardly groaned, anticipating the angry response. Yet, it didn't come. Instead, Honey smiled back, almost sickeningly sweet. "Oh, darling.

You better hope he has that kind of endurance because there's already a few of us ahead of you in line."

"Girls," I sighed, stepping forward. "Calm down. Lyn, we *just* talked about you easing up on Honey. And Honey, Lyn doesn't know you're joking around."

Lynriel's smile dropped, and she silently bobbed her head as she drank the remainder of the water. But Honey's face scrunched up, and she looked at me. "I'm not—"

"Babe," Sara called out from the kitchen, cutting Honey off. "Come help me for a minute, okay?"

Honey let out a sigh and sulked her way to the kitchen. That girl. I've gotten used to her and Sara messing around like that. But she doesn't understand that others like Lynriel or Ara might not catch on to the fact that they're joking.

I turned my focus back to Ara, who still stood smiling at me. God, she was beautiful! I don't even think she's wearing any make-up. She's just naturally pretty like that. "The training was good. I'm exhausted, and it'll be a surprise if I can walk tomorrow. There's still a lot to learn, though."

"Have you thought about what you're going to do about the deadline?" Ara asked, her smile slipping as she remembered Wallace's threat.

I shook my head and let out a long sigh. "Not really. I think I'll get y'all out of here first. Somewhere neither he nor the agency will find you. Then I can—"

"Like hell you are!" Honey yelled from the kitchen. She stormed up to me and poked me hard in the chest. "I know *exactly* what you're thinking, Turtle. It's *not* happening!"

"What?" I asked, trying to feign ignorance.

"NO!" She yelled, poking me again. "If I have to tie you to that bed, I will. Don't test me."

Ara gave us a confused look before turning to Honey. "What do you think he's going to do?"

Honey glared at me, daring me to open my mouth. Damn it. She does know me better than anyone. As soon as Ara told her about Wallace's deadline, I'm sure it took Honey less than a minute to figure out what I would do.

"You said they want that…shard thing that's inside him, right?" Honey asked Ara, pointing her thumb at me. "And they couldn't care less about us or even Ms. Pointy Ears over there?"

"HEY!" Lynriel shouted while trying to cover the tips of her ears.

"Yeah?" Ara answered, looking back at me.

Damn it. I saw the light come on behind Ara's eyes as she finally connected the dots to what Honey was accusing me of. "You . . . You're not going to turn yourself in, are you?"

I let out a long sigh, shaking my head. "I mean, it's not my preferred option. I do have . . . someone else I still need to talk to about things. But right now, my best bet to protect all of you is to give them what they want."

You could hear a pin drop. It felt like all the air had been sucked out the room, and the angry gaze of four women bore into me. Have I mentioned before I'm not an intelligent man?

Within the next breath, I had four thunderous voices yelling at me, telling me how stupid I was. Yup, I should've expected that. Though, I never intended to tell any of them this face-to-face. I was planning on jumping them to the other side of the world and leaving a note so they wouldn't do exactly what they were doing now.

I let them get the anger and frustration out for a few minutes before I finally had to cut it off. They had the right to chew me out, but this all really did fall on me. That, and I was fucking starving and wanted to eat already! "Ladies, I hear you. I'm sure the neighbors heard you. I promise I'm not giving up trying to figure out something else. But if it comes down to y'all or me? I'm turning myself over to them without a second thought."

They all got silent. The tension in the air was palpable. I saw the steak had been sliced and was ready to be served, so I smiled and waved back to the table. "Let's eat, okay? Can't we enjoy dinner without any of this drama? Please?"

Each woman nodded and silently returned to work, getting everything to the table. I sat in my seat as Sara stepped beside me, bending over to put the meat on the serving tray. She smiled at me and winked as she shook her ass right beside my face. I'm glad she was getting back into a playful mood, at least.

Ara sat on my left, and Lynriel was on my right. Honey and Sara sat on the opposite side of the table, and we began making our plates. I was so far past starving; I could've eaten everything myself.

Lynriel watched as we made our tacos, and I kicked myself yet again for forgetting she had no idea what any of this was. I quickly showed her how to make the perfect fajita. As she took her first bite, her eyes almost popped out of her face as she stared at the culinary masterpiece. I laughed and nodded my understanding. Yes, Sara's fajitas were worthy of one of those Michigan stars or whatever they're called.

The playful banter returned, and we all enjoyed our dinner, hearing stories from each person. Ara told us about growing up in England and how different it was here in the States. Honey and Sara decided to share a few embarrassing stories about me, much to my dismay. Even Lynriel joined in and told us about a few Realms she'd been to, like one where the entire population worshipped some strange cat-like creature who was the Goddess of Fertility or something like that.

After dinner, Lynriel and I took turns showering to get rid of the sweat and grime from training. Letting the hot water pour over my aching body felt so good. I thought about asking Ara to help with her power but then figured I shouldn't bother her with something like that. I've been sore after workouts before; I can handle it.

Lynriel decided to head to my bedroom and read for the evening. I pulled out one of my favorite fantasy series for her to try. She was eager to begin when I told her the protagonist was an elf warrior princess, just like her.

Honey, Sara, and Ara curled up on the couch to stream some romantic comedy. I lounged in my recliner, half-watching the movie and half-dozing off. It had been a long day, and my body felt it, okay?

Soon, the girls got up and went to their room, and Ara returned to the guest room. I pulled the ottoman over and tried to situate myself on the couch for another uncomfortable night on the too-small piece of furniture. Man, the first chance I get, I'm going to the store and getting a bigger couch!

Before I could get settled, I heard a voice call from down the hallway. "Turtle? Can you come help me with something?"

I stood and made my way to the guest room. The door was slightly cracked, and I saw the warm light of the bedside lamp illuminating the room. I opened the door and walked in, looking around for Ara. The room looked empty, though Ara's clothes were piled on the floor next to the wall. The door slamming shut behind me caused me to jump and spin, my heart pounding in my chest.

Ara stood between me and the door, completely naked. She wore a wicked grin and had a fire behind her eyes that I immediately recognized. She reached behind her to the doorknob and clicked the lock button in. "There, now nothing's going to stop us this time."

Chapter 21

Boom-Chica-Wow-Wow

I know what you're thinking. You think I took one look at Ara's naked body and got an instant hard-on. That when I saw her beautiful, large breasts with their stiff, pink nipples, I popped a tent in my pants. You think that I caught sight of her flat stomach leading down to wide hips and a perfectly hairless slit, and all the blood went rushing straight to my dick. I know that's what you're thinking.

And you couldn't be more right. There was no preamble, no slow build-up. I saw her presenting her fantastic body to me, and I went from six to midnight in less than two heartbeats. I honestly don't know how I didn't pass out from having so much blood shoot that fast away from my brain. I guess it also surprised Ara, causing her to gasp and cover her mouth. Her eyes grew wide as she stared at the bulge in my sleep shorts.

"Oh my," she said with a slight chuckle. "I guess you're just as excited as I am, huh?"

"Probably more so," I laughed.

Ara bit her lip as she trailed her hand slowly down her neck, between her breasts, and across her stomach. She continued all the way until the tips of her fingers rested on top of her glistening slit. "I don't know about that. I've been soaking wet ever since we got back from the facility. I even finger fucked myself in the shower earlier to try to take my mind off you. But all that did was make me want it even more."

Ara slid her middle finger inside her pussy, making sure to inhale deeply to push out her breasts more. It took every ounce of self-control I had not to grab her right then and take her. But, in the shape I was in, I doubted I'd be able to do much. It never fails! Something always has to get in my way.

"Ara," I said, forcefully making myself look at her eyes and not at her hand that was now rubbing her clit while she slowly fingered herself. "I want this *so bad*! But my body's too worn out after today. I wouldn't be able to—"

"Hush," Ara whispered, stepping close and removing her finger from inside her dripping pussy.

She grabbed my shirt and pulled me down, kissing me like never before. Our tongues danced together as I felt the heat of her body pressing into me. As the kiss deepened, I tasted strawberries and felt myself being turned ever so slightly. Before I knew what was happening, Ara pushed me backward.

In a motion that was faster than I could comprehend, she grabbed the waistband of my shorts and yanked them down as I fell backward onto the bed. My cock was now free and standing straight up as I lay flat on my back. I looked down toward her and was surprised to see she was bent over me, staring intently at my engorged member. She had an almost awe-struck expression as she timidly reached out and brushed her fingers across it.

"Bloody Hell," she gasped as she wrapped her hand around my shaft. "This . . . are you fucking kidding me?! This is huge! Have you ever had sex with a woman before? Is she still alive?!"

"You saw it last night," I laughed as she continued to stare and grip my cock.

"I didn't get a very good look with everything going on," she said, licking her lips as a small line of pre-cum began to drip down my shaft. "This is . . . just . . . I have no words."

I chuckled, and a shockwave of pleasure pulsed through me as Ara squeezed. "Yeah, I heard I'm a bit bigger than average."

"*A bit*?!" She half laughed as she rubbed her soft cheek against the head of my cock. "I've never seen anyone this size! At least not in person. You've got to be at least ten inches! And this girth . . . not even my biggest toy is this thick. I won't be able to walk for a week after taking this bad boy."

"We don't have to—"

"*Oh, no*," Ara said, the desire behind her eyes growing even brighter. "Yes, we do! I want this. I *need* this. We both do."

Before I could say anything else, Ara leaned in and licked from the bottom of my shaft until she reached the tip. I moaned in pure ecstasy as she quickly brought her lips around the head and began to lick and suck while stroking my shaft at the same time. I wasn't sure what she was doing with her tongue, but it was unlike anything I'd ever felt before.

At some point in the middle of her giving me the best blowjob of my life, the cooling rush of her power flowed into me. I felt the soreness of my muscles disappear, and my energy levels skyrocketed back up. What in the actual fuck?! Did she really just heal me while taking inch after inch of my cock deeper into her mouth?

I looked down in surprise and caught her eyes, which seemed to convey the smile I knew she'd probably have right then. Just as I was about to thank her, she inhaled sharply and pushed down even further, swallowing my erection whole. She took me deep into her throat, burying her entire face into my crotch.

She nearly gagged, and I felt her esophagus rhythmically squeeze down on my cockhead. Yet, she held herself there for a long moment, working her full lips at my root. I saw explosions of colors dancing in my vision as I felt her throat massaging my cock. No one had ever deep-throated me before. I didn't think it was humanly possible!

"Araaaaa!" I moaned, gripping a handful of her curly hair and keeping her head right where it was. "Fucking Hell. This . . . this is amazing!"

Ara began moving her tongue around the bottom of my shaft, making the pleasure almost too intense. I released her head, and she slowly pulled herself up. Her cheeks were hollowed with suction, and she was salivating like crazy. Her lips revealed a pulsating shaft very slick with her spit as she teasingly pulled up before slowly going back down. Inch after inch of my swollen, throbbing cock disappeared again into the warmth of her mouth.

She hummed in pleased contentment and began blowing me in earnest. Increasing her speed, her head bobbed up and down as she gripped my shaft, stroking me in tandem. She was sucking as if her life depended on it, and all the while, I could still feel her power trickling into me. It was a bizarre experience that enhanced my sensations and filled me with an energy I'd never experienced with anyone else.

"Fuuuuck," I moaned as Ara began going even faster.

The wet, slurping noises she was making mixed with her hums of pleasure filled the room. I gripped the blanket underneath me tightly in both hands, trying to control myself. The pleasure increased as Ara began focusing on licking and sucking just underneath the head of my cock. It took everything in me not to explode right then. As if sensing my approaching orgasm, she shoved my cock down her throat once again, taking every inch to the hilt. I couldn't let it end here. I needed more!

I reached down and pulled the very reluctant Ara off my cock. An audible pop sounded as my cockhead was freed from the suction of her mouth. A line of saliva connected us as she bit her lip; the look of a predator sizing up her prey crossed her face. She pouted for just a moment before smiling and crawling on top of me, locking her lips against mine once again.

I could feel her juices dripping down her leg and realized she must've been fingering herself the entire time she was going down on me. This just wouldn't do! I wanted to be the one to give her pleasure. Hooking my arms under her legs, I pulled her forward while I slid down so that my mouth lay directly underneath her glistening pussy, and she was sitting on my face.

"H-Hey," Ara stammered, surprised by the motion. "I wanted t—"

Her words morphed into an incoherent moan as I took my first taste. I let my tongue explore her blushing pink folds, playing along in slow, superficial laps. Her taste filled my mouth; it was exactly how I'd imagined. I felt Ara shudder as the tip of my tongue ever so slightly brushed over her swollen clit.

I lazily mapped out every bit of her pussy with my tongue. Finding that sweet place I could ease into, I let myself sink deep inside, causing her to gasp out a ragged breath. Pulling out, I made my way back to her clitoral hood and gave her another lick, this time slightly harder.

"Fuck me," Ara moaned. "Oh, God, baby. Don't tease me any-more!"

I smiled, pressing the flat of my tongue into a pad against her slit as I continued to lap at her. Ara moaned again and began rocking her hips, grinding in sync with my movements. I continued with broad strokes, using slight motions of my head and neck to add more pressure with each pass.

"AHH-ahhh ahh!" Ara gasped as she pinched one of her nipples while continuing to ride my face.

Her cries picked up as my tempo increased. Alright, I think she's ready. I wrapped one arm around her leg and gripped her tight ass with my other hand. Pushing my tongue back inside her quivering opening, I used my thumb to start rubbing her clit. She bucked at the sudden sensation and let out another scream of pleasure. That's what I wanted to hear.

"W-W-What ar-are you do-doing to m-meeee?" Ara stammered as I let go of her ass and brought that hand around, thrusting two digits deep inside her.

I hooked my fingers slightly and pressed them up with each stroke. Feeling the soft, warm spot I was looking for, I focused my tongue back on her clit. Reaching up with the hand that had been rubbing her pleasure button, I squeezed her breast while pinching her erect nipple between two knuckles. As I continued licking and sucking on her clit, her body began writhing in convulsions of pleasure. She flailed atop me, her mind overwhelmed with all of the different sensations she was receiving at the same time.

Her breathing was ragged, and she threw her head back to scream. I took that moment to pinch her nipple and twist ever so slightly. At the same time, I thrust into her G-spot and sucked her clit, using the tip of my tongue to strum back and forth over it. Within seconds, I got the reaction I'd been hoping for.

Ara bucked hard and spasmed as she let out a scream so loud, I'm pretty sure the RRS could've heard. Hot juices gushed from her pussy, covering my face, throat and chest. She stayed rigid for several more seconds before her body went limp, and she began to fall. I quickly grabbed her and guided her down to the bed. Her eyes were closed, and she had a serene look of happiness.

After a moment of jagged breathing, her eyes fluttered open, and a smile of pure ecstasy crossed her face. "That . . . I . . . That's never happened to me before."

Her voice was soft like she was half asleep. I smiled down at her and placed my hand on her cheek. She nuzzled into it and closed her eyes. "That was amazing, Ara. Thank you."

Ara's eyes shot open, and she sat up. "Thank *me*?! I . . . No. You just gave me the single best orgasm of my life! No one's been able to make me squirt before."

I chuckled and shook my head, slightly embarrassed by the compliment but also a bit proud of myself. It's been years since I'd made someone do that, and it always filled me with a sense of accomplishment. The fact it was with Ara made me even more excited.

"Well, why don't we get clean—"

"WHAT?!" Ara shouted, and I could see the lust coming back into her gaze. "We're *not* finished. I need that cock inside me *right now!*"

"Are you sure? I mean, we—"

Ara grabbed my neck and pulled me in for a deep kiss. The fact I was still covered in her juices didn't seem to bother her. I had to admit, I was still painfully hard, and this was making it even more so. She laid down and held her legs open, giving me complete access to her dripping pussy.

"Get that thing inside me already. Break me!"

I leaned in and kissed her, a feeling of connection forming that I hadn't felt with anyone before. Reaching down, I rubbed the head of my cock along her slit, lubricating it with the abundance of juices she'd produced. Ara moaned into my mouth as I pressed her slick, hot opening.

I pushed inside, feeling her folds stretch around my cock as I sank deeper and deeper. She moaned even louder as she accepted my length, her body eagerly wanting more. God, she was tight! I would've sworn this was her first time if I hadn't known better. Even with how wet she was, I still had difficulty pushing inside. Trying to be as careful as I could not to hurt her, I stopped halfway to give her a moment to adjust to my size.

Ara continued kissing me, our tongues entangled together as she gave me an almost imperceptible nod. I took that as my sign to keep going and pressed the rest of the way inside. That made me groan as her hot pussy squeezed my cock from every side. Holy fucking God, was her pussy amazing! She was stunningly tight, and the intense wetness from her orgasm and arousal made it feel so much better.

"OH MY GOD!" Ara shouted, breaking our kiss to take deep breaths. "I . . . I've never felt this full before. This . . . this is unbelievable. Fuck me! Please, don't keep me waiting, Baby. Fuck me hard!"

I pulled halfway out before stroking back inside. Honestly, I'm not sure how I didn't cum the moment I entered her. The pleasure I was feeling was unlike anything I'd ever experienced before. That was when I realized Ara was still linking her power to me. I could feel it coursing through my body, giving me more energy to keep going. This woman was going to be the death of me!

I couldn't wait any longer and started fucking her in earnest. As I watched her eyes roll back in pleasure, I knew this was going to be a night neither of us would soon forget. Her breasts bounced with each thrust, and she let out squeals of pleasure each time I pushed inside. I looked down and watched my cock slam into her smooth, pale pussy, stretching it wide with my girth.

I bent down, kissing her neck and then her shoulder, licking some of the sweat that had formed from our activities. She tasted amazing. I felt her hands wrap around me and her lips against my neck. Then, a sharp pain I hadn't expected stabbed into my shoulder. She bit me, and I could feel her sucking my skin as her teeth continued to clamp down.

An almost animalistic, primal urge flowed through me, and I began to pound harder. The wet sound of our bodies clapping together, mixed with the squeaking of the bed and our combined moans of pleasure, filled the air. She raked her nails down my back, and I let out a deep growl into her ear.

I pulled away and grabbed her legs, pushing them up, and just about folded her in half. She gasped in surprise as I held her ankles and pressed them into the pillow on either side of her head. Readjusting myself, I started hammering her now tighter pussy even harder.

"HOLY FUCK!" Ara screamed.

"You like that?" I asked with a wicked grin.

"Yes," she moaned. "I love it so much. Harder! Go harder!"

Well, I can't disappoint the lady, can I? I redoubled my efforts and fucked her even harder. She moaned and screamed unintelligible things as I felt her pussy seize and clamp down in another orgasm. But I didn't stop. She wanted to be broken, so I'll break her.

Before her orgasm was finished, I flipped her over so that she was face down on her stomach. I lifted her bottom half and reinserted my cock back into her quivering opening. Squeezing her hips, I thrust in and was rewarded with another scream of pleasure. Ara gripped the blankets and tried to look back at me. I could see she was far from being done. I smiled and slapped her ass with one of my hands.

The crack of the strike echoed off the walls, and Ara yelled in a mixture of pain and pleasure. "A-A-AGAIN!"

I chuckled and obliged, spanking her even harder. Her pale skin turned red, making me want to do it more. Pulling back, I struck again and then once more. Ara growled and began slamming herself back hard onto my cock. God damn, maybe she actually *did* want to be broken. I didn't see how someone her size was taking it this rough from me.

Reaching forward, I grabbed a handful of her sweat-drenched curly hair by its root. With a firm grip, I pulled her head back, and she moaned loudly as I slapped her ass once again with my free hand. Her pussy squeezed my cock harder as I thrust faster and faster. This was a night I never wanted to end.

"Yes, Yes, YES!" She screamed over and over. "This! YES! FUCK ME!"

Pulling her hair even harder, I made her look back up at me as I grinned down at her. "You like this? You want it rough?"

"YES! GIVE IT TO ME HARD! ROUGH! THROW ME AROUND AND TAKE ME HOWEVER YOU WANT! CLAIM ME! MAKE ME YOURS!"

"Good girl," I growled in her ear.

I know this doesn't sound like what a new couple's first time should be like. People think it needs to be slow and gentle, gradually getting to know each other's bodies and being soft and filled with lots of cuddles and kisses. But not this time. We've had years of built-up sexual tension between us. And apparently, we both were into some of the spicier stuff.

After several more thrusts, Ara's body tensed, and she squeezed down on me so tight I couldn't move for several seconds. A massive shudder washed over her as another jet of hot liquid shot from her pussy, coating my legs and half the bed. We both took several deep, jagged breaths as her pussy continued to spasm around my cock. Looking back at me, I saw a blissful excitement in Ara's eyes.

"My turn," she said, pulling herself off my cock to sit upright on her knees.

Turning toward me, Ara pushed me backward so I was lying flat on the bed. Then, crawling on her hands and knees, she made her way on top of me, giggling. She began grinding on my dick while leaning down to give me another passionate kiss. With every move she made, I wanted more of her.

It didn't take long for her to finally reach down and position the tip of my cock right inside her dripping opening. Without hesitation, she lowered herself all the way down, taking my entire length once again. I saw a slight bulge in her lower abdomen where the head of my cock was pressing inside her, and I got even more aroused. After a couple of breaths to prepare herself, Ara began to bounce and gyrate on top of me.

I gripped her hips tightly and assisted with thrusting up into her as she bounced. It only took a few seconds before we got our rhythm in sync, and she became lost with fucking me. The fleshy smacking of our bodies matched our grunts and moans of pleasure.

Ara's perfect breasts bounced and jiggled with each thrust, and I just couldn't help myself. Reaching up, I pinched her nipple, giving it a slight twist as I did. She threw her head back and let out a deep, guttural moan.

Leaning forward, Ara looked down at me, her smile filled with love and happiness. "I want to see your face when you cum."

Giving her a cocky grin, I pinched her nipple a bit harder. She sucked in a sharp breath and closed her eyes, biting her lower lip in response. "What makes you think I'm anywhere close to being ready for that?"

I watched her smile turn wicked as she looked back at me. That was when I knew I was in trouble. Her pussy clamped down tighter than ever. She began grinding her clit on my pelvis while her insides felt like they were trying to milk my cock dry. I felt the familiar rush of her power flood me, but then it concentrated just into the nerves of my cock. Every sensation increased tenfold, and I clenched my jaw in an attempt to stop from busting right then and there.

"I have my ways," Ara whispered as she leaned down and kissed me. "Now, cum inside me! It's safe, I promise. Fill me up! Make me yours. Only yours."

This was the closest to heaven that I'd ever come to. Her hot, wet folds squeezed tighter and tighter as I wrapped my arms around her. I pulled her close as I passed the point of no return. I thrust a few more times before slamming my cock as deep into her pussy as I could. The floodgates opened, and I released it all.

I ejaculated uncontrollably, feeling thick rope after rope of cum shoot inside her. She pressed her lips into mine and moaned as her pussy tightened and then released over and over. It really was like she was trying to milk me. Shot after shot continued to pour out, and I saw stars as the world spun around me.

After what felt like an eternity of pure orgasmic bliss, the cum finally stopped. The room was quiet now, save our heavy breathing. I held her in my arms with my cock still inside for several minutes. Neither one of us wanted to move. At that moment, all the stress and pressure from everything else was gone. It was simply just us existing in each other's embrace.

But the world doesn't work like that, does it? Soon enough, we knew we'd have to get up, and the spell would be broken. Ara placed her chin on my chest and smiled. Her emerald eyes glistened as we stared at each other. "That . . . was amazing. It was . . . everything I could've ever wanted and more. Thank you."

"Don't thank me," I said with a chuckle, squeezing her ass which was still hot from where I spanked her. "You're going to regret a few things in the morning."

Ara shook her head and smiled wider. She rested her head on my chest, and instinctively, I ran my fingers through her hair. She nuzzled even closer, letting out a soft hum of contentment. "This feels nice."

"Yeah, it does," I agreed.

Before long, we both got up and went to the bathroom. Ara was moving stiffly, so I reached down and lifted her into my arms like before. She squealed and laughed as I carried her across the hall and helped her into the shower. We didn't talk much, but we shared the same content smile as we helped wash each other.

Before things got too hot and heavy again, I turned off the water and wrapped Ara in a thick towel. I carried her back to her room and set her down in a chair while I got new sheets and blankets for the bed. I mean, come on, no one likes to sleep in the wet spot. And there were several after what we just did.

"Stay with me? Please?" Ara asked, grabbing my hand and pulling me into the bed with her.

I chuckled and nodded, turning off the lamp on the nightstand. We curled up together under the blankets, Ara's head nestled perfectly in the crook of my shoulder. We were both still naked, and I could feel her soft breasts against my torso as we lay pressed against each other.

"So," Ara said, trailing one finger across my chest. Her fingers seemed to follow those of my scars, but just like with Lynriel earlier in the day, it didn't bother me. "I guess we should discuss how things are going to move forward and what our boundaries are for this?"

I smiled, though I knew she wouldn't be able to see it in the dark like that. "Okay, hit me."

"Well, I mean, I pretty much already told you," Ara said with a soft chuckle. "I'm fine with you being with the others. I just don't want you to hide anything from me. I won't ever ask you to break confidence with anyone else. Just be open and honest with me, and I'll be fine. I want us all to be equal as well. So, no playing favorites. I don't want any kind of hierarchy between the women in your life, okay? And as far as what I want, I've already decided you're the only man for me. But, I *am* interested in maybe having fun with Sara and Honey, if that's okay with you?"

I nodded and squeezed her tighter. "I trust you and them whole-heartedly. Have all the fun with them you want."

"What about if I was interested in Rui or Lyn?" Ara asked, and I could feel the smile on her face.

I laughed and shook my head at the thought. "You know what, if you want that headache and they're open to it, be my guest! Maybe it'll calm Rui down some."

"Really, Daddy?" Rui said from somewhere in the dark beside me, causing me to almost jump straight out of bed.

"WHAT THE FUCK?!" I yelled, my heart pounding in my chest. "What are you doing here?"

I couldn't see anything in the pitch-blackness of the room, but soon, I felt the weight of someone crawling into the bed. Soft breasts pressed into me on the opposite side of Ara, and I groaned as I realized Rui was also naked and curling up to me under the blanket.

"Rui! What are you—"

"Turtle, it's fine," Ara said with a chuckle. "Let her in already. Just close your eyes and go to sleep with two hotties in your arms."

"Yeah," Rui agreed, nuzzling herself even closer. Her soft cat ear twitched slightly on my shoulder, and she reached out, holding Ara's hand on my chest. "This is nice. Let's all sleep like this more."

I sighed and resigned myself to letting the troublesome Neko do whatever she was going to do. Soon, I felt both women's breathing slow and get deeper as they fell asleep. I listened to the two of them and felt something pulling deep inside me. It was an ever-growing urge to protect them at all costs.

The women in my life were all precious to me, and I couldn't let anyone hurt them. I let out a deep exhale and closed my eyes. I'd made up my mind. If Rui and I couldn't come up with another alternative tomorrow, I'd turn myself over to Wallace to ensure they all stay safe.

Chapter 22

I Beg Your Finest Pardon?

You know how, in the movies, couples enjoy a night of passionate love-making and then fall asleep peacefully in each other's arms, just to wake up feeling ultra-rested and refreshed in the morning? They're usually cuddled together and wake up smiling, ready to jumpstart their day like they'd just gotten the best sleep of their life. Maybe some snuggling or a bit of extra fun before rolling out of bed and making each other coffee. Does that *actually* happen in real life?

Don't get me wrong, my night with Ara was mind-blowing. I've never, and I mean *never*, had sex that intense or passionate before. And having her curl into my arms afterward was like a dream come true for me. But it wasn't just us in that bed anymore, was it?

Let me tell you, anyone who says it's fun to lay between two women in bed is full of shit. It's a pain in the ass to find an arrangement where all three of you are comfortable, which is made even worse when two of those three people flop around like dying fish when asleep. Not to mention how incredibly hot-natured I am, to begin with. I need some space when I sleep, which isn't easy when there's another person in bed with me, let alone getting sandwiched in by a five-foot-nothing, irritating Neko with no definition of personal space.

I stared at the ceiling as the sun began to light up the sky outside. Apparently, Honey and Sara had already taken down the curtains in preparation to turn this room into the nursery. The blinds helped some, but not enough. How can either of the girls sleep so soundly with it so bright in here?

Listening to them both breathing, I found myself smiling again. While I might not have gotten the best sleep, last night was one I'll never forget. Even with the sudden intrusion by Rui there at the end, I felt fortunate to have two women who cared so deeply for me.

As I lay contemplating just how I would get myself out from between them, something unexpected happened. One of Rui's soft ears twitched ever so slightly on my chest, and in a single heartbeat, she disappeared. Before I could register what had happened, I heard a soft click from across the room as the door slowly cracked open. Crystal-blue eyes peered at me from the hallway, and I smiled, raising my hand toward her. As if being caught doing something wrong, Lynriel's eyes widened, and she quickly turned and disappeared from the doorway.

I sighed and looked down at Ara. She was still dead to the world. Her mouth was open, and a bit of drool had dropped onto my shoulder. If my phone hadn't been in my shorts across the room,

I'd have taken a picture to have fun with her later. But maybe that was too much, at least for the first time.

Trying my best not to wake her, I rolled the sleeping woman over and pulled my arm out from under her head. She grumbled and whimpered something but then went right back to breathing heavily. Slowly, I slipped from the bed, doing what I could to prevent the mattress from squeaking or moving too much. From the looks of the sun coming in through the window, it was still early. I grabbed my shorts and put them on as I opened the door. Looking around, I didn't see Lynriel anywhere and figured she probably returned to my room.

The bathroom was my first stop. Seriously, I can't tell you how good it feels to pee after a night like that. I was still relatively clean from the shower Ara and I took, so I just brushed my teeth and then went to my room. I knocked softly but didn't hear anything. Opening the door a crack, I looked inside, but the room was empty. Strange.

I walked in and sat on the bed, thinking maybe Lynriel had gone outside for some fresh air. Hopefully, not out front since we didn't know if Wallace had sent someone back to keep tabs on us again. As I looked at my phone, I saw it was barely after 7:00 a.m. That meant I had just under five hours to figure something out.

Rui's yellow eyes appeared on my screen as I swiped up on the cat paw. The bratty Neko was staring at me with her arms crossed under her chest. At first, I thought she was mad about something, but I quickly saw the smirk she was trying to hide as she looked me over.

"You had quite the workout last night. Did you get some good rest from it, Daddy?" she asked, her voice seeming extra bratty today.

"You know damn well I didn't because of you," I grumbled, trying to push down the irritation that had already started to build. "Can you just . . . come here already?"

Rui's smirk deepened, and I saw a mischievous glint in her eyes. "I can cum for you wherever you want."

Before I could even roll my eyes at the comment, Rui appeared cross-legged on the bed beside me. At least she did it where I could see her and didn't try to surprise me this time. So . . . progress?

"So?" Rui asked, her smile growing wider. "How was it? You two had a lot of fun before I showed up, didn't you?"

"I'm not talking about it with you," I said with a sigh, though I couldn't stop the corner of my lips from curling slightly.

Rui bounced up and down excitedly. "Oh, I knew it was going to be great! I even gave up my physical form so you could have more energy."

That caught me by surprise. "Wait, what? Your physical body takes my energy away?"

Waving her hand in the air, Rui batted the question away. "Eh, not that much. You don't even notice most of the time. But I'm part of you, so *anything* I do takes your energy."

I blinked several times as I thought about that. It was true I hadn't felt a difference, but that was still concerning to hear. What would happen if I was in a bad spot and having Rui try to help me caused me to pass out or something? I needed to be more careful when asking her to do things.

"Why didn't you tell me you were attached to my desires?" I asked, trying to return my focus to what I needed to know.

Rui shrugged and leaned back on her hands. "I didn't know until I was talking to Ara. I told you, things kind of just . . . reveal themselves to me. It's stuff you do or say. When you asked me to explain things to her, that bit just sort of came out. But it makes sense, doesn't it? I mean, the Sh'landriel are fused into the strongest emotion someone's experiencing when they come into contact with it. Your first time was when you were masturbating during the SRE. So, from that point, all your Sh'landriel were attached to your desires because that's what you felt the first time."

"What?" I almost yelled. "I wasn't . . . I mean . . . It's not like . . . How do you know what I was doing?"

Rui rolled her eyes and let out a deep sigh. "I'm inside you, remember, Daddy? You can't keep secrets from me. It's how I know exactly what you did with Ara last night, whether you want to say it or not. It's also how I know all your dirty thoughts about Honey, Sara, Lynriel, and even me. Thoughts that only got dirtier when Ara said she also wanted to do things with us. By the way, I'm *totally* down for all of it! But besides the fun stuff, it's also how I know what you plan on doing today."

I tried to deny everything she said, but the words just couldn't leave my throat. Rui was quite literally the only person I could never lie to. She was embedded into my every desire, so nothing was hidden from her.

I let out a long sigh and shook my head. There wasn't enough time for me to argue with the irritating Neko. Though, wouldn't it be technically arguing with myself? Or would I be arguing with a God? What exactly *is* she?!

"Whatever," I finally grumbled, not wanting the headache of trying to figure all that out now. "Just . . . can you help me out here? Anything to get Wallace and the RRS off my ass?"

Rui tilted her head slightly, and one of her ears twitched a few times. Slowly blinking, her face fell, and her ears drooped. "I . . . don't know. I'm sorry, Daddy. I want to help! But whatever they were using to keep me from accessing the files yesterday seems to have been implemented agency-wide now. I can't even access their security logs anymore."

My heart raced as I looked down at my watch. "What about—"

"Your watches are still okay," she said, reaching out and placing her soft hand on mine. "That's hardware, so I can still control it. I'm sorry, I'm failing you right now."

The sadness in her eyes almost broke my heart. Maybe that primal urge that awoke inside me last night was still around, or perhaps it was just my insistent need to save people, but I wanted to give her any comfort I could. I pulled her over to me and hugged her.

"Hey, you've done so much for me already," I said, stroking her soft, silky hair. "Whatever's going to happen, please know I'm thankful for everything. You might be the most frustratingly irritating Neko I've ever met, but you're *my* frustratingly irritating Neko."

Rui purred loudly as she nuzzled closer to me. "You know, if you wanted, we could . . ."

I felt Rui's hands begin to rub my crotch, and my cock instantly began to grow. I quickly pulled away and crossed my leg over to not allow her access. "And you had to ruin it."

Rui smirked at me, but at least her smile was back. "You know you love me."

"Anyway," I said, clearing my throat and looking around my room. "I guess there's no other option, huh? If I don't turn myself over, the agency's going to burn down the lives of everyone I love. I can't let that happen."

Rui slowly nodded and placed her hand on my knee. This time, it wasn't in any kind of sexual way; it was more of an attempt to show her support. "No matter what, I'll be there with you, Daddy, until the very end. I'll be there even if you can't see or talk to me. But, before that, there's something you need to see."

She placed her hand on my chest, and I felt an explosion of energy engulf me. All the shards I held in my core seemed to come alive, and I felt immense power course through my veins. Everything that had already happened as well as things that were currently happening played out like a movie in front of me. Flashes of images I didn't recognize strobed through, and I instinctively knew they were things that hadn't happened yet. Or, rather, they had the potential to.

Somewhere, in the far distance behind all of it, a shadow appeared. I couldn't make it out, but something about it felt . . . familiar. I tried to focus on it, but the more I tried, the more distant it became. Somehow, I knew I was meant to get to it. Get to *her*. *She* was . . . destiny.

Rui let go of my chest, and everything crashed to a sudden stop. I gasped, trying to catch my breath as sweat poured down my face. I looked up at the now serene Neko, trying to figure out what she'd just done. Rui gave me a tight smile and nodded softly. She understood the confusion I was feeling.

"I don't know who or what she is," Rui said, her voice soft as she peered into me with her big, yellow cat eyes. "But you felt it too. We need to find her. Your story . . . *our* story, can't end here. Besides, it's not like you to just give up when things look tough. That's never been your style. The people you care about most still need you."

I clenched my jaw and nodded. Rui was right. I had too many relying on me just to give up and turn myself over. And now, I had a new sense of purpose driving me forward. Whoever that shadow is, I *have* to find her!

"I still don't know where to start," I said, standing back up and stretching. "But Wallace mentioned yesterday that Ara's mother might be important to the agency. So maybe we should ask her? Any ideas on who she is?"

Rui's head tilted like before, and her ear twitched a few times. "I can't access any RRS files, not even employee records. But Ara has a contact on her phone with the name 'Mother,' and it's linked to an agency-issued device. I can't tell anything else other than it's based somewhere in the Philippines."

I nodded and headed to the door. I hated doing it, but I needed to wake Ara to get some answers. Time was running out. When I opened the guest room door, Ara was already sitting in bed, scrolling on her phone. She looked up and smiled, and it took everything in me not to rush over to have another roll in the hay.

"Good morning, handsome," she said, stretching her arms above her head.

I wasn't sure if it was on purpose or by accident, but the stretch caused the blanket to fall and expose her glorious breasts to me. Jesus, this woman was not making it easy! I felt myself starting to grow hard, and I quickly turned my head to the side, trying to stay focused. There'll be plenty of time for that *after* we get this all figured out.

"Hey, do you think we can talk?" I asked, keeping to the doorway.

"That . . . doesn't sound good," Ara said, and I could hear the fear creeping in her voice. "Is something wrong? Are you regretting last night?"

I looked back and saw she'd grabbed the blanket and pulled it up to cover herself again. Shit! I didn't mean to put her on edge so early like that. "NO! No, it's nothing like that. I mean, last night was amazing. Literally the best night I've ever had! I meant we need to talk about what's happening today. You know . . . the deadline?"

I saw the relief wash over her as she took a long breath. "Oh, okay, yeah. Let me get dressed, and I'll be out in a minute, okay?"

Sighing, I closed the door and walked to the living room. Lynriel was still nowhere to be seen. I poked my head out and looked in the backyard, but there was no sign of her. Luckily, there weren't any RRS surveillance vans out front, but still, where could she be?

As I sat in my recliner, Ara walked in with a big smile. I was shocked to see her wearing an old T-shirt with the logo from one of my favorite bands back when I was younger, Blue September. I didn't even know anyone else had heard of them, as they had a single hit two decades ago and then kind of fizzled out. And I definitely didn't think they'd been played overseas. The shirt she was wearing was from their last show, one that I actually took Honey to see the night before the FRE happened.

The shirt looked a little big for the petite woman, and the bottom of her daisy dukes barely peeked out from underneath. I returned her smile as I motioned toward her shirt. "Hey, that was one of my favorite bands!"

Ara beamed and hopped onto the couch beside me. "I know! I was surprised when Honey told me. I was actually at this concert!"

"Us too," I laughed, shaking my head at what a small world it was.

"So, what do you want to talk about?" Ara asked as her eyes seemed to focus on my bare chest.

I smirked and leaned in, not wanting to risk Honey or Sara overhearing. "Rui said the software or program or whatever's stopping her from accessing those files has been implemented agency-wide. She can't access anything anymore."

Ara gasped, concern finally bringing her focus back from eye-fucking me. "Seriously? But how? Something like that would take months, if not years."

I shook my head and shrugged. "I'm not sure. But that means we can't get any info from them anymore. We need some way to find out what the higher-ups are doing. Maybe that can give me some kind of leverage against Wallace."

Ara bobbed her head in agreement. "Understandable. But how are you going to do that?"

I took a deep breath and locked eyes with her. "Listen, I know you don't like to talk about it, and I don't want to pry into something that might be a sensitive subject. But yesterday, Wallace mentioned something about your mother. That she's important to the RRS?"

I watched Ara's face fall, and she fell back into the couch. It was like someone had slapped her in the face, and she stared out into nothingness. I felt like shit bringing this up, but we didn't have any other options. I knew this wasn't something to rush, so I gave her a few minutes before pressing again.

"So . . . do you think she could help?" I finally asked.

Ara almost winced at the question. "She and I . . . we're not on the best of terms. There's . . . bad blood between us."

I raised both of my hands and nodded my understanding. "Hey, trust me. I get it, okay? I haven't spoken to my parents in fifteen years. I know just how shitty family can be. And, if this weren't absolutely necessary, I'd *never* bring it up. But, we're reaching zero hour here."

Ara clenched her jaw and stared at the wall for a long minute. "She . . . GOD! She's such a . . . you don't understand, Turtle. She slept with two of my boyfriends! I mean, I'm poly, but that's just a line you *don't* cross. Go fuck any girl you want at the bar, but not my mum. And it wasn't like none of them knew, either. They did it *after* I introduced them!"

Wow! I was *not* expecting that. But, hey, at least she was talking about it, right?

"I'm so sorry that happened to you," I said, touching her knee. "I've been in ethically non-monogamous relationships before, and understand that's why you talk about things to set up each person's boundaries. I'm sorry they didn't listen to yours and broke your trust. And I'm really sorry your mother would do something like that to you."

Ara let out a long sigh and closed her eyes. She reached down, gripped my hand, and squeezed. "Thank you. That's one reason I trust you so much, Turtle. You get it. So . . . if you think it'll help, I can get you in contact with her. But I don't know what good she'll be. She retired from the RRS years ago and only does some consulting for them here and there."

I nodded and smiled, glad I finally had a new lead. "That's great! Rui said the only information she could get was that her phone was based in the Philippines. Is that where she is?"

Ara nodded and looked back at me. "Yeah. But I'm not sure she'll answer if I call. Do you want to jump there? Wait, I don't have the coordinates . . ."

I stood and looked around, hoping Lynriel would've returned by now. But there was still no sign of the elf princess. "Don't worry about that. If you put the address in my phone, Rui should be able to get us there."

Taking my phone, Ara pulled her own out and looked up the contact for her mother. She copied the address to my 'Maps' app and returned it to me. Standing from the couch, she interlocked her fingers with mine and smiled. "I'm glad I can do this with you. I don't think I could trust her around another boyfriend. But I know you'd never do something like that to me."

I laughed and shook my head, bringing her close and kissing her. "Never! Even though you've told me you're okay with me and . . . well, either way, I won't ever do anything to break your trust. Now, let me get my shirt, and we can go. I'm excited to meet your mother and see who created such a smart, beautiful woman."

Ara chuckled and shook her head. "You've already met her, dummy."

I did what now? I quickly recalled all the higher-ups I'd ever met from the agency, trying to figure out who her mother could be. None of them had been from England, that I could remember.

"I have? Who is she?"

Ara pulled me in for another kiss and smiled up at me. "The former director of the agency, Annabella Saph."

Chapter 23

Unhappy Reunion

I've done . . . a considerable amount of stupid stuff in my life. Went out to the beach with no sunblock while having the complexion of a jar of mayonnaise. I had Honey frost my tips back when we were in high school. Hell, I agreed to work for an ambiguously evil government agency because a MILF gave me a blowjob. And every single one of those things has come back to bite me in the ass in one way or another.

Listen, I swear to *everything*; I had *no* idea Dr. Saph and Ara were related. They hadn't even been at the Krayden facility at the same time! Dr. Saph retired and moved away almost six months before Ara transferred in. I didn't even know the director's first name until two days ago! Considering I fucked her more than a dozen times over the years, that doesn't make me look too good, I admit.

But I mean . . . *come on*! She was *the* definition of a MILF, and I'm only human! Besides, the last time I had sex with her was during her retirement party, and I haven't seen or heard from her since. Now that I think about it, she did mention a daughter once, but she said her name was Bella or something like . . . fuck. Arabella. ARE YOU FUCKING KIDDING ME?!

My heart froze in my chest as I stared wide-eyed at Ara. I felt all the blood drain from my face as my mind raced to come up with something to say. She and I have only been together technically for two days, and *I already fucked it up*?!

"D-Did y-you say . . ." I stammered, trying to figure out a way to fix this. Ara *just* said that was the ultimate form of betrayal for her. How can I tell her I screwed her mom regularly for almost a decade? "Dr. S-Saph?"

Ara narrowed her eyes at me as she studied my face. I felt a cold sweat pour, and the pit in my stomach began to turn. But before I could say anything to defend myself, Ara sputtered and nearly doubled over with laughter.

"HAHAHA!" She bellowed, slapping her leg as she shook her head. "You should see the look on your face!"

I was so confused. Was Dr. Saph her mother or not? Was she just fucking with me? But how did she know about me and the former director if she was?

"Turtle, relax," Ara said, wiping a tear from her eye. She wrapped her arms around me and squeezed me in a tight embrace. "I already know about your history with her. You don't have to worry."

"Wait, what?" I asked, pulling her away to look her in the eyes. "I don't understand."

"I knew about you before I transferred," Ara explained, pulling up her phone and scrolling until she found a text from her mom.

She showed it to me with a smile. "See? When I told her I wanted to transfer out of the UK facility, *she* was the one who told me to come to Krayden and pretty much begged me to join your team. That's one of the biggest reasons I hesitated about my feelings for you this whole time. But we're all human, and we all have pasts. Sex is sex; it's not like either of you were in love or anything. While it's not ideal that you've slept with my mother, I can't hold it against you, considering we hadn't even met yet."

I stared her down, looking for any sign that this could be a trap. It felt like a trap. It's probably a trap. Right?

"Uh," I said, still waiting for the yelling to start. "That's . . . are you sure? I mean, I don't want things to be weird between us. And I *really* don't want you thinking that—"

"Turtle! Hey, it's completely okay," she reassured, giving me another warm hug. "You're mine now. Well, mine and possibly four others. But mine nonetheless."

"Four?" I asked, returning the embrace. "I think your math's wrong there. I have you, and then there's that weird bound thing with Lyn. Rui's . . . well, I don't even know what Rui is. But that's it. Honey and Sara are just messing around; they're not serious about any of that stuff."

Ara let out a long sigh and shook her head. She turned and walked back toward the guest room. "I swear, you're so thick-headed . . ."

"Where are you going?" I asked, following her down the hall.

"Well, I can't go to see my mother like this," Ara said, gesturing toward her clothes but not turning back to face me. "Give me ten minutes to fix myself up. If you finish before me, can you make some coffee?"

I chuckled and went into my room to also put on more acceptable clothes. I couldn't face Ara's mother, who also happened to be my former boss and booty call, wearing just whatever. My room was still empty, with no sign that Lynriel had returned. Rui was also gone, but that wasn't surprising.

Since I was going to see the former director for the entire RRS, I opted to change into my standard work uniform: khakis, my RRS polo, and heavy-duty steel-toed leather boots. A heavy thud echoed off the floor just as I finished tying my last lace. I quickly looked over and was shocked to see the shining silver of my S&W 500 lying on the ground a few feet away.

Growing up in small-town Texas, I'd been around plenty of firearms and had gotten pretty good with most of them. But since something didn't allow us to jump with those kinds of weapons, they rarely were used these days. Especially since we had the Swords and Shields now. But I still liked shooting once a month, and Honey had gotten me this brand-new 500 Smith and Wesson Magnum for my birthday last year. It had one of the hardest kickbacks I'd ever felt, but that was to be expected with any cartridge that shoots a bullet measuring a half-inch across.

"What the . . ." I muttered as I searched the room to see where it had come from.

I was still alone, as far as I could tell. Yet I knew for a fact that the revolver had been in a locked gun case on the top shelf of my closet. How the hell did it end up on the floor?

Carefully picking it up, I checked the cylinder and was even more surprised to see it was loaded. I *never* kept it loaded when I wasn't actively shooting it. What was going on?

"Ooo," a voice cooed from behind me, causing me to jump and spin in fright. Rui was sitting on my bed, looking at the gun I was holding. "That's shiny! Why don't you carry that with you?"

I grabbed my chest to calm my racing heart at the woman's sudden appearance. If I didn't know any better, I'd say she was legitimately trying to give me a heart attack. "FUCK! STOP DO-ING THAT!"

I took several deep breaths before turning around to put the gun back in its case in my closet. "You should already know why. We can't take firearms into the Rift. Every time someone tries, whatever they're trying to take is just left behind."

Rui stepped beside me and placed a hand on the closet door, stopping me from opening it. "But you're not going into the Rift, are you?"

I stopped and thought for a second. Wasn't I? I still wasn't sure how this in-realm jumping worked. My core activated, and I felt the pull of the Rift, but I didn't actually go *into* it. Shaking my head, I looked back down at the gun.

"Okay, but why would I take it with me?" I asked, turning my focus back to Rui. "We're just going to meet with Dr. Saph. I doubt I need a .50-caliber magnum for that."

Rui shrugged and let go of the door handle. "I don't know. Just feels . . . kind of important that you have it."

Looking back at the gun, I debated about taking it. There really wasn't a need for it. But Rui seemed rather insistent. And with everything going on, wouldn't it be better to have some way to protect myself? I wouldn't last five seconds against any of the Swords if they used their powers on me.

I sighed, opened the closet door, and grabbed the holster I kept on the shelf beside the gun case. I strapped it in and secured the revolver at my waist. There wasn't any harm in having it, I suppose. Turning around, Rui stood back, smiling warmly at me.

"You look so handsome," she said, her tail flicking playfully behind her back.

I chuckled as I reached up and scratched her head between her ears as I walked past. "Thank you. Are you staying here with the girls or coming with us?"

"I'll stay, just in case," Rui said, a soft purr in her voice. "Lynriel's gone, though. I don't sense her anywhere."

That made me stop in my tracks. I spun and stared at Rui, who looked like she was waiting for me to yell at her. "What do you mean she's gone?"

Rui half shrugged and motioned around. "I knew you were looking for her earlier. But I can't sense her anywhere close by. I think she jumped somewhere."

Fuck. What was that woman thinking? I'm sitting here trying to do whatever I can to keep her out of the RRS crosshairs, and she just jumps somewhere without telling anyone. Was she that upset that I slept with Ara?

I pinched the bridge of my nose and closed my eyes to stave off the encroaching headache. "Jesus Christ. I . . . I don't even know what to do with that."

"I'll keep searching in the area, but I won't go too far so I can be close to Honey and Sara," Rui said, giving me a hopeful smile. "Was there anything else I can do for you, Daddy?"

Once again, I scratched her head and tried to smile in return. "No, thank you. Just do whatever you need to to keep them safe, okay?"

Rui purred and nodded her head. In the blink of an eye, she changed from being the 20-something-year-old Neko to the orange tabby. She meowed and walked out of the room as I opened the door. Ara stared down at the prancing feline as she walked past, chuckling softly.

"It's so weird knowing that's not actually a cat," Ara said with a slight shake of her head.

"Tell me about it," I grumbled, adjusting my shirt to cover my new addition to the uniform. "Just imagine how it feels to have that constantly trying to jump your bones. That's a whole new level of weirdness that I don't even know how to begin to unpack."

Ara laughed and placed her hand on her hip. "Well, how do I look?"

She apparently had the same idea as me and wore her RRS uniform. Hers looked much better on her, though. Her ample chest stretched the fabric of her polo, and her khakis were tight against her firm ass. She'd put on a bit of make-up, but not much. She already had a natural beauty, though, so she didn't need it. But

I've been told it's more of a self-esteem thing for many women, so who am I to say anything?

"Stunning," I said with a smile.

Ara beamed up at me and hopped over, grabbing my hand like she'd done countless times when we jumped. Her fingers interlocked with mine as she smiled up at me. "I'm ready, then!"

"Don't you want some coffee?" I asked, secretly hoping she'd say yes because I *really* needed a cup.

"No, it's fine," she said, shaking her head. "I know we're in a hurry, and I'm hoping we won't be there too long. We can make some breakfast when we get back. Sound good?"

I sighed and nodded. Goddammit, I need my coffee! But she was right. We needed to get this done ASAP so we could focus on whatever else.

"Alright. Let's go say hi to Mom," I grinned as I pulled out my phone and hit the Map icon.

Ara groaned and buried her face into my chest. "*Please* don't call her that!"

I laughed as I hit the address Ara had given me. The familiar pull of the Rift opened my core, and the world blurred for barely a heartbeat. Then, just as fast as it started, everything settled. We now stood outside the doors of a massive estate surrounded by tall trees on three sides.

This house was insane! It was four stories tall, had one of those fancy circular stone courtyards with a big fountain in the middle, and even had armed security walking around. I found that last one out when a giant spotlight slammed on and pointed directly at us. We heard men yelling and even a dog barking somewhere in the distance. *What the hell*?! Was Dr. Saph a drug kingpin now or something?

Ara held her hands toward the light but didn't seem scared by the men rushing toward us. On the other hand, I was two seconds away from jumping us out of there. Maybe we should've just video-chatted or something. But I decided to trust in Ara and followed her lead, holding my hands up as well.

"Stop right there!" A man yelled as he rushed toward us.

"We're not moving!" Ara yelled back in irritation. "My name's Arabella Anderson. I'm Anabella's daughter."

Five men surrounded us, each drawing automatic weapons. Shit, this didn't go very well. I was actually shocked they had the weapons. Before we could say anything else, a speaker next to the door behind us crackled to life.

"Bella? Is that you?" a woman's voice called out, and I saw Ara cringe as she turned.

"Yeah, it's me," she said, motioning toward the men still pointing their weapons at us. "Can you call off your goons already and open the door?"

There was a brief silence before I saw one of the men touch his ear and listen to something. He held up a hand and made a circular motion with a finger. "Stand down! Everyone go back to your stations!"

All the men lowered their guns and turned around as if we weren't even there anymore. The bright light kicked off, and my eyes were left with white spots as I tried to readjust them to the dark. A few seconds later, the house door opened, and a familiar face greeted us.

Dr. Saph was now in her mid-fifties but still had an incredible body. Her red hair had some strands of gray throughout, and there were a few more lines on her face that weren't there the last time I saw her. But otherwise, she looked almost exactly the same. And now that they were together, I couldn't believe how similar the mother and daughter looked.

How could I not see it before?! They had the same thin frame and wide hips. The same hair, eyes, and even nose! If Dr. Saph wasn't wearing three-inch heels, I bet they'd even be the same height. The only difference was their chest. Dr. Saph always had some of the largest breasts I'd ever seen, and they were completely natural. Ara was a solid C-cup, while her mother was easily a triple D, if not larger.

"Bella, what are you doing here?" Dr. Saph asked, wrapping a shawl tight around her body. She looked over at me, and I saw her eyes widen ever so slightly. "Tom? What's going on here?"

"Can we come in?" Ara asked, pushing past her mother without waiting for a response.

With a long sigh, Dr. Saph stepped aside, motioning for me to follow. The foyer of her house was bigger than my backyard; I'm not exaggerating. What in the actual *fuck* is happening? How can a *retired* government employee afford something like this?

Dr. Saph walked ahead and led us to a den lined floor to ceiling with books. A large fireplace was set into one wall, and a massive mahogany desk stood in the middle of the room. I couldn't even point out how cliché it was; I was just so enamored by it all.

Ara quickly sat in one of the leather chairs in front of the large desk, so I followed and sat in the other. Dr. Saph walked over to a desk off to the side of the room that held a glass decanter of what I assumed was whiskey of some kind. It didn't skip my notice that it was almost identical to the one in Wallace's office.

"Can I offer either of you a drink?" she asked, pouring herself a finger into a crystal glass.

Ara scoffed and crossed her arms. "No. It's not even 8:00 am."

Dr. Saph snorted and bobbed her head as she turned and sat across the desk from us. "So, how are things going in Krayden?"

Rolling her eyes, Ara leaned back in her chair. "Listen, we're not here for pleasantries, okay? We came here because you're our *last* option."

Dr. Saph stared at her daughter for a long moment before turning her dazzling green eyes to me. The corner of her lips curled slightly as she looked me over. "Well, it seems my daughter still hasn't learned any manners. But I know you have them. How are you, Tom?"

Fuck. I didn't want to be put on the spot here. I could feel Ara's gaze burning into the side of my head, but I kept my eyes on the woman across the desk. Ara was right saying she was our last option. That meant I needed to play nice.

Smiling, I tilted my head toward her. "I could be better, ma'am. You're looking well, though. Retirement suits you."

Dr. Saph snorted and took a sip of her whiskey. "Retirement. Sure."

"Don't tell me you miss the facility?" I asked, hoping to ease the tension a bit before going straight for the meat of it.

With a long sigh, she sat back in her chair and studied me. "Yes, I do miss it. And you're a smart man, Tom. You should've figured out that I didn't actually retire. I was forced out."

I nodded. It was pretty well known that Wallace had maneuvered his way into the position. Of course, we had no idea what he actually did, but most of us understood that her leaving was not a mutual decision.

Looking back at her daughter, Dr. Saph folded her hands across her lap. "Bella, I can tell you're still holding your grudge against me. So, why are you here, and why did you drag the poor Rifter into this? You know you can get into a lot of trouble having him jump here without authorization."

Ara clenched her jaw and crossed her arms under her chest. "Believe me, I don't want to be here! But we're all in danger, and you're the only one that might be able to help."

That seemed to catch the woman's attention. Dr. Saph sat forward, furrowing her brows in concern. "What do you mean? What danger?"

Letting out an exaggerated sigh, Ara motioned toward me. "It'll be better if Turtle explains it."

Great. There's nothing I love more than cherry-picking through a highly complex story to give just enough information so we can get help, but not so much that it might backfire on us later on. But there was nothing I could do about it now. I leaned forward and began the story as best I could, starting with our first jump to the new Realm.

A solid forty-five minutes later, I sat back and exhaled deeply. That was a shit-ton of information. And to her credit, Dr. Saph seemed to take it all in stride. Now, we just have to hope she can help.

"So Lyn's the Ellyssian they're after, but the shards are already inside of your core," she said, tapping her now empty glass as her eyes seemed to not focus on anything.

Something about the way she said that tickled the back of my mind. She's acting so nonchalant about this. It's almost as if she'd already known all of it and was just pretending to listen to us. One of the things that stuck out most was her using the name Lyn when I'd only referred to her as Lynriel. Was it just a weird coincidence? I'm not sure, but something really isn't adding up here.

I nodded, hoping I hadn't just made the biggest mistake of my life. At least I remembered to leave out everything to do with Rui, the phone, and the more intimate details. Even though I was sure Dr. Saph wouldn't be working with Wallace, there was still something about her I wasn't entirely comfortable with.

"Hmm," she hummed, pulling her laptop in front of her. "Tell me, what do either of you know about the First Rift Event?"

Now, that was not something I was expecting her to ask. I looked at Ara, who returned my glance, and we shook our heads. "Other than the Rift happened, a giant tentacle almost killed me, and the 'miracle' saved me? Nothing else really comes to mind."

After a few more seconds of typing, Dr. Saph spun her laptop around and showed us her screen. It was some weird diagram with a bunch of numbers and symbols that my high school diploma didn't teach me. Ara leaned forward and studied the image, her brows furrowing the longer she looked.

"Wait . . . Is that . . ." she gasped before looking horrified at her mother. "Are you saying that *you* caused it?!"

"Well, me and about two dozen others at the agency," Dr. Saph said nonchalantly. "You have to understand; we didn't intend for *that* to happen. We were just trying to find a way to access to the Pathways."

The passage from her book flashed in my mind, and I shot up in my seat. "You wanted to create a proximate node."

Both Dr. Saph and Ara turned to me in surprise. I wish I could've gotten a picture of the dumbfounded look on the good doctor's face as she stared at me in disbelief. "I . . . Yes. How do you know that?"

I tried to put on my cockiest smile and sat back in my chair like it was no big deal. "Eh, I have my ways."

"So, wait," Ara said, her anger returning as she looked back at her mother. "You were the cause of . . . *all* of this?!"

Dr. Saph simply shrugged one shoulder in response. Ara looked like she was about to blow a gasket, so I knew I needed to step in. I placed a hand on her forearm and squeezed. I know I don't have the same abilities as her, but I hoped my touch would help some. And it looked like it worked, at least a little bit.

Ara clenched her jaw shut and turned away from her mother in disgust. I looked back at Dr. Saph, and a million questions were going through my mind, but none were as crucial as this one. "Why are you telling us this now?"

The woman sighed and pulled her computer back. "Because I've spent the past several years trying to *stop* Gram and his cronies from doing it again. Over the years, they've been collecting shards. But instead of studying them or trying to learn how to use them to better society like the RRS was supposed to, they've been holding onto them. Gram believes humans are 'superior' to all the other races and wants to dominate the Realms. He believes that with the shards, we can trigger a Rift Event big enough to flood our Realm with so much power, none of the others would ever be able to stand against us."

I stared at her in utter disbelief. "Are you *fucking serious*?! Was he not around for the *first one*? How many people died? How much damage are we *still* cleaning up a decade later?"

Dr. Saph sighed and sat back in her chair, nodding. "Exactly. That's exactly why I've been trying to stop him. I've had enough influence with the council to keep the vote from happening. Until yesterday."

"What happened yesterday?" Ara asked, a new kind of fear filling her voice.

"I was locked out," her mother said. "Gram used this threat of the Ellyssian to scare those still hesitant. Lyn's realm is . . . old. And no one knows how powerful they really are. He argued that causing another Rift Event using the shards we have at the RRS will give us the power to stand against anyone, including them."

A quiet ding sounded from the laptop, and Dr. Saph began typing again. She clicked a few times and then started reading. Her brows furrowed deeper and deeper the longer she read. Well, that can only mean good things, right?

With a heavy exhale, she sat back in her chair and rubbed her eyes. "Damn them all."

"What?" both Ara and I asked in tandem.

"They have Lyn in custody, and Gram received final approval from the council to move forward with his plan. You have less than three hours before all Hell gets unleashed on Earth."

Chapter 24

Prison Break

Benjamin Franklin once said, "Anger is never without a reason, but seldom with a good one." This is true in most circumstances. But the key word in that quote is 'seldom.' Because taking an innocent woman prisoner and then causing a potential world-ending catastrophe just because you want to feel more powerful is a pretty good goddamn reason for me to get angry!

I shot to my feet, my heart racing as I tried to think about everything that needed to be done. First, I'd get Honey, Sara, and Ara somewhere safe. Then, I had to find Lynriel and get her the hell out of there. Finally, I'd track down Wallace and beat his ass until not even the Healers can fix him.

"Ara, we need to go," I said, reaching for her hand.

The woman was still in shock but allowed me to pull her up from the chair. I pulled out my phone and was about to hit the home button when Dr. Saph grabbed my arm. I glared at her, my jaw clenched tight in anger. She saw the rage in my eyes and quickly pulled her hand away to step back.

"Tom . . ." she said, her voice soft as she looked down at the ground. Before I could tell her off, she held up a finger and returned to the other side of her desk. "Here, take this. I'm not sure if it'll help, but it might."

She opened a drawer and pulled out an old RFID card. I hesitantly took it, turning it over in my hand. It was just a gray, plastic rectangle the size of a credit card. There weren't any identifying marks on it to indicate what it was for.

When the Krayden branch opened, I recalled that most doors used card scanners. But now, they've all been linked to our watches for the past seven years, so the RIFD cards were no longer needed. Hell, I don't even remember the last time I saw a door with a card scanner in the facility.

"They're keeping your friend in Wing E," Dr. Saph explained. "The shards . . . well, they're going to be a little harder to find. You'll need to go down Corridor 42 in the admin wing. You'll see a door without any kind of identifying marks, almost like a janitor's closet. There isn't a scanner next to it either, but if you place that badge four inches to the left of the handle, you should hear a buzz, and the door will open. That's only if they haven't fully removed me from the system yet. Take the elevator down to Sublevel 9. You . . . you shouldn't have any problems finding it from there."

I stared at her for a moment before giving her a single nod. Yeah, I would've never found it. There are nine sublevels?! Is the RRS some kind of hive or something?

Putting the card in my pocket, I grabbed Ara's hand again and hit the home button on my phone. In the blink of an eye, we stood in the middle of my living room. Honey and Sara were sitting at the dining room table, and both jumped slightly at our sudden appearance.

"Jesus, Turtle! Don't just—"

"Both of you, go get dressed right now," I said, letting go of Ara's hand and heading down the hall to my room.

"Wait, what?" Honey called out, and I heard footsteps running after me. "What's going on?!"

I slammed into my room and walked to one of my bookcases. I'd built a secret storage compartment into the wall behind it several years ago on the advice of a friend I gamed with online. He was one of those Doomsday preppers and was absolutely bonkers regarding most things. But he made a compelling argument about having emergency money and supplies as a 'just in case.'

Finding the crease, I shoved my fingernail in and pulled down the slat. I'd wanted a cushion to fall back on in case anything happened and the Rift disappeared one day. So, I pulled out a bit of cash from each paycheck and hid it there.

"Holy shit!" Honey exclaimed, seeing the stacks of cash I had in the secret cupboard. "What's going on?"

I pulled out all that I had in there- a total of $59,543. It wasn't a lot, but it was something. Turning, I dumped the stacks of cash into an empty gym bag and handed it to Honey. "Take this, and get a bag with some of your stuff together. You have five minutes. GO!"

Honey was frozen, seemingly torn between fighting me for answers and doing what I said. Sara and Ara both swooped in and decided for her. Sara wrapped an arm around Honey's waist and pulled her toward the door while Ara grabbed the money bag and followed them, explaining what was going on as they went.

I heard their door open just as an orange tabby cat strolled into my room. I blinked, and Rui stood with her arms crossed in front of her chest, a worried look on her face. "I heard everything through your phone. You can't do this on your own, Daddy."

"I don't have a choice," I said, walking to my closet and pulling out more ammo for my gun. One of the most significant drawbacks to a revolver is limited round capacity. "I'll get them to safety, and then I'll get Lynriel out of there."

"And, what about the Event?" Rui asked, continuing to stare me down. "How do you plan on handling that?"

I sighed and shook my head. "I . . . I'll figure something out."

"You should call Lana," Rui said, leaning against the wall beside me. "She's smart. She might know what to do."

"No," I shook my head. "Though . . . you can use my abilities, right?"

Rui smiled and nodded. "Yup! And then some."

"Good. Can you do me a favor? Since Lana already knows who you are, will you jump there and bring her back here? I'm going to take them all somewhere safe."

"There is no 'safe' if an Event that size happens," Rui said, growing more serious. "I don't know how many Sh'landriel they have, but considering the First Rift Event was created with less than one . . ."

She let the implication hang in the air. *Fuck my life.* The world was about to get thrown into the very definition of Hell. *I fucking hate Gram Wallace!*

"Well, it'll at least be safer away from major cities," I pointed out. I opened the box of ammo lying on my closet's shelf and sighed. Only seven more rounds left. *Fuck.* "I'll take them to one of the coffee plantations Sara's funding. It's away from almost everything. They should be at least somewhat safe out there."

Rui stared at me long and hard, thinking about something. It really wasn't fair that she got a front-row seat into my head, yet I couldn't tell what she was thinking. Though, with how she was, maybe I didn't want to know.

"No," Rui said before walking to the other side of the room.

"What? What do you mean, 'No?'" I asked, turning on her.

"I mean, no. I won't bring Lana here," Rui said, continuing to walk to the door. Before I could argue, she turned and gave me a warm smile. "I'll take them all down there for you. You need to focus."

"But Honey and Sara—"

"I'll handle it," Rui said with a wave of her hand.

She blew a kiss and gave me a wink before turning and walking out of my room and down the hall. Sure enough, I heard the two women scream a few seconds later. "Who the hell are you?!"

It wasn't long before I felt the pressure of the Rift opening, and the house grew eerily silent. A wave of fatigue washed over me, and I sat on the bed to steady myself. Rui had mentioned using my energy to do things, so I guess that was what it felt like. It was strange having my core activate when I wasn't using it. Yet I still felt as fatigued as if I'd just jumped several times in a row.

I closed my eyes and took a few deep breaths, preparing myself as best as I could. I was about to break into the RRS and declare war on them. In all likelihood, I was about to have to fight people I've known and worked beside for years. And I bet most of them don't have any idea about the shit Wallace was really up to. They were innocent. But that wouldn't stop me from tearing through them if it meant protecting those I care about.

"So, what's the plan?" Ara's voice came from my doorway, causing me to bolt up in surprise.

"What are you doing here?" I asked. "You were supposed to—"

"Leave you to do this on your own?" Ara scoffed, walking up to me and touching my chest. "Turtle, I told you I'm here with you. No matter what. You can't face the entire RRS by yourself. So, I'm coming along, even if it's just to make sure you get out in one piece. Besides, who knows what condition Lyn will be in? She might need a Healer if they've done anything to her."

I stared into her eyes. I didn't want to risk her in any way. But, deep down, I knew she was right. And to be fair, I was somewhat relieved that I wouldn't be alone.

Ara smiled and grabbed my shirt, pulling me into a passionate kiss. Her lips were so soft and warm. My desire to protect her grew even stronger the longer we embraced. One way or another, Wallace was going to be stopped.

We broke away and smiled at each other. "Okay, but you stay behind me, understand? You're only there for support in case I or Lyn need a bit of your power. You're not fighting anyone!"

Ara's grin grew dark, and I saw a fire in her eyes. "No promises."

I sighed and pulled out my phone. To my surprise, the Contacts for the RRS had all been grayed out. Was that because of the new software keeping Rui out? Whatever the reason, I could now only access the general map of the building. I didn't have any of my coordinates for the facility, either, so I couldn't jump out of Realm and back in to get closer. That left us with only one of the entrances.

Wing E was not too far from the gate I usually go through, so I tapped the button for that one as I gripped Ara's hand tightly. In the blink of an eye, we stood just feet outside the entrance. It was clear that the security team hadn't expected us just to appear, and two of them jumped in surprise.

This wasn't an opportunity we could pass. The doors had just opened to let someone in, so we bolted inside as men screamed orders to close it. They were too late. We busted through and ran down the first hallway, bypassing several other security guards who still hadn't caught on to what was happening. That didn't last too long, though. An obnoxiously loud alarm rang throughout the facility when we reached the second hall.

"BRAVO BRAVO BRAVO. ALL PERSONEL, CODE BRAVO WING D. BRAVO BRAVO BRAVO."

"FUCK!" I yelled as two security guards came rushing towards us.

One was a human woman, and the other a male Garatos. The Garatos people were . . . well, imagine a crocodile and a gorilla had a baby, and that baby was beaten with every ugly stick you could find. They stood around six feet tall and had thick, green scales all over their body. Their long snouts were filled with razor-sharp teeth, and they had hands like you and me, just tipped with sharpened claws.

Ara grabbed my arm and pulled me down another hallway, and we continued running. The pair behind us kept in pursuit, and it sounded like others were joining them. Thank God none of them carried guns! Most of the security teams only used some kind of electrified baton, which was strong enough to put down a charging elephant. The downside to that particular weapon is that you have to be close to use it.

An explosion to our left almost sent us to the ground, but I was able to grab Ara and keep her upright. We glanced back and cursed again. One of the Swords was also chasing us now. I couldn't remember his name, but I'm sure it was a douchey one, like Brad or something. They're all assholes anyway.

We lost some momentum, but we pushed forward. Turning a corner, Ara pulled me into a small room, shutting the door quickly behind us. It was a storage closet that could barely fit us both, but we squeezed in as far as we could, trying to catch our breath. We heard the stampede of security come around the corner and continue down the hall, several shouting that we went one way or another.

We waited another minute until we were sure they were gone before stepping back out. I looked each way before ushering Ara down the opposite way the security had run. This was the corridor that connected to Wing E. We ran but tried to stay as quiet as possible. There were security cameras everywhere, so we knew it was only a matter of time before someone called in where we were.

Just before reaching our destination, a massive figure at the end of the hall stepped in front of us, causing us to stop dead in our tracks. I stared at the hulking figure as he sneered down at me. He crossed his giant arms over his chest, making it clear we weren't going anywhere.

"Fuck. Hey, Gregg," I said with a coy smile.

"NOT GREGG!" The Winly guard roared before charging directly at me.

Well, I couldn't say I was too surprised. I imagine that Gregg had a lot of anger to take out. He'd probably beat me to death with my own arm if he could. But I just didn't have time for that.

I drew my revolver, quickly braced myself as I aimed, and fired. I'd learned over the years that most of the other Realms hadn't used weapons like guns for hundreds if not thousands of years. They relied solely on the gifts awoken by the Rift. Firearms had even become rare in my Realm since most of the world's conflicts stopped after the FRE. So even if Gregg had known what a gun was, there'd be no way he'd expect me to be so accurate with it.

My bullet struck the charging Winly in the knee, pretty much severing his lower leg and sending him barreling to the ground. He screamed as dark blue blood poured across the white tile floor. I ushered Ara past the writhing guard just as he lunged out at me. Damn it, Gregg! Just take the L.

I jumped as I pointed my revolver again, letting my anger aim this time. I squeezed the trigger and blew Gregg's manhood clean off his body. His screams increased tenfold as he tried to clutch at the gaping hole that was once his crotch. I knew he wouldn't be a problem for us anymore. He'd bleed out long before any Healers could get to him. Sorry, Gregg. Play stupid games, win stupid prizes.

Ara and I pushed forward and started looking through all the observation windows to the rooms in the security wing. Before we got too far, a shot rang out, and a bullet hit the wall beside my head, causing me to spin in surprise. Since when does the RRS carry guns?! I saw a human man wearing a security outfit pointing a 9mm pistol at me. 'Man' might be a stretch there. He looked more like a boy barely old enough to shave, let alone be security for a place like this. His hand was shaking as he stared wide-eyed at me.

"STOP RIGHT THERE!" He screamed, keeping his gun pointed right at me. "PUT DOWN YOUR WEAPON AND GET ON YOUR KNEES, NOW!"

I held up my hands, pointing my revolver up at the ceiling. This kid was jumpy, and I couldn't risk him firing and possibly hitting Ara. "Hey, it's okay! I'm putting it down. Just . . . relax."

"DOWN! NOW!"

I sighed. This kid was going to get someone hurt or killed. I know saying that after what I did to Gregg might be a bit hypocritical, but . . . leave me alone, okay? That was justified.

I began crouching, slowly lowering my revolver down to the ground. I needed to figure something out. We couldn't get caught this easily. I took a deep breath and tried to judge if I could rush him. But he was too far and would be able to fire at least once before I could close the distance. Yet, if I jumped?

Focusing like Lynriel had tried explaining, I felt for the push and pull of energies. My blood was pumping hard in my veins, and that damn alarm blaring overhead was making it hard to concentrate. I gritted my teeth. I could still only feel the pull from the Rift somewhere above. How the fuck am I supposed to do this?!

I felt an all-too-familiar pressure build and was shocked to see Lynriel appear just behind the security guard. Before he realized what was going on, she grabbed his arm and twisted it up and then backward before slamming him face-first into the wall. The boy crumpled into a heap on the ground, unmoving. Lynriel's eyes locked onto mine, and something inside me stirred.

Before I knew it, Lynriel was in my arms, pressing her lips hard into mine. A sensation similar to when Rui activated the shards flooded through me. I felt a power rush from deep inside, and my muscles rejuvenated. My fatigue from Rui using my ability and the run through the facility vanished as Lynriel pressed herself into me.

We slowly broke our kiss, but the princess stayed in my arms, staring at me with a look of wonder. "You . . . You came for me?"

I smiled, trying to be as reassuring as I could. "Of course I did. I told you I'd protect you."

Before we could say anything else, shouts from several people echoed further down the hall. I heard Ara curse loudly from somewhere behind me, and I knew we were out of time. "Shit! Guys! We got to go!"

I turned and was shocked to see that Ara was much further down the hall than we were. Or, to be more specific, I was no longer where I had initially been standing. Without noticing, I'd apparently used my ability and jumped over to Lynriel. Seriously?! It won't work to save my life but for a hot chick? No issues!

"Corridor 42!" I shouted to Ara as I grabbed Lynriel's hand and pulled her down the hall.

This was going to be a lot harder than getting into Wing E. Corridor 42 was three wings over in the administration building. If we were walking a straight line, it would be about half a mile away. But we had to navigate the massive facility's twists and turns, all while having security and Swords chase us down. No problem, right?

We raced out of Wing E and back down the hall toward the Rifters prep rooms. I knew it would likely come down to us needing to take the shards, and I didn't want to risk anyone overloading and dying or, worse yet, blowing up the entire Realm. We needed a containment case to get it out of Wallace's hands.

Loud footsteps thundered from around the corner in front of us, and I cursed, pulling Lynriel to a stop. Ara looked around and pointed to a cracked-open office to the side. We busted in and closed the door, hoping no one saw us.

Heavy footsteps grew near before stopping somewhere just outside. Shit! They're on to us. I readied my revolver, preparing to shoot when the door opened again.

"Go for Sword KIA," Kyle's voice boomed outside.

Fucking Kyle! I was almost looking forward to putting a bullet in this asshole. No, you know what? I *was* looking forward to it.

"What do you mean all the cameras are down?!" Kyle shouted. "How's that possible?"

Holy shit! Maybe there was a God out there looking out for us. The fact they had no cameras meant that they'd have to rely on line of sight. And there was nowhere near enough security to watch every hallway. We might just be able to pull this off!

"FINE!" Kyle shouted. "I'm on my way! Keep at least three of my men posted outside his damn prep room, just in case. We still haven't gone through it to see if the shards are there."

Well, fuck. So much for getting the containment cases. We'd just have to make our way to the administration wing and hope we can find one along the way.

We listened to his heavy footsteps thundering down the hall until he was far enough away. Once again, I waited a minute before cracking open the door. The hall was empty, so we bolted and headed toward the admin wing. But as we turned the corner, we almost ran directly into two more security guards.

I raised my gun but stopped as Lynriel dashed ahead and kicked the side of one man's knee, snapping his leg in half. Before he even hit the ground, the elf princess spun and punched the other guard in the stomach, causing him to double over. She reared back and kneed him in the face, sending him falling backward, unconscious. The first guard was screaming in pain, grabbing his knee when she swiped back with her leg and kicked him in the temple, silencing him for good.

I was dumbstruck. Ara and I stared with mouths open as Lynriel checked both men to ensure they were no longer a threat. She glanced back at us and gave me a confused look. "What?"

Shaking my head, I let out a long breath. "Just . . . just reminded that I'm lucky we're on the same side."

Lynriel smirked, placing a hand on her hip. "And don't you forget it."

Pressing on, we encountered three more security groups. Like the one before, Lynriel made quick work of them all. After almost half an hour, we made it to the administration wing.

Of course, there weren't any signs to help us figure out where Corridor 42 was. The admin area was one of the largest in the entire facility. If I remember correctly, Dr. Saph once mentioned there were over two hundred different hallways.

I'd only come here a few times when she and I were randomly hooking up and once or twice to meet with Wallace. The director's office was in Corridor 7. And that's about as far as I ever got.

We began looking for anything that might point us in the direction we needed to go. A flash of movement at the end of one hall caught my attention, and I spun, raising my revolver. Yet, looking down, I saw that it was empty. Somewhere deep inside, a strange pulling sensation began to tug at me.

I looked at Lynriel, who was also staring intently down the hall. "Do you feel that?"

She slowly nodded her head but kept her eyes focused. "Yes. It feels . . . familiar. Almost like the Sh'landriel."

Nodding, I looked back at Ara, who was keeping watch behind us. She turned and arched her brow at me, shaking her head once. It was only Lynriel and I who felt it.

I motioned for them to follow as I slowly continued down the hall. As we reached the end, a door creaked open, and I spun, ready to fight whoever was about to come out. To my surprise, a small, red face peeked out from the room.

"Hal?!" I asked, placing a hand on Lynriel's shoulder to stop her from attacking the little imp.

"T-Turtle?" Hal's voice was shaky, but he looked relieved to see me.

Hal poked his head into the hall and looked both ways before stepping out. He was still wearing that same mustard yellow button-down and clutching something tightly in his fist. He looked up in amazement at Lynriel, his eyes growing wide.

"I-It's true," Hal gasped. "Ellyssia has come to save us!"

Lynriel furrowed her brows in confusion, looking down at the little man. "What? I'm not here to—"

"This is Princess Lynriel, right?" Hal asked, turning his focus back to me.

What the fuck? How did Hal know who Lynriel was? And what did he mean she was here to save us?

"Uh, yeah," I said, looking between the two. "Do you . . . know her?"

Hal giggled. Like, a legit 'school girl got a crush on someone' giggled. He clenched his fists tighter and danced excitedly in place. "Oh, yes! Yes! We're all saved!"

"HAL!" I snapped, the uneasy feeling making me grow impatient. "We're in a bit of a rush, bud. What's going on?"

Stopping his little jig, Hal smiled broadly and reached out his hand with a folded piece of paper toward us. "This is for both of you. Hurry!"

Lynriel and I exchanged a look before reaching out to grab the paper. Just as it did before, the entire world seemed to stop. Lynriel looked back at me, confused, as I opened the note. "You have Pridictonatori working as . . . messengers?"

I shrugged and looked at the paper. It was the same block lettering as the first note and the same sequence of numbers and letters. The coordinates to a place that was *way* outside my jump radius. Why the hell is Hal giving this to me again? Who keeps sending it?

Lynriel looked over and read, gasping in surprise. I turned, studying her face as she gently touched the paper. "What? What is it?"

"How?" Lynriel asked, looking down at Hal and then at me. "How does he have this?"

"I don't know," I said, shaking my head. "He gave me something similar once before, and it burst into flames after a few seconds.

And since his race goes through a memory wipe after every Time Stop, he doesn't remember who gave it to him. What is it?"

"This," Lynriel said, pointing to the numbers. "This is . . . Ellyssia. But what's more confusing . . . this was written by my hand!"

Looking down at it, I studied the lettering. It was very uniform. I would've said it was printed if I hadn't known better. How did she know she was the one who wrote it?

I looked back at her, the question evident. She touched the numbers, which seemed to glow a faint blue in reaction. "I can feel my power behind the ink. But . . . I've never written this before. There's no way this can exist!"

Looking between the paper, Lynriel and Hal, I sighed deeply. Seriously? Don't I have enough on my plate right now?

I noticed something small written in the top corner of the page, but it was obviously written by someone else. In fact, it looked suspiciously like my handwriting. I read it, and even more questions popped up.

"Left, Straight, Right, Left. 15 min."

What. The. Fuck?! What is this? Who keeps sending this stuff to me?!

The edges of the paper began to smoke, and like with the first note, everything was consumed by a flash of flame. Then, the world returned to normal, and Ara looked at us, confused. "Where's the paper you were just holding?"

I sighed and shook my head. It was doubtful that she'd experienced a Time Stop before, so it would be hard to explain now. "I'll tell you later."

"Who gave that to you?!" Lynriel heatedly asked, taking a step toward Hal.

Hal looked frightened and stepped back as he stared wide-eyed at the towering woman. "G-Give m-me what?"

"Lyn, I told you, memory wipe," I said, pulling her back from the cowering imp. "Hal, I know you don't remember the note, but you just gave us one during a Time Stop. You don't remember anything about who might've given it to you, do you?"

Hal thought hard but shook his head after a few minutes. "Sorry, Turtle. I don't remember anything about a note."

"Figures," I sighed, looking back down the hallway we faced. "I guess let's—"

An alarm sounded, but it wasn't coming from the overhead speakers this time. Ara's phone and mine went off, followed by Hal's less than a second later. We all pulled them out, and my stomach dropped as I read the message.

RRS ALERTS

"PREPARE FOR RIFT EVENT IN 15 MINUTES."

Chapter 25

Zero Hour

15 minutes. 15 minutes until all hell breaks loose. 15 minutes until the entire world gets thrown into utter chaos that it won't survive. No pressure, right?

"FUCK!" Both Ara and I yelled at the same time.

"What?" Lynriel asked, not understanding what was going on.

I looked down the hallway and back at her, my heart pounding. "They're planning on using a *lot* of shar—Sh'landriel to burst open the Rift."

A look of pure terror washed over the shocked woman. "WHAT?! Are you serious? That's . . . That's insane! It'll destroy this Realm!"

"Yeah, that's why we're trying to find where they're keeping them," I said, looking around. "Fuck. We haven't come across any jump supply closets to get a contaminant case, either. I might have to—"

Both Lynriel and Ara grabbed my arms and squeezed. Ara shook her head vigorously, and I could see the fear behind her eyes. "You *can't* jump without containment! Rui already told you what happens when someone's overloaded, and you have so many already. It'll kill you and most likely everyone else in whatever Realm you jump to!"

"I understand! I just don't know where we can find a containment case over in this Wing."

Hal perked up and turned, ducking back into the room he'd come from. We heard some rummaging around and a curse or two, but the little red imp quickly reappeared with a broad smile and carrying a containment case. "For some reason, this was sitting on my desk when I got in this morning. I have no idea who put it there or why, but feel free to take it if you need it!"

Ara took the metal case from Hal and smiled at me. "I'll hold on to it for right now. You focus on getting us to where we need to go."

I nodded my appreciation and looked back down the hallway we were facing. That note was strange, and I don't know who sent it, but it had to mean something. It warned me about the 15-minute deadline. Could the directions be something as well?

"Hey, Hal," I said, quickly glancing at the imp. "Do you know where Corridor 42 is?"

Shaking his head, Hal shrugged his shoulders. "Not really. They might've told us the numbers at some point, but none of us pay attention to that kind of stuff. Do you know what offices are near there? Those I know by heart."

"No," I said with a long sigh, shaking my head. "Just some unmarked door that requires one of the old RFID cards."

"Sorry, Turtle," Hal apologized. "I don't know of any doors that still take the old keycards."

Well, fuck it. It's not like we have any better options to find Corridor 42. We just have to hope whoever sent that note isn't full of shit. I motioned for them to follow me as I ran down the hall. Remembering the directions, I followed them at each juncture, hoping I wasn't wasting precious time.

Just before we reached the end of the last hall, we heard raised voices from around the corner. "I don't care what it takes! Find them, now!"

I knew that arrogant voice anywhere. Wallace was around the corner. Which means we were most likely in the right spot. I held my hand up for the others to stop while edging toward the corner.

Peering around, I was both relieved and disheartened at the same time. Halfway down the hall was an unmarked door, just like Dr. Saph had said. But standing right in front of it was both Kyle and Wallace. Neither one looked pleased at the moment.

"If they don't find the Ellyssian soon, I'm holding *you* personally accountable!" Wallace screamed, jabbing a finger into Kyle's chest.

"Me?!" Kyle yelled back, his face growing a dark red. "This is your incompetent security team's fault. If you listened to me in the first place, none of this would've happened! You should've killed that coward yesterday, and we could've made one of his bitches tell us where he hid the shards. One of them knows, I guarantee you. My men and I would've fucked the answers out of them in no time. But noooo, you wanted to pretend to still be innocent in all of this."

Wallace glared at the man. "Watch your tone when you speak to me, boy. I'm still your father, so you'll show me respect!"

Say what?! Wallace and Kyle are related? That ... actually makes perfect sense. It's no wonder Kyle got put in charge of the Swords despite his constant breaking of protocol and jeopardizing both missions and co-workers. Fucking nepotism.

"Now," Wallace said, trying to smooth the thinning hair over his sizeable bald spot. "I'm heading down to start the machine. You stay here and make sure no one, and I mean *no one*, interrupts. Do you understand?"

Kyle gritted his teeth hard but seemed to hold back his anger. "Yes, sir."

Wallace tapped a small gray card on the wall beside the door, and I could hear a slight buzz as he disappeared inside. I turned around and took a few steps away from the corner, lowering my voice so Kyle wouldn't be able to hear us. "Wallace just went down to start ... whatever it is that's going to cause all of this. The bad news is Kyle is standing guard."

"Fucking Kyle," Ara spat out, glaring daggers at the corner of the hallway. I grinned at her, which took her by surprise. Her eyes grew round as she began to get nervous. "W-what? Why are you looking at me like that?"

"Nothing," I said, shaking my head. "I just love you."

Ara's eyes grew even wider, and her jaw fell open. "Y-you ... love me?"

Well, fuck me. That just slipped out. Now I have her freaked out on top of the stress we're already going through. Before I could say anything, Hal raised his hand and waved it like a kid trying to get the teacher's attention in class. I looked down and cocked an eyebrow at the strange little man. "Uh, Hal? You don't have to raise your hand, bud. This isn't grade school."

Hal lowered his hand and looked nervously up and down the hall. "Turtle, this is all way past my pay grade. Would you be too offended if I . . . go hide somewhere now?"

I sighed and tilted my head back down the hall we'd come from. "Yeah, That's a good idea. We'll try to stop this from happening, but if we can't, find one of the Shields. Or at least some of the security guards, and stick with them. That'll be your best bet to survive whatever happens next."

Hal bobbed his head in agreement before hurrying back faster than I'd ever seen him move. I couldn't blame the guy too much. I mean, I didn't really want to be there, either. But there's nothing I can do about it now.

"So, what's the plan?" Ara asked, thankfully no longer focused on my little Freudian slip.

Looking back down at the corner, I pulled out my revolver. "I'll go distract him. Maybe if I can get off a shot or two, it'll at least slow him down, and I can try to lead him away. You two get downstairs and try to stop Wallace however you can. Break the machine, kill Wallace . . . anything! Worst comes to worst, Lyn, grab the shards in the containment case and jump as far away from this Realm as possible. If you want them to be safe, return them to Ellyssia. It seems everyone's afraid of your Realm, so that's probably where they'll be safest."

Lynriel grabbed my arm and spun me to face her. She stared intently into my eyes for several breaths, not saying anything. I could see determination in her gaze, and I felt that pit in my stomach tightening even more. "I came here today and turned myself in to save you and the others. I won't stand by while you're fighting a fight you can't win. I'm stronger and faster than you. *I'll* lure him off, and *you* go stop this madness."

Before I could object, she grabbed my shirt and pulled me into a kiss. Like before, I felt the power activate in my core and a boost of energy shot through me. Breaking off the kiss, Lynriel gave Ara a quick smile before disappearing right before our eyes.

Less than 2 seconds later, we heard Kyle yell, followed by a loud crash. I quickly ran to the corner, looked around, and saw Kyle lying on the ground, more than twenty feet from where he'd originally been standing. Lynriel was charging at him, clearing our way directly to the door. I cursed under my breath at her but knew she was probably right. She *was* better suited to handle him.

Ara and I ran to the door as I pulled Dr. Saph's key card from my pocket. I pressed it to the wall and moved it around, trying to find where the hidden scanner was. I held my breath, hoping they hadn't taken her out of the system entirely. Otherwise, we were already fucked.

To my relief, I heard a slight buzz, and Ara yanked open the door. Further down the hall, we heard a loud explosion, and Kyle bellowed out his rage as Lynriel continued to dance around, landing strike after strike against him. That woman was something else.

The room behind the door looked like a miniature lobby with two elevators against the far wall. We ran up to one and slammed the down button, hoping it wasn't one of those that took forever and a day to come up. To our surprise, one opened immediately. Hopping in, we pressed 9, and the doors slowly closed. I was dumbfounded as I stared at all the buttons lining the wall. Apparently, the RRS had 13 sublevels! How the hell did they build all of this in such a short amount of time?

I looked at my watch and hissed out a curse. All of that had already taken seven minutes. There were less than eight to go. I quickly emptied the spent cartridges from the chamber of the revolver and reloaded. Gaming 101: Always reload your weapon before a boss fight. Yes, I know this isn't a game! But the rule still applies.

"So . . . you love me?" Ara asked, poking my arm.

Fuuuuuuck! Why did I have to say that? Stupid Turtle!

I gave her a small smile but felt my cheeks burning with embarrassment. "I . . . Can we talk about this after?"

Ara chuckled and leaned her head on my arm. "I'm just teasing. Besides, I think I—"

She was cut off by the elevator dinging and the doors sliding open. What we saw outside was unbelievable. We both stared in amazement at the large chamber behind a thick sheet of glass less than ten feet before us.

Enclosed within was a pedestal with three metal arms sticking up, holding a shimmering object that looked all too familiar. Just like the one Lynriel had, it didn't hold any specific shape or form but fluctuated consistently. The light within was radiating a kind of peace that we could feel even through the glass. The most significant difference between this one and the one Lynriel carried was the size. Hers was roughly the size of about half my pinky finger, while this was the size of a baseball.

Didn't Rui say that Lynriel's was seven pieces combined? If that's the case, *holy shit*! This one had to be dozens! How the hell did the RRS get so many? I'd never heard about *one* being found, let alone all of this.

"YOU!" Wallace's voice echoed, drawing my attention away from the shards.

He stood off to the side next to a large control panel, his face crimson as he glared at me. "After *everything* I did for you! After I gave you chance after chance after chance. *This* is how you repay me?"

"What the fuck are you talking about?" I yelled back, squaring up in front of the portly man. "You threatened me *and* my family, tried to arrest Ara, tried to imprison an *innocent* woman, and now you're about to unleash *hell* on a world full of unsuspecting civilians! You're lucky I don't just put a bullet in your head right now."

Wallace shook with rage as he continued pointing his chubby finger at me. "You're just too *stupid* to see. We *need* to be stronger. Those . . . *things* keep coming here, year after year, and we just . . . *accept them?! We* are the superior Realm! Humans are the only ones that matter! You'll see. I'm going to bring forth an age of—AHHHHH!"

He screamed out in pain and grabbed at his foot, which I just shot in the middle of his monologue. Bad guys are so stupid. Don't fucking monologue, it's not that hard!

Wallace crumpled to the floor, writhing in pain as he gripped the nub that was once his foot. I ran past and looked at the control panel, hoping to stop whatever it was he started. So . . . have I mentioned I'm not the best when it comes to technology? I saw buttons, knobs, levers, screen displays with a bunch of numbers, and all the blinking lights. But did I know what *any* of it was? Not so much.

"Ara," I called back, waving her over to me. "Can you make sense of any of this?"

"Me?" Ara asked as she frantically looked all over the panel. "I'm a nurse, not tech support!"

Frustrated, I saw a giant red lever and pulled it. Red means 'Stop,' right? An alarm began buzzing even louder, and the arms holding the shard lifted it off the pedestal. *Wrong lever, wrong lever!*

"ACTIVATION INITIATED. STARTING POWER-UP SEQUENCE NOW."

"SHIT!" Ara screamed, looking between the chamber with the shard and the control panel.

With no other options, I decided to do what I do to every alarm. Break it. I pulled Ara back, raised my revolver, and emptied the remainder of the bullets into the machine. The alarm stopped, but the arms holding the shard continued to move.

"FUCK!"

A massive explosion ripped through the room from behind us, sending Ara and me slamming into the wall. We crumpled to the ground as smoke began to fill the air. That was *not* fun. I felt a sharp pain in my shoulder, and I knew it was probably dislocated. I looked up and saw Ara rapidly blinking, a cut on her forehead dribbling blood down her face.

Forcing myself up, I reached down to help her when something hard hit me from the side. I crashed back to the floor with whatever struck me landing on top. Looking up, I saw blond hair slick with red blood, and my heart froze. Ara quickly appeared above me and helped pull Lynriel's unconscious body off.

"LYN!" I yelled, turning her over to get a better look at her injuries.

Her face was starting to swell, and there was so much blood I couldn't tell where it was coming from. Ara was already on it, though. She held either side of Lynriel's head and had a focused look on her face. The crunching footsteps from the now-ruined elevator drew my attention back that way.

Kyle stepped out of the smoldering debris, a look of pure hatred filling his glare. "Fucking COWARD! You couldn't even face me yourself? You had to send a woman to do it for you? YOU'RE PATHETIC!"

Fuck this guy! I held my dislocated shoulder as I stood back up. Ara was too focused on Lynriel and hadn't noticed Kyle's arrival yet. I needed to keep him away from them at all costs.

"ME?" I spat back at him. "You think you're a big man beating up someone smaller than you? You're the biggest coward of them all. You couldn't even get a job without your daddy's help, could you? You're nothing but a scared, *weak*, *pathetic* daddy's boy."

So, I've heard the term 'don't poke the bear' before, okay? I know what I'm doing here. I've dealt with bullies like Kyle my entire life. Hell, my whole *family* was worse than this dipshit. My main focus was to keep his attention on me.

The rage behind Kyle's eyes grew a hundredfold. I could literally feel the anger radiating off him. His fire ability was making the room uncomfortably hot. But Wallace was still lying on the ground just to my side, so I doubted Kyle would do anything too rash with his dad so close.

"FUCK YOU!" Kyle yelled, raising his palm and conjuring a fireball.

Shit. I *really* underestimated his stupidity. The ball grew larger and larger until it was the size of a volleyball. *No!* That would kill *everyone!*

My mind raced as I thought about what to do, but a sudden fatigue washed over me. I felt woozy, and the room spun, yet I managed to keep my feet. Kyle threw his hand forward, and I knew I was too late. This was the end.

I closed my eyes and flung myself on top of Ara and Lynriel. There was little else that I could think of. Maybe they could survive if I take the brunt of the blast. But I knew that wasn't likely. That fireball was too big. We were all about to be turned to little more than ash.

Something that sounded like a giant stone hitting a thick metal sheet rang through the room, followed by another massive explosion that rocked the ground underneath us. Pieces of the ceiling began to drop all around, and my ears rang like I had been standing next to a stick of dynamite that had just gone off. A slender hand gripped my arm, and I looked up in confusion.

Big, yellow cat eyes peered at me through the thickening smoke, and it took me several seconds to make sense of it. "RUI?!"

"Hi, Daddy!" Rui said, pulling me off of Ara and Lynriel.

I heard Kyle scream and what sounded like someone hammering on a thick metal slab behind me. I turned but was not prepared for what I saw. Shiny plate armor glistened in the firelight, dancing around in the smoke-filled room. Chet stood between us and the rampaging Sword, deflecting Kyle's fists with his obnoxious shield. Well, I guess I shouldn't call it that anymore, should I?

"Ch-Chet?" I asked, looking back at Rui for answers.

The Neko smiled and winked as she knelt and laid her hands on Lynriel beside Ara's. "I told you he was still alive, Daddy."

I slowly stood, trying to make sense of . . . anything really. A whooshing sound drew my attention back to the chamber with the shard. Kyle's fireball had not only shattered the glass separating us from the pedestal but damn near destroyed the entire wall as well. The arms of the machine were now pulsing electricity into the shard, and it began glowing brighter and brighter with each passing second. Well, that can't be good.

There was no more time. I looked around the floor but didn't see the containment case anywhere. Fuck. This was *not* how it was supposed to go.

"She's awake!" I heard Ara yell, slowly lifting Lynriel.

The elf princess blinked several times, obviously with a concussion. I stared at her and then Ara. They were both so beautiful. Thoughts of Honey, Sara, and Lana rushed in, and I knew I was their only hope. Rui's ears shot up, and she spun, a look of pure terror on her face.

"DADDY, NO! YOU'LL DIE!"

Ara and Lynriel looked up at me, and I saw the realization on their faces. I couldn't wait any longer. Giving them one last smile, I ran through the broken wall and grabbed ahold of the shard. Electricity shot through my entire body, and I felt like every inch of me was being torn apart over and over again.

I opened my core and let the Rift rip me out of the Realm, and everything went black.

Chapter 26

Aftermath

Bright sunlight poured through the windows as I stood in the middle of my living room. What does Honey have against curtains? The yellow paint on the walls made the light that much brighter as I looked around. Something felt off, but I couldn't tell what.

I listened intently, trying to see if I could hear Honey or Sara in their room. But there was nothing. It was completely silent. That's weird. Maybe they had to run errands? But they didn't tell me anything . . .

I looked down at the ground and grew even more confused. Why was I wearing my work uniform? I didn't have to work today. Wait, did I? What day is it?

"Hello, Tom," a woman's voice said from behind me, causing me to jump and turn in fright.

"JESUS!" I screamed, clutching my chest. "Don't do that!"

A strange woman was sitting on the couch, smiling warmly at me. She wore sheer blue fabric wraps and what looked like one of those headbands with orange cat ears on top. Wait . . . she looked familiar. I just couldn't place it.

From somewhere far off, I thought I heard someone calling out. "Daddy! Don't . . ."

Daddy? What's going on? I didn't think we had any neighbors with kids. Great, Sara's going to make us introduce ourselves. She does this every time someone new moves into the neighborhood. That's probably where they were. Damn it, she's going to be pissed I'm not there!

"Who are you?" I asked, returning my focus to the strange woman. "What are you doing in my house?"

She continued to smile at me, and that was when I noticed she was also wearing contacts to imitate big, yellow cat eyes. Man, this chick was really leaning into the whole Neko cosplay. Was she a friend of Sara's? Maybe she was one of their play partners?

"Come, take a seat," the woman said, motioning for me to sit in my recliner. That's weird; who moved it to in front of the couch like that? "There's some things we need to talk about.'

"DADDY!" The voice from outside called, seeming a bit louder but still far off. "DON'T TR—"

"Tom?" the woman arched an eyebrow at me, drawing my attention back to her.

I shook my head and took a seat. I'm not sure why, but something deep inside was telling me to run away. That's weird. Looking back at the woman, I waited for her to say something. I've seen enough movies to know when you don't know what's happening, keep your mouth closed unless absolutely necessary.

"You have questions," the woman said, slightly nodding. "Unfortunately, I can't answer most of them right now."

"Listen, lady," I said, shaking my head. "I don't know who you are or what you're talking about, okay? What questions am I supposed to have right now?"

The woman's smile never faded. It was both reassuring and unsettling at the same time. "Something's happened to you—the *real* you. Your mind couldn't handle the sudden influx of power, and it's unclear whether your body will survive as of now. So I've brought your consciousness here—temporarily, of course. Consider it a mercy in case the worst happens."

Shaking my head again, I let out a long sigh. "That doesn't make any sense, lady. What happened? What do you mean you pulled my consciousness here? I mean, I'm here! Me."

The woman slowly reached her hand out, offering me her palm. I stared at it for a long minute, wondering what her game was. Somewhere outside, I heard the voice call out again, this time sounding like it was coming from a static-filled radio. "DA . . . DDY! DON'T . . . TRUST H—ERRRR."

I placed my hand in the woman's palm, and she squeezed. A tidal wave of images flooded my mind. I saw the events from inside the RRS and the chamber with the shard. Kyle and Chet were fighting, Ara and Rui were healing Lynriel, and I grabbed the shard and jumped into the Rift. When she let go. I gasped out and sucked in air as if I'd just come up from deep underwater.

"W-What the fuck?" I sputtered, looking back up at the smiling Neko. "RUI?!"

"No," the woman said, gently shaking her head. "Though, at the same time, yes. What you know as Rui is just a fragment of who I am. This was just the form I thought would be best for communicating with you. You seem to have a strong connection to that fragment of me."

I blinked several times, trying to understand what she was saying. "Wait . . . if Rui's part of you . . . that makes you . . ."

The woman slowly nodded. "I have a lot of names. I think what you've been calling me most often is . . . The One?"

My heart froze. I was literally in the presence of a . . . God? Goddess? Deity-thing?

"Uh," I said, not sure what to do.

The woman chuckled and shook her head. "Don't worry yourself too much about it, Tom. You won't remember any of this anyway."

I looked around the empty living room, trying to figure out what happened. "Did . . . did I die? Is this, like, heaven or something?"

The woman laughed again, shaking her head. "No, Tom. There's no such place. You're alive. Well, sort of. You're more in a state of in-between. Your body took in a lot of power—more than someone of your species is ever supposed to. But it didn't instantly kill you. Which is why we're talking right now."

"Wait a second," I said, leaning back in my chair. "I thought you were supposed to be broken up into the shar—ah, Sh'landriel? Lynriel told me she's been collecting them to bring you back, with her as your vessel."

"Indeed," she said, nodding her understanding. "My consciousness and power were broken between the pieces you call shards.

The amount you absorbed just now was a rather large portion. It's not enough for me to be reborn yet, but it was enough to allow me to come back in a small way."

We stared at each other. I studied her hard, trying to figure out what was so special about her. She looked *just* like Rui! Maybe she was acting more mature, but she still looked just like the Neko I knew. "Okay, so why are we talking?"

"I'm here to offer you a choice," she said, her smile never slipping. "Like I said, your kind isn't meant to hold the amount of power you just took in. It was the Ellyssian construct Lynriel who was to collect them and become my vessel. She was specifically created for that purpose. But you've now stolen that destiny away from her."

"I didn't—" I tried to defend myself, but I was silenced as she held up a hand.

"I know it wasn't intentional," she said. "Nonetheless, you did. Now, with the amount you absorbed in your attempt to save your Realm, you have a rather large percentage of all my pieces inside your core—a core that should hold less than a fraction of 1%."

I stared hard at her, wondering what she was getting at. "Okay . . . so, where do we go from here?"

"Like I said, I'm going to give you a choice," she said, holding up one hand. "Choice number one. I send you back before your people tore into the Pathways—before you received your piece of my power. You'll have the chance to live a long, happy life surrounded by the people you love. You could have children, grandchildren, and even great-grandchildren before you die. And when your time comes, it can be peaceful, surrounded by those who love you most."

Above her palm, a blue ball of light formed, and I saw a younger version of myself hugging Honey. The image shifted and showed me lying in bed, Honey on one side and Sara on the other, sleeping soundly. As it switched to another time, I saw myself at my current age. I held a toddler with dark, curly hair while leaning down to kiss a baby's head with blonde locks. Shifting again, I was probably in my late fifties, sitting at a table with Honey and Sara on either side of me. Five people who looked to be in their 20s were also sitting at the table, all laughing and sharing a meal. They were our children, and two had babies of their own. The last image was me, wrinkled and old, lying in a hospital bed with an oxygen mask on. Like the other images, Honey held one hand and Sara the other. At the foot of my bed stood several people ranging from their 50s to a red-haired toddler holding a stuffed sloth toy.

I stared in disbelief. Was she really offering me the life I'd always dreamt about? "How? I thought you said you didn't have enough power to—"

"Sending one human back in time doesn't take much," she said with a chuckle. "Time isn't that complicated. You see it as this convoluted, linear *thing* when it's not. Time simply *is*. The past, present, and future are all relative to the one experiencing it. I, on the other hand, am eternal. I exist in all time. While conversing with you, I'm also watching the formation of the first cells that created your world while simultaneously experiencing the supernova of a star six million years after you walked on Earth. Don't try to understand it, Tom. Just trust me when I say time isn't hard to manipulate when you have the know-how."

I thought about what she was saying. Not about the time stuff—that was *way* over my head. No, I was thinking about her offer. I've always wanted a simple life and to be surrounded by people who loved me. I just never thought something like that would be in the cards for me. But a literal *Goddess* was offering me the chance to have all that and more.

"You said I *could* have that?" I asked, raising an eyebrow at her. "Not that I *will*. It's not a guarantee?"

The Goddess nodded her understanding. "While I can place you in the most favorable position for all of it to happen, *you'll* be what dictates the outcome. Every action by those with free will can alter the course of the world around them. Because of this, the future is ever-changing and cannot be guaranteed. I believe your people refer to this as the Butterfly Effect?"

Another thought popped into my head, and I focused on her again. "What about Ara and Lyn?"

Shaking her head, she pursed her lips together. "I'm sorry, Tom. They'll have their own lives to live, and you'd most likely never cross paths again."

"And the shards the agency had? Wouldn't that put you right back with them?"

She smiled again and turned to look out the window. "One good thing about being eternal is I don't have to worry about time. The RRS will eventually gather my pieces as before, and they will change your Realm forever. But the path I set you on would give you the best chance to avoid as many negative ramifications from that as possible."

I stared her down, wondering if I could actually trust this woman. I remember mythology, okay? Not all Gods are good. In fact, most were total dicks. I just wasn't sure where she fell on that spectrum.

"What's the other option?"

She held up her other hand, and a red ball sparked to life above her palm. "The other option is to send you back to your current timeline. You'll return to your body, and *If* you survive, you'll be more powerful than you could possibly imagine. But be warned, the toll it'll take on your body and mind is uncertain. Your species was never meant to hold so much power. You'd be able to shape not just your Realm but all of them if you so choose. That is, *if* you're able to master my gifts. You could single-handedly bring peace to the entire universe or burn every Realm until nothing is left but ash."

The images flashed in the new ball of light showed me hailed as a savior to countless races. Then, the next showed entire worlds on fire and unimaginable horrors being released on innocent people. It switched to show me sitting on a massive throne overlooking a grand hall. Then, it changed to lines of people from numerous races being dragged through the streets with chains around their necks.

"You would also become a beacon," she said, closing her hand and causing the light to disappear. "Your mere presence would draw them in like moths to a flame. Beings of great power will look for you, either to aid or destroy you. Keep in mind, even I was defeated at one point."

I gulped as a massive pit formed in my stomach. "But, can't you just tell me what to do?"

She shook her head and gave me a sad smile. "I'm sorry, Tom. As I said, there isn't just *one* future. There's an infinite amount, each either coming into existence or not, by countless decisions made by countless individuals. And even if I could tell you what path to take now, you won't remember any of this when you return to your body."

I sighed and sank back further in my chair. Fuck. My. Life. I weighed my options. Go back and have the ideal life I've always wanted? Or, take my chances surviving with a power that can shape the very fabric of existence, inevitably painting a cosmic bullseye on my back for every big bad out there?

Thoughts of Honey and Sara ran through my mind, and I smiled. Maybe they really weren't just messing with me all these years. The three of us looked happy together until the very end. But then I thought about Rui, Lynriel, and Ara. Could I give them up so easily? And on top of it all, the RRS would win. No one would be there to stop them from unleashing a literal hell on earth. Even if my loved ones were safe, could I, in good conscience, let that happen?

"Daaaddddyyyy!" Rui's voice echoed from somewhere outside, suddenly becoming much harder to understand. "DA...DD..Y! DON'T DO I . . .T! DO . . . N'T TRU . . .ST H . . ."

I sighed and leaned forward, looking the woman directly in the eye. "Okay, I think I know what I want."

Imagine, if you will, the world's worst hangover. I'm talking about that head-splitting, soul-crushing kind that makes you wish for nothing but the sweet release of death. The ones that have you regretting every single life decision you ever made and would have you happily pay someone to end your miserable existence right then and there. Yeah, that kind of hangover.

That doesn't even come close to how I was feeling as I slowly regained consciousness. Everything HURT! My fucking hair hurt! Do you know how bad it's got to be if your hair hurts?!

The darkness swirled around me as I slowly rejoined the land of the living. Instinctively, I tried to take a deep breath to stop the world from spinning. That was a mistake. A sharp, stabbing pain shot through my chest and sent me into a massive coughing fit. Yet each time I coughed, even worse pain coursed through my body.

Something heavy was lying on top of me, and for some reason, I couldn't move one of my arms. Knowing I would end up just regretting it, I forced myself to open my eyes. Everything was dark save for a soft red light somewhere in the distance. My heart began to pound harder as I realized I was pinned underneath something. The fog that had just filled my mind cleared, and the memories of the fight came rushing back.

Quickly looking around, I searched the room for the threat. Even though Chet had been holding him off, Kyle was on a rampage. There was no way the girls wouldn't be caught up in it. But the more I became aware of, the more confused I got.

First of all, everything was silent. There were no sounds of fighting, the alarm, or anything else for that matter. It was eerily quiet. In fact, now that my eyes had started to focus, I realized I was completely alone. I was still in the sublevel where they kept the shard, but it had been demolished. Two dim red lights along the far wall were the only source of illumination for the entire space.

Wait a second. Why was I still here? I grabbed the shard and opened my core. I felt the currents of the Rift rip me out of the Realm, but what happened after that? Where's the shard and how did I end up back here?

Looking down as best I could, I saw a chunk of concrete double the size of my body, pinning me to the ground. Great. How the hell am I going to get out from underneath this?

Resting my head back against the cool ground, I closed my eyes again. God, I felt like all my bones had been turned to dust, and battery acid was getting pumped through my muscles. I would kill for some aspirin. Or some really strong whiskey. Preferably a combination of the two.

Thinking about my situation, there was just too much that wasn't adding up. But I knew laying there wasn't going to solve anything. Maybe if I could make a jump . . . except I don't have any coordinates. So I'd be essentially guessing at where I was going.

Knowing my luck, I'd end up back in that godforsaken Realm with the Marrog again, and I was not in any shape to deal with that.

Well, it's time to cowboy up and do this the hard way. Steeling my resolve, I gripped the edge of the concrete slab with my one good arm and pushed. I'm not sure if I still had a bunch of adrenaline in my system or if that concrete was just a lot lighter than it felt lying on top of me. But as soon as I pushed, it flew off and cleared at least ten feet before crashing onto another pile of rubble.

What in the actual fuck? You know what, never mind. I don't have the time, energy, or even care to deal with that right now. My priority is to find out what happened to the girls. Where the hell is everyone?

The chamber was dark and cold, which was also weird considering how much heat Kyle was putting out. I slowly got to my feet and steadied myself. I know I already said this, but it bears repeating. EVERYTHING HURT!

Now that my senses were returning, I could make things out better. I felt a pit in my stomach grow as I saw a dried pool of blood on the ground several feet away. Was that from Lynriel? Or could it have been Wallace? Who was in that area again?

"Ara?" I called, my voice scratchy and my mouth dry. I felt like I hadn't had water in weeks; I was *so* thirsty. "Lyn? Rui?"

No answer. But considering it was all just a single open chamber now that Kyle had demolished the place, there weren't many places anyone could hide. My left shoulder throbbed, and I flinched with the reminder that it was still dislocated from Kyle's first attack. Reaching down to pull out my phone, my heart skipped when

I couldn't find it. Checking my pockets and looking all over the floor, I realized it was nowhere to be found. Well, that's probably not great, seeing that it's my link to Rui and all that.

I let out a long sigh and pinched the bridge of my nose in frustration. This day couldn't possibly get any worse. I was in so much pain I could barely think straight, the device connected to the powers of a literal God was missing, I had no idea where any of my friends were, and on top of it all, I had no clue as to what happened with the shard. It wasn't lying next to me when I woke up, and I didn't feel that sense of peace it's known to give off.

Fuck it. I just need to get out of here before Kyle shows back up and cremates me once and for all. Slowly, I shuffled over to the elevator. One was completely destroyed, most likely from when Kyle had first arrived. Hopefully the other was still working.

I hit the button and, to my relief, heard the engine start. Finally, a break! As I waited, I tried to look myself over the best I could without a mirror. I was covered in cuts and bruises. But somehow, the blood was already dried from all the wounds I could see. That was when I finally noticed that my watch was also missing. Man, this day just keeps getting weirder and weirder.

While the elevator grew closer, a random thought crossed my mind, causing a new pit to form in my stomach. What if there were more security or, god-forbid, Swords up there waiting for me? Looking around the room, I saw no sign of my revolver anywhere. Well, double fuck me.

Soon enough, there was a soft chime as the doors to the elevator opened. I was relieved to see it was empty. At least my luck is holding out!

I got on and hit the ground floor button, leaning back against the cold steel to steady myself. As hard as I tried to remember, I still couldn't figure out what happened after I grabbed the shard. My biggest fear was that the RRS had somehow recovered it and followed through with their crazy plan. But, since the control panel and machine were utterly destroyed, I wasn't sure how they could accomplish that.

The elevator slowed and then stopped, chiming as the doors opened. I braced myself once again. The fake lobby outside the doors was empty, and I sighed in relief. I can't wait to get the hell out of this place once and for all.

Holding my shoulder to keep it stable, I slowly shuffled out of the elevator and toward the door that led back into the facility. This was going to be the moment of truth. I was deep in the heart of the administration wing and needed to figure out which way led out. It would take a miracle for me to go unnoticed, especially in the shape I was in. I'm sure everyone is still on high alert, and this time, I don't have my weapon or even Lynriel to help.

I gripped the door handle and froze, realizing something was wrong. The alarm wasn't blaring overhead anymore. Silence filled the air as I waited, listening as intently as I could. There was nothing: no alarm, no announcements, no footsteps.

After what I could only assume was several minutes, I gritted my teeth and pulled the door open. If they had set a trap for me, this was the perfect spot for it. But to my surprise, there was nothing. The hall was not only empty, but the normally bright white fluorescents were all off, and only a few red security lights along the wall illuminated the corridor, just like in Sublevel 9.

The air was thick, and there was a slight scent of mold mixed with something else I couldn't place. It was metallic . . . copper maybe? I saw several holes in the walls and floor with scorch marks around the edges as I looked around. No doubt Kyle's handiwork. Most likely from his fight with Lynriel.

Shaking my head, I shuffled back down the way we'd come from before. Luckily, my brain wasn't too fried, and I remembered the directions from Hal's note earlier. I just needed to reverse them, and I could hopefully find my way from there. Yet, as I continued down the corridors, an even stronger sense of unease began to fill my stomach. Something was really not right here.

I passed several offices along the way, with doors either kicked in or ripped off their hinges. My heart dropped when I turned into the hallway where we'd met Hal and saw the floor and walls covered in dried blood. What the hell happened here?!

Forcing myself to speed up, I tried to ignore the carnage I passed as I continued. Though, when I came across the first rotting corpse, I almost threw up on the spot. A human, most likely a man, from what I could tell, had been torn limb from limb. Body parts were thrown all over, and what remained of his security uniform was caked in blood and worse.

What the fuck happened in the eight minutes I was down there dealing with the shard?! And again, where the hell is everyone?!

The putrid smell of decay and death filled the air as I moved on, trying to navigate my way back to Wing D. I knew how to get out from there, so I just needed to keep going.

I passed more dead bodies and destruction, my heart pounding in my chest as I wondered if any of them were people I knew. Luckily, none resembled any of the girls, so that was at least one saving grace.

It took me almost forty-five minutes to finally get out of the facility. I nearly cried out in relief once I saw the open security doors at the end of the final hallway. A frigid breeze blew fresh air in, and I couldn't help but smile. Yet, as I got closer, my instincts began screaming that something wasn't right. Wait, it was the middle of the day and hot as balls when we arrived earlier. How is it dark outside, and why is it so cold?

I slowed my pace and tried to creep my way toward the open door leading outside. Once again, I was at a loss when I looked out. It was dusk now, and the sky lit dark red, casting long shadows as the sun sank deep into the horizon. But what made my heart freeze was the pillars of smoke in the distance that rose high into the air from all over the city. Not only that, but the massive concrete wall that surrounded the RRS had been almost entirely destroyed. All that was left was large piles of debris littered with even more corpses.

Fearing the worst, I looked at the sky to inspect the Rift. I sighed in relief when I saw that it looked the same. It hadn't opened or even grown, which meant there hadn't been any new Rift Events. But then, what the hell was going on?

A terrifyingly familiar howl cut through the air, causing my blood to freeze in my veins. Before I could move an inch, the massive creature stepped into view, staring directly at me from across the courtyard. My worst nightmare stood mere yards away, snarling at me with its long, jagged fangs. Raising one of its clawed hands high overhead, it let out an ear-shattering roar as a bright ball of fire the size of a basketball formed inches above its palm. As if that wasn't frightening enough, within seconds, a dozen more Marrog emerged from the darkness beside it, all glaring hungrily at me.

Well . . . shit.